Copyright © 2024 by Amy White

Cover Design by Beetiful Book Covers (beetifulbookcovers.com)

This is a work of fiction. Any resemblance to actual persons, living or dead, or actual events is purely coincidental.

All rights reserved.

No part of this book may be reproduced in any form or by any electronic or mechanical means, including information storage and retrieval systems, without written permission from the author, except for the use of brief quotations in a book review

For my Mother

The Matriarch

Amy White

Part One

Childhood

Jenna sat on her beloved screened porch listening to her three children playfully poking fun at one another as they lounged comfortably in the adjacent den. Even though they were only separated by an open door, her kids seemed unaware of her presence. She was merely a fly on the wall in the background.

It was rare for them to all be home at the same time and even rarer to have nothing on the agenda but spending time together.

Jenna could hear them reminiscing about their favorite childhood memories that seemed to have happened so long ago, even though their combined ages of twenty-two, eighteen, and twelve would not qualify for a senior discount at Denny's. They were teasing each other about past embarrassing moments, and she allowed herself to go back in time and remember along with them.

They howled with laughter recalling the time her oldest daughter, Heidi, caught her hair on fire while lighting the grill only a few minutes before her high school crush came over to study. Thankfully, her husband, Paul, had quickly extinguished the flame before Heidi was injured but not before the stench of burned hair wafted through the air and filled every square inch of their on-post quarters.

All three of her children seemed to remember exactly what smoldering hair smelled like and could describe in detail the look of total humiliation that had planted itself on Heidi's face when she opened the front door for her study date. Her cheeks were beet red, and she kept apologizing repeatedly for the odor. The young man had been very polite and tried to concentrate on World History, even though everyone knew he was distracted by the awful smell.

They cackled about the day Brett, her middle child, sat on a pencil in such a way that it somehow lodged itself squarely in his buttocks.

Jenna also chuckled at this memory from the porch as she recalled having to take him to the doctor to have it removed. She had driven her minivan in a panicked state as Brett moaned from the back seat, unable to sit down fully. The dumbfounded look on the nurse's face in reception as she stared at the pencil sticking out through Brett's pants was unforgettable. It had seemed like a scene straight out of *Saturday Night Live*.

They next recounted the time the baby of the family, Olivia, impulsively belly flopped off the raised front porch onto the bushes in front of their house, just to see "what would happen."

They each took turns describing the body print she left in the neatly manicured hedges, with each description being more wildly exaggerated than the last. Thankfully, they lived in Colorado at the time, and it had been cold. Olivia had been wearing a thick puffer jacket, which acted like bubble wrap, protecting her from the pointy sticks and branches that comprised the bushes.

When the laughing subsided, her children moved on to talking about the many homes and places they'd lived in over the years as a military family, always on the move. Every story they told began with

"Do you remember that time at," then fill in the blank with Fort Carson, Fort Jackson, Fort Hood, Fort Drum, and so forth. The list of Army posts was long.

There was no ill will amongst them about moving so many times during their formative years. They loved their childhoods and wouldn't have had it any other way. Each move meant new adventures, new experiences, new friends, and new opportunities.

The two older children mischievously ruffled the hair of the youngest and tried their best to get a rise out of her in between stories. Olivia, after all, was very easy to rile.

Days like this seemed to happen less frequently as the children aged and lived extremely busy lives. Jenna was thankful for Fall Break for Brett and Olivia, and equally glad Heidi had been successfully able to sneak away from her job in South Carolina to come to Northern Virginia for a visit home. All her chicks were safely in the nest, even if it was only for a few days.

She quietly prayed the love and joy they felt being in each other's company would always be there, and when they were old and gray with grandchildren of their own, they would still sit together and share their lives with one another. She also prayed they would always laugh and joke without reserve. Laughter was the best medicine for the soul.

She asked God to grant them relationships that would sustain them through all of life's trials and challenges. It was a big order, but she knew God was more than capable.

As Jenna recalled the tales her children were telling, she couldn't help but think of her own childhood. It could be argued it was somewhat idyllic. She had a mom, a dad, an older sister, a beautiful home, and doting grandparents who all lived well into her adult years. She had a plethora of aunts and uncles and nine first cousins who felt like siblings.

She was allowed to participate in sports and was a more than decent soccer player. She had won many medals and trophies and proudly displayed them on a shelf in her room as a teenager next to her George Michael and Patrick Swayze posters. She had good friends and enough money to enjoy some of the finer things in life like jeans from The Limited, a portable CD player, and a lip-shaped phone in her room with a fifteen-foot cord. She wasn't rich by any stretch of the imagination, but her family was firmly in the comfortable department.

She made good grades, was considered pretty enough by most standards, and was given a used, blue Chevy Cavalier that smelled like cherry air freshener on her sixteenth birthday. She enjoyed lavish vacations each summer, because of the generosity of her paternal grandmother, and was lucky enough to have her private school university education and sorority dues funded by her parents.

Jenna's mom, Grace, was a guidance counselor at a local high school, which gave her the luxury of having summers and school vacations off with her kids. She could now appreciate her mom usually spent most of this time off from work shuttling her daughters between friends' houses and to and from sports practices and competitions. She took little time, if any, for herself.

Jenna's father, Tom, worked hard to provide for the family by selling real estate. He had moved up the corporate ladder of success by working round-the-clock and earned just enough for his daughters to take things for granted. He mowed the lawn each weekend and kept it so manicured one had to physically step up to get onto the grass surrounding the long, winding driveway in front of their suburban home. He attended soccer games and family get-togethers whenever he was instructed to do so by his wife, barbecued from the back porch when requested, and then would retire each night to the den to study the ups and downs of the stock market.

Jenna had an older sister, Katie, whom she adored and admired for her free spirit and her adventurous nature. The two sisters rarely fought growing up and were comfortable confiding in each other all the normal secrets of childhood. Since Katie was six years older than Jenna, she was the epitome of coolness to her younger sister.

When Jenna was the age of her children now, she would never have dreamed the direction her family, the one she had been born into, would one day go. She didn't think it would have been possible for her seemingly perfect family to fall apart—children and parents pitted against each other and destroyed past the point of reconciliation.

A tear sprung to her eye as she thought about what her poor mother, who had been fully devoted to her family, would think if she could look down from Heaven and see what had become of her life's work.

Within five years of her passing, the family completely crumbled, much like a mountainside avalanche, with each falling boulder creating irreparable damage.

Jenna brushed away the tears and tried to convince herself that her mother cannot possibly know what happened here on Earth because there is only joy in Heaven.

Heaven is not a place for heartbreak.

She missed her mother so much even though more than a decade had passed since she last saw her beautiful face or held her soft hands. To this day, Jenna has never touched another hand with skin as soft as her mother's. Perhaps it was because her mom put Oil of Olay on her face every night and rubbed the remaining cream on her hands, or maybe it was burned into her brain because her mother's hands were representative of her love—soft, comforting, gentle, and memorable.

Jenna's mother was far from perfect and certainly had her faults. She could fly off the handle in an instant, become emotionally overwhelmed, talk or laugh too loud, and sometimes let her competitive spirit go too far, but there was never a doubt she loved her family deeply.

She was the kind of mom who set her alarm clock to make sure her daughters never missed a dose of Tylenol in the middle of the night when they had a fever. She helped her girls with their Chemistry homework and pressed on determinedly even when there were tears or meltdowns over equations and formulas. And as Jenna and Katie aged and became mothers themselves, she transformed into a friend they could call any time of day or night. She would drop everything for them without a moment's notice, and was always there to lend a listening ear, offer a warm embrace, or give them a dollar—or a thousand—if it would be beneficial. She was an excellent mother, despite her human shortcomings, and an even better grandmother.

Grace valued quality time with her grandchildren and spoiled them with love and personal attention. She especially loved reading out loud to them and found great joy in transporting them into fictional worlds brimming with fantasy and adventure.

Before DVR's or streaming services were a thing, she would spend countless hours recording each grandchild's favorite TV show on VHS tapes so they could always watch what they wanted at her house. She would even delete the commercials, which was a very daunting task to say the least. Jenna thought about the number of hours her mother must have spent watching *Power Rangers*, *Barney*, and *Elmo's World* for the sake of her grands and it warmed her heart.

Grace also faithfully attended every lacrosse game, gymnastics meet, and guitar recital, even if it meant flying across the country, and built a pool with a slide and a diving board so her house would be more fun when they came to visit.

Grace Evelyn Jacobs was the definition of selflessness and the beating heart of her family. And just as the body relies on the heart to pump life-giving blood to all its parts, Grace kept the Jacobs family alive and well.

After Grace's death, Jenna became painfully aware she had taken her mother, and the important role she played in the family, for granted. She missed her tremendously and would have given anything to tell her mom how much she had appreciated her and what a wonderful role model she had been.

Without Grace, the Jacobs family struggled to survive. Holidays were suddenly spent apart, large family trips each summer came to a stop, and the feeling of being welcome in each other's lives dissipated rapidly and painfully. And when the patriarch of the family remarried the devil, a selfish woman with a personal agenda, the final nail in the family's coffin was driven.

The family, as Jenna knew it, might as well have been buried in the plot next to her mother's grave. The matriarch was gone, and the once stable family was in shambles.

The Porch

The wind blew lightly against Jenna's skin, snapping her back to the present and refocusing her thoughts on her children's conversation and their laughter coming from the other side of the door.

She shook aside her thoughts about her own childhood and her parents and allowed her eyes to wander around the porch as she listened to Brett telling the story, for the hundredth time, about how he had broken his leg when he was nine because Olivia had toddled out in front of him while he was riding his bike. He had crashed to avoid hitting her, and when he hit the pavement, his tibia had snapped like a twig. Jenna heard him exclaim with great dramatic flair, "I gallantly sacrificed myself for you Olivia, my dear little sister!" He was clearly hamming up his injury and his chivalry to make the story better.

As Jenna listened to her son's performance, she noticed the fade resistant curtains mounted along the top of the screen porch were gently moving up against the wicker patio furniture but made no noise, making it easier for her to hear Brett. Even the curtains and the wind seemed to understand Jenna's ability to focus on her children was all that was important at this moment.

The porch was her happy place where she liked to sit for hours and enjoy a cup of coffee or a glass of chardonnay. She spent hours out there reading, playing mindless games on her phone, watching the TV that Paul mounted to the brick wall, or listening to the sounds of the neighborhood.

The porch was also Paul's happy place. They liked to sit there together and talk about their days and dream out loud about their plans for the future. They also enjoyed sitting in complete silence without saying a word.

Jenna had adorned her outdoor sofa and loveseat with happy, bright lemon-patterned pillows in shades of blue and yellow. Whenever she looked at the pillows, she thought of the adage "When life gives you lemons, make lemonade." She had made a lot of "lemonade" in her life and so had her mother.

She realized her children shared that ability and had clearly made lemonade out of endless moves, embarrassing moments, and childhood injuries. They had the beautiful ability to focus on the good, sweet parts of life and let the sour parts go. This was evident as she listened to them recalling their memories. She was glad they learned this from her and hoped their optimism would last their whole lives.

She could now hear Olivia teasing her older brother with just as much cinematic theatrics as he had exhibited only moments ago. She said, "Brett, if you were a better bike rider, you wouldn't have fallen and broken your leg. You are trying to blame your total lack of coordination on a three-year-old!" Brett rubbed his leg and groaned as if it still pained him all these years later.

Her kids' laughter continued as they bantered in good spirits back and forth with each other, and the faint smell of meatloaf cooking in the kitchen reached her nose. It was a family favorite, and the kids lovingly joked it was better than Paula Deen's.

Heidi, Brett & Olivia Miller

Jenna and Paul's oldest daughter, Heidi, had recently graduated from college and was now working full-time as a church secretary while also pursuing a master's degree in divinity.

She had been a fun-loving and creative child with evolving passions. She was always the life of the party, filled with energy and fully invested in whatever her interest was at the time—guitar, figure skating, sorority politics—her heart was always all in. Her true passion, however, was in the church, and she knew she was being called to ministry since the young age of fifteen. This passion, unlike the others, only grew stronger each year into an undeniable conviction.

She made some missteps as a teenager, as most teenagers do, but bounced back from girl drama and poor choices that resulted in being grounded, with relatively few lasting scars. She made good friends easily and surrounded herself with people who understood the true meaning of friendship. She wasn't good at keeping her room clean or managing time wisely, but she excelled at relationship building, which was far more important in the scheme of life, and a skill most people did not possess.

Jenna admired her daughter for many reasons. Heidi had a love for living. She could make the most socially awkward feel at ease and could probably get a rock to talk if she tried. She could charm even the most stoic of personalities and make them smile.

If Jenna was asked to describe her oldest, she would say, "My dear Heidi is a White Claw drinking, adventure seeking, kindhearted girl who loves Jesus with all her heart and soul. She loves all God's people and is brave beyond her years." A truly amazing combination as far as Jenna was concerned.

Heidi also had an unshakeable faith, which Jenna longed for in herself. When it came to Jenna's faith, she allowed herself to be plagued with moments of doubt or anger directed at God. She didn't understand why bad things happened to good people, and it often made her question her entire belief system. Thankfully, just as quickly as she decided to be a non-believer, she would believe again. Her daughter's rock-solid faith always grounded Jenna and brought her back to the fold. It was obvious why God had called her to ministry.

After completing her undergraduate studies, Heidi moved into a place of her own near the family's previous duty station, Fort Jackson, and stayed even when the rest of the family moved to Fort Belvoir, Virginia, on military orders.

She met the love of her life the summer before graduation and was now engaged to be married in the spring. Her fiancé, Caleb, was a kind-hearted young man, working hard to make it in the corporate world. He loved his family, he loved God, and he definitely loved Heidi.

Heidi was beginning her own life, and the choices she was making brought great joy to Jenna and Paul. Even though she was eight hours away from them, she called multiple times a day and texted even more. She valued her parents' opinions, respected their advice, and modeled many of her own behaviors after them—a compliment that was not missed by Jenna and Paul. Heidi missed not seeing them every day, but knew she was where she needed to be, in South Carolina.

The relationship between Jenna and Heidi was one to be envied. They had an unbreakable mother-daughter bond that grew stronger with each passing year. The two women were honest with one another, told each other the good, the bad, and the ugly when it came to their lives and loved each other unconditionally. There was a feeling of safety between them, and Jenna considered it one of her greatest blessings. She was grateful every day for a daughter who successfully transitioned from childhood to adulthood and became her best friend.

Heidi was the spitting image of Jenna, only better, and it always amazed her how much of herself she could see in her.

Paul and Jenna's middle child and only son, Brett, was a freshman, referred to as a Knob, at The Military College of South Carolina known as The Citadel. The campus was set in the beautiful and historic city of Charleston. The buildings looked like castles and surrounded a grand parade field flanked by cannons. It was a picturesque place and fueled his desire to join the Infantry, following in the footsteps of his father, a career Army officer. He was ambitious, quick-witted, and excelled in physical fitness.

Brett had been a dream of a child with an unusually good sense of humor. He understood the art of sarcasm from a very young age and always kept the family in stitches with his timely quips. He did, however, challenge his parents frequently as a teenager. He wasn't a partier or into drugs or alcohol, but rather he liked to exert his opinion and always wanted to be right, like many typical teenage boys.

He would argue the sky wasn't blue or water wasn't wet just to get a reaction and often failed to prioritize schoolwork. However, he was also the most kindhearted boy one could imagine, protective of his family, and had gone through several personal trials, solidifying he was a young man of great character.

Brett had successfully navigated the difficult world of travel lacrosse and high school sports politics and came out the better for it, despite the emotional abuse it inflicted.

Jenna admired her son for his never-quit attitude, knowing she would have thrown in the towel many times over if she had experienced even half of the pressures of sports Brett had endured.

Perhaps these experiences with lacrosse had prepared him to excel at a military college that made strict demands of the Knobs.

Jenna had also seen him stand up for her and others when he felt they had been wronged. It was rare for a teenage boy to be so concerned about the way people were treated, however, Brett was the exception and always wanted justice for everyone. He was very perceptive and always noticed when someone's feelings were being hurt. He also had an extra special place in his heart for his mama that never seemed to wane.

He was the most sensitive of her children. Even as a young child, Brett modeled compassion naturally, often taking time to stop and play with children in the neighborhood or at school with disabilities so they would feel included. He never felt playing with them was an act of charity. He enjoyed their company and considered them friends.

As Brett aged and matured, he felt he had an obligation to be the man of the house if his father was away on military orders. This came from a place of love, not parental expectation.

Jenna was pleased her son thought being a man included standing up for those who were hurting, defending his family, and embracing confrontation when needed. He had the idealistic viewpoint that people could argue and then work things out. He believed in forgiveness, which he learned from his dad.

Brett was working very hard at The Citadel, and much to Jenna and Paul's delight, his need to argue with his parents had somehow miraculously been satisfied since leaving for college. He channeled his passion for arguing into his business law major and was finding ways to be a productive leader in the corps of cadets.

Jenna and Paul were proud of his work ethic, his willingness to share his life with them, and his future goals. He was only halfway through his first semester and already on track for making the President's List and earning a gold star for academics.

Likewise, he was making a name for himself with the upper-class students because of his mental toughness under pressure, his physical ability to keep pushing on no matter how many pushups they assigned him or how long they expected him to brace, and his ability to laugh when they pulled pranks on him. He considered being the butt of a joke a compliment in the serious environment of The Citadel.

He knew the seniors liked him when he was given a frog one night and told it would now be an inspectable item he was responsible for. He had scrambled to find a box to keep it in and checked on it throughout the night. He found it hilarious when the seniors forgot about the poor creature and never asked about it again.

Brett was the perfect combination of Jenna and Paul, often to his chagrin. As a teenager he wanted to procrastinate like Jenna, while simultaneously being a perfectionist like Paul. A procrastinating perfectionist doesn't always work out well. He was emotional like Jenna but had a temper like Paul. He inherited both of his parents' strongest traits, good and bad, which were complementary in two people but difficult to manage in one body. Thankfully, Brett was learning to manage his strong genetics and to capitalize on his strengths. He was becoming an amazing young man, reflective of the best from both parents.

Olivia, the youngest of the Miller children, was the kind of person everyone wanted to be like. She was more intelligent at the age of twelve than most adults. She was extremely disciplined in her academics and competitive gymnastics, and she was a talented artist. It is a rarity for someone to be considerate, disciplined, brilliant, and artistic all in one package, yet that was Olivia in a nutshell.

She often won competitions and was good at everything she tried, yet she kept a humbleness about herself that was noteworthy. She also loved to genuinely praise others for their accomplishments or their efforts. She was quick to point out her lack of musical talent to others but still confidently belted out her favorite songs, even though she couldn't carry a tune in a bucket.

She was obsessed with Taylor Swift and couldn't be more thrilled she had the same name as one of Taylor's cats. Little things made her happy. She made lemonade.

As an almost-teenager, she had already mastered talking on the phone and FaceTime and loved being social. She knew how to be a good friend to others and built solid relationships at each duty station, lasting even after every move. She loved going to church and made sure to keep her parents on track when Jenna or Paul felt like sleeping in on a Sunday.

Her determination to succeed and desire to work hard were characteristics she inherited from Paul, as was her need to excel in school, which often resulted in her being too hard on herself. There was no denying Paul was her father because they were two peas in a pod, and despite their shared Type A personalities, for that Jenna couldn't be happier.

Jenna could see glimpses of herself in her youngest daughter, too, like the way she danced to music in her head, laughed out loud at her own jokes, got excited for a theme party, and loved to play board games.

Olivia was also very much like Grace—even though she really couldn't remember her grandmother since she died when she was only two.

Genetics is a fascinating thing. You learn in school your eye color, hairline shape, and blood type are all direct results of your genes, but to truly see the spirit and personality of one person shining through another is mind blowing.

Sometimes, Jenna let her imagination freely invent scenarios that could have been had her mother not succumbed so quickly to breast cancer at the age of sixty-six. She could easily picture Olivia and her mom working on a jigsaw puzzle together, racing to see who could solve riddles the fastest, or rolling out pie crust dough with flour splashed all around the kitchen. She could almost smell the apple pie baking or see the Sunday crossword puzzle splayed out on the kitchen table with two pencils laying on top.

Oh, how different things would be now if her mother was still here. The family of Jenna's childhood would almost certainly be intact. *Why had God taken her mother from them?* It seemed so unfair.

Jenna and Paul Miller

Jenna considered herself extremely blessed because she had been able to be a stay-at-home mom for so many years. She officially quit working when Heidi was three, and never returned to the office. She had been able to take her children to the park regularly, do elaborate craft projects with them, help them with their homework, and listen to the events of their days as she drove them back and forth between school and extracurricular activities. Perhaps driving carpool wasn't as bad as it seemed. In retrospect, it had given her an opportunity to hear what was going on in her children's lives and to get to know their friends better.

She was still driving Olivia to and from school and gymnastics and savored every moment she had with her in the car. Time together without distraction from the world was a gift she would gladly accept.

Jenna loved looking at scrapbooks and seeing pictures of Heidi, Brett, and Olivia covered from head to toe in dirt or paint because it meant they explored the world around them that day and experienced the freedom of childhood through their own hands.

Her favorite photos were not the ones where they were dressed up in fancy clothing or every hair was in place. Rather, she treasured the pictures of her children buried in huge leaf piles, covered in makeup stolen from her purse, or hanging upside down from the swing set. These photos captured their personalities, the essence of who they were.

She used to say if a child didn't require a bath at night, they had a terrible day. Her three were no strangers to mud puddles, dirt under their fingernails, making slime with glitter, or fingerpaints. Nothing reasonable was off limits because she had the time to allow it—and the patience, most days, to handle it.

She knew she had done the best she could raising the kids, along with Paul, who somehow managed to work ridiculously long days, deploy seven times, and still make more time for her and the family than most of her friends' husbands. He even cooked, did laundry, and did the dishes of his own accord.

However, she couldn't help but feel a nagging restlessness in the back of her mind. *Would their efforts be enough to keep the family together after they were gone?*

Jenna and Paul were not perfect parents by any means and had more than a few faults. If someone recorded every mistake they'd made along the way, the list would be so long it would surely stretch for miles. Some days their parenting game was strong, and other days they failed miserably. After all, they were only humans and did not possess any supernatural parenting powers.

Jenna and Paul both let cuss words fly more often than they would like to admit, probably daily if they were being honest. They let the kids spend too much time in front of the TV if they were busy or too tired to play, and they angered more quickly than they should have at the sight of a messy room or dishes left in the living room. They had not always handled zeroes in the gradebook rationally and often put too much pressure on their kids for various reasons.

Because of the Army, the family moved so many times, and Paul and Jenna sometimes lost sight of how difficult that could be for children. They expected them to suck it up and press on regardless of their location.

And only by the grace of God, they had.

Jenna was most proud of the marriage she and Paul modeled for her children. They fought as every married couple does, but they always forgave one another completely. There was no room for grudges in their household, and they made sure their children knew that. They had a marriage that was an example of teamwork, unconditional love, and total forgiveness. It wasn't perfect by anyone's standards, but it was solid.

After a quarter of a century of marriage, Jenna fell deeper in love with Paul after each passing year. When the two married at ages twenty-one and twenty-three, they knew they were in love. However, it is not possible for such a young couple to understand how much love can continue to grow. With each trial and success of life, love either grows or diminishes.

It is often said that marriage is when two become one. Jenna always thought this was a reference to physical love, however, she was thankful to understand it on a deeper level now.

She was blessed with a husband who brought out the best in her, supported her, and worked his tail off out of love for their family. She could not imagine who she would be without him and didn't want to. He was truly a part of her and gave meaning to the phrase "my better half."

Sometimes they drove each other crazy or made each other infuriatingly mad, but they never doubted their love for one other. They could trust each other fully and prioritized their marriage in their daily lives. Together, they survived pregnancies, sleep deprivation, fourteen moves, great losses, deployments, financial hardships, rearing children, family drama—so much family drama—and serious illness.

Jenna wholeheartedly believed after teaching her kids about Jesus, modeling a healthy marriage was the next best gift a parent could give a child. It had taken Jenna and Paul years of hard work, commitment, love, and forgiveness to get where they were today, and it had all been worth it.

Paul was a wonderful example to their girls about what they should look for in a husband, however, he was an even stronger example to their son of how a husband should treasure his wife.

In addition to an unparalleled work ethic, Paul never failed to amaze Jenna with his care and concern for her. He worked hard to make her feel appreciated and genuinely believed every dollar he earned was a team effort. He never made Jenna feel like a second-class citizen because he was the only breadwinner for the family. He often said, "My darling, your contributions to the family are far greater and more valuable than my paycheck. You have the most difficult job in the world." Jenna would argue this opinion, but she loved him for having it, nonetheless.

He regularly walked in the door after a grueling twelve-hour day with flowers in hand from the grocery store or a handwritten note in a carefully selected card. He spun Jenna around the kitchen as they danced and listened to music on their Alexa almost daily and was quick to text her a link to any new country song with lyrics about love. Most recently, he had sent her Chris Stapleton's hit song, "The Joy of My Life." Jenna had cried when she listened to it on her iPhone because the simple song confirmed to her Paul was her soulmate.

Paul kissed her every morning before he left for work, even if she was sleeping, and greeted her with a kiss and the words "Hello, My Love" or "Hello, Beautiful" every evening when he returned.

She was always on his mind, and that was a wonderful place to be.

Paul never judged her if there were dishes in the sink or laundry piles on the floor. He was not the kind of husband who expected dinner the instant he walked in the door or pressed shirts hanging in the closet.

Although he was extremely disciplined in his own ways, he understood Jenna had a less scheduled way of doing things. She didn't write down copious notes in little green notebooks to keep track of things like he did, but, somehow, she got everything done and their household ran smoothly. She paid the bills, managed the children's needs and schedules, and kept him informed about everything he needed to know regarding family operations. He thought she did a wonderful job managing their family, and he was better because of her efforts.

He also appreciated that Jenna supported his career choice and happily devoted countless hours to volunteering on behalf of Army families.

Paul was thankful he could trust Jenna to take care of things at home when he was on a deployment or on a field training exercise and never doubted her faithfulness to him or her ability to handle any circumstance life threw at her. He had seen so many Army families fall apart during forced separations, but he never feared this would happen to his own.

Donna Thorn

Donna Thorn scrolled through countless pictures of men who had made profile pages on the popular dating website Christian Companion.

Men on CC were usually naïve, white conservatives who were lonely with money to burn. They were often tied to traditional values which appealed to Donna because they would be more likely to be compatible with her strong, Christian morals. She frequently made Facebook posts about her conservative values so others would know where she stood on any number of controversial topics. Social media was a wonderful tool for her to use to publicly distance herself from anyone she deemed as unworthy. She had no interest in following Jesus's repeated pattern of hanging out with the poor, well-known sinners, those of different cultures, or social outcasts.

Donna claimed to be a member of the modern Assembly of God church even though she had never formally joined. She ascribed to most of its doctrine but didn't feel it necessary to abide by its antiquated views on modesty. She was proud to tout her unofficial affiliation with the denomination and enjoyed showing off that she knew more about the Bible than most regular Protestants and Catholics. She believed she was more devout than most Christians and this greatly pleased her.

Donna thrived on the attention she received for her Christian deeds. She felt she was a generous woman and deserved accolades anytime she gave to a charity, and public accolades were certainly the best. Pride and vanity might be sins, but they didn't apply to her, only to inferior Christians.

At age fifty-four, Donna was tired of working every day, even though she mostly enjoyed her coworkers and her job. She would like to retire but didn't have enough in the bank to make the transition into the leisurely retirement she deserved.

She was ready for some of the finer things in life and had a great figure for someone her age. She never had children to broaden her hips, and she religiously dyed her light brown hair jet black, like a raven, to hide the grays mother nature kept sending. She never went out in public without foundation because she didn't want anyone to see the sprinkling of freckles across her nose or the small birthmark on her jawline. She preferred her skin to look flawless, like porcelain. She always splurged and had her nails done. Keeping up the perfect persona was sometimes costly, but she viewed it as necessary, and she was worth it.

She also had an excellent sense of style. Donna was partial to dark-colored clothing because it complimented her hair and skin color. She knew how to use costume jewelry and accessories to give the illusion she, too, had money in excess. Just the right amount of sparkle could go a long way.

She wanted to look like the total package because she believed she was the total package. She was a catch, like Audrey Hepburn or Jacqueline Kennedy Onassis. Beautiful, smart, poised, and classy.

She continued scrolling through photos and made judgments based solely on a quick glance—too fat, too bald, too ugly, too poor, too old. Swipe left, swipe left, swipe left, swipe left, swipe left.

She wanted a man who was well established and free from any baggage of past relationships gone wrong. There was no room for a former girlfriend or ex-wife in her plan and especially no room for anyone collecting alimony.

Most of all, she wanted a man who could take care of her—which meant spending his money on her. The more he had, the better it would be for them both.

Tom Jacobs's picture stared at her from her laptop screen. He was a decent looking man in his late sixties and recently widowed. He had dark blond hair with minimal graying at the temples, a neatly trimmed beard, and was in better than average shape. He looked tall, which she liked since she was five foot nine without heels. She guessed he was at least six foot two. His picture warranted a deeper look than the men she had quickly swiped away.

She was intrigued and decided to read his bio. It gave some background information on his life including his age, pre-retirement occupation, and hobbies. His profile picture showed a beautiful Sea Ray Cruiser Yacht behind him with the name "Commission Casanova" painted on the side. It was apparently a play on words, referencing his career as a successful real estate agent but also wreaked of just enough conceit to catch her attention. She liked a man who was a little full of himself because he could appreciate how she felt about herself. She also liked any man who owned his own yacht, even if it was a small one.

He devoted a whole section of his bio to highlighting his successful career and listing his professional accolades. She was impressed to see he had been listed in "Who's Who in Georgia Real Estate" more than a handful of times. He had also sold several multi-million-dollar mansions, made a number of well-known commercial property deals in Atlanta she knew were extremely lucrative, and proclaimed himself to be "Georgia's Favorite Realtor."

She judged him to be one who believed respect was given to people in proportion to the size of their bank account.

Perhaps they did have a few things in common. Perfect.

Money equaled respect in her opinion too.

Tom Jacobs clearly valued his reputation. Any drama threatening his image of devout Christian and financial success would destroy him.

She easily surmised if he were to remarry, he would try make the relationship work no matter how bad it got because he would view divorce as a public failure. Tom Jacobs didn't like to fail.

That would work nicely with her plan.

Was God sending her a successful, Christian man who would devote all of himself and his resources to her? Was she finally being rewarded for her faithfulness?

A quick Google search showed he owned a beautiful home in Peachtree City, near Atlanta, and a luxurious vacation home in St. Simon's Island. He had never been divorced or filed for bankruptcy. He had bought and sold more than a few properties over his lifetime as real estate investments, which made sense considering his career. He was a card-carrying Republican and made donations here and there to several highly publicized charities.

He, too, had an affinity for appearing on donor lists and usually contributed the minimum amount to be named. He paid his property taxes on time and there were no outstanding warrants. Thank God for public records. She didn't want to waste any of her time on a deadbeat.

His Facebook page showed he had children, grandchildren, and a handful of friends.

She was able to see a picture of his deceased wife. Her name was Grace, and she had allowed gray hair to infiltrate her head and seemed not to bother herself with manicures or accessories.

Donna was more put together than Grace and wore a much more stylish wardrobe. She would never be caught dead in a T-shirt that said, "My favorite people call me Grandma." She couldn't imagine why any woman would want to call attention to her age. The word "grandma" was synonymous with old. She would never be old and was willing to do whatever it took to ensure her body did not match the number of candles on her birthday cake.

The last picture of Tom's wife showed she'd clearly faded away from some sort of illness with her family by her side. Donna guessed she died from cancer because her scalp was covered by a fabric head wrap, making her believe her hair had fallen out completely from chemotherapy. She also noted her once active body was obviously frail, and she was wheelchair ridden. It was sad to say the least, but at least she wouldn't be looking for any payoffs.

Tom's bio on CC fixated on finding a new wife and touting his own biblical knowledge. Letting others know he was deep in the Word was as important to him as it was to her.

He was abundantly clear with what he was looking for—a Christian woman who loved to travel, cook, spend time on the beach, and would allow him to fish and play golf whenever he wanted. He dreamed of traveling to far off places, which meant he had the funds to bankroll the trips.

Mostly, he desired to find a woman that would provide him constant companionship and take care of him—and if she did, he would take care of her.

Tom's "wanted" list suited Donna well, with the only exception being she didn't want to travel. She was mildly afraid of flying and was content, for the most part, to stay on Georgia's eastern coast. Other than that, they seemed like a perfect match. Donna could easily fake interest in seeing the world though, until she reeled him in fully.

Donna had a knack for attracting men and was good at convincing them she deserved to be spoiled. However, the spoiling never lasted long. She had a problem getting the men to stay for the long haul.

She told herself, *this time will be different*.

Donna was looking for a life partner so she could finally get off these ridiculous dating websites. She wanted someone who would pay for her bi-weekly manicures forever and keep her company. Tom Jacobs seemed like a good candidate.

He could give her the lifestyle she dreamed of, and perhaps they would even get along. If he did as she wished, they could both be happy. She longed for a secure relationship with a man who was completely devoted to her and who would treat her like a queen, make her financially secure, and make her happy.

One last look at his tanned face and bio and she swiped right.

Time to hit him with a Bible verse, make his mouth water with tales of her amazing cooking abilities, and start the methodical planning of becoming the next Mrs. Jacobs. She was convinced this arrangement could work out quite nicely for them both as she worked out a plan in her mind.

Mr. Right

Donna had been close to catching a different "Mr. Right" two summers ago and had even gotten engaged. She found him on the dating website, eUnion.com, which catered to more experienced daters who were a little savvier than those on Christian Companion.

Frank Wilson, an accomplished trial attorney, had been married once before and didn't want to make a mistake a second time. His first divorce cost him a fortune and had left him with a broken heart and a bad taste in his mouth.

When he saw Donna's picture, he had an immediate attraction and decided to ask her out for a date despite his initial reluctance. He would tread cautiously but was optimistic he could find love for a second time.

In the beginning of their relationship, Frank enjoyed spending time with Donna and thought they were compatible. He couldn't believe his luck. He showered her with gifts and liked treating her to the town. They even had many shared hobbies and interests.

She rushed him to propose, and he did so to make her happy, against his better judgment.

He quickly realized, though, nothing was ever enough for her. She always wanted just a little more. More attention, more time, more things, more control. He quickly grew tired of her endless requests and began to view her constant demands as excessive.

Donna's controlling tendencies bothered him immensely. The more she sought to control the relationship, the more he pulled away. The more he pulled away, the more she sought to control the relationship. It was a vicious cycle destined for failure, but she couldn't see that.

The constant emotional outbursts when she didn't get what she wanted, the way she dictated how they spent their time and who they spent it with, and the way she threw his money around like it grew on trees became exhausting. He tried to address these issues with her but there was no compromising on her part. She became wildly upset if he even attempted to bring up any problems, and a rational discussion was impossible.

Frank, like his American Express card, finally reached his limit. He told Donna he wanted to end the relationship and asked her to give him back the engagement ring.

She became hysterical and threw the three karat Tiffany diamond at him, hitting him with it in the shoulder. As he stared at the ten-thousand-dollar ring that had landed on the floor a few feet in front of him, he knew she was truly crazy. He calmly picked up the ring, put it in his pocket, and told her to get out. He also told her she was jealous, selfish, and manipulative. It felt good to get that off his chest.

Donna was enraged by his accusations, even though she knew many of them were true, and stormed out of the home that had almost been hers. Frank had felt bad for hurting her, but he mostly felt relieved. The sound of the door slamming behind her as she left was music to his ears.

Donna didn't like confrontation, especially from men, and was shocked Frank had broken up with her. She hadn't seen it coming. She was even more shocked by his ugly and disrespectful words.

Donna viewed anyone with a different opinion from her as being emotionally abusive—whether it was true or not, and equated getting her way with being loved.

Frank wasn't the first person to call her selfish or think her behavior was crazy. Her ex-husband, Todd Thorn, had made similar comments, and it led to the downfall of their ten-year marriage. She believed that he, too, was cruel like Frank, even if he was the one who filed for divorce.

How did she keep getting in relationships with men like this?

For the life of her, she couldn't understand how Todd had found a woman to marry him after her, and how they seemed to have the perfect life on Facebook—four kids, a dog, a goldfish, a house, and perpetually smiling faces.

She knew her rage, outlandish emotional outbursts, and her need to control were a little over the top, but she accepted this was how God made her. Any partner would have to accept and embrace these traits. Perhaps she had dodged a bullet with Frank.

Donna also believed he was spiritually weak. She decided he had been influenced by the devil to end the relationship because Satan wouldn't want to see a decent, Christian woman happy. The devil may have taken a hold over Frank Wilson, but it was God who saved her from a mistake.

It wasn't Donna's fault he was too naive to see marrying her would have been to his benefit. Although she was not from high society, his friends would have been jealous of him with her on his arm. In her opinion, she looked like a million bucks, even if her bank account balance had a lot less zeroes.

As for his money, she would have deserved it for putting up with him. *Aren't relationships about give and take?* Of course, she always preferred the man to give and her to take.

Todd Thorn and Frank Wilson were fools to let her slip away.

Donna half expected Frank to call her and beg for forgiveness, but he never did.

Tom Jacobs would be different from her previous relationships. He met all her criteria and appeared to be much more spiritually sound. She had learned from her mistakes with Frank and wouldn't let her perfect persona falter for even a minute until they said, "I do," joining them till death do they part. She would keep sweet and play the part of the adoring woman until there was no way out.

She was slightly concerned Tom had adult children and grandchildren who might try to compete for his time or money. A small hiccup at best. She'd assess the situation once she got things rolling and figure out what course of action would be necessary for the brats.

For now, it was time to hit Send and see if love, happiness, and financial freedom were on the other end of the direct message.

The Funeral

Grace Jacobs had been a devoted spouse and was, quite frankly, a saint, for making her marriage to Tom work for so many years. She had been good at covering up her husband's inherently selfish nature and shielding the family from his narcissism.

Jenna had always gotten along decently well with her father but had had very few serious conversations with him over the course of her life prior to her mom's death. She always counted on her mother for advice or a shoulder to cry on when life was tough. She never sought out her father for counsel or comfort, and he never tried to provide it. Her dad had been a constant presence in her life, but he was rarely emotionally engaged.

Growing up, Jenna brushed aside her father's propensity for rudeness and never let it bother her because their relationship was largely superficial. She didn't even realize the lack of depth between them until her mom was no longer there to provide the substance.

Grace had given strict instructions from her deathbed that her husband, Tom, should not speak at her memorial service. It wasn't because she didn't love him. She did. Very much, despite all his faults.

Rather, it was because public speaking brought out the worst in her husband.

Whenever Tom was asked to get up in front of crowds, especially in a church setting, he would turn it into a Christian revival. Grace did not want him turning her funeral into an episode of the *700 Club*. She wanted a peaceful service where her husband, children, grandchildren, and friends could remember her and say goodbye.

She knew if Tom was given the chance to speak, he would transform himself into the all-knowing evangelist, stinking of hypocrisy and self-righteousness, and she would become an afterthought.

For once, Grace wanted to be the focus of her husband's attention. She wanted people to leave her funeral talking about her and the many contributions she made to the world. She wanted just one day to be about her, even if she wasn't there to see it.

Grace did not want the crowds talking about what a wonderful eulogy her husband had given or talking about how passionate his speech was. She didn't want them talking about Tom at all—unless it was to say what a lucky man he was to have had Grace as his wife.

She simply yearned for a sendoff acknowledging her as a person and leaving people feeling glad they had known her.

Tom assured her he would grant her last request, and she died believing he would keep his promise.

Despite his pledge to Grace, Tom secretly arranged with the pastor presiding over the service to speak at her funeral. He purposely did not tell his girls because he knew Jenna and Katie would have tried to stop him. He was flagrantly disregarding his wife's final wishes and his secrecy meant he knew he was wrong, but he didn't care.

Most Christians consider lying a sin. If someone asked Tom if lying was wrong, he would say, "yes," but he would mean, "it is wrong for others to lie." He had an uncanny level of justification for his own lies and rarely considered any of his own actions sinful. As far as he was concerned, his relationship with God was superb. Above average. Superior. He thought it was okay for him to be a little deceptive here and there or to tell a white lie now and again if it were for the glory of God.

He fervently believed defying his wife's wishes was the right thing to do because her funeral was an opportunity for him to witness to others. It was also a chance for him to put his own righteousness on display, which brought him great pleasure.

Tom even rationalized Grace wasn't fully in her right mind when she made her request because of her heavily medicated state. Surely his wife, and fellow disciple, didn't really mean it when she said, "Tom, keep your mouth shut at my funeral."

He even considered it was the devil who put these words on her lips, trying to prevent him from testifying about the goodness of God. Jesus commanded His followers to become fishers of men, and Tom, His ever-humble servant, needed to obey. It was far more important for Tom to take orders from Jesus than his wife.

On the day of the funeral, Reverend Cartwood opened the service by giving some brief remarks about Grace—impersonal and filled with stories from decades ago.

Jenna was dumbfounded by his eulogy because he barely mentioned Grace's role as a mother, wife, guidance counselor, or grandmother. It was painstakingly obvious he had been fed stories from her father, and they were all from the early days of their marriage. They were not reflective of the life Grace lived or who she was when she died.

As Jenna sat in the front pew wondering why every story had been about her mother when she was in her early twenties, she saw her father stand up and start to walk toward the front of the church. Her heart started racing because she knew in her gut something bad was about to happen.

She quickly prayed her father was about to tell the true story of Grace Evelyn Jacobs's life and surprise them all with a beautiful eulogy more indicative of who she had been, even though he had been instructed not to.

As Jenna pondered what her father was about to say, it dawned on her that neither she nor her sister had been asked to speak at the service. Furthermore, Reverend Cartwood had not asked them or any of the grandchildren to share stories with him he could incorporate into his eulogy.

Jenna and Katie had picked the casket, the flowers, and the programs but were not included in the service at all.

It suddenly became crystal clear to Jenna her mother's funeral was about to become the Tom Jacobs Show, and she was just an audience member. Chills ran down her spine.

Within thirty seconds of reaching the mic, Tom turned Grace's life story into that of a struggling Christian who found Jesus on her deathbed. He began to tell the tale of how he led her to make the decision to renew her baptismal covenant just one month before her death.

Jenna's whole body numbed with anger and disbelief. This was exactly what her mother had feared. Her dad was turning the focus of the funeral away from Grace's life. The service was now a recruitment effort, and he was looking for new soldiers to join the Lord's Army.

Tom avoided making direct eye contact with her and with Katie, indicative of his awareness of his betrayal.

Less than forty-eight hours after Grace's death, her only wish was being disregarded. Her life was being reduced to a fictional salvation story of a sinner saved at the last minute, thanks largely to her husband and his unwavering faith.

Tom's lips quivered as he spoke, and his voice was shaky with emotion. He went off on a tangent about salvation, and Grace was nowhere to be found in his words. He was giving a Jerry Falwell level performance, and Jenna's chest grew tighter and tighter as each second passed because she knew some people were swept up by his charismatic gestures and his cracking voice, believing his words about her mother to be true.

Jenna half expected him to make an altar call so he could save everyone in the congregation, although she couldn't think of even one person in attendance who wasn't already a Christian.

Jenna thought, *it is much easier to witness to people who already believe, isn't it?*

There was still barely any mention of the amazing acts of kindness her mother regularly committed, and nothing about her sense of humor or her intelligence. There was not one word about how she lovingly cared for multiple family members until the time of their deaths like a combination of Florence Nightingale and Mother Theresa.

Hardly anything was uttered about the impact she had on countless students who struggled in school or with life's circumstances until they met her.

The role she played in her grandchildren's lives was also glossed over. Her "babies" as she called them, had been her world, but that was not apparent at her funeral.

Jenna wasn't sure her mother had been mentioned at all. She felt like she was listening to a speech about a stranger.

The last words spoken in public about Grace Jacobs weren't about her. What a disservice to a wonderful woman who lived a beautiful life. On a day when she should have been the star, and those who loved her dearly should have been able to mourn, the focus was on Tom and his self-righteous crusade to make believers better believers.

The truth regarding Grace's personal faith journey was she always believed in Jesus, from childhood to the grave. Her compassionate nature and deep ability to love was an obvious byproduct of her Christian faith. She was a servant in every aspect of her life who walked the walk but kept her talk to a minimum because her husband always drowned her out.

Jenna never said a word to her father about her anger over her mother's funeral. She thought it was best to just let it go. She knew her dad was also hurting and somehow his ridiculous funeral speech made him feel better. *What good would it do to scream and yell at him?* The deed could not be undone.

When he handed her a DVD of the service a few weeks after the whole catastrophe, in case she wanted to watch it again, she pushed the rage that bubbled up down into the deepest depths of her stomach.

How could he think she would want to watch him make a mockery of her mother's funeral for a second time?

Tom obviously thought his performance was worth watching again.

Jenna took the DVD he gave her and tossed it in the trash when he wasn't looking. She decided to honor her mother by never thinking about that disgrace of a funeral again.

God & Glory

Tom took a job with an affluent real estate agency in the mid-1980s and the Jacobs family moved from a small town in western Georgia to Peachtree City, a suburb of Atlanta. Tom and Grace found a thriving Presbyterian church and hoped it would be a good fit for the family. They wanted their girls to grow up in faith, and this church was known for having a fabulous youth program. Its congregation contained many well-known socialites and included more than its fair share of doctors, lawyers, and successful businessmen.

After only a short time, Grace began to feel unsettled. She wasn't as impressed with some of the members of the congregation as Tom was, namely the ones in their forty-something Sunday School class.

The class was heavy-handed with successful men who had chauvinistic tendencies, big egos, and trophy wives who adoringly listened to their husbands speak and kept their mouths closed.

Grace disliked the way the men in the class fueled her husband's desire to be seen as a "Super Christian" and agreed with everything he said, regardless of if his opinions were biblically sound. He did the same for them.

They often made racist or sexist jokes and spewed elitist comments that made Grace's blood boil. They were quick to judge others but were incapable of looking in the mirror.

Grace confronted Tom about his behavior and said, "I feel like you are starting to have a God complex, thinking your every thought is of God." Tom dismissed his wife and said, "That is absurd. Perhaps you could try to be a little more like some of the other women in the class."

The church was full of good people too, but Tom didn't seem to click with any of the members who were more to Grace's liking, and she felt like an outsider if she tried to join other couples at fellowship events without her husband by her side.

Tom's head grew larger every Sunday morning, and his behavior was the opposite of what it should have been. He enjoyed showboating more than living right and exhibiting godly behavior.

Tom was making more money than ever before in the real estate world and liked others to see his prosperity. He wrote checks loudly for the offering plate.

Because of his professional success, he had been accepted into the circles of those who had already established themselves as wealthy pillars in the community. He liked rubbing elbows with other professionals and thrived on the attention he was receiving from them at church. He felt like a bigwig who was making a name for himself in society. His newfound status was certainly a step up from lowly farm equipment salesman.

Grace was bothered by Tom's ever-increasing ego. She didn't feel he exuded the fruits of the spirit at all, especially when he was at Sunday School. Love, joy, peace, patience, kindness, goodness, faithfulness, gentleness, and self-control weren't always evident in his actions or in his soapbox preaching.

Grace begged him to try a new church, but he was happy where they were and didn't want to consider a change. His ego was being stroked, and he had been judged as a "worthy Christian" by his peers. He didn't notice his wife felt stifled, unappreciated, and lonely.

Their girls were also happy with the youth program, which was living up to its reputation, so Grace just retreated for their sake and to appease the big headedness of her husband.

She was relieved her children did not see the ugly side of their father because they spent all their time in the youth building, far away from the disingenuous adults she was forced to endure.

When the girls aged out of the youth group, Tom finally agreed to move to a new church. It wasn't a decision made to placate Grace. He didn't like the pastor recently assigned to their church because he had liberal views and was a Democrat. Tom talked about him behind his back and questioned if he really was a Presbyterian.

Tom wanted to follow some of the other men he had befriended who shared the same opinion. They were forming their own startup church and he wanted to get in on ground level. "Founding member" had a nice ring to it.

The problems he and Grace experienced with the first church continued at his new church. It was the same people in a different building. The issues simply moved with them. Tom was quick to blame Grace for not trying hard enough to fit in and accused her of having weak faith.

Ironically, the institution of church, which was supposed to bring out the good in people, brought out the worst in Tom, even though he couldn't see it in himself.

Church became a source of great strife in Tom and Grace's marriage.

Grace stopped going to church completely because of the pain and isolation she experienced there. She didn't pull away from God, rather she pulled away from the man her husband was at church.

Thankfully, it was mostly only an issue on Sundays because that's when Tom was on display. He didn't know Grace spent every Sunday morning deep in prayer at home talking to the Lord and praying for her husband and her marriage while he was singing loudly and off-key in the church pew.

In the last months of her life, Grace made it a priority to let any resentment that had accumulated during her marriage to Tom go. She was determined not to leave this Earth with any unresolved arguments or hurt feelings. The closer she got to death, the easier it was to absolve him from his sins.

They had been through more than four and a half decades of ups and downs, and even though they had problems, they still loved each other very much. Tom and Grace were both committed to their marriage and were living their vows out to the fullest. In sickness and in health, in good times and in bad, for better or for worse, until death do us part.

Tom even put aside some of his selfishness to focus on his wife. He took his role as caretaker seriously, and she was grateful.

Grace and Tom had disagreed about church for more than twenty years, and it was time for the conflict to be settled once and for all. Grace knew she was dying, and the next time she would physically be able to attend church, she would be in a coffin. She was running out of time, and she knew the most meaningful gift she could give her husband was to request she be baptized again.

When she told him she wanted to do this, he cried with joy. Tom equated her lack of interest in the church with lack of faith. A baptismal renewal meant she was once again a believer washed in the blood. No matter how many times she tried to explain her feelings about church had nothing to do with disbelief, he could never understand. He would have had to acknowledge his own faults to fully comprehend what she was saying, and that was beyond his capability.

Grace allowed Tom to make all the arrangements for the ceremony. He invited Pastor Cartwood to come to their home to rededicate her and invited the whole family and her closest friends to attend.

Grace knew this would be her last party and smiled for pictures despite her fatigue and pain. She tried to make small talk with all who had come. She was truly glad to see everyone one more time. Those in attendance were her closest friends and family. She hid her fear of dying as best as she could and made sure she comforted everyone who was present.

She was more afraid than she had ever been in her life, but trusted Jesus would be waiting for her on the other side. He never failed her in the past, and He wouldn't fail her now. The baptism had been a gift for Tom, but it also gave her peace as she prepared to meet her Savior.

It was scary for her to think of leaving this world and her family behind, but she knew she was going to a better place.

Tom Jacobs

Tom sat in his home office, focused on conducting his normal checklist of computer tasks. Clear email inbox. Check. Run software updates. Check. Look at his stock portfolio to see how it weathered the day. Check.

All seemed to go smoothly as he completed this series of to-dos for the third time that day.

Unfortunately, he was no stranger to technical trouble with his computer, router, printer, or anything technological. His children teased him because he needed computer help so frequently, he added Microsoft's tech support hotline to his saved auto-dial numbers in his phone. One touch of a button and he would hear the familiar words, "Microsoft Technical Support, how can I assist you?"

Today, though, he had no trouble and clicked his mouse with ease, navigating the many different tabs and software programs he had opened.

Unlike the first three times he sat down at his desk, he had one new task on his list to check off. He was anxious to get to this final item and was glad everything else was done. He had taken care of business first, but his fourth task was for pleasure.

He closed all the tabs that were open on Microsoft Edge and typed into the search bar www.christiancompanion.com.

As the site loaded, he stared at the picture of his late wife in the gold frame on his desk. It was taken on picture day at the high school where she was a guidance counselor and had been printed in the yearbook on the staff page. He couldn't remember what year it was taken, but it was at least fifteen years old. He kept it on his desk because he liked seeing her when she was vibrant and healthy.

It was hard for him to look at photos from her final days because she had withered from the cancer and seemed so small and weak.

In the photo she had a genuine smile on her face, and she was wearing one of her favorite polka dot shirts.

Grace had been a beautiful woman, particularly in her younger years, and Tom had been proud to be her husband.

As he looked at the picture, he felt like Grace was looking back at him with understanding. They had discussed the possibility he might want to date again once she was gone. She was okay with this possible course of action and even blessed off on him remarrying if he found the right woman. Just because her life was over, they both knew his was not. He was thankful she had been a practical woman, so he didn't have to feel any guilt about reentering the dating world.

Tom missed his wife immensely. Her breast cancer diagnosis had been unexpected and her decline swift. It was still unfathomable how she had a "clean" mammogram at her regular checkup but only five months later was diagnosed with stage four, metastatic breast cancer. The disease had gone undetected in her dense breast tissue, despite her regular mammograms, and spread rapidly to her spine. It was only discovered when she went to the doctor because she was experiencing intense back pain.

The tests they ran indicated she had cancer with estrogen receptors, meaning the origin was the breast. By the time it was found, it was too late. She died less than a year later. The whole ordeal had been a living nightmare for the family.

As much as he longed for her to be there, he was also simultaneously glad it was all over. Seeing her condition worsen each day had been excruciatingly painful.

They had shared over four decades with each other as a married couple and almost another decade courting prior to that. He had loved her since they were students at Abraham Lincoln Junior High, and he never imagined a life without her prior to her diagnosis. Grace's mother and father had both lived well into their nineties. He had expected longevity to be in her genes, but it was not the case.

If she had still been alive, she would have been in the den watching *Jeopardy*, talking on the phone, or mindlessly playing a game on her handheld Nintendo Gameboy. She was especially good at Tetris and could play for hours, moving little puzzle pieces across the screen with her thumb.

Tom didn't understand video games or their appeal, much like Grace didn't understand why anyone would want to track the stock market daily, but they were content to allow each other to have their own hobbies.

Even though they would have been doing their own thing, the house would have felt less lonely, and his checklist would have seemed more satisfying. He would have had no need for Christian Companion. The Tetris theme song that continuously played as long as blocks were falling would have carried through the air and perhaps the smell of chicken pot pie, her signature dish, would have been drifting down the hall.

Grace had been an excellent cook. The thought of his wife's culinary abilities made his mouth water and his stomach growl. He would need to make dinner for himself soon.

When she was well, their home was full and comfortable. But now, without her, the house was quiet, still, and void of anything delicious cooking in the kitchen.

The house was a two-story, white brick home with navy shutters they designed together in the 1980s. Grace and Tom had enjoyed picking out every detail, from the light fixtures to the hardwood floors, and were proud of the home that was constructed on a beautiful two-acre lot in Peachtree City, Georgia, a half hour outside of Atlanta. Tom was doing well at his new job as a real estate agent when they broke ground and began building. They felt like they had finally made it.

During the design phase, Tom and Grace wisely put their bedroom on the ground floor of the house and the girls' bedrooms on the second level. It was good to have some distance between parents and teenagers. The girls had been allowed to choose their own carpet and wall colors, and each had their own bathroom. After many years of sharing a bathroom in their old house, they were both excited to have their own space, complete with large mirrors and vanity chairs.

After they grew up and moved out, their oldest daughter's room was converted into Tom's office, where he spent the bulk of his days, and their youngest daughter's room became a playroom for the grandkids and a craft room for Grace, who loved to sew.

The kitchen, dining room, guest room, oversized family room, and den with a large bay window were all on the ground level. The back of the house had a large, screened porch with multiple access points. The porch led to the pool, which was added in the early 2000s.

However, as lovely as the house had been for more than two decades, he no longer found peace in much of it.

Tom was sad when he went into the kitchen, knowing his wife would never make lemon meringue pie or homemade apple fritters there again. Her cookbooks still occupied the top shelf of the walk-in pantry, but he never used them.

He was sad when he entered the den because he saw her empty Lazy Boy recliner. Her Game Boy and the book she had been reading when she died still lay on the end table next to the chair. More reminders.

And he was especially sad when he was in his bedroom, the room he and Grace had shared. Despite all the good memories they had made in that room, all Tom could think about was saying goodbye to her forever there and watching her take her last breath. Tom was glad Grace peacefully passed at home under the watchful eye of hospice, but it was troubling trying to sleep there now.

After she was pronounced dead, the nurse left. His oldest daughter left to tell her children about Grace's passing because they had been wracked with worry and needed their mother to comfort them, and he quickly retreated to the guest room.

His youngest daughter, Jenna, waited alone with Grace's body until the funeral home arrived. He did not consider how Jenna may have felt sitting there by herself with her mother's dead body while he was just down the hall.

Tom had heard the hearse pull into the driveway, but he didn't come out to greet the men who would take Grace out of the house for the final time. Jenna was the one to open the door and lead them to his wife. He knew if he had seen Grace leave on the rolling stretcher, he would never have been able to set foot in his room again.

He shook away his sad thoughts and considered moving permanently to the beach.

He and Grace had built a lovely life together, one he had taken for granted, and with her absence, he was lonely. Desperately lonely.

Tom was sure the only remedy for his sadness was to remarry. He wanted to find someone who would cook nice meals for him, enjoy his grandchildren, and travel with him. If he found a new wife, she might also be able to bring new memories into his old house and help erase his loneliness. Maybe he could even enjoy his bedroom again.

In addition to Grace's presence in the house, he missed traveling with her. In between caring for their aging parents, who were all gone now, and spending time with their children and grandchildren, they found time to enjoy one or two nice trips a year. They had been to almost every continent, except Antarctica.

He did all the planning for their vacations and spent hours online researching potential destinations. He liked to personally contact the Chamber of Commerce or local tourism bureaus in whatever location he selected and ask for a visitor's guide to be sent via mail to ensure they didn't miss anything the location had to offer. He would also ask whoever answered the phone for their personal recommendations for restaurants or attractions.

While Tom was busy making travel arrangements, Grace was content playing her Game Boy. He was the one to plan trips, she was the one to make plans with the grandchildren, and that worked for them. Tom loved to explore nature, and Grace liked to relax by the pool with a good book. With so many trips under their belt, Tom knew how to make the perfect itinerary that would satisfy both.

He was so detailed in his planning, he would even research gas stations to see which ones were known for having the cleanest restrooms if they were driving. He would add something like "11:17 a.m., pit stop at Shell, exit 49" to their itinerary, which he kept neatly organized in a binder. Grace always appreciated a clean bathroom.

Most of their trips had something go wrong because he notoriously booked a little too much adventure into each one, despite the fact neither of them were world class athletes nor adventurous in their daily lives. He often overestimated their physical capabilities.

He almost slipped off a mountain trying to take a closer look at a goat in Switzerland. He dangled by the guard rail until he could get his footing and pull himself back up. They got into trouble on a whitewater rafting trip in Colorado and had to be rescued by emergency personnel in helicopters, and they both got food poisoning on a vacation in Jamaica that included eating at some questionable restaurants noted for being "regionally authentic."

Despite all this, they had stories to tell about their travels and always looked forward to the next trip. It was their time away together. Away from the grandchildren. Away from church. Away from life's responsibilities. They were happy when they traveled.

Tom worked very hard his whole life and was ready to enjoy his retirement. He had earned this time. But with Grace's passing, all his plans were sidelined. He was eager to have a companion accompany him on trips so he could get back to his hobby of collecting postcards.

He loved looking at them when he returned from a trip almost as much as the trip itself. He especially liked ones that showed the beauty of the land, gorgeous stained-glass windows in historic churches, or native wildlife in their natural habitats. He had an eye for good photography, and many of his postcards were like miniature works of art. His favorite one was of a lavender field in Provence, France. The vibrant purples jumped off the card and served as a beautiful reminder of his favorite trip with Grace. When he looked at the postcard, he could almost smell the lavender.

Tom attempted to travel alone a few times after Grace's death, but the only thing lonelier than his stagnant house was checking into a hotel room by himself or asking for a table for one at a restaurant. It was painful hearing happy couples outside his suite while he watched TV alone. It was even worse watching them laugh and converse as they ate while he stared at an empty chair on the other side of his table. He was eager to fill his days with companionship and home cooking. Eating meat from the grill and opening canned carrots each night was getting boring.

When he wasn't tinkering with something at the house, Tom filled his days by visiting his oldest daughter Katie and her three children as often as he could because they lived only fifteen minutes away.

Katie was a considerate daughter and always tried to include him in the hustle and bustle of their lives. She regularly invited him to dinner, soccer games, and dance recitals. She also tried to drop in at his house for a quick visit whenever possible. She knew he enjoyed her company, and her visits meant a lot to him.

Tom's door was always open to his daughters and grandchildren, and they knew they were always welcome.

Jenna called and checked in on him routinely from afar. She and her family lived in North Carolina because Paul was stationed at Fort Bragg.

Tom knew the open-door policy went both ways, and he had a standing invitation to both of his daughters' homes. He also knew if he needed anything, either girl would be there for him. He simply needed to ask.

Jenna accompanied him the year before for his annual checkup. However, it had been embarrassing for him when he was asked to change into a hospital gown in front of his daughter. The nurse incorrectly assumed Jenna was his wife! She had been embarrassed when she realized her mistake and asked Jenna to step out of the room to give him some privacy, but the situation had been awkward for everyone. It was equally embarrassing when the doctor asked him questions about his sexual health and hemorrhoids in front of his daughter. He decided he would go to the doctor alone after that appointment.

As much as his girls tried to support him, they were busy with their own lives and certainly at a very different stage of life. He loved them and enjoyed spending time with them and the grandchildren, but it wasn't the same without Grace. He was still lonely and ached to have a wife continuously by his side.

Tom made the decision to try online dating. It had been over a year since Grace's death, and he was ready. He knew he was rusty since he hadn't dated anyone other than his wife since his teenage years. However, he was hopeful the new computer dating websites would make the process easy for him. *How hard could it be to find a Christian woman who could seamlessly fit into his life?* He thought of himself as quite a catch and had a lot to offer. He liked to think of himself as the James Dean of the sixty-plus population.

He refocused his thoughts on the desktop computer that was before him and saw the Christian Companion website was now fully loaded on his screen. Tom quickly entered his login and password information. He was anxious to see if he had received any new messages or if any new prospects recently made accounts. If he had multiple messages, the need to eat dinner would lessen, and he would feel a little less lonely in his big, empty house.

When he created his account, he carefully selected the perfect picture of himself. It showcased his decent looks, good hair, and his yacht in the background.

He dreamed of finding a woman who enjoyed boating and fishing, something Grace did not. A woman who did not get seasick easily or sunburn quickly would also be a bonus. A partner who liked to play golf, too, would be icing on the cake.

His bio also let prospective matches know he was a committed follower of Jesus and church was a priority in his life. His perfect match had to be a strong Christian. This was non-negotiable.

Grace had not shared his love for church, and it had been a source of contention during their marriage. He was thankful she recommitted her life to Christ only a month before her death. It gave him great comfort then, and it still comforted him now because he knew for certain that she was in Heaven.

Shortly after Tom made his profile on CC, he began receiving messages from women expressing a desire to get to know him. Some of the women were divorced, some were widowed, and some had never been married. They came from a variety of backgrounds and denominations. He read every message he received and scrolled through bios and pictures of women who met the parameters of his search, even if they hadn't contacted him directly. They should be between fifty-three and sixty-eight, white, and live in Georgia.

With each picture or message, he became more confident finding a new wife wouldn't be hard. He had a thing for dark hair and preferred a woman who appeared to be in shape. After all, he was looking for an active life partner. He prided himself on the fact he could still hike, get up off the floor easily, and bend over to tie his shoes. Much better than a lot of men his age.

Within the first few weeks he was on CC, he quickly zeroed in on a lovely woman just a few years younger than him named Cheryl. She was a widow, had two daughters, four grandchildren, and lived only an hour away in Marietta. She was attractive and had a natural smile. Apparently, he appealed to her as well since she made the first move by sending him a friendly message. After just a few short messages back and forth, they made plans to meet in person.

Tom was very nervous for their first date, but all went surprisingly well. Maybe there was something to be said about Christian Companion. The algorithm for matching couples seemed to be spot on.

Tom and Cheryl met at a lovely restaurant in Atlanta, halfway between their respective cities. He ordered a glass of Pinot Gris to lessen his nerves and she ordered a glass of chardonnay because it paired well with shrimp and grits. The conversation flowed easily and naturally. They shared stories about their grandchildren and their previous spouses.

Cheryl's husband Edward had succumbed to lung cancer after a short but difficult battle. He fought valiantly, but lost his fight, just as Grace had lost to breast cancer. Tom felt there was an instant connection, particularly with their parallel stories.

They continued to date regularly, often playing golf and dining at the country club where Tom was a member. Cheryl didn't mind driving over to Peachtree City for the day.

Tom was confident they were fully moving toward marriage.

After a few short months, he was ready to begin talking about their future. He was surprised to learn she wasn't interested in making a long-term commitment. He had been so certain they shared the same end goal.

She enjoyed his company, but also enjoyed her current lifestyle. She wanted to keep things the way they were. She was blessed with good friends and spent many of her days with her own daughters and grandchildren. She had no intention of moving out of the home she had shared with Edward or remarrying. She made a profile on Christian Companion simply because she was looking for companionship and nothing more.

Tom was devastated and broke things off permanently. There was no point to dating if it did not end with marriage. He needed to get on with his life, and to do so, he needed a wife. He felt he had wasted precious time on Cheryl and wanted to be sure that didn't happen again.

After their breakup, Tom began dating as much as possible. He was a man on a mission and put himself into a dating frenzy. He was on a relentless quest to find his next bride and would not stop until his goal had been accomplished.

It was not uncommon for him to date three different women in a week. He wasn't looking for any cheap thrills, rather he was intentionally dating with purpose. Dates usually included dinner and sometimes, if things were going well, a movie. He figured he should date as much as humanly possible for two reasons. The first was obviously to find a wife, the second was so he didn't have to eat alone.

Tom wanted to date efficiently, so he devised a foolproof questionnaire designed to let him know if a woman was a good match for him, and thus a potential candidate for marriage. He didn't print the series of questions out and give them a number two pencil, but he memorized them and made sure each one came up in conversation. This questionnaire was the best way to guard his heart. If their answers didn't align with his, they were out. Failing to answer even one question correctly meant they were not a suitable match. He did not want to risk falling in love with someone who wasn't right for him and subject his heart to rejection again like he had experienced with Cheryl.

Specifically, he wanted to know their five-year plan. Were they willing to relocate for love? What were their views about religion? Can they recite from memory their favorite scripture? And lastly, were they Republican or Democrat?

If their plans did not include marriage, travel, Christianity, a Bible verse spewed out with great emotion, or the word Republican, he promptly paid the bill and wished the woman well. No point lingering with a mismatch.

Several women seemed to answer his questions correctly, so he couldn't understand why they didn't eagerly return his call for a second date. Tom was unaware his relentless questions put many of his dates on edge and made them feel as if they were on a job interview.

He didn't understand the art of getting to know someone and letting conversation flow naturally. Tom thought small talk was a waste of time with no purpose, and he avoided it at all costs. He didn't chitchat with clerks in the grocery store, and he rarely engaged in conversations with his neighbors. A wave was sufficient. He didn't even care to talk on the phone to his daughters when they called for no specific reason. Tom didn't think "I just wanted to hear your voice," "just to talk," or "because I was bored" were justifiable reasons to call someone and interrupt their day. He didn't have time to waste on "nothing."

His approach to dating was no different. Just as he thought one should have a reason for calling, he believed everyone on CC should have a legitimate reason for making a profile. The only acceptable motivation was because they wanted to get married. Anyone with a different agenda was simply a distraction from him finding a wife.

Mrs. Right

Tom spent almost an hour on Christian Companion mindlessly looking at profiles of women, ranking them by age, looks, and his first impression.

He thought he had come to a natural breaking point in his search just as his stomach reminded him hadn't eaten dinner yet, and he was about to call it a night. But as he moved the mouse pointer across the screen toward the logout button in the upper right corner, he heard the familiar "ding" sound go off, indicating he had a new message. He pushed aside thoughts of leftovers and opened the message.

He was pleased to see a photo of a lovely looking woman with dark hair staring back at him. In the picture, she wore a tailored black top that accentuated her curves and slim fitting black slacks. Her neck was adorned with a shiny, silver necklace and a matching silver belt was draped around her waist.

He was immediately impressed by her looks. His first thought was how put together she looked. She obviously knew how to take care of herself, and it showed.

He glanced at her bio and learned her name was Donna. She lived near St. Simon's Island, only a short distance from his vacation home, and she worked a respectable career as a manager in an upscale women's boutique.

He was captivated by her decision to include a Bible verse on her profile page. Specifically, she had chosen Romans 8:28 (NIV) which said, "And we know that in all things God works for the good of those who love Him, who have been called according to His purpose."

He felt instantly she was a godly woman, and he became even more enthusiastic about her message. Despite the fact this was a Christian website, many women failed to reference the Bible in their bios.

Was she the woman he had been searching for?

She was attractive, had a successful career, and from outward appearances seemed to have her act together. And best yet, she was a true follower of God. She said so herself.

He put her into the first spot on his ranking sheet.

Her message began, "Hi Tom. I saw your profile pic and bio and was immediately drawn to you. Please excuse me for being so direct. I'm sorry to learn you have recently been widowed. I imagine it is difficult for you to reenter the dating world. Congratulations on being brave enough to make an account on Christian Companion! It's nice to see a man who is willing to take life by the horns and make a new path for himself."

Her words made him feel proud, and his chest puffed up ever so slightly as he continued to read.

She continued, "I joined CC because I am looking for a Christian husband of my own, someone I can enjoy life with. I'd love to get to know you better. No pressure, of course." He was drawn in by her compassionate nature and respected her for her forthrightness when it came to disclosing her motive for using the website.

Although she made no indication she considered him a possible prospect yet for marriage, his mind was already heading down that path. She had already answered one of his questions from his questionnaire correctly. He quickly responded, "I'd love to get to know you better too." He felt a warm rush of excitement surge through him.

They continued to chat back and forth. The more they chatted, the more excited he became. He was thrilled when he found out she loved the beach and boating, had an impressive golf handicap, and was a whiz on the tennis court. He also learned she'd lived up north for many years, but much preferred the warmer Georgia climate where she could spend most months outdoors.

He scrolled through her online photo album and found a picture of her in a swimsuit. She looked very nice in a solid, navy one-piece and matching sheer navy coverup. She also wore a large blue-and-white striped sun hat which accentuated her bold, red lipstick. She was beautiful with long, shapely legs and appeared happy standing on the beach. She was conservative and sexy at the same time.

She was an avid birdwatcher, had many good friends, and loved to cook. She was apparently a master in the kitchen and enjoyed nothing more than cooking for others. She was a devout Christian, and this was apparent in her language and frequent usage of scripture. Tom was unfamiliar with what it meant to be a "modern member" of the Assembly of God church, but he wasn't concerned about denomination. He also wasn't bothered she was divorced. Her ex must have been an idiot to let a woman like her get away.

Tom was more than intrigued by Donna and knew he needed to meet her as soon as possible. He had been faithfully praying for someone to come into his life, and out of the blue, Donna appeared. Mark 11:24 (NIV) came to his mind, *"Therefore I tell you, whatever you ask for in prayer, believe that you have received it, and it will be yours."*

Fishing for Love

Tom and Donna communicated for only a few days before a meet up was arranged. They were both excited about their first date, and when they saw each other in person, they felt an instant connection.

Donna aced his dating questionnaire. She couldn't have given more perfect answers if she had studied. She seemed to say everything Tom wanted to hear and was not put off by his intrusive questioning. They spoke easily to one another, and Tom quickly decided she was the answer to his prayers.

Donna felt the same way for different reasons. She knew she was checking off every box on his wish list, and he was checking off every one of her "must haves."

Tom detected a slight midwestern accent in her from the first time they spoke but couldn't tell what state it hailed from. He was surprised to learn she was originally from Ohio. He enjoyed hearing about her life in Cincinnati as a child and then about the years she spent in New York.

She moved to the Big Apple as a young adult, only weeks after completing her bachelor's degree in fashion merchandising, because New York City is the epicenter of the fashion world.

She met her first husband in Manhattan and fell in love quickly. They got married after dating for only a few months.

After several years of harsh winters, they decided to move to Georgia where the weather was much warmer and where they could embrace a more laid-back lifestyle than that of the city. They both loved peanuts and peach cobbler and dreamed of a simpler life.

Todd wanted to start a family, but Donna did not. She wasn't ready to have a kid underfoot. She didn't know if she would ever want to have a child. The thought of another human being occupying her body was bothersome and she didn't want to lose a wink of beauty sleep with midnight feedings.

Tom was glad Donna moved to Georgia so many years ago so their paths could now cross. Perhaps it was destiny. God always had a perfect plan in place.

Tom's family was originally from the North. They moved from New Jersey to Georgia when he was a very young child. The weather in the South was better for his older sister's health because she frequently suffered from various respiratory illnesses. They left the pollution of Trenton for the beautiful Georgia countryside. His parents found much success as small business owners, running a restaurant supply company that catered to high-end establishments across the state.

Even though he had lived in Georgia for more than sixty years, Tom's Jersey accent still lingered in his speech, giving away his roots. He never developed a Southern twang.

The relationship between Donna and Tom moved at a very rapid pace. The two began spending as much time together as possible, even though she lived several hours away on the east coast of Georgia and he lived south of Atlanta. He was willing to drive for the right person.

Luckily, his vacation home was only twenty minutes from her house. He began spending more and more time there so he could be near her and less and less time at the home he had shared with Grace. It made sense for him to go to her more often than the other way around because she still worked full-time, and he was retired.

He was able to enjoy the beach and pool at his vacation home while she worked, then see her in the evenings. After her working day was done, they easily found things to do in the St. Simon's area and took advantage of the plethora of nice, local seafood restaurants. Some establishments were even accessible by boat and allowed patrons to dock onsite.

They ate out most nights and then would walk off their heavy meals by taking a stroll along the seashore. His home away from home had a private boardwalk that led to a gorgeous, private beach, devoid of tourists. The shining stars above, the repetitive sound of crashing waves, and the silky sand beneath their feet created the most romantic backdrop for getting to know each other.

Tom hoped if they married, she would give up her job so they could spend the days together, as well. He had saved more than enough from his job as a real estate agent, wise investments, frugal living, and inheritances to keep them comfortable. He wouldn't want to eat out every night if they were married because that would be unreasonable, and besides, Donna was a fabulous cook. However, for now, it was a wonderful way to begin their courtship. They found each other attractive, and Tom felt less lonely when he was with her. Donna also felt happier when she was with Tom because she was quickly becoming the center of his universe.

With each passing day, Tom grew in affection toward Donna, and she, in turn, became more confident this match would work.

She seemed to say everything Tom needed to hear, and they had more mutual interests than he could count. They both loved black and white movies, art museums, French dining, and fine wine. They both disliked olives, fast food, and waiting in lines.

He lavished her with gifts, which pleased Donna immensely. Tom caught on quickly Donna adored surprises. Beautifully wrapped packages with elaborate bows or a dozen of the reddest roses brought her great joy. In the first few months of dating, he gave her a gold necklace, a pearl bracelet, a teddy bear that said, "I like to give bear hugs" when you squeezed its stomach, Christian Louboutin shoes because he knew she always wanted a pair, and countless bouquets of fresh flowers.

He had time in the day while she worked to look for gifts that would make her happy. She was quick to post pictures of the things he gave her on Facebook for her friends to see. He thought it was sweet she wanted the world to know she was falling in love with him. In addition to her happiness, he also liked the credit he was given on social media. It made him look like a keeper and appear exceptionally generous.

After his traumatic experience with Cheryl, Tom wanted to make sure Donna would not become another one "who got away," and if that meant buying gifts and flowers regularly, he would do it. He could slow down on his spending once she had a ring on her finger.

He was a fisherman at heart and wanted to make sure he figuratively reeled Donna in. He considered her quite the catch and would do whatever it took to make sure she didn't slip off his hook or break his line.

He couldn't believe his luck she was still in the pond.

Love Languages

Tom rarely bought gifts or flowers for Grace because she thought they were a waste of money and went against her frugal nature. He stopped surprising her with presents early on in their marriage because she would complain he spent too much on them. She was more interested in building up their savings account and did not equate gifts with love.

Since Grace was so practical, Tom didn't feel an overwhelming need to romance her. He was the father of her children and believed that fact provided sufficient proof he loved her.

Tom never considered there were other ways to show her love she would have appreciated that didn't cost money.

Grace had tried to tell him about a book she once read called *The 5 Love Languages*, written by Gary Chapman. She found his theories interesting and mentioned to Tom the book taught her different people liked to be shown love in different ways. He assumed she was just making small talk because Grace had no reason to feel unloved.

He did not give it much thought when she said her love language was quality time. *They spent plenty of time together, didn't they?* After all, they had been married for more than forty years at that point and they lived in the same house.

When Grace was diagnosed with cancer, life as they knew it came to a stop. They suddenly began spending hours together because he was her caretaker and she physically depended on him for everything. He accompanied her to all doctor's appointments, brought her meals she pecked at, and sat by her side.

During the last months of her life, Tom and Grace were inseparable. And during those dark days, they shared a closeness and a non-physical intimacy, deeper than any of the days that came before. Tom was finally giving his wife what she needed to feel fully loved. He was giving her quality time and it meant the world to her. Sadly, there wasn't much time left for them.

If Donna had taken *The 5 Love Languages* quiz, gifts would certainly rank as number one on her love scale. Tom could already tell Donna would require more effort than he was used to giving. Unlike Grace, his new girlfriend liked to be pampered and spoiled. Thankfully, gifts was the easiest love language to satisfy and he had a lot more disposable income to spend at this stage of his life than he did when he married Grace eons ago.

Insert New Grandma Here

When Grace had been alive, there had hardly been a day that went by she and Tom didn't see Katie or her girls because they lived only fifteen minutes away from each other. Tom and Grace also made regular trips to see Jenna's family—no matter where they were stationed in the world.

Because of divine intervention, the only possible explanation, Paul received orders for Fort Benning, Georgia, only days after Grace's cancer diagnosis and the Millers moved back to their home state.

Jenna was thankful the Army gave her family the opportunity to live only an hour and a half away from home when her mother was sick. It was the closest to Peachtree City she had been in years, and this allowed her to spend as much time as she could with her mom before her death. Jenna didn't know what she would have done if her mother was dying and she was living far away from her. It would have increased the agony of the situation and would have made the nightmare even worse.

Shortly after Grace died, Paul received orders for Fort Bragg and they moved to North Carolina.

Tom thought it would be nice to get back to his regular routine with his family because he hadn't been able to spend much time with them lately. He had been very preoccupied with dating. He hoped Donna would get along well with his daughters and his grandchildren and fit in perfectly like a missing puzzle piece. He didn't expect her to replace Grace, but he did expect their roles in the family to be similar despite their differences in personalities. He also wrongly assumed Donna would love the opportunity to become a stepmother and step-grandmother since she never had children of her own. Tom never once considered she had chosen not to have children for a reason.

Katie was more than willing to accept her father dating but it was difficult for Jenna to wrap her brain around. The idea of her father with a woman who wasn't her mom felt wrong to her and seemed like a betrayal to Grace. She knew this wasn't true and her father had dutifully fulfilled his vows, but she couldn't help her feelings. It broke her heart when her dad announced he would no longer wear his wedding ring and she cried the first time she saw his finger bare.

Tom was thankful for Katie's understanding and told her all about his dating journey. It was awkward for Katie to listen to stories about the women her father was dating, but she remained quiet about her discomfort and stayed steadfast in her support.

Tom decided he would wait to tell Jenna about any women he dated until he found "the one" because she was so emotional. He asked Katie to let him be the one to break the news when he found his perfect match and asked her not to say anything about his dating escapades to her younger sister.

The first meeting between Tom, Donna, Katie, and her family went very smoothly. Donna poured on the sweetness and was extremely polite. She even doted over the children. Katie was warm and welcoming in return. It seemed like both women got along well, and Tom was hopeful this was the beginning of good things to come.

Tom didn't know Donna had zero desire to be a mother figure and considered herself much too youthful to be a grandmother.

There were about a million other things she would rather be doing than sitting here with his family and playing pretend. She longed to be entertaining friends on Beachview Drive, where Tom's vacation home was located, or listening to live music at one of St. Simon's lovely restaurants. Peachtree City was much less scenic and so suburban she could barely stand it.

Despite Donna's real feelings, she knew it was imperative for her to play the part of grandmother to perfection if she was going to garner a proposal from him. Her acting was so good even Katie believed her to be genuine upon their first meeting.

Donna could have won an Academy Award for her performance as a loving grandma that day. However, she wasn't looking for a gold statue, she was after the diamond engagement ring.

Tom watched her interact with his grandchildren with peace and happiness in his heart. Even though they had only known each other for a few weeks, he knew he had found his next wife.

God was making it easy on him, rewarding him for his faithfulness.

Donna was honestly surprised at how friendly Katie was because she had expected her to dislike anyone who wasn't her mother. After the first meeting, Donna decided she could handle interacting with her and the grandchildren from time to time if it was necessary. An occasional visit would be bearable and would give her the opportunity to play grandma on Facebook. Tom had gorgeous grandchildren, and she was sure she would photograph nicely with them. Her friends would be impressed.

She was certain Tom only visited them with such frequency because he had nothing else to do before meeting her. Grace had forced him to focus solely on the family and he had forgotten how to pursue other interests. Things would be different for him now. Things would be better for him with a little guidance from her. She had almost completely convinced him to sell his home in the suburbs and move to St. Simon's permanently. Geographical distance between Tom and Katie would be beneficial for everyone, especially her.

Donna thought she could tolerate Katie and her kids in small doses if her name was on all of Tom's assets. It would be much easier to enjoy them once inheritance wasn't an issue anymore. In the state of Georgia, a surviving spouse got everything—as long as their name was on the property or account. She knew Grace and Tom had given each other rights of survivorship on everything they had, and she expected he would do the same for her.

Donna hoped she and Tom could play the part of parents and grandparents on birthdays and, perhaps, quarterly for dinner, and that would do the job. After all, Tom was done raising his kids, and if they required him at all now, it meant they were simply not self-sufficient or just plain selfish.

Both reasons were problematic.

She might need to point this out to Tom so they would be on the same page. His children owed him tremendous respect for all he had provided them when they were younger, and neither Katie nor Jenna should have any more expectations of him. It was time for him to enjoy his retirement and do the things he wanted to do without them interfering.

It never occurred to Donna that Jenna and Katie wanted their father to live out his retirement fully and enjoy the fruits of his labor. It was not his fault their mother died, and they didn't want him to be alone. They wholeheartedly supported their father fishing, traveling, golfing, spending time with a new significant other, and discovering new hobbies.

They, however, also wanted him to include them in his life—like he had always done. They loved spending time with their dad and wanted to continue important family traditions that meant so much to them and their children, like taking trips together.

Donna didn't comprehend Tom enjoyed spending time with his family. He didn't visit them only because he had nothing better to do, but because he wanted to—he loved them. She also didn't understand being a parent didn't end when your children reached the age of eighteen. There was no finish line.

Donna knew countless people regarded children and grandchildren to be tremendous blessings from God. Many of her friends thoroughly enjoyed their grandchildren. However, none of them lived as close to their adult kids as Tom did Katie. They were able to pick and choose when they saw their families and didn't have to worry they might show up in the driveway whenever they saw fit.

She would put a stop to the open-door policy once she and Tom were married. Just appearing without invitation at someone's doorstep was disrespectful and frankly rude. She also couldn't believe Katie thought it was okay to just open the front door at her father's house and let herself in without ringing the doorbell. Apparently, Grace had not taught her daughters manners when it came to calling on people.

Donna would never be a "regular" grandma because her social calendar was much too full. She didn't intend to sit around knitting and babysitting. *No thank you.* The grandchildren would have to work around her schedule.

Donna also did not truly understand the bonds between parents and children or how excruciatingly painful it would be for everyone involved if they were broken.

Donna's childhood had been very different from Jenna's and Katie's. Her father had done the best he could with her and her brothers, and she loved him for that. However, he had been very harsh on them and was quick to anger. Her family experienced extremely lean times during her youth, and rather than lavishing her with material things, Donna's father had taught her how to do without. Her upbringing showed her the importance of taking care of yourself— above all else.

Donna's mother was not a June Cleaver or Claire Huxtable type of mom. She was overwhelmed with motherhood and pushed her children onto her husband because she was unable to deal with them. And when she became overwhelmed with life in general, she willed her organs to shut down and died, leaving her children motherless.

Until Donna was forced to hear about Grace Jacob's superstar status as mother, she thought those types of moms only existed on television.

Despite her challenging childhood, she turned out just fine. She was successful enough in her career and she knew how to get what she wanted out of life. She also knew with certainty it was time for Katie and Jenna to grow up and for Tom to cut the apron strings.

Tom had been very close with his own parents and spent a considerable amount of time with them when they were alive, even when he was an adult and had a family of his own.

He and Grace had turned to his parents a number of times for help over the years in varying capacities, either with the children or for financial reasons, and they were always happy to oblige. They were wonderful grandparents by all accounts.

Tom's mother, Helen Jacobs, was the definition of a go-getter and loved to take her grandkids on adventures any opportunity she got. She took them to amusement parks, museums, playgrounds, and any place that sounded fun. And when she wasn't out gallivanting with them, she kept them busy with arts and crafts.

She taught the girls how to make candles from scratch and showed them how to carefully pour the hot wax into molds. She also taught them how to create suncatcher window ornaments. Even as adults, Jenna and Katie could recall their grandmother helping them place tiny glass beads with tweezers into metal frames shaped like butterflies and flowers. Once the beads were in place, they would all gather around the oven, and peer through the door watching them magically transform into stained glass.

After Tom's father passed, Helen started a family tradition of taking the entire family on a vacation every year. She wanted to make sure they carved out time for one another and made lasting memories.

Grace's parents had also been supportive and willing to help in any way that was needed. They were generous with their time, money, and love. Grace's mom and dad loved to take the family out to lunch whenever they visited, hosted Easter Egg hunts each year on their large country property and encouraged their grandchildren to follow their passions. They even bought a cello for Jenna when she expressed a desire to learn how to play when she was eleven years old.

Tom and Grace modeled their parenting and grandparenting style after their parents, and it worked for them. They had good relationships with their daughters and grands and did not consider them to be burdens, even if they needed help on occasion. They had been happy they were able to help, and they loved them with all their hearts.

As Tom and Donna's relationship grew, so did Donna's feelings of animosity toward Tom's family. She quickly realized neither Tom nor Katie was used to a "sometimes" relationship, and Donna wasn't comfortable with the amount of time Tom devoted to his family.

She wanted to put some distance between them to make it more difficult to see each other so often. One could only tolerate attending so many high school football games, band concerts featuring pimple-faced teenagers, and trips to the candy store.

She and Tom weren't adolescents anymore and had more refined interests. Donna needed to make Tom see she was far more deserving of his time than his kids or grandkids. She could offer him fun, adult experiences that would surely be more pleasurable. His family had counted on him for years, and it was now time for him to follow his own dreams. God had granted him a second act and she didn't want him to waste it!

She began to systematically plan dates and events that conflicted with those of his grandchildren and was pleased to see he almost always chose her plans over his family's. Her pouty lips and flirtatious sulking assisted in persuading him to choose her.

Donna was a master at puffing up Tom's ego. The more she puffed, the more he came around to her way of thinking. He began to say things like, "I really have spent a lot of time sitting in uncomfortable high school bleachers, haven't I?"

Donna didn't care if constantly saying no hurt Katie or her girls' feelings, and Tom didn't notice the more he said it, it did.

They missed his presence in their lives.

Katie believed there was room for all of them and a reasonable balance could be found, but Donna Thorn didn't play second fiddle to anyone.

Tom, much like a teenager with a crush, wanted to be with Donna every moment. He put his family on the backburner and gave in to the excitement of new love and the hope of constant companionship.

On occasion, Tom insisted on dropping by Katie's for a quick visit if they were in Peachtree City, even if Donna didn't want to. She made sure he didn't stay long by refusing to get out of the car when they arrived at Katie's house. She knew if she stayed in a running vehicle, he would be forced to leave quickly because it would be rude to leave her sitting out there alone for too long. It was very hot in Georgia.

She told Tom she just wanted to give him "alone time with his family." She would say, "Don't worry about me, stay and visit as long as you like, I will be perfectly fine in the car."

He was so enamored with her he convinced himself she was being overly considerate and didn't want him to be forced to divide his attention between her and his family. He didn't see the devious nature behind her behavior, but Katie did. She was much more adept at understanding social cues and catty women than her father. The red flags were starting to appear before her eyes like a matador's cape being waved wildly at a bull, but she still supported her father's happiness—even when she caught Donna smirking at her from the front seat when she looked out the window.

Despite Donna's attempt to sabotage Katie's relationship, Tom's oldest daughter didn't fade away into the background as easily as she'd hoped.

Donna knew she needed to up her game, so she used every forced interaction with Katie to dig for information. She was on a hunt for dirt about her family, her finances, her relationships, and even Katie's mental health considering she recently lost her mother.

She grilled Katie every chance she got, and when they weren't together, she asked Tom countless questions about her. She pried into her past and was thrilled when she discovered Katie had a rebellious streak during her teenage years.

Tom thought she was taking an interest in his daughter and was pleased. He answered all her questions in great detail and inflated his own role as a parent, making Katie's normal teenage and young adult issues seem much larger than they actually had been.

Donna was looking for a way to turn any past grievances Tom had with Katie into relevant issues of today. *Nothing like ripping Band-Aids off old wounds to get emotions flowing.* It didn't matter who Katie really was, only who Donna made her out to be.

Donna was building an arsenal of weapons and was preparing for the first battle in what would become a very long war. She was gathering ammunition and looking for the right time to hurl the first figurative grenade.

She couldn't wait to watch it explode.

Ready, Set, Go

Jenna was looking forward to a visit from her father. She was particularly excited for him to come because she had signed them up to participate in The Rainbow Run in Fayetteville, North Carolina.

When she told her father several months ago about the event, he seemed excited to participate and agreed to give it a try. She purchased runner's bibs for herself, her dad, and all her children. Paul was unfortunately going to be away for military training the weekend of the race and would miss out on the fun. Training exercises at Fort Bragg, home of the 82nd Airborne, never seemed to slow down, and Saturdays were just another day in the life of a soldier. Thankfully, though, the weekend was surprisingly open for Jenna and her kids. The race would be the highlight of their weekend and a special time with her dad.

Jenna thought the run was an excellent early Father's Day gift. Even though it wasn't exactly on Father's Day, it was close enough. It was common for her to purchase experiences rather than gifts from a store for her dad because they enjoyed spending time together, and he wasn't in need of anything. A few of the things they had done in the past included attending hockey games, dinner theaters, and comedy shows. Each experience had been memorable, and Jenna expected The Rainbow Run to be as well.

Participants would travel along the 3.2-mile course at whatever pace they chose and would be splashed with brightly colored packets of cornstarch at various checkpoints along the way. She thought the kids would get a kick out of being turned pink, blue, yellow, and green and would enjoy the fresh air with their grandfather. She looked forward to taking before and after pictures.

Jenna hadn't been doing much running since her move to Fort Bragg and planned to push Olivia in the stroller if she got tired. She was only a preschooler, and 3.2 miles might be a little far for her, even though she was already showing signs of athleticism.

Jenna fully expected to walk most of the race and thought her father would walk beside her because he wasn't a runner either. She imagined Heidi and Brett would sprint ahead, but they had lots of friends running the race and knew they would always be under someone's watchful eye, so she wasn't concerned. Her dad would be her walking companion, and they would both enjoy seeing Olivia's reaction as they passed through colorful clouds along the path.

Her dad arrived on Thursday afternoon and planned to leave two days later, on Saturday, after the race. He normally stayed longer than that when he came for a visit, but Jenna was grateful for whatever time they got.

Her father seemed different than usual from the moment he arrived at her home in the Normandy housing area of Fort Bragg. He was preoccupied and kept excusing himself to talk on the phone. He was also regularly checking his text messages and stepping outside so he could respond via voice text privately. He was so tied to his phone he reminded her of a teenager.

He didn't offer any information about who he was communicating with, and Jenna didn't pry. She thought it might be his stockbroker. He hadn't shared with her he had found anyone yet to date, so it didn't occur to her he had a girlfriend on the other end of the line.

Katie had kept her promise and hadn't said a word to Jenna about Donna yet.

On the morning of the race, Jenna and her kids loaded up into her minivan while her father put his luggage in the trunk of his car and insisted on driving separately. She thought they would all ride together, but he indicated he would be leaving immediately after the race to go to his Beachview Drive home. He explained he had business in St. Simon's he needed to attend to.

Jenna had wrongly supposed they would all come home after the race and shower because they would be covered with cornstarch. She also thought he would stay long enough to at least enjoy a nice lunch together before he got on the road.

When they arrived at the race, they took a few pictures in their clean, white race T-shirts to mark the "before" part of the race and found the starting line.

Jenna planned to push Olivia, if need be, in a large jogging stroller so she headed to the back of the crowd. She didn't want to block the way for any serious runners, even though the overall feel of the crowd was less than formal. It was primarily filled with families and couples, and there was a festive mood in the atmosphere. Everyone seemed to be there just for fun—except for Tom. He seemed restless for the race to begin promptly at eight o'clock. He kept looking at his watch as if time was moving like molasses. He stood in front of Jenna and Olivia, and behind Brett and Heidi, who had joined their friends just ahead of them.

The race gun fired right on time, and The Rainbow Run was on.

However, much to Jenna's surprise, Tom took off like a bat out of hell and left her and Olivia in the dust. She thought he may have been trying to catch Brett and Heidi and expected to find him later along the course. She was sure he would slow down so he could get doused with color alongside Olivia. There was no way he could keep up that pace for the duration of the race.

It wasn't until Jenna and Olivia reached their third checkpoint, where they were hit by a cloud of yellow, that she began to doubt if she would find her father before the end of the race. They had already been through pink and blue and only had green left.

When Jenna and Olivia finally reached the finish line, quite some time after the rest of the family, they saw Brett, Heidi, and several of their friends cheering for them. Everyone in the crowd had cornstarch packets of their own they were about to throw to make sure the finishers were good and colorful.

Even though Jenna and Olivia had walked the majority of the race, they both ran across the finish line with their arms waving above their heads in victory, laughing as clouds of every color exploded around them.

Tom, however, wasn't smiling or cheering. He wasn't enthralled with the runners crossing the finish line like the rest of the crowd. He was noticeably agitated to have colored cornstarch staining his skin and he was trying to wipe it off his arms and legs with a paper towel. He kept looking at his watch and shaking his head, just as he had done before the race, with an obvious air of irritation on his face.

Tom had run the race as fast as possible in hopes of getting on the road quickly that morning. He was dripping with colored sweat. He had forced himself to sprint and had a nagging cramp in his side which was making him even more irritable. He was annoyed it had taken Jenna so long to finish the race and made no attempt to hide his feelings. He wanted her to try catch him to get this over with faster, and that is why he kept up his speedy pace for as long as he could. However, she had made no effort to finish quickly.

He smiled for one "after" photo following the race in the parking lot and quickly said his goodbyes. He couldn't get to I-95 any faster if he tried. Jenna could have sworn he kicked up dust and rocks with his tires as he peeled out of the event parking lot. He left Jenna, Brett, Heidi, and Olivia standing by their minivan, bewildered at what had just happened.

They had technically run the race together, but at the same time they hadn't.

She Seems Nice

Jenna put her bruised feelings behind her quickly and didn't tell her dad how sad his lack of interest in spending time with her and her kids at The Rainbow Run had made her feel. It was just a fun run, and obviously her dad had something important on his mind. She was hurt, but it was nothing when compared to the way she felt after her mother's funeral. If she could get over that and move forward without saying anything, surely, she could get past this too. After all, they were both just humans and deserved forgiveness and grace.

She decided to forgive and forget and made plans for her family to visit him at the beach in July. He was delighted they were coming and seemed to be looking forward to their arrival. She was confident the dad she was used to, who spoiled her kids with attention, would be waiting when they got there.

A few days before they loaded their suitcases into the van to make the trip, Tom finally worked up the nerve to call and tell Jenna there was someone he wanted her to meet.

As Jenna and her father spoke, she felt a pit in her stomach growing at the news but knew she would have to accept someone coming into her father's life. He deserved to be happy, and she didn't want him to be alone. He was desperately lonely without her mother. She made up her mind at that moment that she would like the woman no matter what, for her dad's sake. *How bad could anyone really be?*

She now knew the reason he had been so distracted on his last visit to North Carolina. It suddenly all made sense. Jenna would call Katie before going to St. Simon's to see if she had any insight on their dad's new love interest.

When the Miller's arrived at Tom's vacation home, the kids were thrilled to hit the pool and the sand. Jenna and Paul unpacked the car while Heidi, Brett, and Olivia quickly put on their bathing suits and searched for shovels, buckets, and boogie boards.

The plan was for the family to spend a few hours at the beach with Tom, and then Donna, his new girlfriend, would come over for dinner. Tom and Paul would cook steaks at the poolside grill, and Jenna and Donna could prepare side dishes in the kitchen. The kids could swim again after the meal and the adults could spend the evening talking and getting acquainted with one another.

The evening went by without any hitches. Donna was polite and easy to talk to and didn't raise any immediate red flags. Jenna's first impression of her was she was friendly, confident, and very put together. She was dressed in a dark green, high-necked, sleeveless blouse and dark green capri pants accented with a shiny, black belt and an oversized black necklace. The outfit was casual, yet very chic. She dressed more hip than Jenna had expected. She had bright red nails that were neatly manicured and matching red lips.

Everyone enjoyed the meal, and as the women cleaned up the table, the men supervised the children in the pool. Jenna and Donna only spoke about unimportant things like the weather and things to do in

St. Simon's. When the kitchen was clean, the ladies joined the men and the children at the pool.

Finally, around nine o-clock, it became obvious Tom wanted to talk with Jenna privately. Paul rounded up the kids and took them back inside the house for brownies, Donna told everyone goodbye and left, and Tom and Jenna remained on the pool deck, sitting in the lounge chairs with custom blue-and-white striped cushions. They each sipped on a glass of cabernet sauvignon.

Jenna already knew in her heart what her dad was about to say. She knew without a doubt he wanted to propose to Donna and wanted her blessing. Jenna thought the relationship had been a whirlwind, and it seemed a little early to propose, however, at his age, people didn't always need to take so much time making decisions.

Katie had mentioned that Donna was good at backhanded compliments, could be domineering, and sometimes seemed like she enjoyed pitting her and their father against each other, but Jenna assumed nothing was so terrible it couldn't be tolerated or worked out over time. She and Katie would have to adjust to their dad being in a new relationship with someone other than their mom. It was different. It was strange. It would take some time to get used to.

Nevertheless, Jenna knew no matter what either of them thought, her father had already made up his mind. She could see he was clearly smitten and seemed happier and more at ease than he had in months.

When Tom asked her what she thought about Donna, Jenna simply said, "She seems nice." And that was all he needed to hear.

Those three words were the gold seal of approval Tom was looking for. The conversation was over. Jenna had nothing else to say anyway. She didn't know Donna from Adam. She had spent approximately two hours with her and was now being asked for an opinion on a lifetime decision. She could only pray this was a good match, and the family would come to think of Donna as a missing link.

Tom had already purchased the engagement ring anyway.

It's Getting Hot

The engagement between Tom and Donna came swiftly upon Jenna's family's departure from Georgia.

Before the Millers could even get back to North Carolina, the engagement photos were posted on Facebook and the relationship statuses had been changed to "engaged." Donna posted a number of photos from various angles of her smiling and showing off the enormous rock that now sat upon her left ring finger.

Jenna couldn't help but notice Donna's ring was ten times the size her mother's had been, but of course she rationalized her mom's had been purchased when her father was just starting out in life as a farm equipment salesman. Money had been much tighter then, and a ring like Donna's would have been far out of reach.

Although Grace's diamond was small, she had never asked for a replacement. Her wedding ring was beautiful to her and meaningful. She had worn it almost every day of her adult life. When she was in her fifties, she had her engagement and wedding rings soldered together because the bands were starting to wear thin after so many years of rubbing together on her finger.

Jenna still felt a little sick over the whole engagement, but she was happy for her father. She pushed aside her discomfort because her father had a genuine smile on his face and seemed quite content in all the photos. Jenna convinced herself the bad vibes were simply coming from her own insecurities and the grief she still felt over losing her mother. She reminded herself her mother had approved of her dad remarrying, and she felt confident he would take her advice and choose someone who would complement the Jacobs family. *She just didn't know Donna well enough yet, right?*

Jenna didn't know this was the beginning of the end of the family she had known her whole life.

Her father was dancing with the devil, and it was about to get hot.

It's Better to Give

Before her death, Grace made Tom promise her he would take care of their daughters in his will. Tom and Grace had worked hard during their lives together, and she wanted to leave a financial legacy to her children and grandchildren.

Together, they decided—at minimum—whatever money they had on the day of her death should be the value of what he left for Katie and Jenna in his will, minus what he needed to live a comfortable life, and barring no catastrophic event occurred that required him to use up all they had saved.

Grace hoped any additional money he brought in would also be divided amongst the girls but left that up to him. She knew he would have to learn to make decisions on his own. She didn't expect him to hoard the money and not use any of it. He deserved to spend some of it, even if she couldn't.

She encouraged him to upgrade his boat to a small yacht, spoil grandchildren with cars if they needed one, and made him promise to take the whole family on fabulous trips like his mother had done. She hoped he would use some of their savings to keep family traditions alive and to fund experiences where they could make new memories even though she wouldn't be a part of them. Tom had assured her he would take care of the girls and the grandchildren.

It was just like Grace to be thinking of everyone else in her final hours.

The first year after Grace's death, Tom abided by her wishes. He bought himself the Sea Ray and was generous to his daughters. He also happily supported his grandchildren's school and sports fundraisers, and decided to buy Sydney, Katie's middle child, a car sometime over the next year for her sixteenth birthday. Tom enjoyed spoiling his grandkids, and he looked forward to spoiling great grandchildren one day too.

He even took the family on a wonderful vacation to Grand Cayman, where they visited a sea turtle farm. They climbed into a tank of baby turtles and took turns holding them. It was an amazing experience, and the joy on his grandchildren's faces as they held the little turtles made every dollar the trip cost worth it.

Olivia, who had only been three at the time, had been so excited when she found out she could hold the turtles she literally jumped out of her stroller so quickly she got tangled in the plastic footrest and fell to the ground in her attempt to run toward the tank. She skinned her knees and palms badly but forgot all about the pain when it was her turn to enter the tank. It was a magical moment for her to have the baby turtle resting in her little hands, and the whole experience had been made possible because of her grandfather and his promise to her grandmother.

The family enjoyed the gourmet food on the island and stayed in a luxury resort with exquisite on-site restaurants, family-friendly entertainment, and an infinity pool. They also booked a sitting with the resort's professional photographer. They had not taken a family portrait since Grace died, but it seemed like the right time for a new one. They were making new memories and still living. It was just the next chapter of the Jacobs family, and it was what Grace wanted.

They had no idea the picture taken at the resort would be the last time they would all happily pose for a photographer and say "cheese."

Pictures, Postcards, and Prenups

Tom took the family on the trip to Grand Cayman seven months before he met Donna.

When she asked about the family portrait the first time she came over to his house, he excitedly told her all about the wonderful vacation. He shared stories about the turtle farm and about the fantastic magician at the resort who had made Brett disappear. He laughed at the memory and said, "Olivia was so worried she cried. She was afraid her brother was gone forever!" He continued, "She literally jumped for joy when Brett reappeared holding a white rabbit."

He revealed to her he especially enjoyed taking his grandchildren to souvenir shops whenever they traveled and would let them buy whatever trinkets caught their eyes—drums made from coconuts, maracas, T-shirts, or stuffed animals. It was something special he liked to do with them.

He continued, "While they pick out their souvenirs, I peruse the postcard rack looking for unique ones to add to my collection. You won't believe how many I have accumulated over the years."

Donna made a mental note about the postcard collection, which she thought was a hobby more fitting for a child than an adult of his means, but said nothing about it.

Tom said, "Traveling has always been an important tradition in my family. I hope there will be many more trips in the future."

He smiled at her. It was clear he was insinuating he hoped she would be on the trips too.

She sheepishly smiled back.

It was evident to Donna that Tom's family clearly meant a lot to him. The garish picture was proudly displayed front and center on the mantle in his living room. It was in a standard frame, likely purchased from a discount store, and was a little too small to sit above the giant stone fireplace. She thought he should take the cheap-looking portrait down and replace it with artwork that would be more impressive to visitors—but decided to keep this thought to herself.

Tom was convinced his future was looking brighter now that he met Donna and let himself imagine what might lie ahead. He dreamed of making new memories that included her and of taking more family pictures on vacations that had yet to be booked.

This would never happen.

Tom wanted to honor Grace's memory and planned to follow through with his promise to her to continue to take care of the family. He was going to request a prenuptial agreement with Donna. He just hadn't discussed it with her yet.

He wanted to make sure his original family was taken care of and his and Grace's legacy of generosity would live on. Of course, he also fully planned to take care of Donna, particularly in the event he died before her. He would make sure she was quite comfortable for the rest of her life.

Tom didn't know how to approach Donna about his plans for the prenup, so he kept it to himself for now. No need to spoil the joy of their recent engagement with financial business. There would be time for that later.

Tom was sure Donna was a woman of great character and would fully understand. She would expect him to provide for his family, especially when she saw he fully intended to care for her too. She would admire him for his generosity.

Respect the King

A few weeks after their engagement, Tom casually mentioned to Donna, "I have been thinking about buying a car for Sydney for quite some time now and I'm finally ready to do so. I think I will go to a few car lots this weekend and see if I can find anything suitable."

He had recently made some wise investments and had the cash on hand for this type of expenditure. He knew it would have pleased Grace, but he left that part out when he mentioned it to Donna.

Tom had noticed since their engagement, his fiancée seemed to get angry at the mere mention of Grace's name. When they first started dating, she listened to all his stories with great interest, many which included Grace, and was happy for him that he had been married to a lovely woman for so long. She seemed to understand that although he loved his first wife, he also loved her and was excited for their future together.

But now, whenever Tom mentioned Grace, it was as if she thought of him more like a victim of a bitter divorce with an awful ex-wife worthy of being despised, instead of a widower.

Donna didn't like Tom to talk about any portion of his life that included Grace. She preferred for him to talk about his childhood or the years after Grace's passing—but nothing in between. She thought it was best for their relationship to pretend the years Tom spent married to his late wife never happened.

Tom thought her request was odd and somewhat off-putting. *How could he ignore the fact that he had been married for more than forty years?* The majority of his life had been spent with Grace by his side.

However, since Donna's disdain for Grace was so strong, he tried his best to limit his stories to the time periods she found acceptable to discuss. He also thought it necessary to take down any pictures of Grace that were in his house to keep from upsetting his future wife. He privately concluded Donna felt threatened by Grace, but he could not understand why. She was clearly not a threat to the relationship. She was dead and was never coming back.

Donna hated Grace because she represented family, motherhood, service, frugality, and selflessness. All admirable qualities that Donna did not possess.

Grace was loved by everyone who knew her, whereas Donna had a long list of ex-friends, ex-family members, and ex-romantic partners. Donna was afraid she would not be able to compete with Grace's memory and would lose Tom, forever. It was best for her if he forgot about his first wife completely.

Tom was quite taken aback when Donna became incensed at the mention of him buying a car for his granddaughter, a reaction he never anticipated. He had expected her to be delighted and to say something like, "Oh, Tom, what a loving and generous man you are!"

Instead, she said, "Katie and her family already demand so much time from you, and now they are taking advantage of your money. I cannot believe your daughter is pushing you into this!"

He tried to explain it was his idea, but she didn't care.

She said, "It is a bad idea no matter where it came from." Donna believed Tom had been more than generous to his children and their offspring over the years. It was time for him to take care of himself and his new bride. Building a new life with her should be his only priority, and to do it right would cost a pretty penny.

Tom mistook her anger for concern and assumed she wanted to protect him financially. There was no way for her to know how much money he had because they hadn't disclosed their net worths to one another yet.

He found her concern endearing and said, "Darling if you are worried about me, don't be. Buying this car for Sydney will not create any sort of hardship for me."

The fact he had a yacht and a vacation home should have been a clue he was okay in the money department, but he incorrectly assumed his fiancée had no idea what either of these luxuries had cost him. He supposed she must have drastically underestimated their value since there were certainly bigger yachts and bigger vacation homes.

He believed since Donna had no experience making purchases such as these her only knowledge about what they cost came from TV shows about extremely wealthy people who threw money around like it was confetti. He found her female naivety cute.

Tom never considered her emotions to be fueled by selfish, ulterior motives.

Anyone with a brain would have considered this a possibility, but not Tom Jacobs.

He believed Donna was the perfect woman sent to him by God. He was not willing to accept she had any flaws or lapses in moral character. He refused to see the possibility that she was angry because she was greedy and wanted all his money for herself.

Tom explained he didn't plan to buy a flashy, luxury car. He said, "I only intend to buy a practical, used car appropriate for a teenage driver," thinking this would calm her down.

However, she remained angry and said, "Anything you buy will be too much." Donna did not subscribe to the idea that giving was better than receiving. She viewed the gift of a car as a slippery slope. *Would all his grandchildren expect one? That would be six cars in total!*

All Donna could see was thousands of dollars wasted on greedy children with selfish parents and less in the bank to be spent on her. *That would never happen if she had anything to say about it. It was time for Tom Jacobs to learn to tell his family "No!"*

She realized it was time to turn on her powers of manipulation to make sure Tom didn't carry through with his plan. She also wanted to gauge how much power she had over her fiancé.

She was confident if she said and did the right things, she could persuade him buying Sydney a car would be a terrible mistake. She was also certain she could even convince him squashing the purchase was his idea.

Donna didn't consider herself selfish or uncompassionate, rather, she viewed herself as worthy and street-smart, capable of sniffing out when someone was being taken advantage of—especially when it threatened their ability to be generous to her! It was a dog-eat-dog world.

As they sat on the couch talking, Donna praised Tom for giving his children such wonderful childhoods. She said, "Tom, your daughters are the luckiest girls on the planet! You were a wonderful father to them, giving them a life of luxury."

She shared tidbits about her childhood with him, confessing she hadn't been as blessed as Katie and Jenna. Donna said, "My parents had very little money, but it was enough. I am glad I wasn't spoiled as a child. God provided all we needed." She said proudly, "Growing up without much made me humble."

Proud humility is an oxymoron, but Tom was oblivious to this contradiction in his fiancée's character. He was listening intently to her every word like a cobra listening to a snake charmer playing their flute.

She said, "Surely your girls owe you the deepest respect because of all you provided." She paused to let her statement soak in.

Donna continued, "It is surprising Katie doesn't model her own behavior after yours. She isn't nearly as generous of a parent with her children as you were with her and Jenna. She obviously did not learn much from the example you set, or she doesn't work hard enough to be able to adequately provide for them. I think she just expects you to take care of everything because you always have in the past. She takes you for granted, which is a sign of disrespect. I'm afraid you spoiled her with your generosity."

Donna had no idea what Katie's financial situation was like, how much she did for her children, or how much money a fourth-grade schoolteacher made. She didn't know Katie always went to work early, stayed late, and created the most thoughtful and engaging lesson plans for her students on the weekends. Katie also respected her father immensely and appreciated everything he and her mother had ever done for her.

Donna made assumptions and accusations to fit her own narrative, without any facts to back them up.

Aware she was building momentum, she asked Tom to give her examples of some of the expenses he had incurred on his children's behalf. She said, "I'm curious what it takes financially to raise a family since I never had the opportunity."

As he began to try to recap every dime he had ever spent on his girls, she made sure to interject at appropriate moments. She said things like, "Tom you were such a good father to pay for Katie and Jenna's braces. It was so generous of you to support their vanity," while stroking the back of his neck with her perfectly manicured fingernails, which he had paid for.

He failed to see the irony but acknowledged her praise.

As he droned on about college expenses, she said, "Did you know private universities cost twice as much as public institutions? It's a shame Katie and Jenna took advantage of you. They could have easily gone to a state school and saved you thousands of dollars of your hard-earned money." And "Wow, you paid for sorority dues? Weren't your daughters capable of making friends for free?"

She urged him to talk about the expense of designer clothing, name brand shoes, hosting birthday parties, personal computers, video game systems, and the cost of playing competitive sports.

She decided not to bring up weddings, because she didn't want to remind him how expensive they were.

Donna said, "Your daughters are lucky they didn't incur student debt like I was forced to take on. I worked two jobs to get my education, and I am better because of it. I also learned how to reinvent hand-me-downs, which is where I developed my love for fashion. Sadly, there was no extra money for me or my brothers to play sports just for fun. We only had the necessities and worked for everything we had."

Donna casually questioned the work ethic and morality of those who had things come easy in life, like it was an afterthought—but it wasn't. Every word she said was carefully premeditated.

Tom found himself suddenly casting doubt on the thankfulness of Jenna and Katie. *Had he done too much for them? Did they respect him?*

He was drawn in by Donna's charismatic speech and by the allure of the accolades she was heaping on him.

She manipulated the conversation masterfully, and painted Katie and Jenna out to be ungrateful, entitled brats, spoiled through and through, raising the next generation of spoiled brats. She also put the idea out into the universe that there was no limit to their willingness to take from their father.

As Tom registered Donna's words, he seemed to forget he and Grace willingly made the choice to provide braces and educations to their children because they wanted the best for their daughters. Jenna and Katie didn't demand anything.

He forgot Grace shopped clearance sales and consignment shops when the girls were little, before he became a successful realtor, and continued to do so even when they had more money because she was conservative. They taught their girls how to use coupons whenever they could, look for bargains, and encouraged them to save for a rainy day.

Tom and Grace urged their daughters to play sports and started them out on the soccer field when they were very young—much too young to make decisions for themselves. They strongly believed making their daughters play sports was an excellent way for Jenna and Katie to learn teamwork and self-discipline and to develop good work ethic. Both girls had worked very hard to become accomplished athletes and spent countless hours practicing their skills and conditioning their bodies. They had also served as team captains at various points of their soccer careers, developing their own personal leadership styles.

At this moment though, all Tom could recall about youth sports was writing checks for soccer tournaments, sporting equipment, and coaches fees.

Tom also became unable to recognize that parents often did things for their kids just because they loved them or because it was their duty. He was completely under Donna's spell.

Donna could feel her barrage of "innocent" questions was having a huge effect on her fiancé. She was pleased with her progress so far. She nestled in even closer and rested her head on his shoulder and let out a long, breathy sigh.

This was the perfect opportunity to remind Tom of every mistake or bad decision Katie ever made in her life. He was currently putty in her hands. *This was the moment she had been waiting for!* Tom was in a vulnerable state, and it was time to strike like a venomous cottonmouth rattlesnake.

It was time to use all the information she had gleaned over the past few months about his oldest daughter as ammunition. She was going to take the first official shot at Katie even though she wasn't there to defend herself and had done nothing to provoke it.

If she was going to stop Tom from buying Sydney a car and setting a dangerous precedent for the grandchildren, she was going to have to throw Katie under the bus. If she also caused some damage to Tom and Katie's relationship, that would be a bonus.

The popular phrase *hashtag, sorry, not sorry* crossed Donna's mind for a moment and made her laugh to herself. She prided herself on keeping up with current social media trends. *Not many grandmas could make that claim, could they?*

She brought up the stories Tom had told her about Katie's rebellion as a teenager, one by one, pointing out every example of selfishness and poor decision making she could. She said, "I believe I see a pattern with your oldest daughter, Tom."

He seemed to forget every teenager who ever lived, including himself, had at some point been egotistic or made a bad choice. It was a natural and normal part of growing up. It was to be expected.

After trashing Katie for what seemed like an eternity and making old sins that had long ago been forgiven feel fresh again, Donna circled back to money. She said, "Tom, have you ever thought about how much money you have spent on your girls and grandchildren over the course of their lifetimes?"

As he tried to come up with a dollar amount, he began to equate success as a parent in proportion to the amount of money one spent on his children. When he was satisfied with a ballpark figure, he suddenly felt like he was eligible for the Father's Hall of Fame.

Donna gently began rubbing her perfectly polished fingernails up and down his arm again and said, "Tom, your girls must owe you unconditional respect because the tally of their accounts is quite high. After all, the most important part of being a father is commanding respect. Right, Tommy?"

She had never called him Tommy before, and it took him by surprise. He liked it. Grace never called him Tommy a single time in all their years, occasionally "Thomas" if she was angry, but never Tommy, mostly just Tom. Hearing Donna say it made him feel younger and more attractive instantly.

Donna knew her fiancé liked to be on the receiving end of praise, and often let his ego get the best of him. It was his easily identifiable Achilles heel. Humility didn't come naturally to him.

Donna had already used his love of money to her benefit and stroked his over-inflated ego. Now, it was time to play to his religious side if she was going to change his mind once and for all about buying the car. The only thing he liked better than feeling rich and powerful, was being recognized for being a strong Christian.

Tom Jacobs cared about three things—money, himself, and God. In that order.

Donna continued by saying, "Just like Christians are taught to respect their Heavenly Father, children on earth need to respect their humanly fathers." Donna saw the look on Tom's face and knew she was winning. She was getting to him, and he was clinging to her every word.

She explained even though her father had not always been perfect, she loved him and gave him the respect he deserved simply because he was a father and a man. It was her biblical obligation.

Tom began to fixate on the idea of deserving respect and said, "You are right Donna, the role of father in a family is equivalent to a king—or even to God. I hadn't fully considered that before and I am glad you pointed this out to me. It is imperative for children to show their father unconditional respect."

If Donna had been unsure before, she was now certain she knew the formula for winning an argument with Tom or getting him to do things her way. Step One: display an outburst of anger or emotion to unsettle him, Step Two: soften him up with physical touch, and Step Three: add some ego stroking followed by a biblical reference that compares him to God, and he will do whatever she commands.

The best part of it all, he will think giving her what she wants is his own idea.

After one conversation with Donna, Tom managed to lose sight of what parenting was about, despite his forty plus years of experience, and allowed the idea of deserving respect to permeate all his thoughts.

He also forgot God was a loving, forgiving Father, not a tyrannical king.

Tom's new mindset would be another pivotal factor in the demise of the Jacobs family and would create as much havoc as a shifting of the San Andreas fault. With Tom under Donna's manipulative trance, he became blind to the fact that both of his girls had a great deal of respect for him and loved him dearly.

He elevated his position in the family from Dad and Grandpa to king and God, supreme ruler of all.

If he had stopped to think rationally for even a second, the smoke cloud Donna's words produced would have cleared. He could have made the realization that generosity and respect were not exclusive to one another, and being a good father had nothing to do with money. But he didn't stop to think.

Donna was pleased with her performance when Tom told her he had changed his mind about buying a car for Sydney. It was time for him to show Katie some "tough love." She was amused he was using her words as if they were his own. Donna had repeatedly said, "tough love" throughout the evening, yet he didn't seem to realize this.

He said, "Tomorrow night, when Katie and the kids come to dinner, I will tell her I no longer plan to purchase a car for Sydney—or for any of my grandchildren for that matter—because it isn't my responsibility." I will also tell her, "It is time for you to stop taking advantage of me and show me the respect I deserve."

Tough Love

The next night, Katie and the girls came over to Tom's home in Peachtree City, fully expecting a lovely dinner and a night of total relaxation like they had countless times before.

His home was like a second home to the kids because they were there so often. They even had pajamas and bathing suits in a drawer in the guest bedroom. They were always prepared for an impromptu sleepover with their Pop Pop or an unplanned dip in the pool.

The girls would either swim after dinner or settle down and watch a movie while the grownups talked and enjoyed an after-dinner night cap. It would depend on everyone's mood and the temperature of the pool.

Donna called everyone to the table, and as they began to sit down, she gave Tom a look that told him it was time to talk to Katie. She wanted him to speak to his daughter as soon as possible to ensure nothing got in the way of him making his announcement. She also didn't want to give him time to change his mind.

Tom said, "Katie, will you please step outside with me for just a moment?"

She replied, "Of course," and dutifully followed her father into the garage and then out to the driveway.

Katie prayed he didn't have bad news for her and quietly whispered, "Please God, let my father be healthy." She couldn't bear the loss of another parent. The family couldn't go through another battle with cancer. She was concerned by the serious expression on his face he had heard something concerning from his doctor. *What else could he need to speak to her privately about?*

Tom pulled a lawn chair out of the garage and motioned for her to sit down, but did not get one for himself. This made Katie even more afraid because she presumed whatever he was going to say would upset her. *Cancer, it must be cancer. He must want me to sit down in case my knees buckle instantly upon hearing his news.*

Katie slumped down into the chair. Her heart was pounding. She could feel a trickle of sweat on the back of her neck.

Tom did not pull out the chair out of concern for his daughter like she thought. This act was intended to be an intimidation factor. He planned to stand over Katie while he delivered his announcement. Donna had convinced him to do this because she thought it would make him look more authoritative.

Tom began his lecture by staring down at Katie and saying, "I have called you out here tonight to talk to you about fiscal responsibility."

Katie instantly felt on edge and knew her concerns about his health were unnecessary. It was clear he had prepared his speech ahead of time and was speaking from memory. She wouldn't have been surprised if he had notecards in his back pocket with every word written on them.

She sat there in disbelief when he said, "I have come to the realization I have been overly generous with you. I have also come to believe you expect this of me. Some tough love seems to be in order." He continued by saying, "I will not let you take advantage of me anymore, and as such, I will not be buying Sydney, or any of your children, a car." He also began to rehash the many times Katie had been irresponsible in her youth but did not allow her to defend herself.

Katie was dumbfounded. She never asked him to buy the car for Sydney and never expected it. It had been his idea. *Where was her loving father, and where was this coming from? Why was tough love in order?*

She had done nothing to deserve this lecture, but he was making her feel embarrassed and ashamed. *Why was he bringing up mistakes she made fifteen years ago as a teenager? Why did he seem like a stranger at this moment?*

It was clear she was to listen and not speak. This was not meant to be a conversation.

When his lecture was over, he casually turned his back to Katie and headed toward the house. He returned to the dining room where the rest of the family was eating, as if nothing had happened, and took his place at the head of the table. Donna served him a piping hot plate of ziti and gave him a "good job" pat on his back.

Meanwhile, Katie remained sitting in the lawn chair, crying in the driveway. Alone. Stunned. Confused. Angry. Devastated.

She couldn't understand why her dad felt this harsh tactic had been necessary at all. He could have simply told her he changed his mind. There was no need for this power trip over her. No need to demean or insult her. No need to make her feel like she was a bad daughter.

It took Katie a moment to collect herself after Tom's vicious attack. She felt two inches tall and was deeply troubled. When she finally regained her composure, she reentered the dining room where she was met by Donna.

Donna Thorn had an overly large, fake smile plastered on her face. It was so big Katie could see her back teeth. Perhaps it could have been better classified as a sneer. The image of a snarling bulldog popped into Katie's brain, and it seemed apropos.

Donna handed Katie a plate of baked ziti, served on Grace and Tom's wedding china, and said, "I have prepared a homemade meal for you. I know you don't like to cook much yourself. I hope it isn't cold." She did not offer to heat it up for her.

The words she spoke were dripping with judgment and condemnation.

An unnerving chill went down Katie's spine as she took the plate from Donna's hands.

Donna purposely chose to use Grace's wedding china to send the message she was in charge. Totally and completely. Things would no longer be done in this household the way they would have been done in the past. Frivolous giving was over.

As Katie stared at her mother's white china, smeared with red sauce—which had only been used on the most special of occasions when Grace was alive—she knew their lives were about to change forever. The plate reminded her of a bloody crime scene, and her appetite vanished.

Katie noted the look of satisfaction on Donna's face when she looked up from her plate and locked eyes with her. It was abundantly clear to Katie who was responsible for tonight's turn of events. This felt like the beginning of a war, and Donna had attacked first with an ambush. *But why?*

While Tom naively thought Donna used the china because she wanted to serve his family a beautiful dinner, Katie knew otherwise. Love was the furthest thing from Donna's mind. She could see the truth as plain as the nose on her face and knew every move Donna made was calculated.

Katie left as quickly as possible after dessert. There would be no swimming, no movies, no talking, and no after-dinner cocktails. The scotch would remain in the liquor cabinet, and the girls' bathing suits would not be removed from their place in the guest bedroom dresser drawer.

Katie only stayed for dessert because she didn't want to disappoint her children. They were looking forward to sampling the warm cookies that had just come out of the oven. A lovely smell of chocolate drifted out of the kitchen and permeated the entire house, but Katie was too sick to her stomach to be enticed to try one.

The second the children finished eating, Katie announced it was time to leave, and she did not offer to help clean up. The kids were noticeably confused since the plans that had been laid out for the evening were changed without explanation. However, they could see their mother was in a bothered state, so they put on their shoes to leave without arguing.

Even they could feel the tension and the shift in the family atmosphere that had happened since Donna came into their lives. She was like a cold wind blowing through and giving everyone chill bumps.

Katie could feel with every fiber of her being she wasn't welcome in her own childhood home anymore, even though her dad still lived in it. Her mother was gone and the house that held so many wonderful memories had changed. It was no longer a place of refuge or a safe harbor. She needed to leave as quickly as possible. The house felt dangerous.

As Tom and Donna watched Katie's taillights pull out of the driveway, Donna slipped her arm around Tom's waist and complimented him for doing the right thing. She reminded him that sometimes as the head of the family he had to take charge. She said, "I'm proud of you Tommy." She catered to his ego by telling him, "A tough man is a sexy man."

Puff. Puff. Puff.

She said, "Katie knew you were right and that's why she left so quickly. She was embarrassed you called her out on her selfishness."

Puff. Puff. Puff.

Tom believed the words spewing so effortlessly out of Donna's mouth and pushed away the concern that had started to creep into his mind somewhere between dinner and dessert.

For a few fleeting moments he saw the obvious look of pain on his daughter's face and noticed she barely even took a bite of her dinner. He briefly considered he might have made a mistake. He also knew Grace would not have approved of the events of the evening. He had been harsh on Katie, and his lecture was unprovoked. He could have possibly approached the situation in a softer way. He purposely ripped the scars open on some very old wounds for no reason other than to assert himself as dominant and remind her he deserved respect. However, Donna was convinced this was necessary and he trusted her fully.

Donna said, "I'm sure this will all be forgotten soon. You and Katie always worked things out in the past, and you will this time too. Hopefully she will take note of what you said and start showing you the respect you are entitled to." She gave him a quick kiss on his cheek to reassure him and then sighed and said, "I guess I will clean the kitchen since Katie didn't even offer to help. Her selfishness is unbelievable."

A month later Tom bought brand new his and hers matching cars for Donna and himself. The only difference between the two vehicles was the color. His was electric blue and hers was candy apple red. He was convinced it was solely his idea to buy them, but Donna knew better. She only had to complain a few times about needing to get an oil leak fixed in her old Buick, which she had driven for the last decade, to get the wheels turning in Tom's head.

She knew he would be concerned about her safety and wanted the best for her. He loved to shower her with expensive gifts and got pleasure out of seeing her happy. When Tom offered to buy her a new car, she adamantly refused at first, but allowed him to "wear her down."

She knew exactly what she was doing.

Donna slipped behind the wheel of her sleek, red BMW and gripped the leather steering wheel. It was fully loaded with every bell and whistle she could need or want. The bright red looked good next to her raven-like hair and would complement any outfit she wore. She glanced in the rearview mirror and thought, *I need a root touch up soon to hide the light brown and gray that is starting to peek through my scalp.*

The BMW was definitely an upgrade. Perhaps the next car he would buy her would be a Limited-Edition Mercedes convertible. *Yes, she had chosen wisely with Tom Jacobs.*

She couldn't wait for a reason to swing by Katie's and show off her new vehicle. Tom would take it as a gesture of friendliness and thankfulness, but Donna knew it would be her victory lap. *Maybe she would even offer to take the kids for a spin and let them stick their hands out of the sunroof.*

She had the car, she had the man, and she was in control. It would be satisfying to remind Katie of this and to point out the generosity of Tom—to those who appreciated him.

When Tom signed the paperwork for two cars at the dealership, he didn't give the horrible night when they had all eaten baked ziti off wedding china a second thought. He had forgotten about the whole situation and wrongly assumed Donna and Katie had also moved on.

Forgive and forget, right?

No Expense Spared

As soon as Tom and Donna were engaged, the bride-to-be began making elaborate plans for the wedding of the century. Donna couldn't contain her excitement, and Tom was pleased to see the joy planning their life together brought his fiancée. He couldn't wait for them to be married and to know his lonely days were over.

No expense was being spared, and Tom was satisfying his bride's every whim.

Donna decided they should be married at the Atlanta Whitehouse. It had a reputation for being one of the most elegant event venues in Georgia and was designed to look like the actual Whitehouse in Washington, D.C. Its grandeur was unparalleled in the area. Donna fell in love with it the first time she laid eyes on it. She exclaimed, "Oh Tom, it's breathtaking! Our guests will undoubtedly be impressed by the spectacular architecture from the moment they arrive. Everyone in attendance will feel like a V.I.P. when they enter through the iron gates!"

She became even more excited when she learned they could be married outdoors in the luxurious garden, painstakingly cared for by a team of Master Gardeners, so long as weather permitted. There was even a stunning double staircase coming from the second floor of the main house, leading outside to the garden. Donna could make a grand entrance, descending the stairs on one side, like a goddess coming down from the heavens, her long train trailing behind her. She would then walk down the grassy aisle, flanked by hundreds of red and white roses, and meet Tom at the custom altar. When the ceremony was over, white doves would be released from gilded cages and a classical harpist would play the recessional.

The reception would be held indoors in the ballroom with marble floors, crystal chandeliers, gold accents, and ample space for dancing. The wedding would be so fancy it might even be photographed for the society page in the newspaper.

Donna hired a highly recommended wedding coordinator to make sure every detail was perfect. She was expensive but knew exactly what it took to pull off a buzzworthy wedding in Atlanta. She also had personal contacts with every newspaper and magazine published in Georgia. If everything went the way Donna hoped, their wedding would be the talk of the town for months. She could already visualize "Thorn-Jacobs Nuptials, Wedding Perfection" splashed across the headlines.

The whole affair seemed a little over the top to Tom since this was a second marriage for them both. A smaller, more personal ceremony in a traditional church and a modest reception in the fellowship hall would have been just fine with him. The only thing he cared about was marrying Donna. He couldn't care less about society pages, media coverage, or doves. He really didn't care about doves.

However, he wanted to give his future wife everything she ever dreamed of in a wedding and start their marriage off on the right foot. He gave in on every request for flowers, music, world class photographers, birds, and even a Rolls Royce to drive the bride and groom away from the reception.

The Rolls Royce was extravagant since they would be spending the night at the hotel next door to the Atlanta Whitehouse. They would only be driving around the block. But Tom agreed to it anyway. He was marrying for love and being given a second chance for happiness and that was all that was important. His days of loneliness were about to be over forever.

He paid the necessary deposits, gave her a credit card she could use for wedding expenses at will, and smiled when she told him about every detail. He was happy she was happy.

However, the wedding bills were mounting steadily, and the costs were beginning to reach levels he never imagined possible. He couldn't help but think, *maybe she isn't as concerned as I thought about my financial security*. He dismissed his thoughts and decided she was just so excited about the wedding she didn't realize how quickly it was all adding up.

The Prenup Meltdown

Tom knew he shouldn't put off telling Donna about his desire for a prenuptial agreement any longer, but he was having trouble finding the right time to spring it on her. It would be unfair to hit her with it just before the wedding, so he knew he needed to work up his nerve and just get it over with. The prenup was just a formality, but he couldn't help but be afraid Donna would view it differently. For some reason, he equated telling her about it with diving into icy water at a Polar Plunge.

It wouldn't kill him, but it sure would be uncomfortable!

He hoped his bride-to-be would understand it was just a practical matter with no reflection of his love for her, because that is exactly what it was to him. It was just legal paperwork, nothing more.

One evening over dinner at Donna's house, Tom felt a surge of bravery and decided it was a now or never situation. He blurted out, "I contacted my lawyers and am having a prenup drawn up. Don't worry though, you will always be taken care of in the way you deserve."

The moment Donna heard this she became angry. These words felt like a sucker punch that had come out of nowhere—forcefully and fiercely. A prenup was a powerful reminder to her his dead wife and annoying children still had control over him. This was intolerable.

She erupted in rage. Mind blowing, unadulterated rage.

Tom didn't even know how to respond as she yelled, cursed, and cried. He had seen her mad before, but this was beyond comprehension. She seemed like a completely different person, almost maniacal, and he was afraid.

He had no idea his suggestion of a prenup was completely derailing the plan she had put into motion since the moment she messaged him for the first time on Christian Companion.

Donna was seething from anger from the depths of her soul. *How dare he do this to her?* She even began to question whether they should be married at all and impulsively shouted this at him.

Was this relationship going to end the same way her relationship with Frank Wilson had ended? A prenup was disrespectful to her as a future spouse and an act of betrayal.

Tom tried again to explain to her she would be taken care of fully, but it was no use. She was in a complete fit of rage and behaving illogically. She heard nothing he said after "prenup."

Tom learned over the course of his lifetime you can't deal rationally with someone who isn't rational, so he just watched her meltdown with no idea what to do. He wanted to honor Grace's wishes and simultaneously respect his future wife. It was a tough situation to say the least.

At this moment he wished Donna was a little more practical like Grace, but of course, he would never say that out loud because of her loathing of his late wife. This was certainly not the time to bring her up. He also wondered why providing for her for the rest of her life wasn't enough. *She did love him as much as he loved her, didn't she?*

Was she marrying him for who he was or for his money? Surely, that could not be the case.

Donna screamed and yelled for what felt like forever to both of them. She fully expected he would retreat quickly and withdraw his desire for a prenup because he wouldn't be able to bear her dramatics for long, but after an hour, he still hadn't backed down and showed no indication he was thinking of changing his mind.

Donna couldn't keep up the act any longer, so she stormed off to her room and slammed the door behind her, leaving him standing shellshocked and alone in her dining room. She needed to figure out what to do to make this go away. She had invested way too much in this relationship to let it go. She had also examined every bank account and brokerage statement he left haphazardly lying around on his desk and knew exactly what she would be losing.

Donna had never seen Tom stick to his guns like this before, and it concerned her. It was clear her normal tactics for getting her way weren't working this time, but she knew she would eventually find a way around this obstacle. This was only a setback. She would never win if she called off the wedding entirely, so she was going to have to concede eventually.

She decided she would stay in her room for the rest of the night, making him fear he was losing her, but would have to come out in the morning if he hadn't changed his mind yet. She was confident he would spend the night on her couch because he wouldn't want to leave her so upset. She couldn't protest any longer than one night, though, and risk Tom losing patience with her and calling off the whole thing himself. She needed to remain in control.

She also had a nail appointment at ten o'clock in the morning and didn't want to miss it. It was time for a fill.

As she sat in her room waiting to come out at the best moment for dramatic purposes, she pulled her phone out of her pocket and did a Safari search for her wedding dress. She typed in the designer's name and style description, and it immediately came up on her screen. She had already ordered it through the most popular bridal boutique in Atlanta, but she wanted to view it again. It made her heart race just to look at it.

It was a long, white, formfitting lace gown with sheer sleeves and pearls and Swarovski crystals adorning every seam. The accompanying train was six feet long with matching pearls and crystals handstitched every few inches.

Some people could argue it was a style only appropriate for a much younger bride, but she was positive she would turn heads in it and couldn't wait for the attention she was sure to receive. She had curves in just the right places—she liked to remind herself of this often.

Maybe once her self-induced isolation was over, she would use her wedding credit card to purchase some killer stilettos or expensive jewelry to match the dress. Tom would owe her some pity shopping.

The Fair Game Column

The next morning, much to Tom's delight, Donna slowly opened the door.

As she expected, he was waiting for her on her living room sofa. He looked like he hadn't slept all night. He had bags under his eyes and his dark blond hair was disheveled. He was still wearing his clothes from the previous day. His normally perfectly-groomed beard was slightly scruffy.

She allowed him to put his arms around her and comfort her while she pretended to cry.

Donna decided the best course of action regarding the prenup was to tell Tom she would accept it and apologize for her behavior. She laid it on thick, saying, "I'm sorry I flipped out on you, Tommy. I must have seemed like I was off my rocker, but when you said you wanted a prenup, it felt like you don't love me as much as I love you. I was heartbroken because I assumed you were trying to leave yourself an open door if you ever wanted to walk away from our marriage. I am in this forever. You are my soulmate. I can't even fathom losing you, my love."

He kissed her on her forehead. It felt good to be so loved. He was sure she was the right woman for him.

She continued, "Sweetheart, you know how emotionally abusive my first husband was. I was triggered by your request because it felt like you were trying to exert power over me or make me feel inferior, just as he did."

Tom accepted her apology and her explanation. He felt badly she had equated him with her ex. He detested being compared to him and would spend the rest of his life trying to be a loving husband who was emotionally supportive. He said, "We are equal partners. Donna, I am not Todd Thorn. Please don't ever doubt my love for you. The prenup is just legal jargon." He hugged her tightly.

He followed up with his attorney later that afternoon. The prenup was ready for signing. They made an appointment to go in the next day and take care of it. They both agreed as soon as the ink was dry on the paper, it was a done deal and that it no longer needed to be discussed.

When they arrived at the law firm of Martin, Buchanan & Carter, Donna carefully read each word of the prenup that was laid out on the mahogany conference table in front of her. She wanted to have a full understanding of its terms. When she finished reading it in its entirety, Tom told her about the pledge he'd made to Grace just before her passing. He said, "My late wife made me promise I would leave a financial legacy for our family that would be worth, at minimum, the amount we had at the time of her death. This is the reason for the prenuptial agreement. Being a Christian man, I intend to honor my promise."

Donna wanted to scream with excitement! This news was like manna from Heaven because it meant all his money wasn't included in the prenup!

Thank God Grace had been a considerate woman and left her a loophole.

Normally, Donna couldn't even stand to think about Grace. Everyone seemed to think of her as a hero, and the mere mention of her name ticked her off. *Grace this. Grace that. Blah. Blah. Blah.* However, at this moment she sent a little "thank you" up to Heaven.

She reached for the blue pen and signed Donna Thorn in beautiful penmanship in every spot designated with an X.

Donna was fully aware Tom had made money off his investments after Grace's death, a staggering amount. His constant studying of the stock market paid off big from time to time. She knew about a recent sale of stock that had netted him more money than she made in five years. She was confident this was the only reason he wasn't complaining about wedding expenses.

Tom didn't know Donna was aware of his recent good luck with the market. But she was. She definitely was.

Unbeknownst to Tom, Donna was being careful not to go over his payoff with her wedding plans because she feared he would put a stop to everything if she did. She had no problem spending all his proceeds but wouldn't go a penny over so as not raise any alarm bells.

Because of Tom's obsession with making money, he continuously bought new stocks that weren't in his portfolio when his late wife was alive. Donna would point this out when the time was right. That certainly was not today though, and she would keep her mouth shut in front of his lawyer.

Donna decided it would be beneficial to her if Tom sold off as many of his personal belongings as possible; the earnings from these sales would be money accumulated after Grace's death. The proceeds would be fair game for her to save or to spend. Donna would begin the shifting of Tom's assets from the "covered in the prenup" column to the "fair game" column, systematically, methodically, without him realizing her true motive.

She had already convinced him to sell his house in Peachtree City, one of his biggest assets, and to move to the beach permanently. They would start the next chapter of their lives in St. Simon's, together. Selling off his furniture and household goods would be a logical next step.

Donna had much better taste than Grace, as far as she was concerned, and wouldn't be sad to see his stuff go. Everything in his home seemed like it belonged in the eighties or nineties, and she had moved into the new millennium a long time ago. She was ready for some Ethan Allen upgrades.

Whenever they took romantic walks on the beach, she would hold his hand and say, "Won't it be nice when we live here together all the time." She would kiss him and say, "We will walk along the beach every night together, hand in hand." He liked the sound of that.

Tom had agreed easily to the idea of selling his home in Peachtree City because he had been unhappy there ever since Grace died. He had come to the realization the house he shared with his first wife wasn't a suitable match for his second wife. He was ready for a fresh start.

Donna didn't want to live in Tom's vacation house permanently because her future husband had stayed there many times with his late wife. It was tainted with Grace's memory. They had probably even made love in the master bedroom at some point. *Gross.*

She wasn't opposed to letting friends stay there or entertaining there because it certainly was impressive, but she would be damned if she lived in it for the rest of her life. She was also tired of her own house. It was just an average cookie cutter home and she longed for something better.

Instead of confessing her true feelings about the vacation home, Donna told Tom, "I have always dreamed of building a home on the intracoastal waters of St. Simon. Wouldn't it be nice to build one together?"

Tom liked the idea of creating something new with her and was touched when she said, "The first thing we should design is a private dock for you! Nothing would please me more than for you to be able to walk out the back door of our home and get on your yacht any time your heart desires! You will no longer need to keep the Commission Casanova stowed at the marina."

Donna also convinced him his vacation house on Beachview Drive would be a perfect property to turn into a short-term rental and provide them with an additional income stream—except when friends or family wanted to use it. She even offered to be in charge of scheduling rentals and personal visits. She said, "Tommy, I could be your own personal leasing agent!" but what she meant was, "I will be the gatekeeper."

He was impressed by this suggestion and praised her for her business acumen. He was glad to see she was looking for ways to increase their wealth. He had often thought of doing this in the past, but Jenna and Katie used it so regularly he had decided against it. Grace only agreed to let him buy the property if it was going to be for the family. However, if he had his primary residence in St. Simon's too, his girls could just stay with them if it was rented out. It would also be nice to put Donna in charge of something to make her feel like an equal partner in their marriage. He was sure Todd Thorn would never have done that.

Tom's only reservation about moving to the coast full-time was leaving Katie and her girls behind. He would miss seeing them regularly.

Donna downplayed this fact and assured him they would visit Peachtree City often, and his family was always welcome to come to St. Simon's. She said, "Don't worry Tommy, the roads go both ways!"

She had no plans to visit Katie unless it was absolutely necessary, and she had already decided if they came to St. Simon's they would stay at the vacation house—not at their new house. Sleeping with those brats under the same roof would be intolerable—but no need to let these little cats out of the bag yet. She wanted him to believe she was being genuine about wanting his family to come visit often, so she said, "Let's buy a floating trampoline for the girls. They will love it!"

Tom was thrilled with this idea and was pleased it came from Donna. Maybe she was beginning to embrace her new role as grandmother.

Tom moved quickly on the plan to put the Peachtree City house up for sale. Even though they were still only engaged, he was ready to start building their new life together and move on from the past. He could move into his vacation home until they got married and built their dream house. He thought it was best if they didn't live together before they were officially husband and wife because he didn't want to give people the impression that Tom Jacobs was "shacking up." He was known for his high moral standards and was proud of his esteemed reputation.

Donna was glad when a lucrative offer too good to pass up came in quickly. It would be easier for her to keep tabs on Tom and limit his time with his family if they were in the same town. She also knew once the sale closed, there would be no turning back for him. He would be unable to change his mind. She would be one step closer to reeling him in fully and proverbially mounting him to the wall like a prized striped bass.

Tom and Donna planned to use the proceeds from the sale of his house to purchase a waterfront lot and to put toward the new house. It was a substantial amount but wouldn't be enough to cover everything. Tom didn't mind getting a mortgage and financing the rest.

They purchased a beautiful piece of land on the intracoastal side of the water and hired an architect to begin drawing up plans. Tom was proud he would be able to provide Donna with her dream home. They both deserved to be happy. They began referring to their new home as the Dom Estate, a combination of their names, Donna and Tom.

Donna got a private chuckle out of this because the word "Dom" is often used to refer to someone in a dominant position. She was quickly becoming the "Dom" in their relationship, but Tom was clueless. The name had a secret double meaning for her, and it delighted her.

Donna also planned to sell her modest home once their new home was constructed but explained to Tom she felt safest keeping the proceeds in a private account because of the prenup. She needed some protection for herself. He chose not to argue this logic. He still felt badly about hurting her feelings and was glad this was behind them now.

Since things were clearly moving in Donna's favor and the "fair game" column was getting longer each day, Donna was careful not to remind him had he not sold the Peachtree City house, it would have been a considerable chunk of the inheritance he could have left for his family.

Donna concluded the next best step in her plan to control Tom's finances was to make him want to dissolve the prenup on his own—and the way to do this was to get his girls out of his life completely.

She reasoned if they weren't a part of his life, he would have no desire to provide for them while he was living or dead. If she could make them appear to be at fault for the breakdown of the relationship, even better. And if she could successfully chase them away, she felt confident she could persuade him to put her name on all his assets.

She would convince him it was for her own financial security, but in reality, it would protect her from his greedy children, who would no doubt come looking for a handout after his death.

Donna knew the laws in the state of Georgia would give her everything if he died first—if her name was on all his assets. Even if the prenup somehow still existed, it would be null and void according to the law. The word "joint" was powerful, and those five little letters would ensure she would walk away with everything.

Donna sang to herself, "Hashtag, sorry, not sorry!" She was finding there were so many opportunities where the saying was applicable. *No wonder it was so popular!*

Her plan was under way, and things were going smoothly with Tom none the wiser. He had already acquired a new car and new boat since Grace's death, so that just made things easier for Donna. She was thankful Grace had encouraged him to treat himself to some nice things.

She really was a considerate woman, wasn't she? Gag.

Once everything was sold, Donna would just have to convince him to dissolve his family trust and get her name on the new house and the vacation home.

The latter would be the trickiest, but she was sure she would eventually get her way. The only reason he wanted to keep it at all was because he wanted to leave it to his daughters. He and Grace had bought the property years ago with the idea it would be passed on for generations. It was his most sentimental asset.

She would change his mind about it if all went according to plan. She just needed to make that beautiful home a toxic place and a source of stress so he would be willing to let it go. As soon as he did, she could put the proceeds in the "fair game" column. It should be worth a considerable amount. Beach front, four bedrooms, outdoor kitchen, amazing view, heated pool, highly desirable location. She could write the listing in her head. *Maybe she could have been "Georgia's Favorite Realtor" if she had chosen to go into real estate instead of fashion?*

Donna figured the worst-case scenario was she would eventually get her name on the deed and it would be hers when Tom died. Her best-case scenario—she would convince him to sell it, saving her all the property tax and upkeep expenses, and her net worth would go up when the profits hit their shared bank account. She also wouldn't have to waste any time being his "personal leasing agent."

The only part of her plan that needed work was figuring out how to get rid of the girls permanently. She was ready to wash her hands of Katie, Jenna, and their brood of offspring. She wanted to own Tom Jacobs completely, and that included controlling his time, attention, and money.

She used to watch a show on TV called *How to Get Away with Murder* and laughed to herself she just needed to write her own show called *How to Ruin a Family*.

Lies & Omissions

Katie tried to move past the troubling evening where her father shamed her about the car, but it was difficult, especially when Donna and her dad pulled up in her driveway to show off their new matching "toys."

It was a slap in the face. Katie knew it. Donna delighted in it. Tom couldn't see it.

Donna took every opportunity she could to demean, insult, or shame Katie. She made snarky remarks about Katie's finances, her appearance, her domestic skills, her decisions, and her parenting, even though she had no experience of her own. Of course, these hits were always out of Tom's earshot or subtle enough he was oblivious to them. Reading the room was not in his skillset.

She picked, poked, and taunted. Relentlessly.

Donna also interjected herself into every interaction between Katie and Tom. She couldn't allow them any opportunity to talk privately because she feared Katie would tell her father about every snide comment she'd made. If this ever did happen, she would be forced to put on a dramatic woe-is-me performance, like she did when she learned about the prenup. She would have to make up stories about Katie that made her look like a spiteful liar. It would be exhausting, but she knew she was more than capable of playing the part of victim, if need be, it was her most perfected role.

Donna didn't know Tom looked forward to running errands alone in his car so he could secretly call his daughters without her knowledge. He had some inkling it was not a good idea to talk to his girls in front of his fiancée, but he never confronted her about this notion. After the prenup fiasco, he avoided arguments with Donna at all costs.

It was easier for Tom to call Jenna than Katie because he could call her during the day. Jenna was more readily available because she didn't work a full-time job like Katie. All he had to do was pretend he needed to run to Home Depot or Wal-Mart since Donna had no interest in going to either of those stores. This would guarantee him some alone time, away from his fiancée's watchful eye. It was much more difficult for him to come up with places he needed to go in the evening when Katie was home, and because of his lack of ability to communicate with her regularly, their relationship suffered.

Donna was pleased her fiancé was speaking less and less to his oldest daughter and took satisfaction in cutting Katie down any time she could. She liked to fill Tom's ears with stories that made his oldest daughter look like a spoiled brat. She especially enjoyed telling tales that made Tom question his daughter's behavior or sanity. She didn't care she was always telling more fiction than fact. Tom hung on her every word like it was gospel.

Donna liked to create reasons for her to interact alone with Katie. It was necessary she have access to her by herself if she was going to successfully drive her away. These visits provided her fodder for reporting back to Tom with outrageous lies and targeted omissions.

For example, Donna invited Katie to go shopping, and against Katie's better judgment, she reluctantly agreed. She knew her relationship with her future stepmother was not in a good spot and the only way to improve it was to try to build a bridge. She wanted to be on good terms with her for the benefit of the whole family.

Donna's motivation for asking her, on the other hand, was to tear Katie down.

Donna had worked out everything she wanted to say in her head long before issuing the invitation. She had been looking for an opportunity to throw word grenades at her future stepdaughter, hoping to inflict some painful wounds. The shopping mall—far away from Tom—would be the perfect place.

Donna told Tom, "I am going to meet Katie in Atlanta for a girls' day. No boys allowed!" Tom was thrilled his fiancée was trying to spend time with his daughter so he said, "I wouldn't dream of barging in on your fun! Enjoy the day and thank you for being so considerate of my daughter!"

On the day of the shopping trip, Katie and Donna met at Phipps Plaza, one of the biggest shopping centers in Atlanta. As they strolled through Saks Fifth Avenue, Donna urged Katie to try on a bold red dress she knew would not flatter her figure. She said, "Oh Katie, this would look lovely on you!" but thought, *if you want to look like a round tomato*.

Katie agreed to humor her and went to the dressing room. The dress was far too expensive and far too red for her taste, but she would play along in a spirit of goodwill. There was no harm in trying it on for kicks.

Just before she closed the door, Donna leaned in and said, "This is so fun, isn't it? Just think, we will probably be shopping together for the rest of our lives—or at least until one of us dies! I know your mother didn't enjoy shopping in nice stores as much as I do, this must be a welcome change of pace for you! There is so much I can teach you about how to dress." She laughed out loud. Then, she said, "I have been meaning to tell you your father confided in me I am the true love of his life, I'm sure your mom in Heaven is glad I have been able to bring him such joy. He told me he is happier now than ever before in his entire life! Aren't you just so happy for him, Katie?" Donna did not wait for a reply to her rhetorical question, she shut the louvred, dressing room door and thought *mic drop*.

The purpose of her comment was solely to hurt Katie's feelings. She wanted Katie to hate her. It was necessary if her plan was going to work. She also wanted to inflate her own role in Tom's life because it made her feel more secure. Even though it was possible for him to have two loves in his life, Donna made sure Katie understood her comment to mean she was his soulmate, and any feelings he once had for her mother had faded or had been ingenuine.

Katie didn't like the way Donna spoke to her or how she tried to demean her mother's role in her father's life. She thought Donna was cold-hearted and insensitive. She also felt Donna's imaginary competition with Grace was ridiculous. As far as Katie knew, her dead mother wasn't competing for anything.

When Donna returned home from the mall and she relayed the story to Tom, she only "remembered" to tell him, "Katie was an emotional mess today and sobbed in a dressing room at Saks because she misses Grace so much. It was embarrassing. She made quite the scene. She doesn't want to accept me as your bride. I am afraid Grace's death has made her unstable."

She made no mention of her inconsiderate remarks or intentional attack.

On another occasion, Donna demanded Katie, and Caroline, her youngest daughter, accompany her on a trip to the upscale bridal boutique where she had purchased her gown. Donna insisted Katie purchase Caroline's junior bridesmaid's dress there as well.

She had searched long and hard to find the most expensive designer dress she could. Her criteria for selecting it was based more off price than its look. The more it cost, the better it was. There were plenty of choices that were more economical and looked similar, but Donna would not compromise. She had made it abundantly clear it was Katie's responsibility to pay for the dress, not her father's, and wanted her to feel the pain when she opened her wallet.

Just as she predicted, when she showed Katie the dress, Katie suggested they look for a less costly and more comfortable substitute. Katie said, "The dress you selected is very beautiful, but would it be okay if we kept looking? Maybe we could find one just as equally nice but more reasonable."

This was Donna's cue.

Pick. Poke. Taunt.

She had been waiting for the chance to shame Katie for poor financial management, and her suggestion provided her with the perfect opportunity. She said, "It is important you buy this exact dress because your father and I deserve only the finest at our wedding. We can't have a discount-store special at the Atlanta Whitehouse!"

Katie tried to argue back but couldn't get a word in before Donna continued, "I can't believe you think it is appropriate to disagree with what a bride wants on her own special day! Are you so strapped financially you can't buy this dress, or are you just being disagreeable and disrespectful again?"

Katie felt like she had just been smacked across the face. She could feel the sting.

Judgment was oozing out of Donna's mouth like sap dripping from a Maple tree.

Katie was only being practical. She meant no disrespect and certainly didn't intend to cheap-out by buying an ugly or poorly made dress. She also knew her father didn't care one iota about a junior bridesmaid's gown. It was silly to shell out huge sums of money for a dress that would only be worn once and would likely rub at the armpits. She had been taught to use common sense her whole life. It was obvious Donna was not a graduate of The Grace Jacob's School of Good Choices.

Donna accused Katie of being selfish. She said, "If you can afford a girls' night out, takeout food because you are too lazy to cook, or an extravagant prom dress for your oldest, you can surely buy this dress to make your dad happy too. It seems you don't consider him at all with your actions." She continued her assault, saying, "I have seen your posts on Facebook, so you can't even deny your spending."

Donna hoped Katie would realize nothing she did went unnoticed. As long as she was in her life, she would be under a microscope. She also hoped it was enough to make her want to withdraw from her completely.

Donna's remarks lacked any understanding and were clearly intended to humiliate Katie. Donna had no idea the posts she had seen were of a friend's birthday party—paid for by her friend's husband as a gift to his wife, a quick meal at Chick-fil-a on a busy night when all her kids had after school activities—and she used a gift card given to her as a gift by a student, and the prom dress had been purchased at a consignment shop because her daughter liked a vintage look.

Katie said nothing, though, because none of it was Donna's business. She had done nothing wrong and did not feel a need to defend her actions, her social media posts, or her bank account balance.

Donna continued the assault at the bridal shop by saying, "Just like you tried to bully your father into buying your daughter a car, you are trying to bully me so I don't get my dream wedding! Your jealousy is sinful. If this dress is truly creating such hardship, you should reevaluate your finances and your life choices."

Her words hit Katie at her core. Seeds of resentment were planted in her soul and were starting to sprout at a rapid pace, but she said nothing other than "I will buy the gown you want." No bridge was being built. Fires were being lit and spreading at breakneck speeds.

Donna turned off her indignation like a light switch and smiled from ear to ear. She knew her strike had inflicted damage and it felt good.

After the ill-fated trip to the bridal boutique, Donna reported to Tom, "Katie must be making poor financial decisions because I only asked her to buy one simple dress, and she lashed out at me. Can you believe her selfishness? By the way, did you notice she had gone out with friends on her latest Facebook post to a very pricey establishment? I wonder how much that restaurant cost? Maybe choices like that are why Sydney doesn't have a car. Honestly Tommy, I thought including her in the wedding shopping would be a bonding experience for us, but she is incapable of accepting me. It just hurts my feelings so badly. I have been nothing but kind and generous." There was no mention of the outlandish price tag on the dress or her onslaught of criticism and condemnation.

She also failed to mention that right after scolding Katie for being selfish and financially irresponsible, she had dramatically whipped out Tom's credit card and bought herself shoes, jewelry, a beaded purse, and a gift for her Maid of Honor.

She omitted the part of the story where she told the lady behind the counter, "She (pointing at Katie) will be paying for the junior bridesmaid's gown. I'm so grateful to have such a loving stepdaughter who will spare no expense for my wedding and appreciates how fashion-forward I am. She had a wonderful childhood, and this is only a small gesture to repay the tremendous generosity of her father. She will be indebted to him for the rest of her life. I am glad my future husband loves spoiling me and I can teach my stepdaughter how to dress her children more fashionably!"

Pick. Poke. Taunt.

Donna also purposely "forgot" to tell Tom she had pulled Caroline aside in the bridal shop and said to her, "I have something very important to tell you. Your grandmother came to me as a ghost and told me she is happy I am with your grandfather. I'm sorry your mom is still so upset I am marrying your Pop Pop, but it really is what your grandma wants."

She thought by telling her this, it would somehow give her power over the young girl and diminish Grace's role as the matriarch of the family. She wanted Caroline to see her as the new head of the family. She was the new Grace.

Caroline was somewhat taken aback by Donna's statement. It's not every day someone tells you they talked to a ghost! However, if Donna thought she could manipulate Caroline with ghost stories, she was wrong. Caroline had had a very special relationship with Grace, and there would never be anything anyone could say that would make her think less of her grandma.

Caroline was open to loving new people and wanted to love Donna too. She had room in her heart for an infinite number of people, but Donna was either too egotistical or too dumb to realize this. Donna was more interested in diminishing Grace's influence than building relationships of her own.

When Katie found out what Donna said to Caroline, she was furious. How dare she bring her daughter into her sick games. Katie was confident her mother had not appeared as a ghost to bring comfort to Donna. The whole idea was either a preposterous lie or Donna was insane. She decided it was most likely both. Although Katie didn't believe this could happen, she allowed herself to imagine her mother haunting Donna and got a good laugh out of it.

Katie knew her mother could have a temper and was sure if she appeared to her dad's fiancée, rather than sing her praises, she would spit in her face.

Donna thought it was best not to mention anything about her conversation with Caroline to Tom because talking to ghosts wasn't exactly in line with her religious doctrine. He believed her when she told him she had the gift of prophecy, healing powers, and was able to speak in tongues but didn't want to push it by telling him she could also talk to the dead, specifically his dead wife.

Out in Thirty Days

It had been a long day, and Jenna was tired. She had been running around town like a madwoman trying to get Heidi to guitar practice, Brett to lacrosse practice, and Olivia to her preschool gymnastics class.

Somehow, she had gotten everyone where they needed to go on time and even managed to stop at the commissary for groceries. She was now on her way back to pick up her children from each of their activities. Her minivan seemed to be in perpetual motion, but such was the season of life.

She was looking forward to Labor Day, which was coming up the next weekend, and hoped she might be able to get some much-needed rest. The kids had several things planned, but Paul would be off and would gladly help with the shuttling of children. He had even mentioned inviting some of the neighbors over one evening to grill out and play cards, something they both enjoyed immensely. There was nothing more relaxing than enjoying a glass of wine, kids running wild in the backyard, and playing cards with friends.

Jenna heard her phone ringing in her purse on the front seat and quickly began to dig for it since she was stopped at a red light. She saw on the caller ID it was her dad. She was a little surprised because he didn't call very often, especially since he started dating Donna. His calls had become even less frequent since they got engaged. The only time he seemed to get in touch with her was if he was out running errands alone and had free time while driving from point A to point B.

Jenna didn't realize he preferred to talk to her in privacy, out of earshot of Donna, and his car was just about the only place he could be alone.

Jenna pressed the green Accept button on her phone and heard her dad's familiar voice on the other end. They made small talk for a few minutes, and she filled him in on all the comings and goings of the day and gave him updates on the kids' activities. She asked him how he was doing, and he said things were mostly the same as usual.

Then he dropped the bomb. "Oh yeah, I forgot to tell you, I sold the house in Peachtree City. I have to be completely out in thirty days."

Jenna knew he had been considering selling, but she didn't know he had made a final decision or even listed it yet. She certainly hadn't expected him to sell so many months before the wedding. She understood he wanted to move to St. Simon's Island full-time and start a new life with Donna, she just didn't expect it to happen so fast.

She also didn't expect him to keep the whole process a secret.

He told her if she wanted anything from the house, she needed to come down and get it. He planned to get rid of everything before he moved.

Jenna quickly thought about her calendar for the next month and realized Labor Day weekend was the only time she could even possibly think of making the six-hour drive home. So much for getting some rest. So much for friends coming over, wine, and cards.

When she told him her availability, he informed her he had made plans with Donna and would be away that weekend. He would not be able to change them, so she would just have to go to the house alone. He told her Katie was also going to be out of town. He had sprung the news on her just before calling Jenna. He said, "It is what it is."

Tom told Jenna it would be helpful for her to go through as much stuff as possible because he was overwhelmed and thought the easiest way to clean out the house was to dump everything. He planned to sell off his furniture and any household items she and Katie didn't want, and everything else would be trashed.

Jenna invited her friend Ashley to come with her for the weekend because she couldn't bear the thought of going through the house and all those memories alone. It saddened her that her father had waited until the last minute to tell her and was unwilling to change his plans. It was also maddening she had such a tight timeline to work with. Jenna would have preferred to have gone through the house with her father and to laugh and cry together as they reminisced about the past.

However, just like Jenna had been left alone in the room with her mother after she died, she was now going to be left alone in her childhood home to decide what to keep and what to toss. She knew she couldn't save everything. Army life didn't allow for pack rats, and her father was counting on her.

The Door

Jenna was grateful Ashley agreed to accompany her on the road trip. They had been good friends for years and stationed together four times. They considered each other family. Ashley had met Grace many times when she came to visit Jenna at various posts, and her mom had considered her a friend. The two women liked each other very much. They shared a similar sense of humor and both had a deep love for Jenna, one as a friend and one as a mother. It comforted Jenna to know she had someone who knew her mom by her side as she embarked upon this difficult task.

After a long drive down to Peachtree City, Jenna and Ashley pulled into Tom Jacobs's driveway, just as Jenna had done thousands of times before. Jenna unlocked the front door with the key that had occupied a place on her keychain since she was ten years old.

As the ladies entered the home, Jenna felt a wave of nostalgia hit her as she stepped over the threshold. This would be the last time she would unlock that door.

Jenna realized the door was a part of so many memories. It stood there silently watching everyone who entered or left the home for the past three decades. It served as the gatekeeper to the Jacobs family, and if it could talk, would have more stories to tell than any one family member because it had been there to see it all.

The door had watched Jenna and Katie grow from children to adults and had been witness to the arrival of the grandchildren. Unlike the people who came and went at the Jacobs' house, the door never changed. The door had been there to greet every pizza delivery driver, plumber, and salesperson peddling their wares. It had been there to welcome every party guest and to let the ones who stayed a little too long out again. It had a front row view of kids riding bikes and roller skating down the long, winding drive and was the only one who really knew who toilet papered the yard when Katie was a teenager.

Jenna giggled to herself when she thought about all the good night kisses after dates that happened at that very front door when she was a teenager and what it would have said about her awkwardness if it could talk.

Jenna's thoughts then shifted to some sadder memories that had taken place by the front door. She recalled the night she said goodbye to Paul before he headed off to Texas A&M the summer after their high school graduation. They had stood under the porch light in front of the door where she cried inconsolably until he had to leave. He was going to school in Texas, and she was going to Emory University in Georgia. It felt like they were going to be worlds apart. The thought of not being together every day was more than their teenage hearts could bear. When Jenna finally opened the door to come in, a few moments after Paul pulled out of the driveway, she found her mother quietly waiting on the other side to comfort her. Grace was also crying because her daughter's sadness was breaking her heart.

The two women slumped down on the floor in the foyer with their backs against the door. Her mother's arms wrapped around her in a protective manner, and she sobbed like never before.

Jenna knew the door had welcomed in the nurses who came to check on her mother when she was sick, as well as the hospice nurse who would ensure her mother passed comfortably.

The door was the first to see the hearse pull into the drive when the men from the funeral home arrived to retrieve Grace's body. The door watched silently when the matriarch of the house was carefully wheeled out on a stretcher for the last time.

And once again, the door was there for Jenna to lean up against while she cried.

Keep or Toss

Although neither Jenna nor Ashley knew where to begin, they knew they needed to get started. Time was ticking. Jenna gave her friend a quick tour of the house, turned on a local country radio station, and pumped it through the house's 1980s monitor system and the pair got to work. Ashley listened to Jenna's stories. She laughed and cried with her and provided the emotional support to keep her going.

Deep down Jenna knew her father was choosing not to come because it was too painful for him to dredge up the memories of the past. His Labor Day plans were just a convenient excuse. He felt Jenna was dependable and emotionally strong when it came to practical matters, like Grace, and trusted she could handle a good portion of the work for him.

Jenna tried to soften her heart with this realization and give him some grace for not being there. Even though he found love a second time with Donna, Jenna was confident he still missed Grace more than he could ever let anyone know.

Tom knew his life was going to be very different with Donna, and he secretly mourned sometimes for his old life where everything was familiar. Selling his home had been very difficult and this is why he hadn't shared his decision with his daughters.

He made the choice to leave the home he built with Grace and start a new life, and in some ways, it felt like he was leaving her behind too. He knew this wasn't really the case and was thankful his late wife gave him her blessing to remarry. Her approval made it easier for him to move forward.

As Jenna and Ashley sorted through decades of stuff, Jenna allowed herself to hope the next chapter of her father's life and the Jacobs family would be as beautiful as the last, when Grace had been at the helm.

Jenna phoned her dad once on his cell to ask him if he planned to toss out her mother's scrapbooks and the framed pictures her great aunt had painted. She couldn't imagine he would but was asking just to be safe.

He seemed put off by her call, but quickly assured her he would store the photos and the paintings, but everything else had to go. He then said Donna was looking for him, asked her not to call again that weekend, and hung up.

It was an odd exchange, but Jenna had too much to do to give her dad's abruptness much thought. She only briefly considered the possibility that Donna didn't know she was there.

Jenna's Great Aunt Sally—on Grace's side of the family, had been a very talented artist. She painted hundreds of pictures over the course of her lifetime and was particularly skilled at painting animals and landscapes. Perhaps, Olivia got her artistic abilities from her great-great aunt. Jenna wondered if being an artist was another genetic trait that had been passed on to her daughter.

Grace had been the lucky recipient of many of these masterpieces and proudly decorated the home she and Tom built with her Aunt Sally's works. Jenna could never remember a time in her life without these paintings adorning the walls of her childhood home. She was excited to show them all to Ashley.

She pointed out paintings of the Eiffel Tower, a zebra with beautiful stripes, a koi pond, a flamingo, a beautiful ocean scene with palm trees, a black horse, and a rendering of her mother's favorite cat, who had been named Boots because she had white paws and an orange body. There were others, too, but those were Jenna's childhood favorites as familiar to her as her own reflection.

Each one was unique and different from the other, but they all seemed to work as a collection. Grace had turned her home into a gallery to showcase the art that was as near and dear to her heart as it was beautiful. Jenna was glad her father would store them for now because she had no room for them in her on-post quarters. However, she would proudly display them once Paul retired from the military and they moved into their forever home. She would hate for them to be lost to strangers because they were irreplaceable, true family heirlooms.

Jenna was also relieved she didn't have to figure out how to load all the paintings in her minivan. She already knew she would be taking her mother's prized rocking chair which would take up considerable space, even with the seats folded down. The rocker had been in her family for generations. Jenna's great grandmother had rocked her grandma in it. Her grandma had rocked Grace in it. Grace had rocked Katie and Jenna in it when they were babies, and she had rocked their children in it too. It had too many miles on it to let it go to a secondhand store.

Tom had been very clear he didn't intend to keep anything except his clothes, the scrapbooks, and the paintings. He trusted her to make the decision of what to keep and what to toss. Some things were easy to get rid of because they held no sentimental value, but other things were excruciating to leave behind, knowing they would be sold or donated, or worse yet, chucked into the local landfill.

Jenna and Ashley were sorting through her mother's closet and were overwhelmed with all the things Grace kept from her girls' childhoods. As a mother herself, Jenna couldn't comprehend throwing her kids handmade gifts into the garbage, so she understood why her mom had held on to so much. There is something very endearing about a child expressing their love through a crayon drawing or a poem they wrote with misspelled words.

As she thought about this, she smiled when she saw a card she made for Mother's Day when she was five. She had written, "I love you because you are a gud mom. You take gud care of me when I have a coff." She had drawn a picture of a girl with a square body, rectangle arms and legs, and a large round head with a word bubble over her that said, "coff, coff."

Although Jenna didn't remember making that card or being sick that particular time, she could recall many times her mother cared for her throughout her life and nursed her through coughs, earaches, and stomach bugs.

Jenna's gaze lingered on the card, but even she didn't know what to do with it. *What was her father expected to do with it?* It wasn't reasonable for him to keep hundreds of pieces of faded construction paper masterpieces that served no real purpose. The children that made them had become adults long ago. Surely her father still had his memories with or without the papers.

Jenna rationalized no one else would want them either and they had no monetary value, so she painfully tossed the card and the whole box into the trash and cried.

Before this moment she had never given much thought to what happens to stored childhood keepsakes when moms die. As long as the matriarch is alive, there is a safe place for yellowing papers that document childhood—stick figure drawings from preschool, homemade cards with painted handprints, and fifth grade graduation diplomas are safe and have a place to rest.

However, when the matriarch is gone, these things that seem to have always just been, suddenly become a burden. The comfortable closets and keepsake boxes that housed them for so long are replaced by trash bins, and they are hauled to the curb. After decades of being viewed as important enough to keep, they suddenly become obsolete.

Tom also had no use for the nativity scene Grace displayed year-round. Some of the pieces were chipped and showed signs of wear and tear. The angel's wing was missing a tip, there was a chunk out of a camel's hump, and a shepherd was missing his nose. The imperfections never bothered Grace and somehow made the set even more special to her. Jenna and Katie played with the pieces as children—and so had all the grandchildren, which accounted for the chips.

Jenna quickly decided she would keep the nativity scene and would look forward to displaying it in her own home. She would be sure to remind everyone each Christmas that it had been in their family for a very long time. And, just like her mother had done, she would turn each piece over to show them how her great aunt had carved her first name "Sally" and the year "1937" on the bottom of each piece when she made them out of ceramics. She vowed to never fix the shepherd's nose either.

Jenna moved on to the many boxes of Christmas ornaments her mother had collected over the years. Trimming the tree had been her mother's thing and her father had always been indifferent to it. His job had simply been to get the boxes out and put them away after Christmas. He did the heavy lifting and Grace did the decorating.

Jenna was certain Donna's taste in holiday decor was very different from her mom's, so she picked out a few of her favorite ornaments with sentimental value and left the remaining decorations behind to be sold or discarded. She was making progress slowly but surely, even though the list of things with their fate resting on Jenna just went on and on.

It hurt to know her father was no longer able to keep her mom's music box collection which had grown so large over the years it occupied space in virtually every room of the house. There were music boxes in the china cabinet in the dining room, on every dresser in the house, and even on the counter in the guest bathroom.

The grandchildren had been fascinated by them, which was why Grace collected them, and they each had their favorite one. Some of the favorites included a dancing monkey, a frog that appeared to jump off a lily pad, a ballerina who twirled, a snowman in a snow globe, a teddy bear with a butterfly on its nose that spun in circles, and a Ferris wheel that went round and round. These music boxes had been wound countless times and served as a great source of joy and calm entertainment for Grace and her grandchildren.

Jenna smiled when she thought of the way Heidi and Brett had stared intently at the music boxes when they played, observing every moving part. They would immediately beg to wind them again the moment the music stopped. They never tired of hearing them play no matter how old they got, and Grace never tired of winding them.

Jenna made up her mind that she would choose one music box for each of her children, her sister, and her nieces to keep—and one for herself.

She realized her father was in a difficult position, moving into a new home with a new wife. It would be unfair to Donna for Tom to fill their house with Grace's things, and clearly the music boxes were hers. Perhaps he would keep just one.

Although it made her sad to know most of the collection would be donated to charity or sold off, it pleased her she could keep a small part to ensure they weren't forgotten forever.

She also let her mind wander, wondering what new and exciting things Donna and her dad would put in their new home that would delight the children.

Jenna had no idea the first time Donna saw the music boxes she informed Tom they were tacky and would have no place in her new house. She thought they were even worse when she learned Grace had collected many of them at garage sales or secondhand shops. *Ew*, she had thought to herself. She was turned off by anything that had been purchased used and much preferred to shop at a mall.

Donna didn't understand the music boxes were a reminder of Grace's love, and it pained Tom to hear her begrudge them. He didn't really care about keeping the music boxes. Some of them were tacky, but they held special memories for him. He decided not to tell Donna about all the times Grace played them for the grandkids. Instead, he simply said, "Maybe my girls will want them," and left it at that.

Donna couldn't imagine why his girls would want those hideous things, but to each their own. She would happily sell them the first chance she got. For one brief moment, she wondered if any of them were valuable. Sometimes tacky and old paid off. She watched *Antiques Roadshow*.

Jenna and Ashley sorted through the toybox in the guest bedroom closet which contained building blocks of every color, baby dolls, McDonald's Happy Meal Toys, and action figures.

A large box that looked like a treasure chest was positioned next to the toybox and contained costumes for playing dress up. In it, they found princess gowns, superhero capes, pirate eyepatches, high-heeled shoes much too big for average-sized children, and accessories like crowns, plastic swords, and magic wands.

Jenna thought about all the times Heidi and Brett, along with their cousins, had donned these costumes and let their imaginations run wild when they were younger. It saddened Jenna to know Olivia wouldn't have these same memories and would never hear Grace call her "Your Highness" or speak to her in pirate brogue.

Olivia would also never remember playing with the large collection of stuffed animals that had been Jenna's and Katie's when they were children. The animals seemed to be looking at Jenna from their position in the back of the closet begging her to keep them.

Sadly, Jenna knew she didn't have room in her house to keep them all. Most of them would have to go. However, she couldn't bear to part with Twinkle Bear, Tilly the Turtle, or her Madame Alexander doll and would have to make space for them. Some of the ones she wasn't taking were literally falling apart anyhow and wouldn't have made the move, even if she had tried.

As she felt the sorrow growing inside her for Olivia, Jenna forced herself to concentrate on being thankful for the memories created by

Heidi and Brett in this house. She also focused on the fact that her father was still alive and there were future memories to be made. She thought, *Maybe Donna will also fill a toy box at their new home with amazing things or buy beautiful new costumes for Olivia to play with when she visits. And maybe, just maybe, she would surprise them all by keeping a few of the special toys Jenna's older children had enjoyed that were currently being left behind in the closet.*

Jenna perked up with this thought. Olivia's memories would be different from Heidi's and Brett's, but no less wonderful.

Jenna turned her focus to the closet in her old childhood bedroom. It contained out-of-style special occasion dresses, a souvenir piggy bank she had been given as a child, a collection of well-loved books that had been read and reread, and an assortment of random odds and ends. Jenna tucked a few of her favorite books in the keep box and left the rest to be donated.

Next, Jenna found her wedding gown that had been preserved and hermetically sealed in a giant box. Her mother let her keep it there because it was cumbersome to move and store with each change of duty station. Clearly, the wedding dress would need to be rescued, but the old special occasion dresses could be donated. Jenna also added her high school letterman's jacket to her keep pile.

After this, she closed the closet door for the last time, knowing everything left inside would go.

It was strange to think after this weekend, she would no longer have a childhood home to return to. She would never again have a reason to pull into the familiar driveway, float in the pool, or rest in the knowledge that her elementary school report cards were tucked away in her mother's closet for safekeeping. She would leave her key to the front door on the kitchen counter for the next homeowners.

Jenna gathered her keep pile and loaded it into her minivan, along with the antique rocker. She and Ashley had worked non-stop for the last forty-eight hours, and it was time to say goodbye to the house for the last time. Jenna took one more lap around and paused in her parents' room. She stroked the paisley-patterned comforter on their bed and ran her hand across the smooth painted wood of her mother's triple dresser. She stared into the attached mirror at herself for the last time and whispered "goodbye."

She found her way to the familiar front door, turned the knob, and left. She stepped out into the front yard and felt the sunshine on her face. She was surprisingly numb. She was all cried out. She had run out of tears.

Gut Feelings

The seven months between Tom selling the Peachtree City house and his wedding flew by fast.

Jenna was not asked to be a part of the planning, and because of this she mainly went about her days without giving it much thought. She rationalized it would have been hard to help from so far away anyway.

When she received the invitation, she dropped it in the overflowing basket on her desk, which also housed bills, school flyers, and junk mail. She went about her hectic life as a mom, volunteer, and wife—pushing her father's impending matrimony to the back of her mind.

Occasionally, she would rifle through the basket looking for a piece of paper with field trip information or a bill that needed to be paid, and she would see the invitation. She would briefly consider what it meant for her family. She didn't allow herself to dwell on it for long though, because she didn't have the time or energy to stir up unresolved emotions about the wedding—or to confront the fear that the match between her dad and Donna was not made in heaven.

She convinced herself her fear came from a selfish place and forced herself to ignore all the warning signs. This marriage was what her father wanted, and she hoped it would make him happy. It had nothing to do with her, so she buried the invitation under permission slips and Publisher's Clearing House envelopes and put off thinking about it for as long as possible.

Her mantra regarding the months leading up to the wedding, taken from the Disney film *Finding Nemo*, was "just keep swimming, just keep swimming." If she could just keep her focus on the routine of her normal life and not allow herself to be consumed with thoughts or emotions regarding the wedding, she would get through it all. She was sure the bad vibes would go away once the ceremony was over. There would be nothing left to think about. Once the vows were said, the next chapter of their lives as a family, which included Donna, would begin—whether she liked it or not.

It was especially easy to push off her thoughts about the wedding for now because she was currently the only parent in her household who was home. Paul deployed to Iraq four months after Labor Day. His battalion was part of Operation Inherent Resolve and was tasked with helping to train Iraqi forces so they could defend themselves against terrorist threats. Unfortunately, he would miss the wedding because he was not scheduled to return for several more months, but there was nothing that could be done about this. Duty called. Jenna and the children would have to go without him.

Whenever Paul had to leave, Jenna worked around the clock to ensure their children's lives were as unaffected by his absence as humanly possible. It was hard on the children emotionally to have their father gone. She was determined not to let his deployment alter the normal course of their days any more than it had to. Since this was his fifth tour, Jenna had become an expert on solo parenting and knew what needed to be done to keep the household running and the children's minds off worrisome thoughts.

Jenna was thankful for the progress that had been made with satellite phones and the internet over the years because she was able to communicate with Paul more easily this time and keep him in the loop on what was happening at home. Communications the last time he was in Afghanistan had been tenuous at best, and it had been difficult.

Frequent communication helped keep her sane and lessened her loneliness. It also made Paul feel more connected to the family, even though he was halfway across the world. Jenna was careful not to burden him with too many problems, because she didn't want him distracted from his work. His safety depended on his ability to remain focused on the mission.

Every deployment meant Jenna became the sole chauffeur, homework helper, housekeeper, errand runner, dinner maker, social planner, nurse, disciplinarian, and comforter by default. It also meant increased responsibility within the Family Readiness Group because she wanted to be sure every family had the information and resources they needed while their soldier was gone.

Since Paul was the battalion commander, she felt she had a duty to be there for the spouses of the service members under his care. Being inundated with so much responsibility and having no relief in sight for the next eight months until Paul came home, made it even easier for her to ignore the wedding looming in the near future.

A deployment naturally took an emotional toll on Jenna too. She deeply missed her husband, who was also her best friend. Some days, the house felt unbearably quiet, especially in the evenings after the children had gone to bed. Having this perspective made her more understanding of her father's situation, and she could easily comprehend his loneliness without her mother. She was glad she had the children to fill her days, unlike her dad, who lived alone. She was also thankful her situation was temporary. Paul would come home in a few months, God willing, and end her solitude.

Jenna felt heartbroken for her father and how he must have felt after Grace died. She imagined the silence he experienced in the evenings was deafening, knowing his love would never return and seeing no end in sight to the quiet. Silence could be a gift or a curse depending on the circumstances that surrounded it, and Jenna could understand why her father was so quick to want to tie the knot with Donna.

Jenna learned early in Paul's career it isn't healthy to live in constant fear. However, she also recognized sometimes fear is unavoidable. It is human nature to fear the unknown and think the worst, particularly when your husband is in a combat zone. Fear and doubt would creep in on her when she least expected it and come over her like a wave she couldn't control. It usually came after a long day that had been particularly trying.

Thankfully, her bouts of fear were usually short lived. Jenna was a positive person for the most part, which helped her cope with Paul's absence. She was able to get through her days without concentrating on the what ifs and focus on what was in front of her. However, every once in a while, no matter how positive her thinking was, she would feel a sense of impending doom wash over her. She knew she had zero ability to see into the future. Prophecy was not her spiritual gift, but in these moments, these unfounded premonitions something had happened to her husband felt so real.

Along with the fear that rocked her to the core, she would feel an overwhelming need to make sure the house was clean. Jenna knew if she received that dreaded knock at the door, notifying her Paul had been killed, it would mean a parade of people would need to come into her home. She would undoubtedly have to open the door for the chaplain, various casualty officers, care team members who would come to comfort her, meal train volunteers delivering food, military counselors for the kids, and for her own friends and family who would come in droves. It was even possible the press would park in her yard like vultures circling prey, hoping to get a picture of the poor widow when the door was opened. She couldn't allow the world to see a messy house. *If her life was about to fall apart, at least her home would be in order. She could control that.*

It was a morbid thought to imagine her husband was possibly dead and all she could do to prepare for the news was to pick up toys or load the dishwasher.

Sadly, she knew she wasn't alone with this thought process because many military spouses had expressed to her they felt the same way. The truth was no one would think less of her if something happened to Paul and dirty laundry was overflowing in the hamper or if toys were scattered across the living room floor. Jenna was grateful she lived in the most supportive community in America, but no matter what she knew to be true, she couldn't change her thinking when the fear came, so she would clean and cry.

Mercifully, as quickly as the dread crept in, it also went away.

Military spouses around the world breathe a collective sigh of relief when ten o'clock at night comes because they know the notification process for the day is done. They have made it through another day and can sleep without fear of hearing the doorbell.

By seven o'clock, the sun rises once again and the fear from the previous evening is replaced by the hope the light streaming through the window brings. The children are awake, and the silence gives way to the normal buzz of the house at full volume. For some unexplained reason, Jenna never worried about receiving bad news when the house was alive with activity, even though that is precisely when a knock on the door is most likely to occur.

Fear and silence always came as a pair for Jenna and were never accompanied by common sense. She imagined her dad also had felt fear and silence in the evenings after her mother died. Fear of being alone and fear the silence would never go away.

If Jenna were truly prophetic, she would have known the panic that plagued her from time to time was unwarranted. She would never know what it felt like to lose her husband in battle. Paul would come home to her, unharmed, just as he had the previous four times he deployed. The only thing that ever came from her occasional bouts of dread and false premonitions was she woke up the next morning to a clean house.

Each night before the kids went to bed, they would mark off another day on the calendar, counting down the days until Paul would return home. It felt like an accomplishment to see the calendar filling up with X's, even though it was still early into the deployment. Every X meant they were one day closer to seeing him again.

With every day that passed, no matter how many remained, Brett, Heidi, and Olivia would celebrate with happy dances and count the X's. They all looked forward to him coming home and wanted to have a "Driveway Dance Party" with their dad when he returned.

Paul invented the Driveway Dance Party as a way to have spontaneous fun with the kids. It is exactly what the name implies, a party where you simply dance in the driveway. No shoes are required, and it doesn't matter what the weather is like outside. Paul loved to surprise his kids by randomly yelling "Driveway Dance Party" whenever the spirit moved him.

At this prompt, everyone would run outside, immediately stopping whatever it was they were doing. Paul would crank up the radio in the car as loud as he could, and the dancing would commence. Jenna always gave Paul "the look" because she was concerned about the neighbors and the noise, but Paul would brush his wife's concerns away with a laugh and turn up the music even louder.

Paul didn't need a reason for celebrating. He had seen so much in his life he wished he never had, so to him, being alive, healthy, and together was reason enough to celebrate. The last Driveway Dance Party they had before he deployed had been held simply because it was raining. The kids had laughed hysterically as they whirled and twirled in soaking wet clothes, singing at the top of their lungs.

Sometimes, for an extra bonus, Paul would let the kids stand on the hood of the car to make the spontaneous party seem even more fun. Jenna also gave her husband "the look" for this because she feared one of the children would fall, but Paul would reassure her with a quick kiss and promise to catch them. As long as he'd been doing these parties, no one had ever fallen, and no neighbors had ever complained.

As Jenna celebrated each X on the calendar with her kids, it forced her to remember her father's wedding weekend was also fast approaching. "Pop Pop and Donna's Wedding" was written in red ink and circled on the calendar. It was only two months away, and she became painfully aware she could not disregard it any longer.

She needed to put on her big girl pants, as her mother-in-law liked to say, and accept the wedding was happening whether she liked it or not. She knew it was time to make room in her schedule to take care of business, like making hotel reservations and figuring out travel logistics. She would play the role of supportive daughter and call her dad tomorrow to offer help and see how the preparations were going.

Brett and Olivia were going to play the parts of ring bearer and flower girl in the wedding. After hearing Katie's horror story about shopping with Donna, Jenna prepared herself for the worst when it came to outfitting Olivia. She wasn't concerned about Brett because he was wearing a standard tuxedo that matched Tom's. Donna surprisingly gave Jenna the freedom to choose whatever flower girl dress she thought was appropriate for Olivia, providing it was cute and white—a stark contrast to how she dictated to Katie what gown Caroline would wear and jeered at her when she complained about the outrageous price tag.

Jenna would come to theorize, months later, that Donna only allowed her to choose Olivia's dress so Katie would look like she was hard to get along with. If her dad asked her if Donna had been difficult to work with, Jenna would have had to respond with "no" if she was answering honestly. This one-word answer would have cast doubt on Katie's story and slanted the whole incident in Donna's favor.

Jenna instinctively felt something was amiss with Donna and her intentions. She oddly felt this way from the moment she found out she existed. However, other than a few stories from her sister she hoped were misunderstandings, and a gut feeling, she had nothing to base this on. So far, Donna had been kind to her. The two women rarely spoke, but when they did, it was friendly.

Jenna hoped her intuition about Donna was as wrong as her false premonitions about Paul.

Perception is Everything

In the weeks before the wedding, Katie confided in Jenna she believed Donna was trying to force her out of their father's life.

When Katie rattled off the long list of things Donna had done to her, it was clear there was already considerable damage to the relationship between the two women. It hurt Jenna's heart to see the strife that was already beginning in the family before the wedding had even taken place. It also pained her to know her sister had been treated so badly. The whole scenario seemed like a *Lifetime Original* movie.

Katie explained how Donna's attacks started just before their father sold the Peachtree City house and had gotten even worse since he moved to St. Simon's. What Jenna couldn't understand though, was why. *Why would Donna purposely try to drive Katie away?* It didn't make sense for someone to be so intentionally cruel.

She wanted to give Donna the benefit of the doubt and hoped her sister was just being overly sensitive, but in her heart, she had the sinking feeling Katie was right.

Katie revealed to Jenna she was even more upset by their father's reaction to the situation. He took Donna's side every single time.

Every. Single. Time. He repeatedly scolded her and accused her of not accepting his fiancée.

She was tired of being told her behavior was disrespectful when she had done nothing to warrant this opinion. She said, "Jenna, honestly, I have never heard the words *disrespectful* or *not accepting* as many times in my entire life as I have over the past few months from Dad. I never want to hear them again!"

Tom was unwilling to listen to Katie's side of the story or consider her viewpoint for even a second, which made her feel like she didn't even matter to him. Katie had done everything possible to support her father and welcome Donna into the family, yet she was being treated like a pariah, unworthy of love, attention, or compassion. She couldn't and wouldn't take it much longer if she continued to be treated so poorly.

As Jenna listened to her sister, she began to wonder if her father being so easily manipulated was the early onset of Alzheimer's. For some reason that would be easier to accept than believing he didn't care if he lost his daughter forever.

Tom wouldn't allow himself to entertain any concerns about his future wife. She was the woman God sent him, and nothing anyone said would change that. He would risk everything he had for her because it was God's will for them to be together—and he couldn't stomach the thought of living alone.

Tom refused to believe Donna was purposely hurtful to Katie and placed her on a pedestal of righteousness. He was frustrated Katie wasn't willing to put more effort into being hospitable to Donna—especially after she had been so kind to her. He expected more from his oldest daughter. There was nothing for her not to like about Donna. She was perfect in almost every way—except her excessive temper, but she had never unleashed it on Katie.

As much as he wanted things to get better between Donna and Katie, he couldn't afford to interject himself into the problem and get stuck in the middle between his daughter and fiancée. He would be in a no-win situation. For now, the safest place for him was standing in solidarity with his future wife.

He didn't want to lose his daughter, but he honestly felt it was up to her to change her attitude, make amends with Donna, and welcome her into the family. It was the only possible solution. There was nothing he or Donna could do to improve the situation. He considered them both blameless.

Tom was hopeful they would eventually find a way to get along. They would have more time to try to work things out after the wedding. He might even be able to play the part of mediator once he and Donna said their vows because he would be less afraid of her leaving him if she had a ring on her finger.

Tom felt protective over Donna, as a soon-to-be husband should, and was concerned Katie might talk badly about her to others or put unfavorable posts about her on Facebook. Women seemed to enjoy publicizing their every thought on social media. The residents of Peachtree City were very good at gossiping. Rumors spread like wildfire, and he didn't want to be the topic of any of them. God forbid the lies traveled out of the suburbs and into Atlanta. One ugly rumor could jeopardize the likelihood of their wedding being featured in the society pages, which was very important to his future wife.

If he could keep Donna's image pristine, it would also ensure his own reputation wasn't damaged by association. He wouldn't stand for that, so he preempted this possibility by taking every opportunity he could to make Donna look like an angel. He figured with enough public accolades he could overshadow anything negative Katie might say about Donna.

Tom wanted to make sure he kept his image of loving husband, father, financial success, good citizen, and devout Christian intact and wanted Donna to be perceived as Heaven-sent.

It was important to Tom that his friends and family, outside of his daughters and grandchildren, like Donna. He wanted them to see she was a loving, God-fearing woman, devoted to him and his family. He wanted them to believe he had chosen wisely. Nothing less would be acceptable. Tom Jacobs didn't make bad choices.

It was obvious to those in Tom's social circle there was contention brewing in his relationship with his oldest daughter, and he needed to come up with a good reason for this if anyone asked.

No one would have even guessed everything wasn't all kittens and rainbows if Donna hadn't put so many cryptic posts on Facebook and Instagram. She perpetually posted quotes about forgiving others even when they didn't deserve it, eliminating toxic people from your life, or about the unappreciative nature of stepchildren—and there was nothing he could do about it. He assumed her reasoning for doing this was because she was female and just couldn't help herself.

She made it clear to Tom her social media usage was an off-limits topic of discussion early on in their relationship. She had told him, "I will post whatever I want, any time I want. If you try to control me in any way, I will view it as abusive."

Tom decided the best tactic for handling questions about his strained relationship with Katie was to make sure others knew Donna was the victim. This would help justify her habitual posting. She had told him so many stories about Katie's unprovoked, irrational behavior it was easy to see why it had taken a toll on her. She was an innocent bystander, and he would defend her fully.

Tom devised a plan based on the premise that the worse Katie looked, the better Donna would appear. He reminded anyone who would listen that Katie had a rebellious streak as a teenager and implied she was rebelling against his relationship with Donna now.

Once a rebel, always a rebel.

He also reported Katie was unwilling to accept his future wife, causing great turmoil and stress in the family. He even accused her of trying to break up his relationship with Donna because she was having a hard time with her mental health. Losing Grace had brought her to a place of inconsolable grief and anger she was unfairly taking out on Donna.

He liked to say, "Donna has been such a loving influence in her life, showering her with attention and patience. She is a good example of a godly woman, but Katie just won't accept her. She has decided embracing Donna means she is betraying Grace. It is a shame for the whole family." He portrayed himself as a loving father, willing to do anything for his children, and at a loss when it came to what he should do to make Katie happy or how to help her overcome her grief and bitterness.

He was pleased when Donna validated every word he spoke about his daughter and patted his shoulder to comfort him when he talked publicly about his love for Katie. They made a good team and were loyal to one another. Tom would never tell anyone he was embellishing the truth about his daughter to keep the peace with Donna and to keep a favorable light shining on him. He would also never admit he had never seen any of the behaviors Donna accused Katie of himself. He only knew about them because of his fiancée's reports.

He ended every conversation with, "I am praying God will intercede and soften Katie's heart so she can fully accept Donna. I'm so thankful the Lord has brought such a fine woman into my life." Tom would also throw in that Katie didn't go to church regularly and portray her as a struggling soul who had fallen away from God.

He compared her to the prodigal son, hoping she would return to him one day. He would always say, "I will be waiting for her with open arms when she wants to come back." He liked to flex a good Bible story any chance he got, especially when he was comparing himself to God.

It was extremely hurtful when Katie found out about the lies he was spreading about her. It was even more hurtful when she found out people believed him.

The rumor mill in Peachtree City was in full swing, and she was its latest casualty. She could feel people staring at her in the grocery store wondering how she could be so mean to her loving father and to his angelic fiancée. People outside of Tom's immediate family had no idea of his hypocrisy or how he treated his daughter. He was an excellent actor when he needed to be and could even cry on cue.

It wasn't important to Katie though what others thought about her. She was different from her father in that way. She held her head high and spoke kindly to everyone she saw, even if she knew they were talking about her behind her back. She was confident the truth would eventually come out on its own. It always does.

She did nothing to stop her father's unfounded smear campaign against her and remained silent. Ironically, she did not post a single thing about Donna on social media and she certainly didn't pilfer any pathetic quotes from Pinterest to announce to the world she was dealing with difficult people.

Others mistook her quietness for admission of guilt, but that was the farthest thing from reality. Tom's preemptive strike was completely unnecessary. But it was extremely damaging.

Chicken is Chicken

Jenna listened to her sister's stories about Donna and her continual attacks. One after another, after another. She felt horrible for Katie but could not fully comprehend Donna's true nature. It was unimaginable for someone to be so willfully hurtful, particularly to the family of the man she loved. *Why would someone purposely try to destroy a family?*

Her sister's stories left her very unsettled though because she knew Katie wasn't a liar. There was no denying, Donna had done some truly awful things to Katie.

In addition to the night she served her on their mother's wedding china, the dress shopping fiasco, and the ghost story incident, she had hurled malicious words and insults at Katie more times than she could count. Her jabs hit below the belt and were designed to inflict pain and dredge up any insecurities Katie had or past discretions she may have committed.

Jenna was flabbergasted when Katie told her about the time Donna refused to eat a meal she had cooked because the chicken had not been purchased at Roscoe's Organic Market, Donna's supermarket of choice.

Before anyone took their first bite, but just after Tom said a long prayer, Donna asked, "Katie, out of curiosity, where did you buy this chicken?" Katie replied, "John's Market, it's a very popular grocery store in Peachtree City and close to my house."

Donna set her fork down curtly and said, "I cannot eat chicken that came from anywhere other than Roscoe's. I have very strict dietary requirements I thought you were aware of. I've certainly been around long enough for you to have noticed. When I am in Peachtree City it is the only place where I will shop. It is simply the best. I guess I wrongly assumed you were aware the, uh—how should I say this?—less expensive stores in this area—are seriously lacking in quality. I'm sorry you didn't feel the health of your children, your aging father, and someone with stomach issues were worth spending a few extra bucks on. Budgeting for quality is very important, Katie."

Donna was throwing shade on Katie's finances and implying she either purposely served them poor quality food because she was inconsiderate, too dumb to know better, or was too cash-strapped to be able to afford organic.

It was hard to miss the accusations being thrown at her, which were both vicious and false, but somehow, Tom was oblivious.

Katie found the whole scenario truly ludicrous.

Chicken is chicken.

She wanted to scream, "It was purchased at a mainstream grocery store where thousands of people shop. I didn't pick it up off the side of the road, but at this moment I would love nothing more than to serve you roadkill!" But she did not. She said nothing.

She stared in disbelief when Donna pulled a Tupperware container out of her bag and placed it in front of her on the table. Donna said,

"Thank you for trying to make a nice meal for us. I know how rarely you cook, so I'm appreciative and I'm sure your children are too." Smile. Smirk. Sneer. "However, I'm glad I had the wherewithal to plan ahead. I was afraid something like this might happen."

Katie thought, *another dig on her skills in the kitchen and on her parenting*. She had gone to a great deal of effort to prepare a beautiful meal for her father and future stepmother. The whole evening was meant to be a peace offering of sorts, even though she had never done anything wrong, but it was quickly becoming a disaster.

She never dreamed her supermarket choice would be used against her. Somehow though, when it came to Donna, everything she said or did was used against her.

Jenna couldn't even begin to imagine Donna pulling out her own Tupperware of food and refusing to taste the meal Katie prepared. Not only was it extremely rude, but it also proved her actions were premeditated.

How could her father not see this for what it was? This was a grand display of selfishness. Her lecture was blatantly offensive. The whole event was a clear attempt to anger Katie and try to provoke a reaction.

Donna wanted nothing more than for Katie to lose her cool so she would appear emotionally unbalanced, falling into the trap she had been laying. If Katie blew a gasket, Tom would believe his daughter was unhinged and Donna's accusations about her emotional instability were true. It would be another win for her and bring her one step closer to fulfilling her plan.

Tom brushed away his fiancée's behavior by saying she had a delicate stomach and chastised his daughter for not being more considerate of Donna's needs. He admonished Katie for not asking if there were any dietary restrictions and said, "You could learn a lot from Donna. She is an excellent cook and really knows how to pick out the finest ingredients. I'm sure she would love to help you learn how to select good meats." He then went on to pontificate for ten minutes as to why chicken from Roscoe's was superior.

It was clear by his reaction Donna had already planted the idea ahead of time that Katie was out to get her. She convinced Tom his daughter would purposely try to sabotage this evening because she was incapable of being polite. It was also clear he had been brainwashed about the superiority of Roscoe's. Until he met Donna, he never stepped foot in what he called "a yuppy, overpriced marketing trap." When it first opened, he even joked, "I don't need to eat a chicken that has eaten better than half of Atlanta its whole life!"

Tom was too naive to see he was clearly being manipulated and too lovestruck to recognize his fiancée wasn't always a perfect angel.

Donna was a player and Tom didn't even know there was a game.

Jenna defended her sister any time her father brought up the tension between Katie and Donna. She attempted to explain her sister's side repeatedly, but her dad refused to listen.

It was clear to both Jenna and Katie their father was marrying that woman no matter what his daughters' thought or what damage she caused in the family.

Tom was concerned Katie might cause a disruption at the wedding and voiced this to Jenna over the phone. He said, "Jenna, you know your sister tends to be overly emotional at times, particularly when it comes to Donna. I am terrified she will have a total meltdown at the wedding and cause us all a great deal of embarrassment. Can you imagine what people would say if she started sobbing hysterically or if she yelled at the bride? She would ruin the entire day!"

Jenna dismissed his fears by telling him he was being ridiculous. She privately noted her father's concerns were about public perception and not about the reason his daughter might be upset. He was clearly more worried about being humiliated in front of his guests or upsetting his bride than he was about his daughter, his flesh and blood.

The Wedding

The wedding weekend finally arrived, and Jenna and Katie made plans to travel to Atlanta. Katie from Peachtree City, Jenna from North Carolina. Neither of them wanted to attend, but they were determined to put on happy faces and pretend like they were excited about the whole affair.

The moment the ladies, accompanied by their children, arrived at the rehearsal dinner, they knew the weekend was going to be unbearable. When they entered the private dining room at the country club where it was being held, Tom and Donna both threw up a casual wave from where they were seated but made no attempt to get up to greet them. The bride and groom were at the head table with the bride's side of the wedding party, children excluded. Jenna, Katie, and the children were left to find seats wherever they could in general seating.

Jenna tried to converse with other guests and made cordial small talk. Her sister kept more to herself and her children, barely saying a word. Both sisters left as quickly as the dinner ended. There was no invitation from their father or Donna to linger or to join them at the hotel for cocktails afterward.

The next day was the wedding. It was a beautiful spring day in Georgia, and the ceremony site was breathtaking. Everything looked picture perfect, like it was straight out of a magazine or from the TV Show *Lifestyles of the Rich and Famous*. The only thing missing was Robin Leach narrating the event with his distinct British accent.

It was clear Donna and her wedding planner thought of every detail. In addition to the venue being the most beautiful property Jenna had ever seen, she was impressed by the beauty of the red and white roses in full bloom that lined the aisle, the programs that were calligraphed by hand, and the unity candle that had pearls and crystals covering every square inch. It glistened when the sun hit it just right and was designed to match Donna's gown. And when Donna came down the grand staircase, even Jenna gasped because she looked like a vision descending from the sky.

Jenna, Katie, and all the children were on their best behavior and had no intention of purposely ruining the wedding. They were there to support their father and his bride and hoped all would go exactly as planned.

Everything ran smoothly until it was time for the vows. Jenna was suddenly stricken with intense emotion when she heard her father promise to love Donna and take her as his partner until they were parted by death. Jenna was overwhelmed with feelings of sadness and grief. Nothing about this union evoked happiness or joy in her, but she knew she was just being selfish. She thought, *get it together, Jenna, Dad deserves this!*

Jenna looked down at her lap and silently caught the tears streaming uncontrollably down her face. She would not allow herself to look up toward the altar, because she knew if she saw her dad gazing into Donna's eyes, her silent tears would become audible bawling. She would not risk letting her emotions ruin her father's special day.

Jenna suspected her sister, Heidi, Brett, and her nieces were also feeling similarly and were all using every bit of willpower they could summon to keep their emotions hidden from view. Jenna thought she saw a tear stain on Caroline's cheek but quickly looked away in case she was right, knowing if they made eye contact it would open the floodgates for them both.

Olivia, who was only six at the time, was the only one too young to remember much about her grandmother. Jenna felt confident her youngest daughter was graciously spared from the sadness everyone else was feeling and was unaffected by listening to the promises her grandfather was making to Donna and God.

Jenna wished Paul was there at this moment to hold her hand or to protectively put his arm around her shoulder, but he was not, so she just had to imagine he was sitting next to her. Somehow, this brought her just enough strength to keep everything bottled up inside.

The ceremony felt ominous and reminded Jenna how much she missed her mother. She noticed one black cloud oddly looming in the distance. This wedding was only happening at all because her mother died decades before she should have been called home to the Lord. It seemed almost surreal for Jenna to watch her father pledging his love to another woman who was not her mom.

How could this be God's plan? Jenna's parents had not divorced. They did not choose to end their marriage. They did not fall out of love. Death made the decision for them, and it suddenly seemed so cruel and unfair. For a brief moment she wondered *what would it be like if it had been my father who died instead of my mother?* She quickly pushed this thought away because it seemed sinful.

Jenna was confident Donna was not the woman her mother would have chosen for her dad, and although it crushed her heart, there was nothing she could do about it but pray she was wrong. It did not matter in the least who Grace would have chosen, it only mattered who Tom chose. This was his decision to make alone. No one else's opinion counted.

Jenna briefly closed her eyes as the officiant pronounced them husband and wife and prayed God would lessen her despair and give her comfort. At that moment, she made the choice to accept Donna. She expected to feel an immediate sense of peace with this decision, but she did not. Her prayer had not been answered instantaneously as she hoped. She could only pray it would come true in God's time.

It was by the grace of God though that Jenna was able to stop her tears before the ceremony ended. She miraculously replaced her tears with a complete void of emotion and felt nothing but numbness when her father and new stepmother turned around to face the guests. She stared blankly at nothing in particular as the pastor announced, "I proudly present to you Mr. and Mrs. Thomas Jacobs."

The crowd erupted with cheers and applause just as Caroline erupted into tears, no longer able to hold them back any longer. Her tears became noticeable to everyone when the harpist began playing and Tom and Donna began to walk down the aisle, arm in arm, back toward the grand house. The tears were pouring from Caroline's eyes like a fountain and she was desperately trying to stifle her sobs.

Many in the crowd mistook her tears for happiness for the new couple, but all the members of Tom Jacobs's direct bloodline knew this was not the case. It was grief showing up uninvited.

Following the ceremony, the whole family was expected to take pictures. However, this plan went south quickly as Caroline continued to sob uncontrollably.

Katie instinctively ran to comfort her daughter and took her into her arms. Caroline clung to her mother as if she were drowning, and both mother and child cried together.

When Jenna saw them holding on to one another, she couldn't help but remember the night her own mother had held her when she was sobbing over Paul leaving for Texas A&M. There was nothing more comforting than a mother's arms, but just as quickly as the thought crept in, she pushed it away again. If she continued to think about her mother, she would surely break down into an inconsolable fit.

While still embracing Caroline, Katie glanced over at Donna and could see her seething with anger. There was no compassion in her eyes, only a look of mortification and disdain. Her eyes even seemed beady like a raven's, matching her dyed black hair, and her nose took on a sharp beak-like appearance.

If looks could kill, Katie and Caroline would have been dead. Stone cold dead.

It should have been understandable to Donna watching Tom remarry was emotionally gut wrenching. It should have also been understandable crying and grief over Grace did not necessarily equate to unhappiness or lack of support for the bride and groom. It is entirely possible to feel conflicting emotions at the same time.

Caroline truly liked Donna and even asked to be in the wedding party. She was oblivious to the way Donna treated her mother and held no ill will against her. She wanted to be included in her grandfather's special day. Preparing for the marriage felt right during the planning phase, but somehow, on the wedding day, it seemed so wrong.

Caroline had no way of knowing her unresolved emotions about her grandfather remarrying someone else would bubble up at the ceremony, and she certainly had no intention of sabotaging the wedding. Her tears were not an indication she didn't accept Donna, rather they were just evidence she loved her grandmother and missed her dearly. She was confused by the tension brewing in her family and felt her role as granddaughter was somehow changing.

Jenna stood silently off to the side with her own children, assessing the situation at hand and afraid to intervene. It seemed obvious to her it would be wise to take a brief pause in the wedding timeline and allow everyone ten minutes to collect themselves before pictures. She could also see this was not going to happen. There would be no compassion or grace offered by either the bride or the groom. They were going to stick to their wedding timeline come hell or high water—or tears.

Her father was barking at Caroline and Katie to stop crying and harshly admonishing them for ruining the wedding. Through clenched teeth he said, "Stop this embarrassing display this instant!" He was angry they were upsetting Donna.

Jenna wondered, *has anyone ever stopped crying when they were being screamed at to stop crying?* She didn't think so.

It did not appear to cross Tom's mind to take a gentler approach. Perhaps giving Caroline a warm embrace, or trying to console her, would have yielded a more positive result. He did not take the opportunity to tell her how much he loved her grandmother and how much he loved her too. He did not reassure her marrying Donna would not change that. Instead, he fixated on attempting to control the situation.

His only concern was for his bride, who was focusing solely on creating her wedding scrapbook and taking pictures worthy of posting on Facebook. Donna gave no visible care for Caroline's heart and made no gesture of compassion.

Katie, knowing her daughter would not be able to gain her composure if she remained at the ceremony site, and offended by her father's cruelty, gathered her children and left. She decided they needed to go for a drive to clear their heads before the reception and would not stay for pictures. She would not subject herself or her daughter to Donna's piercing glares or her father's wrath for another second. She briefly considered going home and skipping the reception altogether.

Jenna, like Katie, saw how mad Donna was when Caroline was crying. She could also see her anger level went through the roof after Katie's departure. She could almost imagine steam coming out of both of her ears like an angry cartoon character.

It was obvious both her dad and Donna felt the display of emotion was ruining the whole wedding, but in reality, only the wedding party consisting of the bride and groom's closest friends had been witnesses to the scene. Tom's yelling had been far more disruptive than Caroline's crying.

All the other guests had been promptly ushered from the ceremony to the grand foyer of the Atlanta Whitehouse for cocktail hour. They were currently drinking flutes of champagne and guzzling Scarlet O'Haras, Georgia's state cocktail—a lovely combination of Southern Comfort and cranberry juice with just a splash of lime. They were enjoying chicken croquettes, extra-large shrimp prawns, and delectable mushroom crostinis.

The guests were blissfully unaware any emotional outbursts were transpiring in the garden.

Jenna thought it was a good thing that no pictures were taken of the full family because it was best to try to forget the moment entirely. There would be future times that would be better, happier, and more photo worthy. She was sure the bride would still have more than enough pictures to fill her scrapbook and create a narrative of a perfect day, even without her sister and her nieces.

Jenna watched Donna taking picture after picture with Olivia. She was confident this series of photos would be posted on Facebook and would garner a hefty number of likes. Her youngest daughter was truly adorable in her flower girl dress, miniature diamond tiara, lace-trimmed socks, and black patent leather shoes with pink ribbon laces. She looked like a little princess, who had no idea everyone around her was hurting. The innocence of a child really was a beautiful thing, making Olivia the most photo worthy person at the wedding.

Brett and Heidi were also feeling the stress of the situation and were wildly uncomfortable. Jenna instructed them to smile and gave them stern warnings to do everything Donna asked of them. It was important they act like robots or risk making the photo shoot even more miserable.

Jenna was keenly aware they, like her, were trying very hard to push their emotions down deep inside. It was natural for them to miss their grandmother on a day like this, and she knew they were sad to see their cousin and aunt so visibly upset. She also knew after seeing Donna and her dad's reaction to Caroline and Katie, it was imperative they keep their emotions in check or risk becoming the next victims of their rage.

Jenna was fearful she, or one of her children, would suddenly lose control and the truth about their feelings might burst out unexpectedly at any moment like a jack-in-the-box.

Thankfully, much to her relief, the final crank never came, and the pictures went off surprisingly well.

The Final Straw

Just as Katie predicted, Caroline calmed down once she left the ceremony site. Katie drove her girls around, going nowhere in particular, blasting the radio until they sang themselves into a better mood. By the time they arrived at the reception, everyone in the family was feeling better.

Katie was pleased the bride and groom were so busy interacting with all their guests they barely had time to speak to the Jacobs family members at all. She didn't feel like talking to her dad or Donna. She wasn't sure if she would ever feel like talking to them again.

Donna enjoyed being in the spotlight and loved all the compliments she was receiving on her dress, hair, flowers, and venue selection. Tom was following his bride around like a lost puppy, but he was smiling from ear to ear because Donna was visibly happy. The scene in the garden was behind them now.

Jenna, Heidi, and Brett allowed themselves to forget about the overwhelming grief they felt at the ceremony and hummed along to the upbeat songs the DJ was playing. He had a great playlist with hits from across a variety of decades. An outsider looking in would have only seen a happening party complete with music, fabulous food, dancing, and a cake so beautiful it was worthy of a feature in *Southern Living*. There was no visible indication to those without internal knowledge that the family of the groom had been at its breaking point only thirty minutes earlier.

Jenna was thankful her kids were now having a great time, and she let herself relax when she saw Brett take Olivia to the dance floor and start spinning her around to Justin Timberlake's song "Can't Stop the Feeling." Olivia was thrilled she had a good dress for twirling, and it showed in her laughter as she held on to her older brother's hands. The photographer swooped in out of nowhere to capture the image.

Jenna even joined her kids on the dance floor a few songs later so Heidi and Brett could teach her how to do the "Cupid Shuffle." She caught on quickly to the dance and soon found herself singing along to the catchy lyrics, "to the right, to the right, to the right…"

Jenna's happiness grew when her sister and nieces joined them and reached new proportions when her father and Donna also joined them on the dance floor. The song "Electric Boogie" by Marcia Griffiths was pumping through the speakers and, together, as a family, they did the popular line dance known as "The Electric Slide." All the kids laughed hysterically and sang out, "And I'll teach you, teach you, teach you, I'll teach you the Electric Slide!"

Tom and Donna surprised them by singing along, and for one perfect moment, everything seemed like it was going to be okay. Jenna saw a snippet of the man she knew before Donna came into their lives, and she saw a less guarded and more fun side of her new stepmother. She let this silly line dance spark hope deep inside her that all the damage that had been done could be undone, and the relationships between Katie, Donna and her dad could be repaired.

Katie danced alongside the family, too, but the thoughts swirling through her mind were very different from Jenna's. She was counting down the seconds until it would be socially appropriate to leave. She would not stay any longer than was necessary. Every moment she was there felt like being sentenced to an eternity in hell.

When Tom yelled at Katie after the ceremony, it was the final straw that broke the camel's back. Katie was done. Her father's need to control and dehumanize her and her children was maddening, and she would not take it anymore. The hurt her father inflicted could not be undone with one line dance.

Katie knew she had to get away from her father and Donna before she began to question her own sanity. Donna manipulated and controlled every opportunity and every person she could and seemed to have a target on Katie's back. She was unpredictable, calculating, and selfish. Over the past year, she had been deliberately savage and deceitful more times than Katie could count.

It was also clear to Katie her father was never going to stand up for her. Never.

He was completely under Donna's spell and believed everything she said without question because he thought she was an honorable Christian woman simply because she said she was. He did whatever she instructed, regardless of how his actions affected his daughter.

Jenna forced her children to stay until the end of the reception, even though it dragged on for at least two hours too long, out of respect for her father and Donna. She was determined to make her relationship with her dad and new stepmom work.

Jenna agreed to have brunch with them the following morning before they left for home in North Carolina. She was convinced sticking it out was the right thing to do and wanted to support her dad, even though it was difficult. It was important to look for opportunities where they could have quality time because it was the only way they would get to know each other better. She already knew her sister and nieces would not be joining them because she was certain they had already left.

The next morning, Jenna and her children rode the elevator down to the restaurant on the ground floor of the hotel where they found Tom and Donna waiting for them. Jenna congratulated them both on the beautiful wedding and gave them warm hugs. She said, "Your months of planning really panned out well. It truly was a fairytale event."

Donna smiled and agreed.

Jenna also made sure to privately point out to her father, when Donna was out of earshot, that despite his fears, Katie had done nothing to ruin his wedding. She said, "What happened during photos did not negatively affect your wedding. It was a beautiful event from start to finish." She said, "Katie is not a vindictive and unstable woman. You should know that, Dad. You probably know her better than anyone."

He defiantly huffed at her comments, then without saying a word, headed for the table where the waitress was seating their party.

As brunch came to an end and the dishes and cutlery were cleared from the table, Jenna once again allowed herself to be hopeful everything would work out. There was a lighter feel in the air, despite the formality of the restaurant, and they even laughed genuinely as they shared stories about their lives with one another. It was the first time since meeting Donna everyone seemed relaxed and comfortable sitting at the same table.

It was hard to imagine Donna was the monster of Katie's stories because she seemed so sincere and likeable. *Was the woman sitting across from her now really the same person who had been shooting daggers with her eyes at Caroline yesterday?* If Jenna hadn't seen it herself, it would have been hard to believe. Jenna hoped she was just acting like a Bridezilla because she wanted everything to go perfectly, as many brides do, and the anger that flashed across her face was out of character.

Jenna would find out the answers to these questions later, but for now, she would rest on the hope that there had just been a lot of misunderstandings that could all be worked out. For the sake of the Jacobs family, Jenna hoped the adage "time was the healer of all wounds" was true.

After the meal was over, Jenna loaded her minivan up to leave. She had a long drive ahead of her back to Fort Bragg and needed to get on the road. As the children said goodbye to their grandfather, Jenna said goodbye to Donna. She was glad the weekend, which started so badly, was ending on a good note.

Donna pretended to be disappointed Katie slipped away without saying goodbye, but she couldn't care less. She knew she had won the war. *Victory*. Her plan to get rid of Katie worked, and Tom was none the wiser. She would be surprised if they ever saw her again.

As Donna waved goodbye to Jenna, she secretly hoped she could get rid of her just as easily as she had gotten rid of Katie.

With that thought, she grabbed her husband's hand and the pair walked back toward the hotel lobby.

One Down, One to Go

Shortly after the wedding weekend, a unique business opportunity was presented to Katie. She was sought out by a startup educational software company based out of Huntsville, Alabama. They were looking for someone with her teaching expertise to assist them in developing and marketing products that could benefit every school in America. They needed someone who understood how children learned and how teachers taught. Katie was exactly the person they were looking for.

The company had a lot of promise, and she and the founder clicked personally. She was confident they would work well together. She jumped at the chance to take on a new professional endeavor. She also liked the idea of putting some serious distance between herself and the new Mr. and Mrs. Jacobs. This job offer was the opportunity she had been looking for to get out from under Donna's controlling thumb and get her out of Georgia. She would be far enough away Donna would not be able to launch anymore sneak attacks against her.

The war Donna started for no apparent reason was finally over. She had survived every battle and was still standing with her dignity intact.

Victory. She was choosing to walk away forever. She didn't want her father's time or money. She only wanted to be free from the abuse.

She put her house up for sale and packed her bags, never looking back. She was moving onto bigger and better things.

Goodbye, Donna. Goodbye, Dad. Goodbye, Peachtree City. Goodbye rumor mill. Goodbye, Georgia.

Hello, Alabama. Hello, new life.

When Donna heard the news that Katie was moving out of the state, she said to her husband, "Tommy, I hope she isn't leaving because of me. I'm sorry she had such a hard time accepting my presence after her mother's death. I truly hoped she would come to view me as a mother one day, but her mental instability made this impossible. Hopefully, with some time and distance we will be able to work things out. A small break might be good for us all." She patted Tom on the head like he was a dog and told him she was going shopping. She didn't wait for a response before heading toward the front door.

Donna hadn't noticed Tom, sitting quietly in the recliner, had barely looked up from the book he was reading to acknowledge her. He had listened to her words and was sure he detected insincerity in them, but decided it was better to convince himself his wife was telling the truth than to ponder the thought he had lost Katie forever. He knew he had done nothing to try to save the relationship, and he would have to suffer the consequence of his inaction.

He also knew Grace would not approve.

Tom felt shame wash over him—and then anger he was in this situation at all. None of this would have happened if Grace was still here. She had gone on to glory and he had been left with a mess.

No matter though, he now had Donna by his side, and he would never be alone again. It didn't do any good to entertain thoughts like this or wallow in self-pity.

Donna got into her Beamer that still had the new car smell and chuckled out loud. She proudly said, "One down, one to go," knowing no one else could hear her. She put the car in reverse and backed out of the driveway.

It was time to do some damage to their credit line.

People Are Crazy

Jenna invited her dad and Donna to come to North Carolina for Mother's Day weekend, the month after their wedding. Brett had a lacrosse tournament and Olivia had a gymnastics exhibition. She thought her dad would enjoy photographing each sporting event and could help her juggle the kids' schedules since Paul was still deployed.

She knew she was going to need another driver because Olivia would need to be at the gym warming up before Brett's game at the lacrosse field across town was over. She couldn't physically be in two places at once, and although Heidi had just gotten her driver's license, she had recently gotten into a minor accident while driving Paul's truck and it was in the shop.

Jenna was relieved when they agreed almost immediately to come. It would be a good time to get to know Donna a little better. They had only seen each other in person a handful of times. She was looking forward to their visit and wanted everything to be nice since it was Donna's first time visiting the Miller home at Fort Bragg. She was disappointed they were only coming for two nights but was glad they were coming at all. She didn't understand why they wanted the visit to be so short. It would have been nice to have some adult company for a few more days.

Jenna planned to cook dinner for them on the night of their arrival and then take them to a Billy Currington concert being held on the parade field near her house on Fort Bragg that evening. She felt lucky to live on a military post with so many wonderful live events and was looking forward to sharing this special performance with her guests.

Many first-rate musicians offered to perform at Fort Bragg and other Army installations they were stationed at over the years to show their support for military families. Jenna and her kids all loved country music and were particularly fond of Billy's newest song, "People Are Crazy." Paul was also a big fan and hated to miss out on the fun.

Jenna knew Donna was a music lover in general and hoped she would enjoy the concert, too, and get to experience some of the perks of Army living. She told Jenna in one of their first meetings she liked all types of genres, and this was evident in the wedding reception playlist. Some of her favorite artists included Amy Grant, Beyonce, One Direction, and Miranda Lambert. Jenna hoped she would add Billy Currington to her list after tonight.

Jenna cleaned the house from top to bottom in preparation for their arrival and even purchased a gift for Donna for Mother's Day. She was torn about what to do about the holiday because it was somewhat unclear what was expected. She had never been in this situation before and wanted to handle it thoughtfully. She knew she didn't want or need Donna to be a replacement mother, but she did want to send the message she was happy to welcome her to the family and was glad to have her in her life.

Jenna finally settled on a rose gold locket, inscribed with a Bible verse, "I thank my God every time I remember you" (Philippians 1:3, NIV). She put a photo of Donna and Tom together inside. It seemed odd to put a picture of her or her children inside—and she knew her sister would have killed her if she put a photo of her or her kids in it. It seemed like a thoughtful gesture with just the right sentiment. Jenna truly wanted to move past any awkwardness between them and hoped to create a tight bond with her. She hoped the gift would touch Donna's heart and kickstart the relationship. She gave it to Donna shortly after they arrived. It was apparent she liked the locket, and it seemed like the visit was getting off to a good start.

Just as Jenna planned, they all shared a nice meal together around her dining room table. Conversation flowed naturally, and Jenna did not see any glimpses of the woman who was so emotionally distraught during the wedding pictures episode. She appeared to be relaxed and in a jovial mood. She also did not ask where Jenna grocery shopped. She ate the chicken parmesan Jenna had made without issue and ate every bite on her plate. The word "organic" did not come up one time.

Jenna chalked up the whole wedding episode up to a Bridezilla moment. So much time, money, and preparation go into a wedding it is understandable for a bride to feel the pressure for everything to be perfect. Any deviation from the plan is enough to send many brides into a tailspin and make them temporarily unable to empathize with anyone else. She was glad a happier woman was here now. She couldn't explain her willingness to eat Jenna's chicken, but she was thankful she was not on the receiving end of one of Donna's lectures.

Once the dirty dishes were loaded into the dishwasher and the leftovers were put away, the family left Jenna's house and traveled the short two-block distance to the main parade field. They set up lawn chairs for the adults and spread a blanket on the ground for the kids. It was a warm North Carolina evening with a slight breeze, and you could see the stars shining like diamonds in the night sky. There were tons of other families sitting on the parade field, and food trucks and vendors surrounded the area. There were dogs on leashes, babies in strollers, and kids playing with glow-in-the-dark frisbees. A comfortable atmosphere of community could be felt. The stage was set, and a warm-up act was playing to get the crowd excited.

As the Miller-Jacobs family waited for Billy to take the stage, Tom offered to take Heidi, Brett, and Olivia over to the funnel cake truck. Jenna and Donna were content to let him take the kids while they sat in the chairs and chatted with one another. Both ladies were still stuffed from dinner and had no desire to wait in the line that was growing longer with each passing second.

Donna said, "Tom, I don't know how you keep so trim with as much as you enjoy dessert. If I ate as many sweets as you did, I would be as heavy as a whale!"

Everyone laughed.

Tom had always liked taking the kids out for dessert. It was one of the special "Pop Pop things" he enjoyed doing whenever he got the chance. It warmed Jenna's heart to see him following this tradition again and adding a funnel cake outing to her children's memory banks. She could remember past trips for ice cream, donuts, cupcakes, eclairs, frozen yogurt, gelato, churros, and McDonald's hot apple pies. There had been countless trips for dessert over the years, and each trip was special.

Jenna knew Brett, Olivia, and Heidi would want their funnel cake topped with hot fudge and whipped cream, and her dad would want vanilla ice cream and strawberry syrup.

The two women watched Tom and his grandchildren as they walked toward the funnel cake truck called "Twisted Dough" and then got in the long line. They seemed to be a happy and cohesive family unit. Jenna thought *everything seems normal for the first time in a long time.*

Olivia was now turning cartwheels in the grassy area beside the line and Heidi and Brett were attempting to teach Tom how to play Ninja while they waited to order. He wasn't nearly as quick as they were with his Ninja moves and was clearly losing the game, but he was trying!

Conversation flowed effortlessly between Donna and Jenna for quite some time until Donna abruptly said, "I would never marry a military man. I once dated a soldier but was afraid he would become mentally ill, so I broke it off. They are so likely to return from a deployment with PTSD. I knew I didn't want to subject myself to that nightmare. You must be brave, Jenna."

Jenna felt blindsided by the statement and was even more surprised Donna chuckled when she said it, like it meant nothing. Jenna was not expecting Donna to make such a derogatory generalization about soldiers, especially not while sitting in the middle of the parade field on Fort Bragg where yellow ribbons were visible from every angle. She was also sure they were within ear shot of several soldiers and their spouses. She looked around to make sure no one was glaring at them.

Jenna was even more surprised when Donna continued, "You just never know what they will be like when they return. I read many soldiers come back from deployments and abuse their wives horribly or cheat on them. Isn't the divorce rate unusually high in the Army?"

Without missing a beat, or waiting for a response from Jenna, she said, "I read an article about emotional support dogs. I believe they could cure all soldiers suffering from PTSD. I don't know why they aren't issued to every soldier upon their return to U.S. soil."

As she droned on very nonchalantly about dogs, like she was an expert on PTSD—and acting as if it was only a trivial problem, Jenna stared at her in disbelief. It seemed like she truly thought a furry friend was the answer to every soldier's problems and that, somehow, they could miraculously reverse all the traumatic experiences so many men and women in our armed services endured—on our behalf. She also seemed to be questioning the mental health of anyone who served and anyone who chose to be in a relationship with them.

It was unreal and it was offensive.

Donna could see she was getting under Jenna's skin so decided to pause for a brief second and stare into her stepdaughter's eyes. She was trying to read her mind and peer into her soul.

Jenna couldn't help but feel like she was daring her to react. It seemed she was willing her to retaliate against her. She felt unsettled, as if she was being gawked at naked. *Was she expecting her to act out in rage about the insinuation that Paul would be a bad husband when he returned? Was she accusing him of being a bad husband? Was she expecting Jenna to chastise her for diminishing the seriousness of PTSD by saying it would all go away if soldiers just had dogs? Was she accusing her of being mentally ill because she loved someone serving in the Army?*

Although Jenna felt defensive, she responded calmly by saying, "I am very happy I married a soldier. Paul is an amazing husband and father. I'm not sure issuing everyone a dog is the perfect answer to curing PTSD. I support their use when it is appropriate, but I do not believe they are the total solution." She paused momentarily and said, "Donna, I hope you understand PTSD if a very complex and very serious issue."

Jenna quickly changed the subject, without giving Donna a chance to reply, by directing her attention to the architecture of the 82nd Airborne Chapel located within view across the field. She said, "Isn't the stained glass beautiful?"

Jenna was done with the previous conversation. D.O.N.E.

Although Donna's statements greatly bothered Jenna, she did not feel it necessary to mention the conversation to her dad when he returned from the food truck, or even later that night. She didn't want to be perceived as a tattletale. Jenna couldn't help but think Donna purposely made these comments to upset her. *But why? What purpose would it serve?*

Jenna had put her foot in her mouth a time or two in her life by mistake and hoped this was simply what happened to Donna. It is easy to say the wrong thing when you are just getting to know someone, and sometimes the more you realize you said something you shouldn't have, the worse you make it. It can be easy to dig yourself into a hole with no idea how to get out. This was the first time the two women spent any prolonged amount of time together, so it was not unreasonable to think this might be the case. It was preferable to give her the benefit of the doubt rather than assume Donna had purposely tried to offend her.

Jenna didn't want to make a big deal about it, so she dismissed it, even though her intuition was telling her Donna hadn't just made an honest mistake.

She looked across the field toward Twisted Dough and could see her kids and her dad walking back toward them with enormous funnel cakes in hand, topped exactly as she had predicted.

The rest of the evening was wonderful. Billy Currington put on an amazing show, and her dad filmed the kids as they sang along, "God is Great, Beer is Good, and People are Crazy!" It was especially funny to see her kindergarten-aged Olivia belting out a song about beer, but she knew every word because it played so many times on the radio.

When they returned to the house, Jenna was surprised to learn her dad and Donna would not be staying with them, but rather at a hotel in Fayetteville. She had wondered why they didn't have any luggage when the first arrived, and now she knew why.

They told her in unison, "We are tired and ready to go check in."

Her father had always stayed with her before, so she was caught off guard. She mildly expressed her disappointment but did not want to start an argument on the newlyweds' first visit to her home as a married couple. Other than the odd conversation on the parade field, the evening had been a success.

Jenna made sure to let Donna know she was always welcome in her home by saying, "I have an open-door policy for family," hoping she would infer a hotel wasn't necessary for future visits.

She thought she saw Donna wince when she said "open-door policy" but decided that must have been a figment of her imagination because she couldn't imagine why that phrase would be off putting. Jenna admonished herself, *stop reading into everything*!

Sit Down, Pop Pop

As they were leaving for the hotel, Jenna bid them goodnight and reminded them Brett's lacrosse game started at eight o'clock the next morning.

As soon as Donna heard the time she said, "We will be there later than that. I don't do mornings."

Jenna was immediately angered by this comment and confused. She thought one of the main reasons they came to visit was so they could see Brett play. Her father had attended many games over the years and had never been late a single time. "I don't do mornings" did not seem like a valid excuse to Jenna. It meant a lot to Brett for his Pop Pop to watch him play, especially since Paul wasn't there to see him.

Jenna expressed her desire for them to arrive on time but didn't press the issue too hard. She could see her persistence was annoying Donna, and she did not want to spoil the lovely evening. Jenna had confidence her father would talk to Donna about this later at the hotel, and they would be on time when she realized how important it was to both Tom and Brett they be present for the whole game.

Jenna also rationalized he had a second game on Sunday that didn't start until ten o'clock in the morning, so in the worst-case scenario, they would see a whole game then. Donna had never been a grandmother before, so Jenna expected there to be a slight learning curve. She was sure once Donna understood how kids' sports worked, she would be more agreeable. It was new territory for her she needed to learn to navigate.

The next morning, Jenna loaded up all three children and all the necessary sporting equipment for the day into her minivan and headed toward the field where Brett would be playing. They left the house promptly at seven o'clock because he had to be there thirty minutes early to warm up. The game started exactly at eight o'clock with Brett playing midfielder.

He loved playing middie because he liked to be in the heart of the action. He was an excellent player with amazing eye-hand coordination, physical toughness, and extraordinary stamina when it came to running.

With every minute that passed, Jenna's frustration with her father grew. It was already the third quarter, and her father and Donna were still not there. Brett was playing his heart out, and his grandfather, who was in town, was missing it because his wife "did not do mornings."

Finally, at the beginning of the fourth quarter, Tom and Donna came strolling up just in time to see Brett get checked by another player twice his size. He fell hard, landing on his wrist. He got up quickly and began running downfield. Another player passed him the ball, but when he tried to cradle his stick, it became obvious he was injured. He was unable to bend his right wrist.

After a quick evaluation by his coach, it was determined he was going to be out for the rest of the game. Everyone was hopeful he could recover before the next game of the tournament the following day because they believed Brett when he said, "I promise it doesn't hurt that bad!"

Jenna needed to leave the lacrosse field to get Olivia to her gymnastics exhibition across town. She, like Brett, had to be there early. Her father promised to bring Brett and Heidi to the gym following the game since Brett could not and did not want to leave before it was over, even if he was no longer playing. Jenna hoped it was just a minor sprain and was comforted knowing it was currently being iced.

As she said goodbye, she heard Donna complaining to Tom about the heat. He was opening an umbrella for her and trying to shield her from the sun. For some reason Jenna imagined a vampire evaporating in the daylight. She thought to herself, *less sun was one benefit of an early game,* and left with Olivia who was anxious to get to the gym.

Jenna was relieved when her dad, Donna, Heidi, and Brett showed up at the gymnastics exhibition on time. She had saved them front row seats and could see Olivia getting excited about performing from across the gym. Jenna smiled when she saw Olivia waving wildly at her Pop Pop after he entered through the double doors. Her enthusiasm was contagious.

Olivia was huddled up with the other members of her pre-team group, who were all looking forward to performing their first skills demonstration. The exhibition was supposed to mimic a real meet to give the athletes some experience. She was wearing a bright yellow and pink leotard, her first GK Elite leo, which made her feel even more like a gymnast. Upgrading from the Target brand to a "real" leotard brought her immense joy and added to her excitement.

This day would serve as good practice to prepare her for competition when she moved on to team in the fall. There was also going to be a cartwheel competition with a trophy for the winner. Olivia had been practicing consecutive cartwheels for weeks and couldn't wait to compete.

Tom, Donna, Heidi, and Brett all found Jenna easily and joined her at the saved seats. Tom unpacked his camera with the zoom lens and settled in, ready to photograph Olivia doing her thing.

Since the gymnasts were all young and new at this, there was a little bit of chaos moving from event to event. Jenna laughed because it seemed like the coaches were trying to wrangle wet cats. Olivia, however, was doing everything just as she was told. She was a rule follower and naturally excelled at gymnastics. She was in her element and soaking up every moment. Jenna could tell she was having the time of her life and was proud of her performances. She could imagine her youngest picturing herself as the next Gabby Douglas in her head.

Olivia executed a flawless back hip circle on the low bar, a straight jump off the springboard, stayed on the balance beam for her short routine, and performed a beautiful, shortened compulsory floor routine. She was crushing all the demonstrations of the day. The event was fittingly called, "Skills and Thrills," and it was clear Olivia was both "skilled" and "thrilled."

After the skills demonstrations, everyone prepared for the long-awaited cartwheel competition. Each gymnast would have one minute to do as many cartwheels as they could while volunteers counted. After the chaotic minute of counting as children cartwheeled in all directions, trying not to plow into one another, it was clear Olivia was going to be the winner with fifty-seven cartwheels. She was one of the only six-year-olds who had continuously cartwheeled the whole sixty seconds and was still able to stand upright. Her practice paid off.

Dizzy children flopped on the floor trying to catch their breath. It was quite a comical scene watching six-year-olds stumble as if they had been drinking all afternoon.

Once the little gymnasts found their footing and began to stand up again, it was announced over the loudspeaker there would be a brief delay until awards were given. The organizers needed a few minutes to move the balance beams and set up tables with the trophies and medals. The children were instructed to move toward a roped off section near the awards area once they could walk in a straight line again.

As they sat there waiting, Jenna noticed Donna whispering to her dad. Suddenly, Tom stood up and announced they were leaving. He said, "We need to go. Donna is hungry."

Jenna was dumbfounded. The awards ceremony had not started yet. There were concessions for sale in the lobby. *Couldn't Donna just go buy a granola bar to hold her over until after the awards?* It would only be a few more minutes until everything was over.

She wanted to say this out loud, but before she could get the words out of her mouth, Heidi surprised everyone by commanding her grandfather to sit down. Heidi sternly said, "Sit down, Pop Pop. You will not leave until awards are given out. Olivia is about to get her first trophy, and you need to be here to see it. She deserves the same attention Sydney and I got when we were her age. You and Grandma were at all our gymnastics meets. You never left early then, and you will not leave early now."

It must have taken her quite some courage to gather the nerve to stand up to him. Heidi was not usually disrespectful, but it was clear she had reached her limit with Donna and her grandfather. She was also feeling protective of her youngest sibling.

Silence fell among the first row, and Tom did as he was told and sat back down without saying a word.

Tom knew Heidi spoke the truth. He would never have left a gymnastics meet early, even if it was only an exhibition and not a real competition, in his former life. He also knew Grace would never have put her own needs ahead of the grandchildrens'.

If Grace was here, she would have been rooting Olivia on, cheering more loudly than everyone else in the gym. He could almost her hear yelling, "Go O, Go O, Go O!" Her behavior would have been a stark contrast to his current wife's.

Tom wasn't sure what to do. He felt like he was stuck between pleasing his family and pleasing his wife, and the two were not on the same page.

Donna was clearly angry and if looks could kill, Heidi and Tom would both be dead, just like Katie and Caroline after the wedding. Donna's eye dagger body count was growing steadily.

Jenna tried to ignore the tension that surrounded her and focus on the awards ceremony that was starting. This was Olivia's moment, and she did not want to miss it because of the ridiculousness that was happening in the front row.

Fifteen minutes later, Olivia had her cartwheel trophy in hand, her participation medal for the day around her neck, and a smile as big as the crescent moon across her face. She greeted everyone with laughter and hugs and posed proudly with her awards while her Pop Pop snapped some photos. He even took a picture of Olivia with Donna for her to post on Facebook later.

Even though she had been bored out of her mind, Donna looked forward to bragging about Olivia's competition like a doting grandma, and none of her friends would be any wiser about her true feelings. If she was forced to spend her whole day at blistering hot lacrosse fields and in stinky gyms, at least she could get something out of it for herself.

Tom announced, "We are going to stop for a quick lunch through a drive through and then go back to the hotel for some rest. We will rejoin you for dinner tonight." He quickly gathered their things and beelined for the door, with Donna leading the way.

Donna viewed Jenna and her children as selfish for expecting them to be at both sporting events in their entirety. She needed to remind her husband she wasn't like a "typical" grandma for the umpteenth time. She didn't intend to let his family dictate their schedule because that was extremely disrespectful.

Jenna was bothered by the events of the day but tried to shake it all off. However, it was harder to ignore her father's unusual behavior was also becoming problematic to her oldest daughter.

Heidi told her mother, "I am deeply bothered Pop Pop missed almost all of Brett's game today and then had the nerve to suggest leaving Olivia's exhibition early. This is not the Pop Pop I have known my whole life." She whined, "Mom, he seems like a stranger and Donna is the most impatient adult I have ever met! I thought grown-ups were supposed to know how to behave themselves!"

Jenna reminded her daughter of the importance of showing her grandfather respect and suggested she give Donna some grace as she learns to become a grandma. Jenna was confident she would figure it all out eventually and maybe even come to enjoy her new role. They all needed to be more compromising.

The family reunited for dinner that evening at Red Lobster.

Tom pulled Jenna aside so he could speak to her privately before they sat down at their table. He said, "Donna needs to eat more often than most people because her blood sugar drops easily. In the future, we would appreciate a little more consideration when you schedule us for hours on end."

Jenna was confident he was giving her a speech scripted word for word by Donna and could tell by the tone of his voice he had experienced a less than perfect afternoon with his wife back at the hotel. Jenna decided there was no point in mentioning the concession stand again or the kids' feelings that did not seem to be considered at all. They were both moot points and it would not do any good to argue. Instead, she said, "Of course dad, I'm sorry."

The party of six was seated and made their menu selections. However, by the time the entrees were delivered to the table it was obvious to everyone Brett's wrist was hurting more with each passing moment. He couldn't even concentrate on the huge plate of fried shrimp the server had placed in front of him.

Jenna decided it was best to go to the emergency room to have it examined by a doctor. Tom and Donna agreed to finish dinner with the girls and then take them back to the pool at the hotel to swim until Jenna and Brett were done in the ER.

Two hours later, Jenna pulled into the Hilton parking lot with Brett in a cast. There would be no lacrosse for him for the next three weeks. His grandfather would not get the opportunity to watch him play this visit.

Upon hearing this unfortunate news, Tom and Donna asked if the family could meet them at eight o'clock the next morning for a quick breakfast at the hotel and for formal goodbyes. Tom said, "There is no point in prolonging our visit since Brett is no longer playing in the tournament. We want to get ahead of the traffic."

Jenna thought, *how interesting Donna has no trouble getting up early to leave but getting up for a lacrosse game is impossible. What happened to "I don't do mornings"?*

As Tom and Donna drove out of the hotel parking lot, Jenna had mixed feelings about the visit. They mostly had a good time, and her father and Donna had been very helpful shuttling the kids between the sporting events and watching the girls while she was at the hospital with Brett, but there were enough things that seemed off to cause concern. Then she remembered her own advice to Heidi to give Donna some grace while learning to be a grandmother and decided to extend it to her dad as well, who was in a pickle. She decided to focus on the positives and let the unpleasant parts go.

Jenna and the kids climbed into their minivan and turned on the radio. Billy Currington was playing on their favorite station. As they started to drive down Skibo Road in Fayetteville, just a few minutes from Fort Bragg, they all sang out loud, "God is great, beer is good, and people are crazy." Jenna laughed out loud.

The Importance of Gifts

The first Father's Day after the wedding snuck up on Jenna. For the first time in her life, she did not have a gift for her dad on or before the exact day. She felt bad about it, but she honestly couldn't think of anything to get him. Since they had no plans to get together anytime soon, an experience gift wasn't possible, and there was not a thing he needed or wanted. She didn't want to waste money on something useless. She was sure he would understand, and with a little more time, she was hopeful she would find the perfect gift. Her dad and Donna were flying out to Barbados on Father's Day for their long-awaited honeymoon anyway, so he wouldn't even be in the country on the actual holiday.

Jenna tried to make herself feel better about not having a gift by convincing herself even if she had mailed something on time, it was likely to sit on the front porch at Donna's home for weeks since her dad and Donna were going to Ohio directly after their honeymoon. They planned to spend several weeks there visiting Donna's friends and family.

Jenna thought it was strange they decided to live in Donna's house since the wedding, instead of at Tom's vacation home, but when she asked her dad about it, he just said, "Donna prefers it that way. She doesn't want to move twice."

He was unaware his second wife was put off by the idea of sleeping in a house he purchased with his first wife. They were still in the planning phase for their new home and had yet to break ground. Tom had also explained to Jenna they were in the process of getting Donna's house ready to be put on the market, so it was helpful for them to live there.

Tom was happy to do odd jobs for her that needed to be done to make her house more sellable. His experience as a realtor was coming in handy. He had suggested adding unique pulls on the kitchen cabinets, updating the light fixtures in the bathrooms, and installing a garbage disposal.

Even though Jenna didn't have a gift, she called her dad to wish him a happy Father's Day and let him know she was thinking of him. She knew Katie would not call him, so thought it was important she did. She didn't want him to go completely unacknowledged.

Her dad and Donna were at the airport when they spoke. They were at their gate awaiting the announcement to board. He didn't have much time to talk, so she told him "Happy Father's Day" and said, "I promise to send you something fabulous in the mail." She wished him and Donna a wonderful honeymoon and hung up the phone.

She thought it was interesting he was taking Donna to Barbados for their honeymoon since he had already been there many years ago with Grace and the family on a cruise. She knew her dad usually preferred to travel somewhere he had never been before when given the opportunity. It was a beautiful place though, with gorgeous white sand and lovely shopping. She would be surprised, however, if Donna would climb on the back of a moped like her mother had done.

She smiled at the memory of the family riding around and grimaced when she remembered how Katie had accidentally driven into a brick wall and bruised her calf severely. She wouldn't fault Donna if she didn't try because both she and her father were quite a bit older than the first time Tom had gone to Barbados. It would be prudent to be cautious. She didn't want them to have the same travel curse her parents had where something always went wrong.

As Jenna thought more about the Barbados trip so many years ago, she laughed to herself when she recalled how sophisticated she felt when she was allowed to purchase a souvenir from the island's well renowned Holetown Shopping Center. The stores were far more expensive than the local outlet mall she was used to, and the exorbitant price tags made her equate it with being better. When she thought of the various stores and their impeccable displays with finely accessorized mannequins dripping with diamonds, she imagined Donna would like it too.

Jenna honestly hoped they would have a good time and enjoy their honeymoon. She was sure she would see hundreds of pictures the next time they got together and was glad her father would have a chance to add to his travel postcard collection, which had been sorely neglected since her mother's death. He probably had collected thousands of postcards from all his travels with Grace.

Jenna didn't know Donna had thrown out every postcard her father had ever collected when he was selling his home in Peachtree City. She had said indignantly, "Tom, there is no place in our marriage for obsessing over memories you made with Grace. It is time to make new ones that are better." She had heartlessly chucked his entire collection into the kitchen garbage can along with the scraps from their evening meal. Once she was done tossing them out, she said, "Honey, these are as useless as Grace's tacky music boxes. Surely, we can find something better to collect."

Jenna didn't give Father's Day much more thought after the phone call. With Paul being gone and her being the sole parent at home, she had a lot on her plate. She felt confident her good wishes were enough for her dad for now. Materialism wasn't important, loving relationships were.

Jenna didn't hold true to her word to mail a gift as soon as possible. Time continued to get away from her, and the gift for her dad was low on her priority list because she didn't think it mattered.

Several weeks later in late July, she came across a website that specialized in handcrafted ornamental vases filled with sand from around the world. She was suddenly thrilled she had found the perfect gift for her dad! She selected a beautiful glass vase shaped like a seashell and requested it be filled with sand from the beaches of Barbados and St. Simon's Island, Georgia. Jenna thought this would be a perfect late Father's Day gift because it was a reminder of where he and Donna started their lives together and where they honeymooned. It would also look perfect in their new house.

She purchased the vase, ignoring the price. It was considered a "one-of-a-kind" piece of artwork and was quite expensive. It really was like nothing she had ever seen before, and it was exquisitely crafted. She hoped he would like it and forget about its lateness. She also thought Donna would appreciate the thought behind it since both of those beaches were surely special to her as well. Jenna chose to have it shipped to her house so she could make sure it looked as nice in person as it did online.

Since it was so late already, Jenna decided she would just mail it with his birthday present in August. *What did another few weeks matter?*

There was no need to spend extra money on postage. She mailed the vase along with a separate birthday present in the same box on the twenty-eighth of August, with a postal guarantee it would arrive by the second of September, her dad's actual birthday. At least his birthday gift would be on time.

On the first of September, Jenna was at a Family Readiness Group meeting at Paul's battalion headquarters where she had prepared a meal for twenty-five people. It was time for their monthly gathering, and she wanted to do something special for the volunteers. She and her beloved "Battle Buddy," Paul's Sergeant Major's wife, were busy setting up the food and preparing for the meeting when Jenna heard her phone ding, indicating she had a text message.

She quickly crossed the room and dug her phone out of her tote bag.

She wanted to see who was texting her in case it was one of her children. They always seemed to need something at the most inconvenient times, but that was just a part of motherhood.

Jenna was surprised to see the text was from Donna, whom she had barely spoken to since her visit last May. The text said, "My husband was devastated because neither you nor your sister had the decency to acknowledge him on Father's Day this year, or the year prior. I am texting to remind you his birthday is tomorrow." The next text bubble that popped up said, "I would hate for you to miss another important occasion." The third text bubble said, "You should be ashamed I feel it necessary to remind you of your dad's birthday."

Jenna was immediately incensed. She couldn't believe she was being scolded like a child. She already felt bad she hadn't sent a Father's Day gift on time, but it wasn't tantamount to a capital crime. *For Pete's sake.*

She texted back, "I did acknowledge the day. I called him when you were in the airport to wish him a happy Father's Day." She hit Send. Her next text bubble said, "Thank you, but I don't need a reminder for my dad's birthday. I have already sent a package and included an additional gift for Father's Day."

Donna responded with "Father's Day was in June."

Jenna felt the anger bubbling up inside her. *Why was so much importance being placed on a present? Would sending him a random tie really have meant that much? Why didn't Donna just call and talk to her civilly about this?*

Jenna started texting again, "The Rainbow Run was my gift the year before." Jenna also typed, "Remember the run where my dad ditched me completely because he wanted to get back to you!"—but thought better of it and deleted the last part before hitting Send. She was not going to engage in a text war. She didn't have time for that, and it wasn't the right thing to do.

Jenna took a deep breath and texted again, "Donna, I hope you can extend me a little grace since Paul is deployed. I have so much on my plate right now. I'm sorry my Father's Day gift is so late."

Donna's response was not one of understanding. She reprimanded her for being disrespectful to her father after he was so generous with her. She also said, "I'm sorry you are so overwhelmed and unable to handle your children without Paul there to help."

Ouch.

There was no offer to help her or to try to understand what she was dealing with, just cold-heartedness. Donna had a complete lack of comprehension when it came to the enormous responsibilities of a parent. Jenna could suddenly empathize more with her sister and some of the stories she had told her about being chastised for her parenting abilities.

Jenna fumed. She could appreciate Donna trying to protect her husband, but those were fighting words. She was Tom's daughter, not his arch enemy.

Jenna showed her Battle Buddy the text to make sure she was not misreading the tone. Her friend agreed wholeheartedly this was a full out attack.

Jenna missed one gift-giving occasion in her life and was being raked over the coals for it. She couldn't even think of a single gift her father had ever given her. Her mother had done all the Christmas and birthday shopping her entire childhood, and since she was an adult, each member of her family received a fifty-dollar check for each occasion. She always used the checks made out to her and Paul to pay bills or spent it on her kids. She and Paul never bought anything for themselves.

She was grateful for the checks; however, her father had never gone to the store to search for something special for her. He never had to package and mail her something, and he had certainly never taken care of three very busy children, a house, and a Family Readiness Group by himself. Neither had Donna.

Jenna wasn't incompetent without Paul, she was just busy and practical, a trait she had inherited from her mother. If smoke could have come out of her ears, it would have filled the battalion classroom. She dropped the phone back in her tote bag and tried to forget all about the nastygram she had just received. She wished the text had been from one of her kids instead. She thought, *it would have been less nerve wracking to find out one of her kids had broken a bone in gym class.*

On the second of September, Jenna waited until eight o'clock at night to call her dad to wish him a happy birthday. It was the first time everyone was under the same roof at the same time all day. She felt it was important for her children to speak to their grandfather on his birthday.

Her dad seemed happy to talk to them and thanked them for his birthday gift and Father's Day gift. He didn't say as much about the vase with the personalized sand as she had expected but she didn't want to bring up Father's Day in light of her recent text exchange with Donna.

Jenna had no idea the time of day she called was being recorded and would later be used against her. Donna was building an arsenal again. Her every word and action were under a microscope, unbeknownst to her.

Jenna ended the conversation by saying, "Paul and I would like to invite you both to his upcoming change of command ceremony."

Paul was scheduled to return to U.S. soil in mid-October and would be relinquishing his command the last week of the month. He had been in battalion command for thirty-six long months—six months longer than usual. It was time. He would be reassigned to another position in the 82nd Airborne Division until the family moved the following summer. He was slated to attend National War College in Washington, D.C., the next logical step in his career path.

Jenna and the children couldn't wait for Paul to come home. They had almost made it through another deployment and were happy they could share their joy with family. Jenna hoped the next visit with her dad and Donna would go more smoothly than the first, but after the insolent texts, she had justified concerns. She pushed away her fears with the power of positive thinking and focused on the excitement of welcoming her husband home.

Welcome Home

P aul arrived home to Fort Bragg from Iraq in October, exactly as planned—it is a rarity in Army life for things to go as expected.

When the plane carrying him and the other soldiers from his battalion landed safely on Green Ramp, the cheers from the waiting families erupted like a volcano throughout the hangar where everyone was huddled together. Homemade posters, balloons, and American flags could be seen waving proudly from every direction. The onlookers were as excited as children on Christmas morning.

The feeling of welcoming a soldier home after a deployment is like no other. Pride, relief, happiness, and feelings of tremendous patriotism wash over you all at once. Jenna felt chills of anticipation running up and down her spine.

The Millers, like the other family members in attendance, were in complete awe when they saw the long line of soldiers deboarding the plane and marching into the hangar. Knowing only one formation stood between them and the moment they could hug Paul created an immense sense of excitement. Waiting even a minute more—after all these months—seemed like more than they could bear.

Thankfully, as soon as the anticipation became too overwhelming to endure any longer, the soldiers were released to greet their families. It was time for hugs, laughter, and happy tears. The deployment was officially over.

Jenna closed her eyes, amidst the chaos surrounding her, and took a deep breath.

Breathe. Paul is home. He is safe. Breathe.

She opened her eyes and saw her husband approaching. She threw open her arms, grabbed his neck, and squeezed him with all her might. She felt his familiar arms around her and kissed him on his familiar lips. He smiled widely and said, "Hello, beautiful." He was the same man who had gotten on a plane to leave many months ago. He was not a stranger. Donna's implication he would return as a completely different man was wrong.

Breathe, Jenna. Breathe. Your love is home.

In the days that followed the soldiers' return, the Miller family relished the joy of being together once again and even had a Driveway Dance Party. Paul chose the song "Courtesy of the Red, White and Blue" by Toby Keith to kick off their party playlist. Although it was mildly inappropriate, all three kids had screamed, "we'll put a boot in your ass, it's the American way" as loudly as possible, and for once, Jenna didn't care about the volume or the cuss word. She sang along with them.

The family quickly fell back into their pre-deployment roles, and all seemed right in the house for the first time in many months. For Jenna, the loneliness of the evenings and the fear of the doorbell were in the past. For Paul, the angst of being away from his wife and kids and the pressures of being in a combat zone were over. For Heidi, Brett, and Olivia, the feeling of safety and normalcy that comes to military kids when both parents are home returned.

Jenna and Paul were also busy preparing for the change of command ceremony and for the party they would host once it was over. They invited friends and family to come to an "Everything Party" that would celebrate the completion of a successful command, Paul's safe return, all the holidays he missed when he was in Iraq, and even his fortieth birthday, which happened months ago.

Jenna and Paul were simple people and didn't want anything fancy. A barbecue in the backyard, a firepit, a keg, a cake, and some good country music would set the backdrop for a relaxing evening where all the stress of the previous months could melt away.

Donna Knows Best

On the day of the change of command, guests streamed in and out of the Miller House all day long, including Tom and Donna—first to meet up with one another before traveling to the ceremony, later to caravan to Brett's middle school football game which was scheduled for that afternoon—directly between the ceremony and the party, and, finally, back again that evening for the Everything Party.

Paul was ready for the change of command. He had practiced his farewell speech several times and was ready to do the official hand off to Lieutenant Colonel Joseph Peterson. He was also looking forward to a cold Samuel Adams Pale Ale by the fire later that night and catching up with friends and family, but he was most excited about being able to see Brett's football game. The hardest part of a deployment for him was missing out on his kids' sports and extra-curricular activities. He loved to cheer them on more than anything in the world—to say he was a proud father was an understatement.

Heidi was also excited to see her brother play. Today's game was the only one she would be able to attend this season since she normally had guitar practice after school—at the same time as his games. However, since she was missing school for the ceremony, her normally busy schedule was free. Heidi loved to support Brett whenever she could and was proud of his athletic prowess. He was quarterback and this felt like a big deal to her.

Jenna felt like a hamster running on a wheel to nowhere all day, spinning her wheels as she prepared for all the events of the day, but somehow everything was going smoothly. The only hiccup came just before Brett's game. Paul announced to everyone who had gathered at the Miller house, "Let's load up! It's time to go. We can caravan to Albritton Middle School. I'll lead, so if you are driving and unsure where to go, follow me."

Everyone—except Donna—scrambled to grab their purses, jackets, and keys and headed toward the front door.

Donna stood in the kitchen watching the other guests stream past her. She pulled Jenna aside and said, "I am extremely thirsty. I don't believe anyone offered me a drink when I arrived. Do you mind getting me something before we leave?"

Jenna suddenly felt like a poor hostess. It had been a very busy day and people had arrived at various times, so it was entirely possible she had failed to offer Donna a drink. This was a simple request—even if it was made at the exact moment the family needed to leave for Brett's game. They were already running late, and this would delay them even more, but she wanted to be hospitable.

Jenna quickly said, "I have sweet tea, unsweetened tea, lemonade, soda, juice, and water." She laughed and said, "I also have beer and wine if that's more to your liking. Bourbon and vodka are in the liquor cabinet!" Jenna thought to herself, *Lord knows, I could use a drink!*

Because of the party scheduled for later in the day, Jenna had more drink choices available than normal and felt like a waitress rattling off the menu. Unfortunately, she didn't have any ice though, because she had dumped her remaining stash into the trash can housing the keg that was going to be put to good use at the party that evening. She wanted to make sure it stayed cold because no one appreciated warm beer.

Jenna said, "I'm sorry I don't have any fresh ice, but all the drinks are cold in the garage refrigerator."

Donna became indignant there was no clean ice and arrogantly asked, "Is there a store close by where I can purchase a proper drink?"

Jenna thought, *are we seriously going to do this right now?* Jenna was normally an ice snob herself. She would drive ten miles out of her way for Diet Dr. Pepper from Sonic because nothing was better to a soda lover than a good fountain drink with crunchy ice in a Styrofoam cup. Diet Dr. Pepper was her one major vice she would probably never give up. Being a fellow ice aficionado, she could understand Donna wanting some, but not when it was an inconvenience to everyone else. Jenna would never choose ice over being at her son's game!

Being on Fort Bragg, the quickest option was the Shoppette, an on-post gas station, but you must be a military ID holder to make a purchase—which meant Tom and Donna could not go by themselves.

Donna's own personal needs were taking priority over Jenna's children, just as they did on their last visit in May. Jenna wanted to shove a solo cup filled with lukewarm tap water in her hand and say, "Get your butt in the car, we're going to be late to Brett's game!" But of course, she didn't. She wanted to appease Donna, so she instructed Heidi to accompany her grandfather and Donna to the Shoppette so she could get a "satisfactory" beverage. Heidi had a military ID and could make the purchase for them.

Heidi was very angry at this request because it meant she would be late to the one and only game she could attend because of ice! *Why did she have to be the one to go?* She didn't understand why Donna couldn't just grab a drink from the garage. She was also annoyed her mother catered to Donna's every whim. She was only a teenager but could recognize when someone was acting like a spoiled brat. Heidi knew if she had asked for a drink her mother would have said, "Seriously Heidi, you're not a princess. Get some water," and the conversation would have been over.

She tried to bottle up her aggravation, knowing she had no choice but to do as her mother asked. However, she became more noticeably angry when Donna selected a bottled drink from the cooler at the store and ironically did not choose a fountain drink with ice at all. Heidi screamed in her head, *are you kidding me?!?*

By the time the trio made it to the middle school, Heidi was clearly mad. Donna had a way of making steam pour out of peoples' ears, and Heidi was fuming. She ran off toward the game, which had started twenty minutes ago, leaving her grandfather and Donna behind.

The game was visible from the parking lot, but Donna made sure to point out Heidi's rudeness to Jenna when they finally made their way to the bleachers. She made it sound like they had been abandoned in the wilderness with no idea where to go, rather than deserted in a parking lot.

Jenna thought, *thank God you had a drink with you. Wouldn't want you to get dehydrated on your treacherous journey.* She said, "Oh Donna, I'm so sorry. Heidi was just so excited to see Brett play. Today's game is very important to her."

Donna replied, "I'm sorry you allow decency and manners to go out the window when your children are excited." She quickly turned her back to Jenna before she could say anything in return, an obvious signal a response would not be welcomed.

Pick. Poke. Taunt.

Jenna couldn't help but notice the much-needed drink that was more important than getting to her son's game on time was still three-quarters full when the time clock ran out after the fourth quarter. Cue ear smoke.

The rest of the day seemed to go by without any major issues and Jenna put the drink incident behind her. The whole ordeal was so absurd it didn't deserve any headspace. What did occupy her thoughts though, was the realization she could no longer deny Donna was very self-centered with little concern for anyone else's time or feelings. She wasn't progressing much on the learning curve. Jenna quickly shut down these ugly thoughts. She would not allow herself to let anything bother her today. *Today was a day of celebration!*

Several days after the Everything Party, Jenna learned others in attendance experienced minor run-ins with her dad's wife. She was surprised, but also not surprised.

Jenna's mother-in-law, Beverly Miller, told her she had gotten into a disagreement with Donna over some pictures. Apparently, while Jenna attended to her fifty-plus guests, Donna had leafed through the plethora of photo albums on the shelf underneath Jenna's coffee table, trying to figure out who was who in the Tom and Grace Jacobs family lineage. Donna asked Beverly if she knew who was on each page.

Bev had met most of the people pictured multiple times and was happy to answer her questions. After a few minutes of cordial discussion between the two women, Donna pointed to a picture of a tall man with light blond hair and a muscular build and said, "Who is this? It must be one of Tom's relatives. He is certainly good looking."

Beverly looked at the picture and said, "No, that is Mark. Grace's older brother. He was a very nice man. Unfortunately, he died a few years ago from a heart attack."

Donna refused to believe her. She was convinced it was not possible for the man in the photo to be blood related to Grace. She said, "Beverly, the man in that picture looks nothing like Grace. I'm sure you are making a mistake!"

When Beverly still insisted it was Grace's brother, Donna said curtly, "I have seen pictures of Mark when he was younger. There is no way that is him. This man is much too tall, more like a Jacobs, and Mark's hair was much darker. We will just have to agree to disagree. I will ask Tom." Donna turned the page of the album and loudly pointed out everyone she did know as if this somehow made Beverly even more wrong.

Donna also asked Bev more than a handful of probing questions about Grace, Grace's family, and even Jenna. The whole interaction disturbed Beverly because she couldn't help but feel there was malice behind Donna's incessant search for information.

Beverly laughed to herself when she saw Donna and Tom looking at the picture of Mark later that evening. She overheard Tom say, "I was only related to him by marriage. That was Grace's brother. He was a nice guy and a very good uncle to Katie and Jenna. I considered him a friend."

Donna glanced over at Beverly with a scowl on her face. She was angry she was wrong and even angrier Tom had liked him. She wondered, *weren't there any bad eggs in Grace's family? Every family must have at least one crazy uncle somewhere.*

Bev pretended she didn't see Donna glaring at her, but she inwardly felt a surge of satisfaction. She wanted to stick her tongue out at her like a child in the school yard and say, "nah-nanny-boo boo, I was right! You were wrong!" But instead, she gloated privately and poured herself a glass of chardonnay.

Donna also argued with Jenna's friend Ashley about military etiquette, even though Ashley was a veteran Army spouse of twenty-five plus years.

Ashley's husband, Nick, had also had a battalion command, like Paul, and had only recently transitioned to a new position. She had been to more change of command ceremonies in the past two years alone than she could count.

Donna, however, seemed to think she knew more in this instance as well, despite having no experience with the military. She completely disregarded Ashley's advice when she suggested it was improper for Tom and Donna to attend the incoming commander's reception.

Donna had the audacity to argue with Ashley. She said, "Lieutenant Colonel Peterson extended an invitation to everyone in attendance to come to his reception during his speech. Didn't you hear him say this? I for one would like to attend a formal military reception while we are here at Fort Bragg. Jenna and Paul are only doing something in their backyard tonight, similar to a child's birthday party. It doesn't seem like a fitting tribute for an officer."

Ashley explained, "Yes, I realize that. Paul had a formal reception when he took command, but tonight is all about fun." She continued, "For your information, it is also protocol for the incoming commander to invite everyone in his speech to his reception, but he doesn't really mean it, he's just being polite. Typically, only friends and family or members of the army or civilian forces who will be working with the new commander go. Peterson has to shake hands with enough people, extra guests he will have no affiliation with just prolong how long he has to stand there and smile."

She then pointed out Paul was still standing by the ceremony site where a large group of people had gathered so they could congratulate him on a successful command. Ashley said, "Donna, it really would be more appropriate for you to be among that crowd. Paul is your family."

Donna said, "Thank you for your advice, but I will figure things out for myself. It is unbearably hot today and I would much rather be in the air conditioning. Jenna and Paul haven't cared about any of their guest's comfort since we arrived." She walked away from Ashley indignantly without saying another word.

Ashley shook her head when she saw Tom and Donna entering Lieutenant Colonel Peterson's reception—and then exiting a few minutes later with a plate of cake in each of their hands.

Donna sought Ashley out at the Everything Party and said, "I just thought you should know, Tom and I went to the reception following the change of command, despite your recommendation we shouldn't. Lieutenant Colonel Peterson was very glad we were there. He and his wife shook our hands and sincerely thanked us for coming. He seems like a fine officer and was very attentive to everyone in attendance. Jenna and Paul could learn a lot from him." She paused for a few seconds and then said, "The cake he had was delicious, and there was lemonade and tea—with ice. It was much nicer than spending the afternoon sweating in a field."

Ashley responded, "Well, I'm glad you went then." She knew definitively at that moment she would never like Donna Thorn and she felt sorry Jenna was stuck with her for the rest of her life. Ashley surmised Donna liked rubbing elbows with people who she thought were important because it made her feel important. Being at Joe Peterson's reception made her feel like she was mingling in high society. He was a good guy without question, but his record certainly wasn't more impressive than Paul's, but Donna was too dumb to know this. She had no clue how highly regarded Paul was amongst his peers because he was humble by nature.

When Ashley relayed the story to Jenna weeks later, she said, "Your dad's wife sure is something!"

Brett also found it difficult to be around Donna for a different reason. Donna was obsessed with talking to him about girls. Every time she saw him, she would say, "Brett, I am determined to set you up with my friend's daughter! The two of you would be a perfect match!"

Brett told Jenna, "She makes me uncomfortable, Mom. Doesn't she know I am only a twelve-year-old kid? It's weird for an adult to try to be a matchmaker for seventh graders who don't even live in the same state. I never want to talk to her about girls again. I would rather talk about sports, music, school—anything else besides girls."

Jenna listened to everyone's stories but decided there was no need to bring any of them up to her dad. No one had been physically injured by any of Donna's selfish or off-putting behaviors, they had only been annoyed.

Trick or Treat

The day after the change of command ceremony was Halloween. Tom told Paul, "Donna and I will be leaving this afternoon, right after lunch. We are going to cut our visit short by one night. Sorry to say this, but we will not be here to see the kids Trick-or-Treat."

Donna wanted to visit her friend Angela, who lived in Statesboro, on their way home. Her friend was much younger than she was and had a son close to Heidi's age and a daughter close to Olivia's age. Jenna had met her at Tom and Donna's wedding and thought the friendship was an odd pairing, but when she learned how wealthy Angela was, it made more sense. Angela Phillips was the sole heir to an enormous railroad fortune. She had tremendous generational wealth and a reputation for being extremely generous.

Paul was very upset about this announcement and called Tom out for it. He said, "Tom, why would you want to spend Halloween with someone else's kids when you could spend it with your own grandchildren? Halloween used to be a family event when Grace was alive." He also said, "Tom, in case you haven't noticed, there seems to be an obvious shift in the family climate that needs to be addressed. Your biological family is playing second string to anything Donna requests. This should bother you deeply."

Paul's words resonated with Tom. He took a moment to remember past Halloweens. He and Grace had almost always celebrated the holiday at Katie's house. Grace would help the girls get in costume, and then, while Katie took them Trick-or-Treating, she and Tom would pass out candy every time the doorbell rang. When everyone returned home and the doorbell stopped chiming, they would eat pizza together and watch the girls dump their buckets for the yearly candy exchange. They would laugh at the negotiations the sisters would try to make. "I'll give you one Almond Joy for one Kit Kat." A trade none of the girls ever wanted to make. When no trade was made, they would happily pass the Almond Joy to their grandma because they knew it was Grace's favorite. She loved coconut. Then they would give their Pop Pop something with caramel.

Tom had nothing but fond memories of Halloween. Candy, costumes, laughter, grandchildren, and Grace.

He decided he would ask Donna if they could stay for the night and go to Angela's tomorrow. He wanted to reclaim one small slice of family normalcy and be with his own grandchildren on Halloween. Donna wasn't happy Tom wanted to stay, but she begrudgingly gave in, which Jenna took as a good sign she was coming around to the family.

Tom took pictures of Heidi, Brett, and Olivia in their costumes. Heidi was a movie star on the red carpet, Brett wore a Gilly suit so he could lay in the grass undetected and scare people, and Olivia was the cutest robot anyone had ever seen in her custom costume, designed and made by Paul.

Paul and Tom offered to walk with the kids from door to door and assigned their spouses to candy duty. Donna helped Jenna pass out candy to the hordes of children who flocked to Fort Bragg's Normandy neighborhood for Halloween. Together, they passed out hundreds of Snickers, Reese's, Dum Dum lollipops, and miniature boxes of Nerds. They had fun complimenting the trick or treaters' costumes, talking with their parents who strolled behind them, and seemed to both enjoy the festive feel of the evening.

There really was no better place to spend Halloween than on an Army post.

When the streets grew quiet because all the trick or treaters had gone home to sort their hauls, Tom and Donna said goodbye and headed for their hotel. They didn't stay for the Miller kids' candy swap, but they had participated in the evening, and it was appreciated.

The next morning, Mr. and Mrs. Jacobs left for Statesboro without stopping back by the house to say goodbye. Donna was anxious to get on the road and to get away from Jenna and her family. She had found the events of the previous evening unsufferable.

The Final, Final Straw

Nine months after the wedding, Katie made the difficult decision to try one more time to repair her relationship with Donna and her dad. She would give it one last ditch effort and hope for the best.

Against her better judgment, she invited them to a New Year's Eve party she was hosting. The party was very important to her because she wanted to commemorate her new life in Alabama and her wonderful new career. It seemed like the perfect occasion to celebrate her happiness and recent success as well as to make a fresh start with any relationships that had been strained.

Isn't that what New Year's is all about?

She had had almost no contact with her dad and Donna since she moved, and she was ready to try again. She missed her dad and so did her girls. Donna, not so much.

Tom was thrilled to be invited and was pleased when Donna offered to provide catering for the party as a gift to Katie. He believed this gesture was proof his new wife also wanted to try again with his daughter, despite the way she had been treated. He loved her forgiving nature. It didn't matter she would be paying with his money, they were married, and he considered all he had to be theirs. He had even added her name to his checking and savings accounts.

Katie thanked her for her offer, even though she was hesitant to accept, and told her she would be in touch with her soon so they could plan the menu.

She hoped she wouldn't come to regret this. Katie instinctively knew there was something other than generosity behind Donna's offer but wanted to believe she was being genuine, despite all the horrible things she had done to her in the past. She wanted to believe Donna, like her, also wanted a redo on their relationship.

Donna kept her real opinion about seeing Katie to herself. She didn't dare let Tom know she wasn't the least bit pleased the little brat had reached out to them again. She thought she had rid herself of her completely once she moved out of Georgia, but here she was again, like a stray cat who kept coming back looking for handouts. She would find a way to get rid of her permanently this time.

She was proud of herself for thinking to offer the catering so fast. She knew Katie would jump at the chance to spend her father's money. This would give her greater access to the planning of the event and the opportunity to talk to Katie by herself. She knew Tom would have no interest in interjecting himself into party planning. That was not an area of interest for him.

Working with her would give her more chances to get under Katie's skin. A little jab here. A little jab there. Her snide comments and subtle put downs had been highly effective when she and Tom were engaged, and she was positive they would work again. It should be easier this time because of their past history. She would ramp up the insults just a bit more, to be sure.

Pick. Poke. Taunt.

Donna needed to make sure Katie didn't find a way to sneak back into Tom's life. The old expression, "keep your friends close and your enemies closer," was exactly the approach she would be taking with her stepdaughter.

Life had been so nice since Katie was gone. They had the state of Georgia to themselves. No one was vying for Tom's money or attention on a daily basis except her, and she liked it that way. There had been no annoying children's activities to occupy their time and no Friday nights wasted sitting on hard, metal bleachers. If she could keep Katie out of their lives, she would be halfway through her plan of making the prenup null and void.

Mama Bear

If only she could get rid of Jenna too. She had suffered through two trips to North Carolina in the last nine months since she wed Tom. At least Jenna and her family lived far away. The principle of "out of sight, out of mind" was easily applied. Donna's plan to chase her away completely was already underway.

She laughed to herself when she thought of Jenna's facial expression when she told her she would never marry a soldier because they were sure to be mentally ill. She had expected her to argue with her, but her ability to stay poised was impressive. She had stronger powers of restraint than she expected. She looked forward to testing her limits. Everyone had their breaking point. Even perfect little Army wives.

Donna had figured out very quickly Jenna was a mama bear when it came to her children. Mess with them and you quickly get on her bad side. Poking a mama bear usually resulted in anger and retaliation, which she welcomed. If she could just provoke Jenna enough, her self-control would go out the window. This was exactly what she wanted to happen. She was determined she would get that mama bear to come out of her den. She would happily play the victim of a bear attack if it got rid of Jenna and her children, especially that imp Heidi, who was intolerable.

Donna knew she had turned the tide in her favor by continuously harping on the fact that Tom didn't receive a Father's Day gift. She had said repeatedly to him, "Tommy, I am so sorry your girls don't respect you enough to even think of you one day a year, especially since you have done so much for them." She continued to make comments like this until he agreed with her that he had been rudely slighted, especially by his youngest daughter who he still had a good relationship with.

He hadn't cared one bit at first, but over time he adopted her way of thinking. He even believed her when she convinced him Jenna had not acknowledged Father's Day two years in a row. Tom had forgotten about the call in the airport and The Rainbow Run the year before. Donna made sure not to remind him.

With just a little more time, both girls would be out of the picture forever.

Right now, though, it is time to focus on Katie. She was a bird in the hand.

Party Planning and Paybacks

Shortly after Donna made the offer to pay for the catering for Katie's New Year's Eve party, she began calling her ad nauseum with endless questions just to get on Katie's nerves. It was fun constantly reminding her how generous she was.

It became quickly apparent to Katie that Donna's gift was more about controlling the menu—and her—than being generous. She was sorry she had accepted the offer.

Donna could tell she was annoying Katie. *Perfect.* She purposely took issue with almost every food Katie wanted to serve and insisted on creating a menu that would satisfy her own dietary preferences. She reminded Katie repeatedly since she was the one paying, she should have the final say. She also scolded her for being inconsiderate again when it came to her food requirements and said her lack of appreciation was disrespectful.

She said, "Katie, I hate to even bring this up, but didn't you learn anything about hospitality after the unfortunate chicken incident many months ago?"

Katie wanted to go off on her. Major ear smoke. However, instead of losing her temper and telling her off, she decided it would be best if she just politely asked Donna to hold off on making any catering arrangements until she had more time to devote to menu planning. She said, "Let's just table planning the food for a while. I have more pressing details to work out first."

Donna was displeased with this request. *How dare she put off someone who was being so generous? No one else was offering to foot her bill.*

Katie booked a large, beautiful log cabin in the Appalachian Mountains for the event and encouraged Tom and Donna to book the smaller one next door from the same leasing company. Katie was trying to be considerate because she knew her father didn't like to drive after dark. If Tom and Donna's lodging was within walking distance of the party, it would be easier for them because they wouldn't have to traverse dark mountain roads at night.

Although the contract said, "no parties," Katie was unconcerned because she was only inviting a small group of people—her closest friends and family. This would not be a rager like a fraternity party. It was going to be an intimate affair with only responsible parties in attendance. She was confident there would be no damage, and the leasing company would be none the wiser if she had a few people over.

Donna hadn't bothered to familiarize herself with the terms of the contract since Tom was the one who signed the leasing agreement for the property they were renting. She had been content to let him handle the paperwork and the deposit while she focused on harassing Katie. However, when Katie mentioned the "no party clause" to her and asked her not to disclose any information about the gathering to the leasing agent, Donna became more than a little interested in the terms of the contract. This was the information she needed to make sure this event would never get past the planning phase. She didn't really want to spend the money on it anyway.

She had been eyeing a beautiful designer bag at Nordstrom's and thought that would be a better use of Tom's cash. The purse was an investment piece she could enjoy for much longer.

Donna assured Katie she wouldn't need to call the leasing agency if Katie remained in constant communication with her. She viewed this statement as a clear warning. It wasn't her fault if Katie didn't take heed.

Donna's initial plan had been to make working with her so unbearable Katie would run away—and this time—never return. She had only hoped to be able to tell Tom nothing had changed between them, and Katie was just too difficult to manage. However, she now had a better idea that would yield much better results. *Thank you, Katie!*

Donna was still so angry at Katie for refusing to take wedding photos and equated the short episode after the ceremony with purposely ruining her entire wedding. Caroline's incessant sobbing and Katie's coddling of her had been an embarrassment. *How dare they cry over Grace at her wedding!*

She was also sure Katie was the sole reason their wedding wasn't featured in any of Atlanta's society pages. The columnists must have witnessed the scene where her stepdaughter dramatically took the hysterical junior bridesmaid away, leaving the bride and groom standing in the garden with only a portion of their wedding party. She was sure they found the display uncivilized. There was no other possible explanation. She had scoured every magazine and newspaper in Georgia for two weeks after their wedding before she finally gave up.

Donna had been determined to get revenge one way or another since her wedding day. She vowed her stepdaughter's disrespect would not go unanswered. It was now time to deliver the punishment. As the Bible says, "An eye for an eye." This time it would simply be "a wedding for a New Year's Eve party." She felt it was biblically justified, and she looked forward to getting revenge.

After her conversation with Katie about the "no party clause," Donna promptly asked Tom for a copy of the contract. She told him she needed it in case the caterer had any questions about the event space for the leasing agent. She also told him she was having so much fun helping Katie plan the event. She said, "Tommy, I feel like a schoolgirl on the prom committee!" She assured him she was getting along great with Katie and they both looked forward to their daily chats. She proudly reported, "We have moved on from the problems of the past!"

She wasn't completely lying because she was having fun—trying to destroy the relationship with her stepdaughter once and for all—and she was moving on from the problems of the past by getting rid of her forever!

Tom, who had no idea about Katie's request to hold off on planning, or his wife's scheming, was pleased to see Donna so enthralled with helping his daughter plan her party. He willingly gave her the contract without any further thought and went into the den to check the stock market for the second time that day. He didn't have a care in the world at that moment, other than the Dow Jones Industrial Average.

Donna called Katie twelve times over the next week, and after the third call, Katie stopped answering the phone. Donna left long messages on her voicemail every time she didn't pick up the phone, which Katie simply deleted without listening to first.

In the final voicemail that Katie never played, Donna said, "Katie, your refusal to speak to me is ill-mannered. You have left me no choice but to call the leasing agent for information since you don't have the decency to answer my questions. It is imperative I get details about the property so I will be prepared when you finally let me hire a caterer. I have narrowed it down to two choices. Of course, the one I am leaning toward is the most expensive one in the area. I should think you would be interested in booking as quickly as possible before someone else snatches them up!"

Without giving Katie time to listen to the message (which she wouldn't have anyway) or respond (which she wouldn't have either), Donna picked up the phone again and immediately dialed the leasing department number listed on the contract.

They, unlike Katie, answered on the first ring.

Donna made small talk with them for a moment, telling them who she was and what date her check-in was, providing all the standard information. She then said, "I am actually calling to ask you some questions about the property next door. You know, the larger cabin." She emphasized the word "larger". She continued, "I am paying for the catering for my daughter's New Year's Eve party that is going to be held there, and I want to be sure I have all the information I might need to share with caterers and invited guests." And just to be sure her point was made, she said, "What fun would a New Year's Eve party be without good company and good food? I even suggested she hire a band!" Her purposeful remarks made Katie's intimate gathering sound like a large-scale event. She was also lying about the band suggestion. She and Katie had never talked about music. Not even once.

Management immediately took this to mean there was going to be a big party, which violated the contract. They informed her they were going to cancel Katie's reservation. Donna pretended to be upset, but she was silently celebrating on the other end of the line. It looked like she would now be free to make New Year's Eve plans with her friends. She had a killer new black jumpsuit she couldn't wait to show off. It had just the right amount of sparkle and would be perfect for ringing in the New Year. Of course, she would need to make a nail appointment. She couldn't wait to get the deposit on the cabin back, the Nordstrom's handbag was calling her name! It was fate!

The leasing manager's reaction was even better than Donna had hoped for. Katie did not deserve a nice party after she ruined her entire wedding day, and this was the payback she deserved. *Karma.*

Donna decided she would play dumb about the whole situation. She would continue to act excited about the party until Tom received the news about the cancellation directly from Katie. At that point, she would act shocked and pretend to be heartbroken. Then in the next breath, she would remind Tom his daughter was willingly trying to break the rules, just as she had when she was a teenager. She would say, "Tommy, it was unreasonable for Katie to believe she could get away with such a violation of the contract. This whole fiasco is her fault. She will have to accept responsibility for her own actions."

Donna was confident Katie would blame her but didn't care—not even a little bit. *Revenge was sweet.* She knew she would be able to masterfully spin this as another unprovoked attack against her. She would cry and demand Tom answer her when she asked, "How many times must I be blamed for your daughter's wrath and poor decisions?" She would also remind him she had done nothing but devote her time and resources to trying to make her party a success.

As she worked the impending confrontation out in her mind, she decided she would end her dramatic monologue with something like, "Katie is so selfish, she is only willing to talk to me when she is getting something from me or spending your money." She was confident her husband would take her side. *He would have no other choice.*

For now, she would just sit back and wait for it all to hit the fan.

You're Canceled

Two days later, the leasing company called Katie to inform her that her reservation was being canceled due to a flagrant disregard of the contract. They refused to make any concessions, even after she explained it was not going to be a big party.

They said, "A rule is a rule for a reason."

Katie was furious and knew without a shadow of a doubt this was happening because of Donna's direct doing. She had been purposely sabotaged because there was no other logical explanation. There would be no more attempts to reconcile with her. She was officially done with her stepmother.

She wondered, *how many times must someone be hurt before they finally walk away forever?* She answered herself, "This many times."

Katie called her father to tell him what happened. Tom could tell she was crying on the other end of the line, and it was obvious she was blaming his wife for the unfortunate turn of events.

Donna, who was standing next to him when he answered, acted surprised to hear the news. Katie began to sob louder, and this was Donna's cue to perform her reaction exactly as she planned.

Tom was once again stuck in the middle with no idea what to do. His daughter was crying on one end of the phone and his wife was now crying on the other.

Fearing his wife's temper would overshadow her tears if he tried to comfort Katie, he made the decision to lecture his daughter for violating the contract. He said into the phone, "I'm sorry this happened Katie, but you need to take responsibility for your actions. Blaming Donna for your problems is unfair."

Tom knew Donna could hear every word he was saying, and he needed to appear to be fully on her side or risk her being angry with him for days. Christmas was coming up soon and he didn't want his only gift from his wife to be the silent treatment. He secretly planned to call Katie later from his car and tell her how truly sorry he was this all happened, but he did believe his wife was innocent—mostly.

After he hung up, he told Donna he needed to go to the store and would be back soon. He mumbled something about needing nails. When he backed out of the driveway, he called Katie on his Bluetooth. Something told him he needed to listen to what she had to say. So, for the first time since he met Donna, he asked Katie to explain to him why she had such a visceral dislike for his wife. He then listened to her lengthy list of complaints calmly without interruption.

And for once, Katie thought her dad might care. She invited him to come to her house for New Year's Eve since there was not going to be any sort of official celebration anymore and made it clear Donna was not welcome. She told him Jenna was also coming because the party had been canceled, and she thought it would be a good time for the three of them to talk about how to move forward as a family.

Tom agreed this was a good idea and told her he would come alone, without Donna. He knew his relationships with his daughters, particularly Katie, needed attention. They had only just reconnected, and he feared losing her again. He also thought it was time to send Donna a message his family was important, and he would expect compromise from everyone. It was time he stood up for his family.

He still wrongly believed none of the drama that had transpired had anything to do with him and he wished for the thousandth time Grace was here. If she were, he would never be in this position.

Following his phone conversation with Katie, Tom called Jenna. He relayed his conversation with Katie and how she had accused his wife of purposely sabotaging her event as retaliation against her for "ruining" the wedding. Katie had also accused her of trying to destroy his relationship with his daughters.

Tom said, "I can't understand why Katie would think Donna would do this. Jenna, my wife is not a vindictive person. She is a loving, Christian woman who wants nothing but harmony in the family. It isn't even rational to think someone would purposely try to wreck a family, particularly when she chose to marry into it." However, in an unusual moment of wanting to be fair to Katie's feelings, Tom asked Jenna, "Have you ever seen any concerning behavior from my wife?"

Finally, after all these months of bottling up her observations, Jenna told him about all the things Donna had done that bothered her. From the nastygram text, to not attending the kids' sports events, to not being able to drink a glass of lemonade without ice. Everything came out like water from a garden hose on full blast. She confirmed all of Katie's complaints and agreed with her it seemed his wife wanted them out of his life. Jenna said, "I'm sorry to say it Dad, but I believe Donna's actions are purposeful and calculated."

Tom was shocked at Jenna's accusations, which mirrored her older sister's. However, for the first time, he paused to consider what he was hearing and realized there was some truth in what they were saying. He had no choice but to agree he, too, had noticed some unfavorable behaviors from his new wife toward his family but hadn't wanted to admit it. He could no longer deny some of the alarm bells he had heard ringing. They were loud and clear.

Jenna, still feeling hopeful everything could be resolved, told her father, "I am willing to forgive Donna for everything because she has a learning curve to overcome. Coming into a family like ours can't be easy." She continued, "She needs time to figure out how to be a stepmother and step grandmother. I'm sure if we all offer her a little patience and grace, she will figure it out."

Jenna hung up the phone, thinking they'd had a productive conversation, and looking forward to a visit with her dad and sister over New Year's.

Telling Secrets

Rather than keeping his newly gleaned information to himself, Tom hung up the phone and immediately went to find his wife. He didn't believe married couples should keep secrets from one another—unless it was for self-preservation. He told Donna everything Jenna and Katie had said.

Donna became infuriated Tom entertained any of this nonsense for even a second. She said, "Your daughters have been out to get me since day one!" She continued her tirade, "I demand you cut off ties with them, and I forbid you from going to Alabama for New Year's." She screamed again for emphasis, "I. Forbid. You!" *How dare she be attacked by his ungrateful, spoiled children, and how dare her husband attempt to appease them again! They didn't accept her, and she considered them toxic. It was time he stood up for her.*

Tom was completely befuddled by her reaction and the rage that ensued. He didn't know what to do to calm her or to rectify the situation. He knew things were going badly, but it all seemed out of his control.

When Donna sensed he was conflicted, she screamed, "If you go to see your daughters, I will divorce you!"

The words hit him like a ton of bricks. *Wasn't marriage supposed to be about sticking it out in good times and in bad times?* However, seeing his wife completely unhinged, he feared she was telling the truth.

Wanting to save his marriage, he quickly decided the best course of action was to assure Donna he would not be visiting his daughters over New Year's and agree with everything she said. He just kept repeating, "Yes, dear." He thought it would help him get out of the doghouse a little faster if he even added a little fuel to the fire and made a few negative remarks about both Katie and Jenna—to make it look like he was completely on Donna's side. His daughters weren't there to hear what he was saying, so it didn't matter if he threw them into the flames. They would never find out.

Donna was pleased to hear his decision but was still mad. She knew he was in a vulnerable state, so she took the opportunity to inform him he would be taking a break from his children so he could focus on his marriage. She said, "This is an order, not a request." She paused briefly, as if trying to figure out what to say next, then continued, "If you love me at all Tom Jacobs, you will do exactly as instructed. Your children's disrespectful attitudes are destroying our relationship. We would be better off without them!"

She faked weakness in her legs and said, "I am retiring to bed to lie down because this situation has caused me to feel physically ill. Your children are now affecting my health too." She then said, "When you try to defend your daughters, who have been so willfully awful to me, it makes me feel like you don't even love me. You do realize withholding love is emotionally abusive and reminds me of my ex-husband."

With that statement, rooted in manipulation, she went into the bedroom and shut the door.

THE MATRIARCH

Tom was left dumbstricken and feeling awful. *Did his wife really believe he was abusive? This wasn't the first time she had made this accusation.*

He couldn't see that Donna, on the other side of the door, had picked up her phone and was casually scrolling through Pinterest looking for passive aggressive quotes about getting rid of toxic people. Her dramatic performance had ended the moment she entered the room. She settled onto the bed and got comfortable. She would be sure to post some of these quotes on Facebook later, so Tom would know she was still upset.

As a bonus, all her friends would think she was being victimized, and they would have to assume it was by Tom's hateful, selfish daughters. She would get a lot of pity. Social media certainly had some advantages, and she planned to use it to publicly build a case against Katie and Jenna.

Now It's Personal

Donna felt confident she was the victor in the whole New Year's Eve party debacle because the party was canceled, and Tom was forbidden from going to Alabama. Even though she came out on top, she couldn't help but keep obsessing over the things Jenna had said about her to Tom over the phone.

She hadn't expected Jenna to launch an attack against her.

The more she thought about it, the angrier she became because it was clear Jenna had it out for her. How dare she insinuate Donna needed to "learn" how to be a stepmother or step grandmother. It was insulting. She clearly had no respect for her father or for her—and she had no room to talk. She certainly wasn't perfect. She couldn't even get a gift in the mail on time.

Donna was confident she wouldn't hear from Katie again but wasn't so sure Jenna would go away as easily. For the sake of her own sanity, it was time to get rid of her. *Enough with the games.* Anyone who dared to assassinate her character was toxic and had no place in her life or her husband's. Jenna's words were verbally abusive to Donna, even though she never said anything directly to her, and she would not tolerate being treated so poorly. She had originally wanted her gone solely for financial reasons, but now it was personal.

Conspiracy Theories and Cuss Words

Donna decided it was imperative she let Jenna know she was no longer welcome in her life. It was time to "break up" with her stepdaughter. She planned to compose a letter, outlining all the horrible things Jenna had done to her and Tom. There would be no way for her to deny anything if it was on paper in black and white. Jenna would have no choice but to admit her faults and retreat. *Good riddance.*

Donna preferred to write letters over talking because she could control the dialogue. She made a firm decision she would never speak to Jenna again and would not put herself in a position to be verbally assaulted.

Donna spent hours looking at Jenna's Facebook posts for any signs of character flaws, rereading emails she sent to Tom in case there were any signs of disrespect—she was glad she knew her husband's passwords—and even pouring through phone bills so she could point out how selfish it was of Jenna not to call her father on his birthday until eight o'clock at night.

Donna wrote at a feverish pace, admonishing Jenna once again for completely ignoring her dad on Father's Day, for allowing Heidi to treat her so poorly, for not being hospitable and providing guests with drinks, for being selfish and expecting her to attend to her every scheduling whim. She questioned her parenting techniques and her character. She told her she should be embarrassed by her behavior and should feel deeply ashamed.

Donna poured out pages and pages of accusations about Jenna and supposed very hateful things, even though they had no basis. As she wrote, she convinced herself Jenna was under the influence of the devil, trying to destroy the life she was building with Tom. Because of this, she felt it necessary to cite every Bible verse she could about how unchristian-like it was for Jenna to be so nasty to her and her father. Every verse she chose reflected favorably upon herself and was meant to shame her stepdaughter.

She would not acknowledge Jenna had bought her lovely Mother's Day and birthday gifts, had invited her to her home on numerous occasions, or had tried her hardest to be a good hostess. None of that mattered because she was evil. No number of fake niceties could make up for her real agenda, which was to see her father divorced. She was convinced this was Jenna's true goal because she was an entitled brat who wouldn't want to see anyone else happy. She probably wanted all her father's money, too, which is why she never even tried to accept Donna as part of the family.

Donna systematically twisted every encounter she ever had with Jenna to make it appear she was the most inconsiderate human being who ever lived. By the time she was done writing, she believed every word she had written. She had created a convincing conspiracy theory about the true nature of Tom's youngest daughter. With as much as she had written, it was hard to believe she had only seen Jenna five times in her entire life. Someone reading the letter would have assumed they had decades of history.

She shared her letter with Tom and made it clear he was in no position to argue with her if he wanted to have a wife by his side in the morning.

Tom quickly adopted her conspiracy theories and played the part of supportive husband. He even helped her think of things to add to her letter to please his wife. He especially loved to look for Bible verses. He knew defending his daughter would ruin his relationship with Donna, and he wasn't willing to take that risk. *He would never go back to the silence.*

When she was finally satisfied she had addressed every issue in her letter, she placed it in the mailbox. Upon her return to the house, she announced, "I never wish to hear the names Katie or Jenna again. As far as I am concerned, they are bad words. The worst of the worst. Just so you fully understand me, the K word and the J word are far worse to me than the F word."

Tom had accepted Grace was a bad word, and now he had to add his daughters to the list. *What had he allowed to happen?*

If he had been a swearing kind of man, he would have rattled a few real ones off.

Merry Christmas

Jenna had no idea her father had shared the details of their conversation with Donna, and therefore, did not know about Donna's rage directed at her. She also never suspected Donna had demanded Tom cut ties with his daughters. Rather, she was still hoping for complete resolution in the family and had an expectation her father would handle the whole situation diplomatically now that he had information from both sides. She was looking forward to seeing him at Katie's and moving forward.

For the time being, she needed to focus on packing. She and Paul were taking the children on a trip for Christmas to Massanutten, Virginia. After the long deployment, they were ready for a family vacation and for some fun.

Their plan was to arrive in Virginia on December sixteenth, Brett's birthday, and stay until Christmas Day. They would spend Christmas morning at the resort, then pack the car and head for home. They would do a quick turnaround and leave the day after Christmas for Katie's house in Alabama. Paul and the kids would make sure to give her space once they were there so she could have some alone time with her sister and dad. They would stay in Alabama until the second of January.

The trip to Massanutten was exactly what the doctor ordered for the Millers, and they all agreed it was their best vacation ever. Olivia learned to snow ski, Heidi got her hair and nails done at the spa, and Brett loved indoor surfing at the water park. They had traveled to nearby Luray Caverns and ate at a variety of amazing restaurants. Santa even found them at the resort.

They were all sad to leave, but once all the gifts were opened, they knew it was time to head for home. Jenna tried to call her dad on speakerphone from the car to wish him and Donna a Merry Christmas. No answer. She called several more times, but each time her call routed directly to voicemail. The fourth time she called, she began to get concerned. She couldn't believe her dad wouldn't want to talk to his family on Christmas Day. She was worried something was wrong.

When they finally pulled into their driveway at Fort Bragg after their long trip home, they unloaded the car and headed into the house with Chinese takeout for Christmas dinner. They had all laughed hysterically when they realized they would be eating Sesame Chicken, Lo Mein, and egg rolls instead of turkey and stuffing, but it was the only place that was open, so they would have to make do.

Jenna decided to check the mail before going into the house because she wanted to be sure she paid any bills that might be due before they left again. As she walked toward the front door, she casually flipped through the large stack that had accumulated since they were gone.

Junk mail, junk mail, junk mail.

And then she saw it—an envelope with her name on it and Donna's name on the return address, Mrs. Thomas E. Jacobs. An unsettling feeling washed over her, and she knew she was about to find out why her father wouldn't answer the phone on Christmas Day.

As she read through the lengthy letter filled with lies, fabricated stories, and completely inaccurate interpretations of the truth, she became increasingly upset. She was being portrayed as a villain, even though she knew in her heart she had always tried to offer Donna grace and understanding.

Jenna had much to do before they could leave again but she couldn't concentrate on any of the tasks she needed to complete. She couldn't get the letter off her mind, so she stayed up until four o'clock in the morning crafting a response.

Donna's sharp words were like an arrow piercing her heart. Jenna was wounded badly, but even amid her pain, she tried to leave room for potential reconciliation. In her response, she pointed out every single inaccuracy of Donna's letter and attempted to set the record straight with the truth.

When she was finally satisfied with her response, she emailed it to Donna and went to bed where she tossed and turned. She didn't sleep a wink.

The next day, the Millers traveled from North Carolina to Katie's house in Alabama, and only upon their arrival did they learn Tom would not be joining them as planned. He had waited until the last possible moment to tell them of his decision. It was a devastating blow to his girls. He had made his choice. He would stand by Donna no matter what the cost was to his family.

Jenna learned Katie had also received a hateful letter from Donna. However, Katie had tossed her letter into the trash after reading only the first sentence. She no longer cared what Donna had to say and wouldn't waste another minute on her. She was done with Donna Thorn Jacobs and was at peace with her decision. She was also done with Thomas Eric Jacobs, formally known as Dad.

Jenna wished she could be more like her sister but still hoped, somehow, everything could be worked out. She wasn't ready to let go. It didn't seem right to walk away from her father, and she was sure her mother would have wanted her to continue trying to repair the relationship.

Just before Paul and Jenna turned in for the night, Jenna heard her email inbox ding on her phone, indicating she had a new message. Even though she was exhausted, since she hadn't slept at all the night before and they had driven such a long way today, she decided to check it before turning off the light. She was shocked to see there was an email from Donna. She had not expected a response so quickly from her. She wasn't sure if she had expected any response.

It was a short message calling her "toxic" and telling her she would have no contact with her ever again. She was also blocking Jenna from her Facebook page. The email instructed Jenna not to contact her father because they were working on their marriage and trying to repair the damage she had caused.

Jenna stared at the message in disbelief. She had hoped her email to Donna would correct some wrongs and open the door for communication, not end the relationship entirely. The pile of misunderstandings and hurt feelings was getting bigger and bigger, and Jenna had no idea what this would mean for the future.

She forwarded the email to her father in case he hadn't seen it. She was surprised when she received an almost immediate response. He asked her not to call him or attempt to contact him again. He was hopeful they could work everything out eventually, but, for now, he needed to focus on Donna and his marriage. He signed off with "Love, Dad."

Jenna wondered what her mother would think about all of this if she could see what was happening here on Earth. She was pretty sure she could hear her turning over in her grave.

Confessions

Several weeks went by after that ill-fated email from Donna with no word from her father, and Jenna began to wonder if she would ever hear from him again.

When he finally called, he expressed his remorse for all that happened. It was clear he was not in a good place.

He said, "Hello, Jenna. I'm calling you from the car because I cannot let Donna know I am reaching out to you. She would be furious if she found out."

She sensed exhaustion in her father's voice, and she felt bad for him. He sounded like he had aged ten years since they last spoke.

He said, "Tensions have been very high between me and Donna, and we have been fighting continuously." He then said, "Jenna, my marriage is in trouble."

Tom could not understand how someone who was supposed to love him would demand he never see his daughters again. Anytime he tried to bring up the topic for discussion, Donna would become extremely angry and lose her temper. The mere mention of Jenna's name was enough to set her off for days. He said, "You won't believe this, but your name is considered a bad word in our house, Katie's too." Tom said, "I feel like I am always walking on eggshells around my wife. I'm terrified of disagreeing with her over anything, especially if it concerns my family. She threatens to divorce me any time my opinion differs from hers." He even confided in Jenna, "things have not been this bad between us since I asked her to sign a prenuptial agreement."

Jenna was shocked after hearing his last statement. *What prenuptial agreement?*

Her immediate response though, was to keep quiet and let him keep talking. She put her hand over her mouth to make sure she didn't speak. He needed someone to vent to who would keep his words in confidence. It was obviously difficult for him to admit his marriage was anything less than perfect. Tom Jacobs never admitted anything.

Jenna had no idea a prenuptial agreement existed and felt Donna's negative reaction to it was a giant red flag. Her dad had kept this information to himself because he knew his daughters would question his wife's motives. He only now let it slip accidentally. Suddenly, it was very clear to Jenna why Donna wanted Tom's family out of his life. In addition to being selfish and controlling, she was also a gold digger.

Tom said, "Anytime I disagree with Donna, she has a meltdown of ridiculous proportions and accuses me of being emotionally abusive. She questions my love for her and compares me to her ex-husband." He continued, "Jenna, you can't imagine how deeply hurtful this is for me."

Donna had yelled at Tom so often he began to question whether her ex-husband was really the emotionally abusive one in the relationship or if it was her. He had even gone so far as to look up her divorce records online and saw Todd Thorn was the one who had filed for the dissolution of marriage, not Donna.

Other than one handwritten comment in the margin by Donna, there was no mention of abuse anywhere in the document. None of it made sense to him based on the things Donna had told him. Her story and the facts didn't match up.

He also shared with his daughter his wife had a long line of broken relationships behind her and, ironically, never seemed to be at fault for any of the fractures. He said, "I see a pattern, and I am concerned."

It was clear his confessions were pouring out like water from a broken dam, and he couldn't hold them back.

When he finally took a breath, he realized his venting had exposed more than he intended. He informed Jenna his priority was saving his marriage. Because of this, it was going to be important for him to keep his distance from her for a while longer. He said, "Although none of this is directly your fault, I have no other choice but to put our relationship on hold until I get in a better place with Donna." He said, "Do not expect any more calls anytime soon."

Jenna now knew what Katie meant when she said she felt like a pariah. She felt like one too. He blamed her for all his marital problems without blaming her for all his marital problems.

Before he hung up the phone, he said, "I have lost all hope of ever reconciling with Katie because she refuses to answer any phone calls, emails, or letters. There is too much damage to overcome."

Jenna had spoken to her sister and knew this was true.

More Confessions

Over the next nine months, Jenna only occasionally heard from her father if he was able to sneak in a phone call to her when he was not in Donna's company. Time was not softening Donna's disdain for her stepdaughter.

In the few sporadic conversations they had, Jenna was able to see her father was desperately unhappy and felt completely under Donna's control. Even innocent comments he made set her off. He had to be careful about every word that came out of his mouth.

He said, "Say the wrong thing and you accidentally start World War III." One time, Donna had asked him to slice some carrots and zucchini for her while she was cooking. He had been happy to oblige, but as he started cutting, he remembered there was a kitchen gadget that could make the job easier. He said, "Don't we have a vegetable chopper?" He began to open kitchen cabinets looking for it.

She flew into an extreme bout of rage.

He quickly realized his mistake. He had owned a vegetable chopper with Grace, not Donna. His use of the word "we" was incendiary and the cause of her tirade. Any reference to his life with his first wife was strictly prohibited, and he had unintentionally violated her rule. Even though it had been an honest mistake, and he meant no harm, he had to deal with the ramifications of her anger for the rest of the evening.

Tom knew if he broke any of Donna's rules, even if it wasn't on purpose, he would have to suffer the consequences.

In addition to not being allowed to mention Grace, he wasn't allowed to visit her grave either. He admitted to Jenna in one of his secret phone calls he lied to his wife once about attending a conference in Atlanta with his church men's group so he could sneak over to the cemetery in Peachtree City where Grace was buried. All he wanted was to make sure the silk flowers on her grave were not overly faded. He only needed five minutes to go to the graveside, but this was against the rules. It seemed unreasonable to him that Donna, after all this time, still felt so threatened by a woman who was dead. She wasn't coming back. Ever.

They were all painfully aware of this fact.

He also confessed to Jenna that Donna believed if he even acknowledged Grace ever existed, it meant he loved her less. It was ridiculous logic and was difficult for Tom to grapple with.

Jenna asked her dad if he still planned to be buried next to her mom when he died. His name was already carved on the grave marker. He pretended he didn't hear her and skipped over the question completely. His avoidance gave Jenna an uneasy feeling, and she didn't know what to make of it.

Tom also revealed he was becoming increasingly concerned about his wife's mental health because she seemed to be extremely paranoid and convinced everyone was against her, particularly Jenna. He didn't know what to do when she worked herself into a tizzy or why she felt this way. She had an uncontrollable temper and could act like she was going mad.

However, when she wasn't worked up or being paranoid, she was a joy to be around and the woman he fell in love with. She was worth fighting for, and he couldn't bear the thought of losing her. His vows required him to be her husband until they were parted by death.

Jenna wondered to herself, *is it really the thought of losing her or the thought of being alone again that bothers him more?*

New Houses, New Beginnings

Major changes were happening in the Miller family—and for Tom and Donna—between Christmas and the following August, but they rarely knew what was going on in each others' lives because of limited communication. Jenna sent gifts though, because, God forbid, she miss another holiday.

Jenna celebrated the big four-o at Fort Bragg. Paul pulled off a huge surprise party with all of Jenna's friends and family in attendance, except of course for her dad and Donna. Olivia, Heidi, and Brett were all promoted with honors to the next grade, and most significantly, the family moved from North Carolina to Annandale, Virginia, so they could be closer to the National War College where Paul would be a student.

Their new town was only thirty minutes from Fort McNair in Washington, DC, Paul's official new duty station. He was looking forward to having a much less stringent work schedule than he had at Fort Bragg and more time to be home with the family. It was only an eleven-month assignment, and the family was excited to be close to so many national landmarks. There was so much to see in a short period of time.

In addition to playing tourist in their new town, Jenna and Paul wanted to maintain the routine of their normal lives. Consistency was important for the children and helped them transition to a new home and town more easily. Brett had already tried out for travel lacrosse, making the team. Heidi slid into the lead guitar position for the band at their new church, and Olivia enrolled in gymnastics at a gym just down the road from their rental house. They all liked their schools and were making friends in the first few weeks after moving. They were resilient children and it showed with their quick adjustment.

As Jenna reflected on the upcoming months, she knew their time in the DC area would be important. Heidi was a senior and would be graduating from high school. She was already applying to college. Her first-choice school was the University of North Florida. She loved how close it was to historic St. Augustine and Jacksonville's beaches and was impressed with its religious studies program. Ironically, the university was only a little over an hour away from St. Simon's Island. Perhaps if she went there, she would be able to reconnect with her grandfather and there would be an improvement in their situation.

This would be the last year the Miller family would all be together consistently under the same roof. Jenna was glad they would be in such an incredible place. She was sure it would be quite a change for the family when Heidi moved out and into a dormitory. Sure, the bathroom would be cleaner, the driveway less congested, and the house quieter—but she knew she would miss her terribly. It wouldn't be the same without her.

Tom and Donna had also been busy since Christmas, building their dream house on the intracoastal waterway in St. Simon's Island. When they weren't looking at blueprints or picking out furniture, they spent a tremendous amount of time cultivating deeper relationships with Donna's friends. Most of Tom's friends were still in Peachtree City or Atlanta, and he saw them less and less. It brought Donna great joy to be around her friends, and Tom liked to see her happy.

They were looking forward to having a housewarming party to show off their home to their friends and extended family. It had just been completed and they were almost moved in. Donna's house was finally on the market, and they expected it to sell quickly for a good price. Of course, Donna would bank this money, but Tom didn't mind. He was very pleased to get rid of it, so they could finally start the new life they planned together.

It had been a tumultuous time lately for them, because of the drama with his family, and he hoped a fresh start in the Dom House would be a turning point for their marriage. Things did seem to be slowly improving.

Tom noted the real turning point for them came when he added her name to the deed for their new home. He wanted her to know she was his equal partner in life, and this was an easy way to show her. This gesture meant a lot to Donna and she cried tears of joy when he showed her the official paperwork. Her reaction touched his heart.

Mr. and Mrs. Jacobs were proud of the beautiful white-and-gray swirled marble floors, bright white walls, the breathtaking view of the water from the second story balcony, and the large screened in porch with custom pull down sunshades. They had carefully selected every decoration, from the nautical themed dishes featuring brightly colored starfish, tropical fish, and seashells neatly displayed inside the kitchen cabinets with glass doors, to the ocean scented candles placed perfectly on the built-ins in Donna's private office.

Just as Donna had thought of every detail for their wedding, she left no corner of the home untouched during the design phase. She pressed Tom to let her make most of the decisions, and he quickly realized it was in his best interest to give her free reign because it made her happy. He would have preferred a little less formality and a little more color on the walls, but these opinions weren't important enough to fight for. The only design element he voiced his dissatisfaction with was concerning her selection of tile in the master bedroom. She wanted a very sleek looking tile that almost looked like glass. Tom agreed it was beautiful, but he wanted carpet. He didn't want to wake up to a cold floor every morning.

Donna, however, was unrelenting and insisted the tile stay. He knew the argument was over when she purchased him socks with grippers on the bottom he could sleep in. She said, "Wear these. If you get up in the middle of the night to go to the bathroom, you won't have to worry about slipping or fumbling in the dark for your slippers."

They reminded him of the socks the hospital put on Grace's feet every time she had been admitted the last few months of her life. Tom grumbled to himself every time he put on the ridiculous socks, but other than that, he had to admit Donna had done a beautiful job designing the home, and they were both over the moon with the results. He also finally had his own dock where he could anchor the Commission Casanova. He loved being able to get out on the water without having to plan ahead.

As Donna prepared the invitation list for the housewarming party, Tom gathered his nerve to ask her to consider adding his daughters. In a moment of extreme bravery, he dared to utter the J and K words in front of his wife. He felt it was time to take a step toward reconciling with them since it had been almost nine months when everything imploded.

Donna was confounded by his request. She had wrongly assumed he had finally realized it was best to keep them out of their lives. *How could he even consider asking her this, knowing his girls did not accept her? They had verbally assaulted her and inflicted a great deal of emotional abuse on her. They had tried to ruin their marriage, and now he wanted to welcome them into their new home—her own personal sanctuary!*

Donna knew she didn't have any intention of willingly bringing them back into their lives. When they were out of the picture, things were easier between her and Tom. He was free to do everything she wanted, which pleased her. She liked things the way they were—without them.

However, she also realized after months of vicious arguing and digging in her heels he should never see them again, it might be time to pretend she was sorry for all that had happened. She knew his daughters' absence was a source of sorrow for him. She decided it would be in the best interest of her marriage to lie she wanted reconciliation, so she agreed to add them to the invitation list. God would understand she was only lying for her husband's benefit. Donna was sure the relationship with Jenna and Katie would not and could not move forward at this point. There was too much hurt to overcome. She would make her husband happy by fueling his hope but wasn't concerned anything would change.

Katie purposely ruined her wedding and Jenna said such hateful things about her for no reason. These were not the actions of women who wanted a healthy relationship. She completely dismissed any of her own wrongdoings, like a classic narcissist.

Despite her hatred toward Katie and Jenna, Donna thought adding them to the list would be a safe thing to do. She would look like she was supporting her husband's desire to see his family, but she was confident neither girl would say yes. When they turned down the invitation, it would prove they didn't love him enough to try to work things out. Maybe this would be the final straw for Tom, and he would never want to see either of them again. She could only hope. If he was officially done with his daughters, it would make it easier for her to bring up putting her name on the Beachview Drive deed.

She was glad they were now renting the vacation home out occasionally through Airbnb because it was bringing in a nice stream of income. It was technically a side business for them, so she could argue she would want to keep it going if something unexpectedly happened to him. That should be enough of a reason to get her name on it.

Tom was thankful his wife was willing to accommodate his request to invite his daughters, and he showed his appreciation with a kiss. Donna promised to put the invitations in the mail as soon as possible.

Hurricanes

As soon as Jenna received the invitation to the housewarming party, she promptly RSVP'd with a "yes." She had been waiting for an opportunity to see her father again, with Donna's blessing, and to try to get their relationship back on track. This was the first genuine step being made toward reconciliation, and she was glad to be invited.

Jenna wanted nothing more than to see her father and his new home. She remembered how she had assumed she would spend many hours there when she was packing up at the old Jacobs house but had lost almost all hope of this ever happening over the last few months. It had been almost two years since Tom sold his home in Peachtree City, but it finally seemed like things were now moving in the right direction. Jenna didn't understand what it was Donna thought she had done that was so terrible, much less why she believed her entire being to be toxic. Other than one conversation with her dad where she voiced concerns, she had never done anything besides try to be accepting and hospitable.

When Donna saw Jenna replied with a "yes," she nearly fell out of her chair. She screamed in her head—*why won't she go away?!?* She was relieved there was no acknowledgment whatsoever from Katie, because to have them both coming would have pushed her over the edge.

Now, she had a dilemma. She had pretended she wanted Jenna to come. She could not change her mind now and object without giving away her true feelings. Tom would know she lied, and this would be bad for their marriage.

Donna told Tom Jenna responded with a yes. She said, "Darling, I am thrilled she accepted the invitation, but I'm afraid she might only be coming because she wants to make a scene in front of our guests and ruin the whole party." She continued, "Tommy, I hate to point this out, but your girls seem to have a knack for ruining special events."

Her paranoia was kicking in, and she was immediately feeling enormous stress. She wanted him to rescind the invitation.

But Tom wasn't regretful of inviting Jenna as she had hoped. Instead, he said, "Honey, I have a great idea to ease your fears. Why don't you and Jenna talk on the phone prior to the housewarming and start working on your relationship." He was confident if they could just talk, Donna would see his daughter was not the devil incarnate she believed her to be.

Donna didn't want to talk to Jenna ever again, and especially not now, but she couldn't admit this to Tom. She begrudgingly agreed to a phone call, praying her stepdaughter would reject the idea of being forced to speak to her. She also begged God to change Jenna's mind about coming at all.

As Tom dialed his daughter's number, she hoped she wasn't home. She could have died when Jenna picked up on the second ring and agreed to a conversation with her. Donna was screaming inside her head again. She was positive Jenna was only willing to talk to her to manipulate Tom. Jenna was conniving through and through.

Surprisingly, when the two women began talking, they were both civil to one another. They were both good actresses. They agreed to put the past behind them and start over. Donna had no choice but to be agreeable because Tom was standing right next to her listening to the whole conversation. He was beaming with a silly grin that made him look like a child rather than an adult. It was a turn off. Donna still believed Jenna had a secret agenda and was amazed she didn't let it show.

Tom was thrilled, because for the first time in nine months, his wife and daughter were getting along. He hoped this one conversation would fix all their problems. He was naïve enough to think this might be possible. He still didn't believe he had any part in anything that had transpired and attributed all the grief to stubborn women.

The weekend the housewarming was supposed to take place, Hurricane Matthew was barreling toward the entire east coast, and Tom and Donna had no choice but to cancel the party and evacuate. Donna felt a sense of relief she wouldn't have to see Jenna. She would rather take her chances with a natural disaster than her stepdaughter. Perhaps, God sent this storm on her behalf. Donna was confident her house was built with safety in mind and exceeded all building requirements since hurricanes were commonplace in Georgia. However, she was not confident she was built to withstand the toxicity her stepdaughter brought into their lives or the gale force winds of Hurricane Jenna.

Even though Jenna was unable to come, she and her dad were now talking freely once again. Tom had even asked his wife to unblock his daughter on Facebook. Donna was not pleased her plan had backfired on her.

Jenna invited both Tom and Donna to visit her family in Virginia. She thought it would be fun to tour some of the national monuments in Washington, DC. Tom jumped at the invitation and said he would come up the next weekend, for his seventy-first birthday, if the weather was amenable to flights.

Donna had no interest in going on the trip and told him he would have to go without her. She was going to plan a girls' weekend. She was furious he was going but couldn't express her dissatisfaction without looking like an unsupportive wife.

Tom flew to Virginia without issue, and they all had a wonderful time together. Jenna decorated the dining room with streamers and balloons for his birthday and baked him a caramel vanilla cake. They toured downtown DC, and before he left, they started making plans for the next visit. They both agreed the next time he came up, they would go a few hours north to Philadelphia for a family vacation. None of them had been there before, and they wanted to see the Liberty Bell and Constitution Hall. Tom hoped Donna would join them, but much to his disappointment, when it came time for the trip, she found a reason not to come.

Two months later, after the Philly trip, Tom invited Jenna and the children to come see his new home in St. Simon's and spend Spring Break in Georgia. With so many visits and trips back and forth, it almost felt like old times.

Jenna thought going to Georgia would be a good opportunity for her and Donna to try to reconnect. They would be on Donna's home turf and hoped this would make her more comfortable. She was determined to make things right between them, so she accepted her dad's invitation to come without hesitation.

She had no way of knowing this would be the last time she would ever see Donna face-to-face in her life, even though she would feel the effects of her presence for years. She also would never have predicted her Spring Break visit would be the last time she would be welcome in the vacation home her parents purchased together—or in her father's house.

Spring Break

The following April, seven months after her dad's first visit to her house in Annandale, Jenna drove from the DC area down to St. Simon's Island, along with Heidi, Brett, Olivia, and two of her teenagers' friends. It was a very long drive and took her two full days with an overnight stop halfway in Raleigh, North Carolina.

When they got to Tom and Donna's house, everyone was excited to get out of the van. Their legs felt like jelly and they desperately needed to stretch. It was their first time seeing the beautiful new home, and they were immediately impressed with its beauty. It was stunning and the view was glorious. There weren't any toys or children's books, but no one cared, including Jenna. There also wasn't a floating trampoline.

It was immediately clear Donna had a more formal style than Grace, and toyboxes and treasure chests would have looked out of place next to her Tiffany lamps and cashmere throw blankets.

The kids were thrilled Tom had arranged for them to canoe in the waterways just behind his home and were looking forward to spending time on the beach. Tom and Donna's home, coupled with the Beachview Drive vacation house, was a perfect environment for Spring Break, even if their boat was on the fritz. Tom kept having motor trouble, so they would be unable to go out on the water in it this time, but there were plenty of other things to do.

Since they were a large crew, Jenna and the kids would be staying at her dad's vacation house. He purposely didn't rent it out that week so they could use it. Donna pointed out this would also provide them all with some privacy. It truly was the best of both worlds to have such easy access to the intracoastal waters and the beach.

Jenna was very impressed with Donna's hospitality, and from the moment they arrived, she felt warmly welcomed. Things were looking up. Any apprehension she felt about seeing Donna quickly evaporated.

Donna prepared a lovely meal of homemade fried chicken, au gratin potatoes, and roasted asparagus for them on the first evening they were there. It was delicious, and Jenna thanked her repeatedly for going to so much trouble. Once they were done eating, Jenna loaded up the children and headed over to the Beachview Drive house for the night. They were all exhausted from the long day and needed to get some rest.

Jenna claimed the master bedroom for herself and headed straight for it to put her suitcases down. When she flipped on the light, she was surprised to find stacks of plastic totes containing her mother's scrapbooks lining the wall. She couldn't imagine what they were doing here. *Wouldn't it make more sense for them to be kept at her father's house since he often rented this house out to snowbirds and tourists?*

When she asked her father about the scrapbooks the next day, he said, "If you want them, take them." His tone was despondent. He looked around to make sure Donna wasn't in earshot and then whispered to her, "I'm not allowed to keep them." Even though they had been stored in the attic, their mere existence bothered Donna. She had given him one month to get rid of them or she would. He had relocated them to his vacation home until he could figure out what to do with them. She wouldn't allow them to be stored there long term, either.

Donna did not believe it was appropriate for him to keep pictures of his late wife in either of her homes. She disregarded the fact there were other pictures of Tom's life also in these books. They told a story much greater than just the life of Grace Jacobs. They were filled with images of Tom's children growing up, his grandchildren, his parents, family vacations, and countless other memories from his life special enough to document.

Jenna thought it was awful he was forbidden from keeping them. She could understand not displaying pictures of Grace all over their house, but banning all pictures completely, even from the attic, seemed extreme. She gladly agreed to take them home with her even though she didn't really have room for them in the van. The kids would just have to cram in tighter on the very long ride back to Virginia.

Jenna suddenly wondered if her great aunt's paintings were also in danger of being banned, since they had belonged to Grace and were from her direct family line. Jenna asked her dad, "Where are Aunt Sally's paintings being stored?"

He replied by telling her, "Don't you remember you and Katie took them all before I moved out of the family home?"

Jenna adamantly refuted this by saying, "No, you promised to store them for us!"

Tom acted like he had no idea what she was talking about and quickly made up an excuse about needing to check on something in the kitchen.

As her eyes followed her dad out of the room, she realized Donna had seemingly appeared out of nowhere. She did not want to ruin the nice visit they were having, so chose not to continue the conversation about the paintings on this trip. She hoped he was storing them as he had promised but hypothesized Donna did not know about them. She knew her dad secretly had her mother's wedding ring stored in a safe deposit box without Donna's knowledge, so it was plausible.

Overall, their visit seemed to be going very well. Donna was trying her best to make the visit fun for everyone, even if she was a little out of touch with the kids' generation and what they liked. Jenna appreciated the effort, though, and happily played along with all of Donna's suggestions. She even participated in her karaoke competition and made the kids join in, despite their protests.

Donna insisted they each take turns doing a solo performance to the song of her choosing. She said, "I will be the judge, and everyone must play. I will award the winner a check for fifty dollars. I am feeling in the mood to be extremely generous. I bet most people you play games with aren't willing to shell out cash to the winner. It literally pays to hang out with me!"

The kids sang conservatively, feeling uncomfortable and not really caring about the potential for a cash prize, but Jenna hammed it up trying to make Donna happy.

As Jenna sang along to a song with somewhat questionable and suggestive lyrics, she couldn't help but feel Donna had created this entire activity with the intent to humiliate her. She noticed she was watching her with an odd look of satisfaction on her face, but Jenna didn't care—she was comfortable in the presence of her kids and wasn't going to do anything that would give Donna a reason to find fault with her.

She would be a good sport if it killed her.

Donna gave her the check after the competition, declaring her the winner. Jenna tried to refuse it and told her it wasn't necessary to give her or her kids money. Finally, after a few back and forths with the check, Jenna decided she would accept it to appease her and use it at a local bakery. She would let the kids each pick out a special treat. She felt this was an appropriate way to use the money because it was keeping in line with family tradition. She would make sure the kids knew the desserts were a gift to them from Donna when she paid the bill.

That night, Jenna also played Yahtzee, Scrabble, and Charades with Donna in her living room and tried to engage in conversation with her as much as possible. Jenna thought they were both having fun. There was laughter, and it felt real. Jenna was finally making progress with Donna and getting to know her stepmother better. They were both letting their guard down, which was more than she had hoped would happen on this visit.

Jenna was determined not to let anything get in the way of her bonding with Donna, and when Olivia, who had had an ear infection before their trip, started complaining about her ear hurting again, she brushed it off as much as possible. Olivia had just finished ten days of antibiotics, and Jenna knew from experience the more she sympathized with her the more it would hurt. She did believe it was bothering her but didn't think an emergency room trip was in order. Jenna was confident her youngest daughter was more tired than in pain, but she wasn't ready to end the fun with Donna yet. She gave Olivia Motrin and told her they would go to a walk-in clinic in the morning for another round of antibiotics.

Under normal circumstances, Jenna would have been more nurturing, however, she was laser focused on building a better relationship with Donna. She had no idea every parenting decision she was making was being silently scrutinized.

A few other minor things happened, like Donna thinking it was Heidi's seventeenth birthday—when it was her eighteenth—while they were there and having the wrong number of candles on the cake. Jenna did not want to embarrass her, so she told Heidi not to mention it. It wasn't important how many candles there were, only the effort and thoughtfulness mattered. It was very sweet of Donna to have such a nice cake for Heidi, and Jenna appreciated it. They could set the record straight later.

Brett also jumped in the brackish water behind their house after Donna told him not to and then rolled around in the grass, wrestling with his friend, resulting in a bad case of hives. There is nothing uncommon about a teenager not listening, and Jenna was used to Brett's allergic reaction to grass since it had been happening since he was a toddler. There wasn't anything that couldn't be cured with a scolding, dry clothes, or Benadryl.

After several days of fun, it was time for Jenna to pack up her crew and head north. She drove away with a happy heart, thinking progress had been made, as did Tom, who waved at them until he could no longer see the taillights.

Jenna would be very surprised two years later to find out Donna viewed the week entirely differently. Every little mishap would be used against her in the vilest way to judge her parenting.

Apparently, Donna only enjoyed the week because it gave her a heap of ammunition to add to her arsenal. It was getting quite large, and no one else even knew about it. The week Jenna had originally perceived as progress would later be viewed for what it was—another part in Donna's plan to destroy the Jacobs family permanently.

Jenna would eventually come to realize the only thing good that came out of her visit to St. Simon's was that God gave her the opportunity to save her mother's photo albums on that trip. If she hadn't rescued them then, they would have been lost forever. They would have been tossed into the trash, and all photo evidence of her beautiful mother, her amazing childhood, and the family she came from, would have been lost.

There would have been no proof without blood tests that the Tom and Grace Jacobs family ever existed.

Not So Happy Trails

Three months after Jenna's Spring Break trip to Georgia, the Miller family received orders for Fort Jackson in Columbia, South Carolina. They made the move from Annandale, Virginia, to the Palmetto State easily, like any true Army family, and settled in quickly. Paul was being pre-positioned for a year before taking brigade command of a basic training unit. Heidi headed off to college at the University of North Florida, Brett started high school, and Olivia was ready for third grade.

Tom came to visit them every so often, and even though Donna was always invited, she never chose to accompany him. She always had an excuse. Tom wanted his wife to come with him on these trips and spend time with his family, but he didn't have it in him to argue with her about it anymore. It bothered him she refused every invitation but didn't know what to do about it. Any time he tried to convince her to come, it would result in a bitter fight lasting for days. They had reached an unspoken compromise that he could see Jenna, Paul, and their kids as long as she wasn't expected to come. Ever.

Jenna didn't really understand why she was so opposed to visiting, because she thought their last visit had gone well. Her father didn't understand it either or was unwilling to tell her the truth. She wasn't sure which was accurate.

On one visit to South Carolina, about ten months after they moved there, Tom came up to see Olivia compete in a gymnastics competition in Myrtle Beach. Since Myrtle, as the locals called it, was a few hours from Columbia where the Millers lived, Jenna booked hotel rooms for them. The meet gave them a good opportunity to take a mini vacation together, their first since the trip to Philadelphia. They went to several tourist attractions after Olivia's meet, and thoroughly enjoyed themselves. They went to Ripley's Believe It or Not and then to the Hollywood Wax Museum where Tom and Olivia posed for pictures with figures of Dolly Parton, Elvis Presley, and Taylor Swift. They ate a fabulous meal at King Kong Sushi and swam in the hotel's indoor pool since it was still too cold to get in the ocean.

When they returned to Jenna's house two days later, so Tom could get packed up for his return flight, they started reminiscing about all the travel adventures they had enjoyed as a family in the past before Donna entered the picture. They recalled trips to Las Vegas, the Hoover Dam, London, and San Francisco. The travel bug had bitten them both because of the good time they had in Myrtle Beach, and they wanted to plan another trip soon.

Tom wasn't sure if Donna would want to go but told Jenna they were going to plan one anyway. He was no longer going to miss out on family vacations because his wife didn't want to be a part of them. They had always been important in the past, and he wanted to bring them back.

Jenna was glad to see her father was finally taking a stand.

Donna told Tom she liked to travel before they were married, but he now knew she was afraid to fly. He wasn't sure why she led him to believe she wanted to see the world when they were dating, because it clearly wasn't true. She would have missed this question on his questionnaire if she had answered honestly, but it was too late now to matter.

She only agreed to go on trips by plane if it was to visit her friends and family in Ohio. It frustrated Tom he couldn't convince her to go anywhere else that required air travel. After their honeymoon, she informed him Barbados was the one and only trip she planned to take with him out of the country and discouraged him from bringing it up again.

It seemed she had a lot of things on her "don't talk about" list.

Together, Jenna and Tom decided Savannah, Georgia, would be a wonderful place to visit, and it was within driving distance for them both. They selected Easter weekend as the ideal time for everyone to travel because the kids had time off from school and Paul had time off from work.

They had been there many times before since they were from Georgia, but it would be fun to go with a tourist mindset. Jenna and Tom got on Google and looked for a wide variety of things to do that would appeal to everyone. They settled on some good restaurants like The Lady & Sons and The Olde Pink House, a day at Tybee Island, shopping downtown on River Street, a visit to the Telfair Museum of Art and the Owens-Thomas House, and horseback riding.

Tom and Jenna both knew Donna wouldn't want to ride horses, but it was only a forty-five-minute trail ride in a seventy-two-hour period. Tom loved horses, and he looked forward to sharing the experience with his grandchildren. He was more excited about the chance to get on a horse than anything else they planned because it took him back to the early days of his marriage with Grace when they both rode often.

When Tom was in his twenties and employed as a farm equipment salesman, he made a deal with one of his clients—he would give him a discount on supplies if his client would let him and Grace ride his horses on the weekends. The customer was happy to make this deal because it served both parties well.

Grace and Tom would ride for hours, enjoying the country landscape that stretched for miles in the small Georgia town where they'd lived. He smiled when he thought about his favorite horse, who had been named Jolly. It had been years since he thought about him, and it made him happy to think of him now. Grace's favorite horse had been named Trotter. She had looked beautiful sitting on his shiny, brown back. They both became very skilled riders, easily navigating across fallen logs, through small streams, and around a variety of obstacles put in their path by Mother Nature. Some of his happiest memories with Grace were when they were on horseback.

Tom was confident Donna would enjoy everything else planned for the trip. Perhaps she would just take pictures of everyone sitting on the horses or relax at the hotel until the ride was over. Tom might even suggest she spoil herself at a spa and get pampered while they were on the trails.

He left Jenna's house happy about the Savannah trip and excited to tell Donna about it. However, he did not get the reaction he expected when he pitched the idea to her.

She was in a terrible mood when he arrived home, as she usually was when he got back from seeing Jenna. He had noticed a pattern with her that she was particularly irritable the week before he left and the week he came back. He didn't understand it but knew the idea of him seeing his daughter bothered her greatly.

Donna was incensed Tom had the nerve to suggest they travel over Easter weekend. She did not want to spend the holiday with his family, and she thought he was inconsiderate for even suggesting it. She scolded him, "Easter is about Jesus, not vacations."

It was not lost on Tom they had spent every holiday since they were married, with the exception of one Halloween night at Fort Bragg, with her friends, but chose not to bring it up at this moment. She was nearing the meltdown stage, and he didn't want to provoke her. He tried to tell her all the fun things that were planned and insinuated Jenna had been the one to select the activities. It seemed safer for him if she didn't know he had also helped plan the itinerary.

When she heard horseback riding was on the agenda, she flew into another rage. She screamed at him, "How dare that selfish little monster plan an activity I cannot participate in! I am sure she did it on purpose for the sole reason of excluding me. She knows I am afraid of horses. There is no way I will go on this trip now that I see how willfully mean your daughter is. I will not travel with Jenna—not now, not ever—and neither will you, Tom. If you do, I will divorce you!"

Tom was too afraid to set the record straight by admitting he was the one to encourage Jenna to find a place that provided horseback riding. He would also never tell her about Jolly or Trotter or the many times he and Grace had ridden together either if he wanted to stay married.

When they had made the plans, Tom really didn't think forty-five minutes would be a problem, and he certainly didn't see any willful disrespect in their agenda. He decided it was in his best interest to keep his mouth shut and let his daughter take the blame entirely. *She wasn't there to see he wasn't defending her, so what did it matter?* They were not going to go on the trip, so Jenna would never need to know about the horrible things his wife was accusing her of.

Donna screamed at Tom, "We will not be controlled by your family anymore."

Although Tom didn't know how anyone was controlling them, he sat back idly and watched her pick up pen and paper. She said, "I am going to write a list of non-negotiable rules so we can all be on the same page." He suddenly understood what his daughters meant when they said they thought Donna was trying to sabotage the family, but there was nothing he could do about it. He wouldn't go back to being single ever again.

Donna's list would continue to grow over the years, making his relationship with Jenna almost impossible. In fact, these rules would eventually destroy all remaining happiness that existed between Tom, Jenna, and her family—and lead to the end of their relationship.

Of course, he had no way of knowing this at that time, so he let his wife carry on, trying not to do anything that would add to her hysteria.

When Donna was done writing down her rules, she read them off to her husband, making it known they were not up for debate.

Rule #1: You will not be gone from me for more than three days at a time.

Rule #2: You will not go on a vacation with anyone but me.

Rule #3: I will not travel with your family.

Rule #4: You will be with me on all holidays and birthdays.

Rule #5: I will approve of all visitors who come to see us in Georgia. I will also approve who we will allow on our boat.

She quickly added, "Jenna and her family are banned from both of our homes and our boat in case that wasn't crystal clear. Your daughter willfully tries to cause problems in our marriage and I will not tolerate it any longer."

Tom didn't know how to respond to his wife's reaction or her rules. They seemed extremely harsh and designed to keep his daughter and grandchildren out of his life. He was heartbroken, but knew he was defeated when she said, "If you break any of these rules, I will call an attorney. They are not up for discussion." Then she said, "Tom, if you love me at all, you will not challenge me on this. I have only made these rules because they are in the best interest of our relationship."

Feeling spent from the emotional conversation, Donna retired to the bedroom for the remainder of the evening.

Tom called Jenna to tell him the Savannah trip was off, and he read his wife's new rules out loud to his daughter.

Jenna couldn't believe what she was hearing, and she certainly couldn't believe her father would agree to these ridiculous rules.

When Easter weekend arrived, Donna made plans for her and Tom to go to her friend's house in the Buckhead area of Atlanta. Her rule about spending holidays with others did not apply to her friends.

It would become painstakingly obvious over the next few years her rules didn't apply to anyone except Jenna, and she had no problem rubbing this in her face. She quite enjoyed grinding salt into her wounds.

Pick. Poke. Taunt.

Donna loved Facebook because of the power it gave her. She was glad Jenna could see her page again. It was a mighty weapon in her war against her stepdaughter. She delighted in posting pictures of her and Tom posing with her friends on holidays because she knew it bothered Jenna. She also loved to share photos of Sydney (the only grandchild she liked and had a relationship with), Tom's cousins, and her friends spending time at their vacation home or on Tom's Sea Ray.

She liked to remind Jenna what she was missing and she was in charge whenever she could. If her stepdaughter had been more respectful, perhaps things could have been different. Then she remembered the prenup and knew things had to be the way they were. She was getting closer every day to her end goal. She had gained complete control of Tom's vacation house since she was in charge of all rentals. It would only be a little longer before her name was on the deed and it was officially hers according to the law.

On the way to her friend's house for Easter dinner, Donna told Tom never to mention the Savannah trip again and informed him Jenna's name was back to being a bad word in her house. You could have cut the tension in the air between them with a knife, but as soon as they pulled into her friend's driveway, Donna miraculously became her happy-go-lucky self.

Tom much preferred his wife this way, so he decided to abide by her wishes and keep his mouth shut. He was getting better and better at avoiding hot button topics because he had so much practice.

Jenna called her dad later that day to wish him a happy Easter, unaware he wasn't at home with his wife.

When Tom saw "Jenna" on his caller ID, he discreetly stepped outside to take the call. When he answered he said, "I can't talk right now because we are at Barbara and Rick's house for Easter dinner."

Jenna, recognizing those names as friends of Donna's, was completely taken aback. Her feelings were hurt. She asked him "How is this possible since it is clearly against Donna's rules?" She was audibly frustrated. "Why is it okay for you to be with her friends on Easter but not with your grandchildren?"

Tom had no answer because there wasn't one. There was only silence from his end of the line. The whole situation was truly unbelievable to them both and made no sense, but Tom felt his hands were tied regarding the matter.

He finally said, "I'm sorry Jenna but it is what it is. There is nothing I can do to change anything. You and Donna will have to work things out yourselves. None of this is my fault."

Jenna was annoyed with his refusal to stand up for her or to take any action. She said, "It seems like Donna made your Easter plans with the sole intention of hurting me."

Tom, not knowing what to say, muttered, "That is ridiculous, Jenna. My wife is an honorable woman. I must go now," and he quickly hung up the phone.

A few weeks after Easter, Donna had the brilliant idea to invite Sydney to come to their house for the weekend. She was now in school at Georgia Southern so it was easy to coerce her to come for a visit.

Sydney was exceptionally beautiful, and Donna loved to share pictures of her on Facebook so her friends could see her "grandmothering." She had to keep one member of Tom's family on her good side so she wouldn't appear to be the problem publicly. Sydney was her choice. Her sole ally.

Donna was glad Sydney hadn't held the whole car thing from several years ago against her. She never made the connection Donna was the one who got her grandfather to change his mind about buying it for her.

Donna decided to sweeten the weekend, and her revenge, by surprising Tom and Sydney with a special gift to make her visit even more memorable and photo worthy. She booked a two-hour horseback riding excursion for them on the beach. Donna couldn't wait to take pictures and post them on social media.

She smiled because she was about to look like the world's best grandmother for planning this experience for her husband and beloved granddaughter. The rest of the world would be clueless as to the real reason behind her "generosity."

Sydney had no idea she was being used as a pawn against her aunt, and Tom never realized this whole stunt was an intentional slap in his youngest daughter's face. He wanted to believe the best about his wife and thought she planned everything to make up for her unreasonable anger over the failed Savannah trip. He never considered how it might make Jenna feel when she learned about Donna's surprise.

As soon as Jenna saw the pictures, she knew the truth. Once again, Donna was making imaginary smoke pour out of her ears. It was another attack designed to inflict damage, and it did. The missiles were hitting closer to home base each time they were fired.

After seeing the post, Jenna lamented to Paul, "Why would Donna do this to me and our children? Doesn't she know Brett, Olivia, and Heidi can also see these pictures on Facebook?"

She raged on, "How dare she try to make my niece a weapon in her war against us!" Jenna was confident Sydney had no idea about anything that had transpired between her and Donna and did not know she was being played like a pawn in a strategic game of chess.

It was detestable to Jenna and Paul that she would pit one family member against another, especially without their knowledge. *How was her dad allowing this to happen? How could he be so naive about his wife's true intentions?* Donna was vindictive. She was spiteful. She was devious.

Flu and Falls and Bunions, Oh My

Over the course of the next two years, Donna regularly added to her list of rules—especially after every visit Tom had with Jenna. She officially named them "matrimonial boundaries" and their sole purpose was to make it increasingly more difficult for her husband to see his daughter.

In addition to her ever-growing boundaries, Donna claimed Jenna was such a source of stress to both her and Tom, that she was single-handedly responsible for any illnesses they contracted or accidents that happened.

Jenna was blamed for giving Donna the flu, even though she hadn't been in the same state as her for years, and she was not sick with the virus herself. The only possible explanation for Donna becoming ill was the stress of dealing with Jenna had weakened her immune system, making her susceptible to illness. Donna would not acknowledge flu is an airborne virus, or that it is scientifically impossible to spread it from more than two-hundred miles away.

She also claimed Jenna was responsible for Tom falling and hitting his head on the bedroom floor, requiring stitches. Since the fall happened only a few days after he returned from seeing Jenna, it was clearly his daughter's fault, and had nothing to do with the fact he bent over quickly trying to pick up his gripper socks that had fallen to the floor and became dizzy. There was also no acknowledgement if they had carpet his injuries would have likely been less serious.

Apparently, Jenna even had the power to give her stepmother bunions because the anxiety she induced in Donna often made her pace back and forth, resulting in podiatric problems.

After finding out she was being blamed for this, too, all Jenna could do was laugh and shake her head in disbelief. Jenna's superpowers became a running joke in her household and Paul teased her by calling her "The Bunion Queen."

It was such a ridiculous list of accusations, but Donna was convinced they were true. She fervently believed her stepdaughter was the source of all their misfortunes. She even began requesting her doctors document her stress, and subsequent ailments, were caused by "Jenna Miller" and place it in her permanent medical file.

When Jenna found out she was doing this, she became concerned. *Was Donna trying to build a legal battle against her? Did she plan to use these medical documents in court against her one day?*

Jenna theorized Donna was systematically trying to build a case against her to fight the prenuptial agreement when her dad died. She wanted evidence Jenna was a horrible daughter, undeserving of her father's inheritance.

Jenna sought the counsel of a lawyer she knew well and explained her concerns. She felt much better when she erupted in laughter after hearing Donna's accusations. She told her not to worry at all—if anything, her preposterous claims would convince a judge she was bona fide crazy!

Square Pegs

Jenna and Tom would continue to see each other from time to time over the next year, of course with Tom always coming to South Carolina. Jenna was prohibited from coming to Georgia to see him, per Donna's rules. She was literally banned from the entire state.

Tom remained hopeful things would eventually change but there was no indication of that happening anytime soon.

Jenna didn't share the same level of hope as her father. Each time Tom came to visit his daughter he would ask her, "Do you like things the way they are, with Donna being out of your life?"

Jenna never knew how to answer his question. It had never been her choice or her intention for the family to be so fractured. She had never done anything to cause the schism but always seemed to be held responsible for it, while Donna and Tom were excused from all responsibility. It was clear her dad thought it was up to Jenna to save the relationship and had no intention of getting involved himself. Tom wanted things to be different but wasn't willing to put his own neck on the line to force change.

Donna also pretended she wanted things to get better, too, even though she refused every invitation she was offered, and perpetually posted cryptic Facebook messages targeting Jenna.

At this point, Jenna was satisfied with things the way they were. She was able to see her dad from time to time, and she no longer saw a need to try to cram Donna, a square peg, into the family circle.

You Are Not Invited

Almost a year after the Easter trip to Savannah was canceled, Tom informed Jenna he and Donna were planning an anniversary trip to Greenville, South Carolina. They would be there for seven days. Greenville was only an hour and a half away from Columbia, where Jenna lived, and a very easy drive.

Jenna asked her father if it would be okay for her family to join them for one day and one night of their weeklong trip. They could all enjoy some of the local tourist sites together and try to rekindle their relationship. Greenville would provide a beautiful backdrop for a visit, and there was so much they could do together. It was chock full of beautiful nature trails and parks and had a booming, recently revitalized downtown with amazing restaurants and shops. It was also well known for having fabulous breweries. It had been two years since Jenna last saw Donna in person, so if they could stay busy it would be easier and the attractions would provide them with great topics for conversation.

Tom loved this idea and hoped this would be the first step in reuniting his family since Donna would actually be in the same state, by her own will, as his daughter. Tom disclosed he and Donna were staying in a luxury hotel in downtown Greenville that required reservations months ahead of time so suggested Jenna book a different hotel for her family.

Jenna agreed to this request. She wanted to give them some space and was sure even if the hotel had rooms available, it would cost more than her budget would allow. Jenna didn't think it was important to ask the name of their accommodations, because it didn't really matter to her.

When Donna learned of the plans Tom and Jenna were making, she became outraged. She thought, *this is an anniversary trip—which constitutes a holiday. My husband and stepdaughter are purposely disregarding my very clearly established matrimonial boundaries. How can Tom think it is appropriate for his family to join us for even one minute? Anniversary trips are supposed to be romantic! Jenna wants to come just to spite me!*

Donna fired off a contemptuous text to Jenna telling her, "You and your family are unwelcome in Greenville. DO NOT attempt to crash our anniversary."

Jenna couldn't help but think of other unpleasant texts she had received from Donna over the years, like the one where she was scolded for missing Father's Day. The tone of this text was similar and just as equally unsettling.

Jenna assumed there was a misunderstanding and replied, "We only wanted to see you for one day," thinking Donna thought they were coming for the whole trip.

Donna responded coldly, "Let me repeat myself, you are NOT invited to come at all, not even for one second—and if you try to come against my wishes, the whole trip will be ruined."

Jenna stared at her hateful words. *How was her mere existence enough to enrage her father's wife?* She couldn't understand how making time for family would ruin anything.

She also felt heartbroken for her children, whose relationship with their grandfather had become almost non-existent since Donna came into the picture.

Jenna immediately contacted her father to tell him about the scathing text. It was clear this was not going to be the trip that brought the family back together.

Tom couldn't understand why his wife hated his daughter so badly. He honestly couldn't think of anything Jenna had done to Donna that was so awful. He also didn't understand why seeing his own family for one day would ruin an entire week, especially when it would make him so happy. He always bent over backwards to accommodate seeing her friends and family, even when he didn't want to, because he knew it was important to her. There was no reciprocity.

Jenna was not going to go somewhere she wasn't welcome and made other plans for the weekend that did not include being anywhere near Greenville. Brett had a lacrosse tournament anyway, and Olivia had multiple commitments. Jenna had no intention of disregarding Donna's request and showing up uninvited.

The Devious Dessert

The day before Tom and Donna were supposed to leave for Greenville, Brett had a lacrosse game about forty minutes from the Miller's home. Jenna was sitting in the bleachers at Lexington High School waiting for game one of her son's multi-day tournament to begin. It was Spring Break, and his team would be playing in at least three games, more if they kept winning.

Jenna rolled up her sleeves, trying to get a small head start on her summer tan, and started thinking about everything on her family's calendar for the upcoming weekend. It was almost overwhelming. Greenville was not on her mind at all.

Her thoughts were interrupted when her phone started ringing. She saw it was her dad. She picked it up and said, "Hello."

Tom told Jenna, "I'm calling to discuss the issues between you and my wife." He then proceeded to beg her to keep trying to work on the relationship.

Jenna thought to herself, *your wife is the issue*, but didn't say what she was thinking out loud.

He said, "There is nothing I can do about this situation, except pray Donna's heart will be softened to you. I just cannot get in the middle of this, so it is up to you to keep trying for the sake of the family."

Jenna replied, "I don't understand the point of trying anymore and think it would be better if you stood up to Donna and explained how important your family is to you. Dad, you NEED to do something about this. Please!"

Tom dismissed this suggestion immediately because he didn't think he was responsible for any of the problems and felt interjecting himself into the issue would make the situation worse. Worse for himself.

Jenna said, "If just being in the same town as someone can ruin an entire vacation, what can I possibly do to change her mind?"

Her father agreed it would be difficult but sounded desperate. He didn't want to give up hope yet that something could change. Jenna could tell he and Donna must have been fighting over the whole situation and that was why he was reluctant to get into it again with her. She didn't want to dash all his hopes yet, so she agreed she would keep trying. With that, they hung up the phone and the lacrosse game started.

Later that night Jenna told Paul about her phone call with her dad. They were both thinking about how to keep trying since Donna wouldn't see them, wouldn't talk to them, and seemed to want nothing to do with them. They both felt it was important, though, to try to honor Jenna's promise to her father. They knew Donna liked gifts, so they decided they would find a local bakery in Greenville and have a dessert delivered to them as an anniversary gift.

Jenna texted her father, "Paul and I would like to send you a special gift for your anniversary. What is the name of the hotel you are staying at so we can make delivery arrangements?"

Tom was pleased with the text, recognizing his daughter's effort on his behalf, and he quickly responded with "The Grand Bohemian Lodge."

Less than a minute later, Jenna received a text from Donna telling her not to send anything.

Jenna informed her she didn't want their anniversary to go unnoticed, so she insisted.

It was clear Donna had no idea her husband had called his daughter earlier that day begging her to reach out to his wife. Donna then told her, "If you must, send it to the house. But I wish you wouldn't."

Jenna couldn't understand why she was being so difficult, especially since she had been ostracized in the past for missing a gift giving occasion. She decided it would be best to just explain to her she wanted to send a dessert from a Greenville bakery, so it wouldn't make sense to send it to their house. It would be inedible by the time they arrived home.

With this, Donna went into a full-on rage. Typical Donna.

She began sending text after text about how devious Jenna was and accused her of trying to ruin the vacation from the moment she found out about it. Jenna's phone dinged over and over again with each new message more heated than the last. It sounded like someone was playing the xylophone.

Donna wholeheartedly believed Jenna was planning to show up uninvited. That was the only possible reason she could think of for Jenna's insistence on getting the name of their lodging. She was convinced Jenna was looking for a way to weasel her way into their romantic getaway. She was furious with her husband for disclosing the name of the hotel so readily.

Jenna knew it was very bad between her father and Donna, because shortly after the texts to her from Donna stopped, her father accidentally sent her one meant for Donna. It said, "Please remember, we made a contract with one another, and you agreed not to cuss or yell at me anymore." He quickly sent a follow up text that said, "Please ignore the previous text."

That, of course, was hard to do. Jenna and Paul had already seen it. They could only imagine the fighting that must have occurred between Tom and Donna that would require them to sign a contract regarding how they should treat one another. Her father's small mistake gave Jenna a snapshot into what it must be like to live with Donna Thorn Jacobs.

Donna was so angry she yelled at Tom, "I no longer want to go on the trip with you at all. You can go by yourself." Then she screamed at a deafening decibel, "GET OUT because you are not welcome in this home anymore!"

Tom couldn't believe he was being kicked out of the house they built together.

Donna was completely out of control, irrational, and now threatening him with divorce. Although she had done this many times in the past, he really thought she meant it this time. He didn't know what to do, so he put his suitcase in his car and drove to Greenville by himself.

He was also angry. He had been subjected to her screaming, yelling, and ugliness more times than he could count. She had created a wedge between him and his daughters. He lost Katie because of her, and now he was losing Jenna. He was also losing his grandchildren. The only one he even had a semi-decent relationship with was Sydney, because she was Donna's obvious favorite. But even that consisted of seeing her only two or three times a year and a Zoom call once a month, a stark contrast to what his life had been like before he married Donna. *How could his wife treat him like this if she truly loved him?*

He was starting to doubt she loved him at all. She certainly didn't model understanding, compassion, or compromise. Everything was always under her control, and it was her way or the highway. He was reaching his breaking point too. *Did he even want to stay in this marriage?*

Tom did not tell Jenna he was going to Greenville; he didn't tell anyone. He needed time to think, and he figured he might as well go to the hotel he had already booked to do it. It was too late to cancel his reservation at the Grand Bohemian Lodge, and he had paid a pretty penny for the room. He needed to figure out what he was going to do. He never thought he would even consider divorce an option, but it was starting to look like a real possibility.

Her behavior, paranoia, and rage were simply not normal, and he could no longer deny that they were. Maybe he had been a little hasty with his proposal.

Three days later, Tom called Jenna to tell her what happened. Jenna felt terrible her gift prompted all of this, but there was no way of knowing a cake would be viewed as a "devious" attack and an attempt to ruin an entire vacation—or a marriage.

Jenna and her father had several lengthy conversations about Donna and exchanged more than a few emails about her. Jenna was convinced Donna had Paranoid Personality Disorder because she exhibited every one of its symptoms, which included holding grudges, distrusting others, being paranoid others were out to get her, hypersensitivity, being easily insulted, and being hostile toward others—just to name a few.

When Tom heard the clinical description, he had to admit his wife checked all the boxes. He also agreed with Jenna she displayed narcissistic tendencies because she believed she was never at fault for anything.

Jenna had never heard of Paranoid Personality Disorder until the night before her conversation with her dad about it. For some strange reason, she woke up from a hard sleep with the certainty Donna was suffering from this disorder. She believed the Holy Spirit was telling her this because she instantly reached for her phone on her nightstand and, somehow, mysteriously knew exactly what to Google.

When she read through the description of the disease, Jenna's anger toward Donna greatly decreased and was replaced with newfound sympathy for her stepmother. Even though she was only making an assumption, with no clinical proof whatsoever, her heart softened, despite all the times she had been hurt. She believed the Holy Spirit had a powerful way of working through people and was imbuing her with empathy.

Tom confided in Jenna he was truly scared his wife would divorce him this time.

Jenna, thinking of the stink Donna pulled over the prenup, told him, "Don't worry, Dad. She is bluffing." She said, "There is no way she will divorce you because she signed the prenup. If she were to walk away from the marriage, she would leave with what she came in with, which isn't very much."

Jenna was confident Donna would not risk losing everything, but Tom wasn't so sure.

Jenna did not tell her dad to divorce Donna and she didn't demand her father choose between his wife or his family. It was important for him to make his own decisions. She counseled him to do whatever would make him happy because that is all she wanted for him, and she meant it.

After a few days of self-reflection and prayer, Tom decided it was time to go home. He loved his wife and wanted to stick it out, no matter what. He had made vows to love her in good times and in bad, in sickness and in health, and that is what he intended to do.

He knew it was possible Jenna was right about his wife but was fearful she wouldn't react well to him suggesting she was mentally ill, so he knew he never would. He was caught between a rock and a hard place and he would just have to accept her the way she was.

Upon his return to St. Simon's Island, Donna demanded he stay in the Beachview Drive house. Thankfully, no renters were currently occupying the property. She was still angry with him and didn't want him to come home yet. He did as she requested until she finally gave in and let him come back.

When Jenna found out she agreed to let her dad go back home again, this was all the proof she needed that she was manipulating him. She had called her bluff accurately. There was no way Donna would ever leave her dad. She had a very good life with him where she was able to have everything she needed and almost everything she wanted, and she knew it. She wasn't going to give that up. She liked having the power to make him think she would leave, but it was a hollow threat.

Tom and Donna eventually rescheduled their trip to Greenville and purposely kept it a secret from Jenna. Donna went so far to try to keep it hidden from her stepdaughter she even created a ruse on Facebook with fake plans about going to a concert in Atlanta. She was so convinced Jenna lived only for the purpose of hurting her and believed if she knew about the trip, she would try to ruin it.

Nothing could have been further from the truth. Jenna wasn't purposely devious; she didn't enjoy hurting people, and she never had it out for Donna. But that was Donna's reality, created by her own imagination or illness, which one—no one knew for certain. Even if Jenna had known they were going, she would never have suggested joining them again.

When Donna finally posted pictures of their trip, Jenna quickly realized the discrepancies in her timeline and knew she was lying about when they went. She was quickly able to figure out when they had actually gone because she posted about attending a city market in downtown Greenville. A quick internet search of area events gave her away.

Ironically, the Miller family overlapped a weekend with them in Greenville because Brett had a lacrosse tournament there. Thank God they didn't run into each other, or else Jenna would have been blamed for that too—even though she had no idea they were going to be there. She was frustrated her father would willingly go along with Donna's plan to deceive her. It didn't feel right to her, but at this point she was starting to not care anymore.

She was also starting to see her dad was becoming more and more comfortable with lying.

Brackish Water Doesn't Cause Hives

Six months after the Greenville fiasco, Paul received a message from Donna on his work email. He was immediately annoyed she contacted him on his government account, which was monitored. Many officers have had their careers ruined by personal emails being discovered on their professional accounts. Of course, most of these officers had also made grave lapses in judgment, and the emails were simply proof of their bad decisions. Paul didn't have any skeletons in his closet to be concerned about.

As soon as he saw the subject line was "Jenna," he was sure he was about to read something ugly about his wife. He was also sure he wouldn't believe it. Paul wasn't concerned about whatever it was his father-in-law's wife wanted to tattle on Jenna for, and he couldn't imagine it would be important enough to warrant an Army investigation into his wife or him because of association.

When he opened the message, he laughed when he saw the reason for the email was "to let Paul know what kind of person and mother his wife really was." It was clear she used his government account because she wanted to make sure Jenna did not see the email in their shared Hotmail account and delete it before Paul could read it.

As he continued reading, his laughter was quickly replaced by anger. Donna informed him she would be "outlining all the egregious things Jenna did when she brought the children down to visit over Spring Break." Paul couldn't even begin to fathom why she was just sending this email now—two years after his wife had taken the trip.

The fact she sat on this "important information" for so long was already an indication she was grasping at straws and just looking for something she could turn into ammunition.

He assumed it was retaliation over Greenville and the "devious" anniversary gift because nothing else even made sense. How a cake caused so much trouble was beyond him. It was clear though, by her tone, she thought she was really going to stick it to Jenna this time.

Little did she know Paul was his wife's fiercest ally, and if you picked a fight with her, you picked a fight with him.

Donna accused Jenna of child abuse for making "poor Olivia suffer with a tremendously painful ear infection. Rather than seeking medical attention, she sat on the couch selfishly playing games and ignoring her child."

Paul wanted to erupt in a rage when he read this. He couldn't believe she had the nerve to make an accusation of abuse against his wife. It was preposterous to even suggest this. And now he was even more angry this was on his work computer because accusing someone of child abuse was certainly enough to raise eyebrows and warrant a formal investigation.

She also informed him "that despite my request for Brett not to go in the water, he still did, and Jenna allowed it, blatantly disregarding my wishes." She went on to say, "many of my friends have brought their grandchildren over and none of them have ever gone in the water or disrespected me like Brett did. I was appalled by his behavior." Then she boldly proclaimed, "If Jenna can't follow my rules or control her kids when they are at my home, they are not welcome."

Paul rolled his eyes because his wife and family hadn't been welcome in a long time, and they weren't just Jenna's kids, they were also his. *Was this the reason they were banished from Georgia? Because Brett jumped in the water on a hot day? Isn't being able to swim one reason for buying waterfront property?*

She continued, "Brett broke out in hives because he was immersed in the brackish water, which is precisely why I advised against it. Jenna didn't even seem to care about him suffering from a terrible rash. Her lack of concern was neglectful, another form of abuse. If she mothers this way in front of others, I can only imagine what she is like behind closed doors."

Donna pretended to care greatly about the Miller children, but he knew that was not true at all. Her actions over the years and her complete lack of interest in seeing them, talking to them, or being involved in their lives was evidence she didn't give a rip about them. Her desire to keep them away from Tom was another mark against her. No one who really cared about a child would make it so difficult for them to see their grandfather.

Paul was confident Donna's story would not match his wife's. He knew Jenna was a loving mother who always cared for her children when they were sick or suffering. He also knew she didn't let them get away scot-free if they were being disrespectful. His wife was a disciplinarian when it was necessary. She wasn't as harsh as he was, but she didn't let willful misbehavior go unaddressed.

Donna also said, "I also want to let you know about something that happened the very first time I visited your family at Fort Bragg when you were deployed. It has bothered me for years. When Tom and I were at your house before the Billy Currington concert, Jenna shared a video of Heidi gagging while she forced her to do the dishes. It was unfathomable that a mother could be so heartless as to demand her daughter do a chore that made her physically ill. She was obviously too lazy to do the work herself and delighted in her daughter's suffering."

Paul was in even more disbelief she was just bringing up something now that happened more than three years ago, however, he laughed out loud when he read this because he knew exactly which video she was referring to.

When his secretary asked what was so funny from her desk outside his office, he said, "God is great, beer is good, and people are crazy."

Alice Myers had no idea what her boss was talking about, so she just said, "Okay boss, whatever you say."

Donna concluded the email by saying to him, "I feel it is important you know this information since you weren't there to witness any of these events yourself."

Paul thought to himself, *does she really think she can cause me to doubt my wife or bring any sort of trouble into our marriage with one email? What does she expect me to do with this so-called important information?*

Paul had been by Jenna's side for nearly twenty-five years as her husband and had loved her for longer than that. He knew exactly what type of wife and mother she was—a damn good one. Donna wouldn't find a husband who was more loyal to his wife than Paul, and she wouldn't find a marriage more unshakeable than the one he shared with Jenna. She was barking up the wrong tree with her ill-planned attack.

He was confident there was no truth in any of the things she was saying and responded to her from his and Jenna's personal email account. He typed, "I know exactly what kind of woman Jenna is and I couldn't be prouder to have her as my wife and the mother of my children. Do not contact me at work ever again." He continued, "If you would like to discuss this matter fully, please feel free to call me anytime and we can talk about it like adults." His message had been short and concise.

When he showed Jenna the email later that night, she was furious.

She said, "How could Donna accuse me of child abuse?" She tried to think back to the trip from so long ago and remember what had happened. She did recall Olivia's ear had been hurting, but also remembered she had just finished her antibiotics and was cleared to swim. She only stayed late that evening because she was trying to befriend Donna. She was certain she had taken Olivia to the walk-in clinic as soon as it opened the next morning and had given her Motrin to ease her discomfort. She never expected Donna to use her desire to spend time with her against her! It was irony at its finest.

She also vividly remembered Brett jumping in the water, because she had been mortified he had broken Donna's rules and was afraid she would be upset. Jenna had pulled her son aside, outside of Donna's view, and harshly scolded him in private so as not to make a scene or call attention to his disobedience. She also remembered being pleasantly surprised when Donna didn't make a big deal out of the incident. She thought she understood that sometimes kids act like kids! Boy, was she wrong!

After his scolding, Brett told her he thought the rule was ridiculous, and she had silently agreed. It was silly the kids weren't allowed to cool off in the water. It had been very hot that day and they were burning up after canoeing. They were all good swimmers, and the water was barely waist high. Having grown up in Georgia, she knew there was no harm jumping in water, even if it was brackish. As long as there weren't any alligators lurking nearby, it was neither dangerous nor hive inducing.

What caused hives though, was grass.

Brett broke out in a rash after rolling around in the yard with his friend. She was very aware of the source of his allergic reaction because it had been happening since he was two. They dealt with it on a regular basis. She recollected her son had dramatically hammed up the whole situation because he thought it was funny to run around and scream like a lunatic.

It was very typical teenage boy behavior to act like a clown in front of teenage girls. He knew Heidi's friend was watching and he wanted to make her laugh. She was a senior and he wanted her to like him. The hives only lasted until the Benadryl kicked in, like always.

Regarding the video she referenced, even Heidi will tell you her aversion to dirty dishes is ridiculous. She had been standing right next to Jenna when she showed Donna the clip and was laughing because she knew she was being overly dramatic. Jenna had seen her daughter share the video with several of her friends herself because she thought it was funny.

It was Paul who was behind the camera the day the video was filmed, not her. She had only shown it to Donna because it was a running joke in their family, and she wanted to include her in some of their humor. She had thought of it as they cleaned up the kitchen together on the night of Donna's first visit.

She also felt confident her kids would be the first to admit they should do more chores and help their mother out more often. No one had ever accused her of being lazy before. Jenna thought to herself, *it is not abusive to make your teenager wash dishes.*

Paul held his wife and told her he had already forgotten everything the email said because he didn't care about it in the least. He was madder Donna contacted him on his government account and that she would even consider for a second he wouldn't stand by his wife.

Donna never called Paul to discuss the matter any further. It was clear she preferred to send cowardly emails and had no intention of talking about anything. She didn't want resolution, she wanted control.

Paul also found it wildly ironic Donna loved to falsely accuse Jenna of trying to come between her and Tom, yet she had taken the exact same tactic and purposely created a divide between her husband and his daughters. She had also unsuccessfully tried to create strife between him and his wife.

Zoom Kaboom

Six months after the accusatory email was sent to Paul's work account, the world shut down for Covid-19.

Tom thought it would be a good idea to make a call with his family so they could all connect, since no travel was possible, and it had been ages since they were all together. Jenna, Olivia, Brett, Heidi, Sydney and her boyfriend, and Caroline and her boyfriend, all joined Tom on the line. Katie and her oldest child refused to participate in the call.

The conversation flowed naturally for a while as everyone reported on how they were keeping busy in quarantine. Games, Netflix, naps, cleaning out closets, and trying new recipes seemed to be the norm.

When the conversation was ending, Tom said, "Sydney, Caroline, if you ever want to come to St. Simon's, you are more than welcome. Feel free to bring your fellas too. Donna would love to see you and meet them. I'll even take you for a ride in the Sea Ray."

After that, they all said goodbye and dropped off the call, one by one.

Jenna disconnected from Zoom angrily. *How could her father be so inconsiderate to offer an invitation to two of his grandchildren, but not the other three that were on the line?* Brett, Olivia, and Heidi had been banned from visiting their grandfather through no fault of their own, and it was mean to remind them of this by notably excluding them from the invitation.

Heidi was also mad and said, "Guess we're still not cool enough to be invited to St. Simon's. Nothing like being blackballed by your own grandfather." Her statement was a clear indication her feelings were hurt, and she had taken full notice of the snub.

Jenna and Heidi were both triggered by Tom's rudeness on the Zoom call because it reminded them of an incident that had happened about one year before Covid. The Miller kids had been begging Jenna and Paul to take them to St. Simon's. They loved it there and couldn't understand why it had been so long since their last visit. Even though Jenna knew it was against Donna's rules, she dared to ask her father if they could go to the Beachview Drive vacation home. She thought it was worth a shot to ask him directly. She called him on speakerphone in the car to discuss the matter. Heidi had been with her that day. Jenna did not expect the response she received. If she had even an inkling about what her father was going to say, she never would have made the call in front of her daughter.

Tom's response to her question was, "I'm sorry Jenna, but you and your family cannot come. Donna and I consider it an extension of our home and we won't invite people we don't like."

Jenna and Heidi had both been shocked by the callousness of his response. Jenna said, "Dad, are we so bad we are now considered people you don't like?"

Tom answered her by saying, "Well, you know I like you, but my wife does not. You can take it up with her."

Jenna asked him, "What have we ever done to Donna?"

He couldn't answer her question.

Jenna and Heidi thought it was abhorrent he would allow Donna to control his family's access to him and the property he had purchased with Grace. It was even more abominable he would consider his own daughter and grandchildren "people he didn't like." They weren't "people," they were family, they were blood.

Tonight's Zoom call brought these emotions back, and Jenna went into her notorious mama bear mode. She fired off an angry email to her dad asking that he never make her children feel left out, unimportant, and unloved again. She typed, "Invite whomever you want to your home or your vacation property but be more careful not to do it in front of people who aren't welcome. It is both tacky and hurtful."

He responded, "It is only you that is upset; I don't believe the children even noticed." He didn't seem to realize they weren't little anymore, and they were very capable of being hurt. Heidi was in college, Brett was in high school, and Olivia was in fifth grade. They weren't little anymore, but he barely saw them and underestimated their emotional maturity.

His email response went on to say, "I can't do anything about it anyway." Then he typed his familiar advice, "You should take it up with Donna." Making it clear she was the one who decides who can come and who cannot.

His response did nothing to make Jenna feel better, in fact it made her feel worse.

The Scapegoat

Shortly after the Zoom incident, Tom texted Jenna, asking if she and Paul would be available for a phone call on Thursday evening at six o'clock. She couldn't fathom why he was scheduling a call with his own daughter and son-in-law like a business meeting. She texted back, "I'm available right now. No need to wait three days." This wasn't the first time he treated her more like an associate than a family member, and it annoyed her greatly. He said he would not be ready until the time he had indicated, so she begrudgingly agreed to the scheduled call.

What did he mean when he said, "he wasn't ready?" There was no telling when it came to her father, especially since he met Donna. Jenna couldn't even begin to imagine what was on his agenda this time.

When he called exactly at the prespecified time, he and Donna were prepared for the conversation. Jenna imagined this is how Katie felt on the night her father requested her presence in the driveway so he could lecture her about tough love and financial responsibility.

Paul and Jenna were on one end of the call and Tom was on the other. It was clear Donna was in the room listening in, but she would not speak or acknowledge her presence.

As soon as Tom opened his mouth to talk, Jenna knew the evening was not going to end well. She was immediately perturbed when her dad started his scripted speech by saying, "It has come to my attention you have accused my wife of having Paranoid Personality Disorder which could be classified as a mental illness. I am here to tell you this is not true and to defend her. I will not let you talk about her that way."

Jenna and Paul's jaws hit the floor.

Jenna had spoken with her father about his wife's irrational behaviors more times than she could count. He was lying when he said they never discussed this. It was obvious at this moment, Tom Jacobs was only concerned about protecting himself and didn't care about his daughter or the truth. Jenna was collateral damage. He was making her the scapegoat to save himself.

Multiple conversations raced through Jenna's head. Tom and Jenna had discussed Donna's abnormal rage and paranoia repeatedly and agreed she exhibited almost all of the symptoms on the PPD checklist. They had talked in depth about the accusations Donna made about her ex-husband and Tom had admitted he had come to believe she was actually the one with the abusive behaviors, not Todd Thorn. Tom let it slip accidentally his wife overreacted to minor things like when he mentioned he and Grace had owned a vegetable chopper, and he was the one who told her Donna's jealousy of Grace was so intense he wasn't even allowed to visit her grave or keep a photo of her in his attic.

But here he was now, pretending as if he had never said anything negative about his wife and acting like he was as shocked as Donna to learn Jenna had the nerve to make such a ludicrous accusation.

As he lectured her, one specific conversation they had had several months ago kept coming to Jenna's mind. Her father had been very discontented with his marriage and had been almost in tears when he called. He lamented he had sacrificed his family for Donna, and it still wasn't enough to make her happy. He was feeling sorry for himself.

His self-pity was particularly bothersome to Jenna that day because it was evident her father believed he was the only one who suffered because of Donna and lacked any sort of empathy for Jenna or her family.

She remembered saying, "As hard as everything has been on you emotionally, Dad, you need to acknowledge you are the one who made the choice to sacrifice your family because you were afraid of the consequences from Donna. Have you considered it is worse to be the one being sacrificed?"

That was how she felt on a regular basis. She was continually being laid on the altar like a calf about to be slaughtered. *Did this make Donna akin to God in the Old Testament?*

Because of Donna's overly reactive nature, her dad sacrificed her and her family over and over and over again. Her analogy seemed to click with him, but he didn't think he had any other choice. Now, here he was again, sacrificing her for his own self-preservation and lying vehemently. Jenna felt like his self-righteous speech was igniting flames and she was the burnt offering. She could almost feel the heat on her skin and smell the burning flesh.

Jenna suspected the reason for this scheduled call was Donna had discovered the emails between her and her dad with her research about Paranoid Personality Disorder, but it appeared she never saw any of his responses. If she had, he wouldn't be able to put on this pompous display of arrogance and maintain deniability.

Jenna wondered, *Why would her dad take the time to delete his responses, but keep her side of the conversation in his records? Had he kept them to use against her later? Had she been baited? Had she actually been emailing with Donna the whole time pretending to be her father?*

Jenna was fuming with anger and hurt. After almost five years of abuse from Donna, she could feel herself starting to lose self-control, and so was her husband. Paul refused to listen to Tom's lies and accusations for even one second longer and interrupted the lecture. He asked his father-in-law to put Donna on the line so they could all hash things out once and for all and try to move forward, but of course she refused.

Paul was tired of Tom and Donna controlling the dialogue with pre-scripted, one-sided conversations. If Donna wouldn't speak, he was going to make her listen.

He began firing questions at Tom. He had completely lost his temper and didn't care. He thought his yelling would be further evidence he wasn't going to stand for his family being treated so badly anymore.

Tom had claimed for years that none of the problems the family faced were his fault, and there wasn't a single thing he could do to make things better but pray.

Paul could no longer ignore his father-in-law's hypocrisy and screamed into the phone, "Most of the problems in this family are your fault, Tom! You allowed your wife to come between you and your family. You sat idly by and watched the destruction of every relationship you used to hold dear."

Paul then brought up the Beachview Drive property and asked why his children couldn't come. "What have they ever done to deserve the cold shoulder from their own grandfather? They are innocent victims in all of this. I never would have imagined years ago that you would not willingly open your door to family. We used to be welcome any time, day, or night."

Tom responded by saying, "Donna and I make joint decisions and if she doesn't approve of someone coming, there is nothing I can do about it. I have changed my open-door policy out of respect for my wife's wishes."

At this point in the conversation, Tom was desperate to regain control, and wanted to get back to his script. He said, "Jenna, you should think about how you were raised and about the marital example my parents set for you. Grandma Helen would disprove of your failure to accept my marriage to Donna."

He thought by taking this tactic, he would shame his daughter and shut down any further conversation, taking the reins again.

To Jenna, it was almost as sacrilegious to use her grandmother as a weapon against her as it was to use the Bible to inflict pain. Another thing he had no problem doing. *How dare he try to shame her!* She had not been the instigator a single time in all these years, and he knew it.

Donna liked to tell everyone Jenna was disrespectful and unable to accept her marriage to her father. This simply wasn't true. She had done everything she possibly could to welcome her into the family. She even subjected herself to being hurt repeatedly, simply because she was trying to do the right thing.

Jenna didn't have a problem with her dad being married, but she did have a problem with every aspect of his life being controlled, including his relationship with her. She should not have to fight for the right to maintain a connection with her father. Jenna was tired of being blamed for everything.

Tom said, "Your grandma wouldn't approve of the horrible way you treat my wife. It isn't very Christian."

Instead of quieting her like he hoped, his comments about her grandmother incited her to find her voice. Through tears she yelled at him, "If anything, your mom would be disappointed in you! You are absolutely right she and Grandpa were a powerful example of marriage that I try to emulate every day. Paul and I have a loving and honest relationship. We respect one another, offer each other support, and do not control or manipulate each other. We value family like she did! I don't see that in your relationship with Donna or in your actions."

Jenna continued, "Grandma Helen was the most powerful example I have ever seen of a Christian woman who modeled unconditional love and devotion to family. She didn't use the Bible as a weapon against people or to try to appear like a superior Christian to others. She turned to scripture for guidance, to give others godly advice and comfort, and as a handbook on how to live her life. I certainly can't say the same about you. I have no doubt she would be proud of the woman I am today, and she would be especially proud of me as a wife and mother."

Paul completely lost it at this point. He yelled at his father-in-law, "Stop trying to blame us for everything. You are an adult and can make choices for yourself. If you want to have a relationship with your family, have one! If you want to have your grandchildren come to your house, invite them! Stand up for yourself and your family and stop letting yourself be controlled! You are the one that has allowed us to get to this point!"

He then said, "Olivia doesn't even know you are a fisherman because she has never seen you fish! Isn't that sad? Strangers know more about you than your own granddaughter!" He shouted out in frustration, "She has never even been on your boat!"

Tom replied, "There are other people who are part of my decision-making process. It is not solely up to me who can go on my boat.

It isn't that simple." He was clearly referring to Donna but wouldn't say her name.

Paul couldn't take it anymore and he started yelling even louder. "Tom, you and I both know that is complete bullshit!"

Tom hung up the phone.

It's Time to Talk

Jenna mulled over all that happened since Donna came into her life and decided to let the idea of ever visiting her dad's vacation home go. She phoned him and told him she didn't care about it anymore and would never ask about using it again. It was no longer a happy place and even the idea of it upset her.

Tom asked her if she would be willing to talk to Donna one more time about it before she gave up completely. Jenna said, "We have talked enough. If a miracle ever happens and she changes her mind about letting my family visit, let me know."

Tom hung up the phone with his daughter and went looking for his wife. When he found her in the kitchen, he said, "Darling, Jenna would like to talk to you about the vacation home. She is willing to make an apology to you so we can all move forward."

Tom knew Jenna hadn't offered to say she was sorry, but it was the only way he could think of to get Donna to willingly talk to his daughter. He knew she liked to be on the receiving end of apologies. If the two women could just talk, he believed everything could work out. If he had to lie a little to facilitate the conversation, so be it.

Donna felt a rush of flow through her. She was truly surprised Jenna was willing to make an apology to her; it meant she definitively had the upper hand in the war they had been fighting for years.

Furthermore, if Jenna was willing to apologize to her, she reasoned she must be desperate to go to the vacation home. Donna thought, *she is probably too cheap or too poor to go on a vacation without Tom's money. I know it just kills her that I am the gatekeeper!*

Donna still hadn't decided if she would say yes to letting her and her disrespectful brood come. It would probably still be a no, but it would be fun listening to Jenna kiss-up to her. She would enjoy every minute of her stepdaughter being forced to brownnose. *Maybe she would offer her a tissue when it was all over.*

Later that day, Jenna received an unexpected text from Donna that said "Your father has informed me you would like to talk about the vacation home. He told me you are ready to apologize to me for your disrespectful behavior towards me and for all the damage you have caused in my marriage. I will be available at five-thirty this evening. After you make a sincere apology, we can discuss the usage of the Beachview Drive property."

Jenna stared at the text in disbelief. She had made no offer to apologize to Donna. Her father had lied—again. Jenna felt strongly Donna was the one who should be sorry. She had attacked her repeatedly over the years and ruined the relationship she and her kids had with her dad. She had also blocked her from the beach home purchased by her mom and dad years ago and loved to throw it in her face with pictures of practically every other person they knew enjoying it.

Jenna texted back, "You can call me at your convenience."

Donna was instantly angry. There was no way she would be the one to make the call. She replied, "If you want to speak to me, you will call me promptly at five-thirty. That is the only time I will accept your call.

And of course, you already know, if you don't abide by my request and sincerely apologize, you will never step foot in MY vacation home again."

Donna's inability to compromise and her use of capital letters in her text was maddening. Jenna had never met someone so unwilling to bend or incapable of extending even an ounce of decency in her entire life.

Even though Jenna was completely put off by the whole situation, she decided she would make the call and attempt to talk to Donna civilly for the first time in years. She purposely called ten minutes before she was instructed to do so, trying to send the message she was not a puppet on strings and would not perform tricks at Donna's request. There needed to be more balance in their relationship if it was ever going to work.

Donna answered the phone by saying, "I understand you are calling to apologize to me for being so disrespectful."

Jenna rolled her eyes and thought *hello would have been nice*. She took a deep breath and said, "I'm sorry about everything that has happened. I would like to move forward and discuss the usage of the Beachview Drive property."

Donna called her out immediately and said, "It sounds like you are only sorry you are in this mess, but you are not apologizing to me directly."

Jenna couldn't take it anymore and said huffily, "I don't know what it is you think I have done to you. I am also wondering if you plan to apologize to me for all the things you have done? I can give you a list of all the times you have purposely tried to hurt me or put a wedge between me and my father."

Donna said, "I can see your emotions are already running high. I hope you will be able to control yourself during this conversation.

People my age cannot handle being put in such stressful situations because it makes us feel ill. I am already starting to feel a little sick because of your tone."

Jenna wanted to reach through the phone and throttle her.

Donna continued, "As far as apologies go, I am sorry I emailed your husband at work; it was wrong of me to send him a communication on his government account. I am not sorry for what the message said, only the address I used. I have never done anything else to you. Your so-called list of transgressions is a figment of your imagination."

Jenna guessed her dad had explained to Donna it was inappropriate to email Paul at work because he could have been fired for it. Jenna and Paul could have lost their livelihood and all he had worked for over the years, including his retirement. They also could have had their children taken away.

Without stopping to take a breath, she said, "I might consider allowing you to use the property if you will formally agree to follow my rules. I know they have been a source of contention for you, but they are not negotiable. Of course, it has been necessary for me to add one more to my original matrimonial boundaries list."

She said, "My new rule is you will treat me with respect. It's a shame that this has to be stated as a rule, it should go without saying."

Jenna said, "Before I agree to your new rule, I would like to ask you a question. Do you plan to extend mutual respect to me? The way you are speaking to me now is extremely condescending."

Donna did not reply.

Jenna continued, "Furthermore, I will gladly follow all your matrimonial boundaries, old and new, if I can understand them fully. Surely, you won't mind if I ask you a few questions."

Donna didn't like the way this conversation was heading. Jenna wasn't groveling like she expected, in fact, it was quite the opposite. She seemed to be taking control of the dialogue.

Jenna said, "Is the rule I cannot travel with my father considered a matrimonial boundary?"

Donna replied, "Yes. I think that has been made perfectly clear."

Jenna then said, "How does me going on a trip with my dad negatively affect your marriage? I cannot for the life of me understand how allowing my dad to travel with me hurts you."

Donna did not answer. There was a long pause.

Jenna could tell her silence meant she was searching for an answer. Jenna continued, "Can you please clarify how you classify travel?"

Donna replied sarcastically, "It means exactly what it sounds like. I prefer your father to travel only with me and it will be a detriment to our marriage if he travels with you."

Jenna pressed on. "Does travel include going to the children's sporting events and music recitals if they aren't in our hometown? How many miles can we go from our house before it is considered traveling? If I book a hotel because we are attending a specific event, but we aren't going sight-seeing, is this considered a vacation?" She continued firing questions at Donna.

Jenna was starting to feel empowered because she could tell Donna didn't understand her own rules. She hadn't considered everything Jenna was asking. She simply created her rules so she could control the relationship Tom had with his daughter. She never expected them to be questioned in so much detail.

Donna was becoming extremely rattled.

Jenna said, "Respect is a two-way street. You have disrespected important Jacobs family traditions by prohibiting any sort of travel or visitation on holidays. Why is it fair you can ban my dad from traveling with his family, yet give no regard to what our family enjoyed before you came into the picture?"

Jenna reiterated, "I simply cannot understand how taking a trip with my dad or my family coming to the vacation house has any bearing on your marriage. It is completely up to you whether you choose to see us when we are there or to accompany us when we travel. My relationship with my dad is unrelated to your marriage."

Donna erupted in rage and screamed over the phone at Jenna, "They are considered matrimonial boundaries because if any of them are violated, I will divorce your father! It will be the end of our marriage!" Then she hung up the phone.

Jenna couldn't believe what she had just heard. Donna's statement was the epitome of irrational. Jenna tried to call her back, but when her voice mail picked up, she knew she would never talk to Donna again. She left a message asking her to call her back and said into the recording, "If you are willing to divorce my dad over anything I do, there are clearly other problems in your marriage that need to be fixed. You are the one who should be ashamed of yourself."

She didn't care if her message hurt Donna's feelings, she had reached her absolute limit.

The Breakup Letter

Two months after the horrible phone call with her stepmother, Jenna got a certified letter in the mail. As soon as she saw the oversized manilla envelope she knew it was going to be bad news because the return address was her dad's and Donna's.

When Jenna opened the envelope, she found a lengthy letter, her mother's wedding ring and engagement ring, which were permanently joined, and her father's wedding ring from his marriage to Grace.

His letter said, "I am writing to inform you I am taking a break from you and your family because you have caused unnecessary stress in my marriage. Your lack of respect is intolerable, and your failure to accept my wife is unacceptable."

He also informed her he had officially changed his will. He put Donna's name on all his assets and dissolved the family trust he had previously created. His wife was now the primary beneficiary of his entire estate. He realized this would make it easier for her in the event of his death, and it was all merely paperwork as far he was concerned. He still planned to honor Grace's request, but if he died first, he trusted Donna to do the right thing in her will. She promised him she would abide by his and Grace's wishes, and since she was such a devout Christian, he had no reason to doubt her sincerity.

He was enclosing the rings because they had been promised to Brett after Grace's death. All the other grandchildren received a piece of jewelry, but since he was the only boy and couldn't wear her jewelry himself, he was giving him the rings with the hopes he would use them one day to propose to his future wife. He also enclosed a letter for Brett on how to be a good husband.

Tom instructed Jenna not to attempt to call him or contact him again. If there was an absolute emergency, she could email him, as that was the only line of communication that would remain open.

Jenna stared blankly at the letter and wondered, *have I just been disowned?*

She had been sacrificed repeatedly, kicked while she was down, called names, treated dreadfully, and now she was being cast out of her father's life and being blamed for all the problems that occurred. She didn't really care about the money, but it stung knowing Donna had prevailed. Her greed and nastiness netted her everything she ever wanted and the prenuptial agreement was now null and void. Jenna knew Donna would have no intention of leaving her, Katie, or their children even one penny. Maybe Sydney, her favorite, would get it all.

Donna wasn't the woman of character her father believed her to be. She didn't even know how he could believe this himself after all she had done to destroy his family. Jenna wished she would have walked away years ago with Katie and saved herself years of torment and abuse.

Brett came into the living room where his mother sat.

He said, "Mama, what's wrong?"

Jenna handed him the letter without saying a word. After all, the rings were intended for him, and her father had left a note for him to read as well. Jenna didn't care about protecting her dad anymore and didn't care if her son read every word. Every awful, terrible, unbelievable word.

Brett read the whole letter, becoming more furious with each line. His heart was broken for his mother and the way she was being treated. His letter wasn't much better. He couldn't understand how his grandfather could be so cruel. He had been taught a parent is supposed to love their child unconditionally, but it did not appear to be true in this case. He could see no evidence of love in his Pop Pop's letter.

Paul was in Saudi Arabia on a one-year assignment when the letter arrived. Because of this, Brett felt like the man of the house and wanted to defend his mother. He went upstairs, and unbeknownst to Jenna, called his grandfather. He left several heated voicemails demanding he call him back so they could discuss this matter.

He apparently even threatened if Tom didn't call by a certain time, he would no longer consider himself his grandson. He had cussed several times, trying to make himself feel older than he was.

Jenna could admit this wasn't the best way for Brett to handle the situation but admired her son for trying to protect her. She was proud of him for standing up to his grandfather on her behalf. He was just a teenager trying to be an adult.

Rather than talking to his grandson, Tom chose to block Brett from ever being able to call him again. He never responded to him and went so far as to classify him as "harassing." He blamed him for causing Donna "undue stress." He never offered him a chance to work things out or to talk things over. He decided to cast him out of his life forever, rather than deal with confrontation.

There was no acknowledgement Brett was upset and his grandfather had hurt his feelings. There was no understanding Brett was barely seventeen. There was no unconditional love, grace, or forgiveness offered, and it hurt Brett more deeply than his grandfather will ever know.

He tried to contact his Pop Pop one more time after this, when he learned he had been awarded an ROTC scholarship to college. It was the biggest accomplishment of his life, and he was angry because he couldn't pick up the phone and share his good news with his grandfather. He felt cheated to have a grandpa who was alive but who he couldn't have a relationship with.

Brett wrote one more email to him in an effort to provoke a reaction and said some nasty things about Donna because he was still so furious at her for destroying the family he loved. He was wrong again with his method, but Tom refused to see the humanness or the hurt in his grandson and decided his decision to walk away from him was for the best.

When Jenna found out about the ROTC email, she was heartbroken for her son again. He felt like his grandfather had thrown him out of his life with no more thought than someone tossing out vegetables that had rotted in the bottom drawer of the refrigerator. All Brett wanted was for his Pop Pop to take some accountability for the damage that had occurred in the family. He wanted an apology. He also wanted his grandfather to tell him he was proud of him.

Brett's intense emotion was clear evidence of his deep affection for his Pop Pop, but Tom was too selfish to see this and too self-righteous to recognize what real love looked like.

Without realizing it, Tom had shown Brett exactly what kind of man he didn't want to be when he grew up.

Part Two

Cancer With a Side of Meatloaf

As the wind picked up outside and blew through the screened porch, Jenna shivered. The coldness that swept over her was a reminder of the unresolved pain inflicted upon her by her father, a reminder of the cancer rapidly growing inside her right breast, and the stabbing feeling that maybe God gave her time with her children when they were younger because he wasn't going to let her have it as they aged into their adult years. She was grateful for all the memories her children were sharing with one another on the other side of the door—but she longed for the opportunity to make more.

Several weeks ago, Paul and Jenna FaceTimed Brett and Heidi individually to tell them about the cancer since they were not in the same state when Jenna received the dreaded call from the doctor. Paul and Jenna at least had the foresight to make sure their two oldest children were not alone when they heard the news. Heidi's fiancé, Caleb, had held her as she cried, and Brett's girlfriend, Sarah, sat with him on a curb in Charleston, away from the watchful eye of upperclassmen who would surely poke fun if they saw him crying because they would have been unaware of the reason for the tears. Olivia was home at the time, and Jenna embraced her lovingly as she sobbed on the same loveseat that she sat on now. This news is what made Heidi and Brett want to come home so badly. They felt the need to be near their mother.

Jenna wondered, *why did her children have to go through this pain?* They had been through enough in their short lives.

Here she was again, questioning God.

Jenna stood up, put a smile on her face, and walked through the open door into the comfort of the house. As she crossed the threshold, she said to no one in particular, "It's getting chilly out there."

She suddenly felt the laughter of her children surround her, the smell of the meatloaf fill her nose, and just as quickly as she had questioned God in the moments before, she sent up a silent prayer of thanks for the amazing blessings in her life. After all, the doctors were certain her cancer was treatable, for now. She was about to fight the battle of her life, but science, medicine, her family, and God were on her side.

Brett looked up at Jenna and affectionately said "Hey, Mama." He had been so worried about her since he found out she had breast cancer but was having so much fun with his sisters his concern for her was temporarily tabled. He got up without even thinking about it to give her a little shoulder hug and then returned his focus to the story Heidi was telling about a road trip where they had all gotten into a fight before even leaving the driveway.

The kids hooted as they remembered how Paul slammed the car into park yelling, "Everyone WILL have a good time on this trip whether they like it or not. Stop annoying each other, NOW!" They all imitated him taking a deep breath, and then as if they had practiced, they said in unison "It's time to REGROUP," a common phrase uttered by Paul at some point during most family road trips. None of them could remember where the Millers were going that time, but they were all sure there was a family sing-along once everyone stopped their fussing and successfully "regrouped."

Paul always liked to kick off sing-alongs with "Pour Some Sugar on Me" by Def Leppard because it always put everyone in a good mood. He then usually played "Don't Stop Believin'" by Journey, followed by "Born in the U.S.A" by Bruce Springsteen before taking requests for Taylor Swift and modern country from the backseat.

Jenna knew it was time to move on from the hurt that had been heaped on her by her father. She also knew today was not the day to dwell on her cancer or entertain worst case scenarios about her future. She was here. Her children and husband were here. She had more in this house at this very moment than many people would ever have in their entire lives. God had been very good to her, despite her current trials, and He would be by her side as she embarked on this journey. She had a treatment plan in place and would be having surgery in a few weeks to eradicate the tumor.

But first, meatloaf.

Love Runs Deep

The days of being together under the same roof had flown by at a breakneck pace, and it was time for Brett and Heidi to return to their daily lives in South Carolina. Brett needed to go back to school, and Heidi was needed at work. Responsibility was calling.

Heidi was taking Brett back to The Citadel, saving Jenna and Paul a lot of driving. Charleston was only two hours from her house, and she was happy to help.

Brett was a much better driver than Heidi, by her own admission, so she would gladly let him take the wheel. They would listen to true crime podcasts and catch up on each others' lives without their mother eavesdropping. The miles would pass quickly, and it would become one more road trip to remember. Maybe they would even do an 80s sing-along.

Neither Heidi nor Brett wanted to leave Virginia. They felt a tremendous need to be near their mom. They were afraid of losing her to cancer, like they had lost their grandmother. They wanted to be with her every second they could. When they stopped to think about the what ifs, it was more than they could bear.

It was Jenna who insisted they return to their normal lives until the day before her surgery. She wanted their focus to be on school and work, not on her. It saddened her to be a source of pain for her children.

Brett and Heidi both planned to come home again for her scheduled lumpectomy and wanted to help take care of her while she recovered, and Jenna was grateful for their support. They both also wanted to be sure they could tell her they loved her one more time in person, before she went in for surgery—just in case.

Jenna wanted to tell them she loved them too. Lumpectomy's rarely go wrong, but there is always risk with any operation.

It was a relief to Jenna her two oldest children would be home on the day of her surgery so Olivia wouldn't have to be alone. Paul would accompany her to the hospital, and the three kids would be together. Jenna worried about her youngest daughter the most because she often kept her emotions bottled up and didn't like to talk about things that were bothering her.

Olivia was only twelve and cancer shouldn't be on her mind at all. She already had to worry about something happening to Paul on deployments, and now, she had to worry about her mom dying too. Sometimes, life just isn't fair.

Jenna asked God again, "Why?"

The Memory Reel

As Jenna helped Heidi pack for her return trip to South Carolina, she remembered she had the suit her mother wore when she left her own wedding reception many decades ago hanging in her hall closet. It was crammed in next to bulky winter coats and cocktail dresses that were rarely ever worn. It had hung in the back of Grace's closet for more than forty years before being relocated to Jenna's hallway.

Jenna wondered if her mom had looked at it every now and then to help her remember what it felt like to be young, beautiful, and in love. She had felt an unexplainable need to keep the suit when she cleaned out her mom's clothes years ago, just before her dad sold her childhood home. She didn't know why she decided to keep it that day, but only knew she couldn't bear to part with it.

She was extremely glad now that she did. Heidi had only been a young teenager then and marriage for her seemed so far off in the future. But here they were, ten quick years later, and it was very much happening.

It seemed the years between Grace's death and now had flown by. As Jenna headed to the closet to retrieve the suit, she threw up a silent prayer of thanks to the Holy Spirit for leading her to pack it up years ago. She knew it would be perfect for Heidi to wear to her bridesmaid's luncheon and a wonderful way to include her mother in the festivities.

Heidi tried on the pale pink suit. It had a high neck, sleeveless top and a matching pencil skirt, very typical of the 1960s. It fit Heidi like a glove and shockingly needed no alterations. It looked like it had been tailor made for her.

Jenna had a picture of her mother wearing it as she and her father had run out the door from their reception. Her mother had her hand over her eyebrows, shielding her face from the rice being thrown at them by their guests, and she appeared happy.

Grace and Heidi had the exact same body shape and were both gorgeous in the suit. The resemblance between the women was strong and another testament to genetics. It struck Jenna at that moment, for the first time ever, that Heidi was now a woman. Jenna's first baby and the child Grace had known when she was alive, had grown up. The little girl she used to be had been replaced by an amazing young woman who believed fully in God's promises and was ready to make her own path in the world.

Heidi's childhood had gone by in a flash. The years had been so short. Jenna's mind suddenly swirled with thoughts of midnight feedings and how she and Paul tried everything they could think of to comfort her when she had colic.

She remembered teaching her to walk and the joy she felt when her daughter grasped tightly onto her pointer finger with her whole hand, trying to put one foot in front of the other. She was wobbly at first but very quickly got the hang of it, and before Jenna knew it—her daughter could run, jump, dance, and do cartwheels. Heidi's hand now had no resemblance to the tiny hand that had clung to her tightly so many years ago. She now had neatly manicured fingernails adorned with a beautiful engagement ring that sparkled when the light hit it just right.

Jenna recalled looking at picture books with Heidi on her lap when she was an infant. She had pointed to illustrations and said things like, "A cow says moo," and "the flower is red." They graduated to nursery rhymes, then easy readers, and finally, chapter books. Heidi learned to read letter by letter, syllable by syllable, word by word—and now she was in graduate school.

Jenna could visualize Paul running along beside Heidi as she learned to ride a bike without training wheels. He steadied her by keeping one hand on the back of her seat and one hand ready to catch her if she leaned too much.

Her mind raced forward to Heidi's teenage years. Jenna could clearly remember clutching the "Oh Crap Handle" above the passenger window in the car and stomping on an imaginary brake in the floorboard when she taught her to drive. The memories began to slam into one another, and Jenna wished she could remember every day of her oldest daughter's life but that was impossible.

She could see snapshots in her mind of Heidi proudly posing for photos in her navy blue-and-gold beaded prom dress, on the stage at her high school graduation in cap and gown, on sorority bid day surrounded by her new "sisters," and when she received her degree from the University of North Florida. Jenna could hear happy screams the night Caleb proposed to Heidi at Ormond Beach, and she could almost feel the tears streaming down her face when Heidi stepped out of the dressing room at the bridal shop in Charlotte wearing the most gorgeous gown either of them had ever seen. They both knew it was "the one" with its long, flowing train, exquisite lacework, and floor length veil.

Jenna had so many memories and was suddenly aware being able to watch your kids grow up was a privilege and one of life's greatest blessings. God had given her so many wonderful days with her children, and she was thankful. She was also aware the old saying, "*the only thing constant in life is change,*" was true.

Jenna longed to see Heidi become a mom herself and experience the joy of motherhood. She prayed God would grant her the gift of becoming a grandmother and that cancer wouldn't prematurely take her life. She already felt an overwhelming sense of love for her future grandchildren who were not even yet conceived and wanted to hold them in her arms and kiss them on the head as she had done with her own babies.

Heidi walked down the hall so she could see herself in the full-length mirror on the back of the bathroom door. When she realized the fit of the suit was perfect, she began to cry. Jenna's tears followed. They both missed Grace enormously. Whenever they thought of her, they were overcome with how much they loved her and how much she had loved them in return.

Jenna spontaneously grabbed her daughter and hugged her with all her might. Heidi hugged back fiercely. They both could feel Grace's love in the embrace. It was as if she was somehow surging through their bodies.

Jenna was sad Heidi only had thirteen years of memories with her grandma but was simultaneously glad Heidi had those thirteen years. It was far more than Olivia had. Heidi had known her, loved her, and remembered her well.

Although Olivia didn't remember her, she knew she had been deeply loved. The legacy of Grace had reached her youngest granddaughter, despite the fact she was only two at her passing.

Olivia knew who the essence of her grandma was because she lived on through stories as familiar to her as they were to the person telling them. She knew far more about her grandmother and the type of person she was than she did about her grandfather, who was alive and well, choosing to live a life without her in it.

Occasionally, Jenna would hear her children reminiscing about the type of man their Pop Pop was before he met Donna, and they would tell a story about something fun they had done together. But mostly when they spoke of him, she sensed they were either sad or mad or both. They talked about him in past tense.

Olivia liked to look at pictures of Grace because they made her feel like she could remember being with her even if it was only in her imagination. She turned the pages quickly if there were photos of her grandfather. She didn't like to think about the fact she lost him unnaturally, since death was not the reason why. It is almost harder to lose someone who is still alive, thinking they don't love you or care about you, than to lose someone to death who you know would choose to be with you if they could.

Jenna knew her mother hadn't wanted to die. She desperately yearned for more years to be with her family, but it was not in God's plan, and she accepted her fate.

Jenna wondered, *will I go as gracefully as my mother did, or will I rebel against God on my deathbed? Will I feel mad and cheated, or will I be thankful for the life I had been given?* What a horrible thought to think, so she quickly prayed God would give her strength to accept His will for her life.

She had been blessed abundantly, and she knew who the source of these gifts was. It was just hard to remember sometimes, especially considering her cancer.

Auditioning for the Part of Granddaughter

Seeing Heidi in her mother's dress made Jenna mad at her father all over again. *Things should not be the way they were. How had the family gotten to this point?* Jenna knew her father and Donna would not be at the impending wedding because they wouldn't be invited.

There was only space for happiness in the pews at Heidi and Caleb's wedding. Jenna wanted the day to be perfect for her daughter and future son-in-law. Heidi and Caleb deserved to be surrounded by friends and family who loved and supported them through thick and thin.

It made Jenna's stomach hurt to think about how her oldest daughter had been wronged so many times by her grandfather and Donna and made to feel like less because of them. It was inexcusable, and Jenna was sorry she hadn't stood up for her sooner.

THE MATRIARCH

When Heidi was a sophomore in high school, she had the opportunity to go on a mission trip to Oklahoma. She had no idea the trip would change the course of her life forever, because that was where she would receive her calling from God to go into ministry.

As she prepared for the trip, she asked her grandfather if he would be willing to make a financial contribution to help pay for some of her expenses. She knew he was a devout Christian and assumed he would be pleased to help her. However, she quickly realized she had made some bad assumptions. He not only didn't say yes like she expected, but he didn't even have the decency to give her an answer at all. He found a way to put her off anytime she asked. Jenna and Heidi were both bewildered by his lack of support—and hurt.

After her first mission trip, Heidi discovered she had a heart for service and wanted to go on as many trips as possible. She was discerning her call and was on fire for the Lord.

Over the course of the next few years, Heidi went on five more mission trips, which is a lot for anyone, much less a teenager. She was passionate about mission work and looked forward to these trips more than anything else in her life. She prioritized them over family vacations, outings with friends, and summer jobs because she truly felt God was calling her.

Each time she planned to go on a trip, she asked her grandfather if he would consider donating, and each time, he ignored her completely. He knew how important these missions were to her, yet he didn't seem to care.

The last mission trip she was able to take in college, the summer before Covid, was to India. It had been a lifelong dream of hers to go to Asia, and she was in awe she was going. God had opened so many doors for her she didn't even know existed to make this happen, and she knew He was sending her there for a purpose.

It was also the most expensive trip she ever embarked on since it was on a different continent, halfway across the world. She had prayed her Pop Pop would help her but knew he wouldn't. She was used to his rejection by this point and left for her trip with much excitement and anticipation.

As she suspected, she was profoundly impacted by the trip. She began planning to return to India as soon as she returned home and was thrilled when she found an organization she could travel back with the following summer.

Since the next time she went was going to be eight weeks long, it was imperative she raise money so she could go. She decided she would ask her Pop Pop one last time if he would help her but expected no response.

She was pleasantly surprised and shocked when he answered her this time with "yes." He told her he would contribute "because he needed to make a few more donations for tax reasons." He explained giving to her "would help him out." He said nothing about his previous rejections. His gift appeared to be more about tax write-offs than supporting his granddaughter. Heidi was hurt by his response, but simultaneously thankful he was finally contributing, regardless of the reason why.

The trip to India was planned for the summer of 2020, the year Covid stopped the world. Her trip was canceled, and her grandfather's money was fully refunded. So, all in all, she went on six mission trips, and her Pop Pop never gave her a single dime.

It was very ironic after refusing to even acknowledge most of Heidi's requests, Tom and Donna decided to sponsor a child from India of all places. A Christian organization visited their church and made an appeal for donors. They were one of the first couples to sign up. It was very coincidental to say the least since this is where Heidi had gone and had hoped to return.

Tom liked to give Heidi regular updates on the child he and Donna sponsored because he knew she loved India and thought she would find his stories interesting. He described in detail all the gifts they showered on the child and explained how they made monthly donations. He also rattled on and on about the huge care packages they sent her for her birthday and Christmas.

Heidi hated feeling jealous of a child from India because she was so blessed, but that's how she felt when she heard her grandfather talk about her. He was so generous to this girl yet so stingy when it came to her.

Heidi was also taken aback when she heard her grandpa refer to the girl as their "adopted daughter." She was glad this child was being helped, but the more she was forced to listen to stories about her, the angrier she became. Her Pop Pop and Donna were over the moon for this girl they only knew through letters and pictures but didn't seem to care about her, their real grandchild, at all.

Jenna asked her father to stop talking about the child from India because it was upsetting Heidi, but he ignored her request. It made him feel good to let others know how generous he was. The pain he caused his granddaughter was lost on him.

His failure to support Heidi became even more difficult to accept when she found out he chose to support other missionaries with their trips. She only knew this because he constantly bragged about it, rubbing salt in Heidi's wounds. For years, he made it known he made regular contributions in support of the mission work being done by the son of someone he attended church with—whom he hadn't even seen in years. He explained he had a donor list and sent out a newsletter to let his benefactors know how his mission was going.

Heidi wasn't mad he was helping him, but no matter how hard she tried, she couldn't understand why her own grandfather would readily support someone he barely knew while ignoring her request for help completely. Perhaps if she had a donor list, he would have been more inclined to give.

Jenna suspected the reason her dad didn't help Heidi was Donna. Either she put a stop to any financial help from him or he was being extremely cautious with his money because she was bleeding him dry.

Donna also hurt Heidi's feelings repeatedly.

Heidi was very excited about her high school graduation and wanted her whole family to celebrate with her. She invited her aunts and uncles, cousins, closest friends, and her grandparents, which included Beverly, Tom, and Donna.

Donna informed Heidi and Jenna she wouldn't make the trip to Virginia if she wasn't guaranteed ground level seating at the ceremony which was to be held in the basketball arena at George Mason University. Donna claimed she was terrified to sit in stadium seats because of her fear of heights and insisted Jenna call the school on her behalf and ask for special accommodations. If they couldn't grant her request for special seating, she wouldn't come.

Heidi was upset with this selfish response because there were also other activities planned for the weekend, including a beautiful lunch on the water in Occoquan and a graduation party at their home. If she couldn't come to the ceremony, she could have joined the family at the other events. She seemed to have no desire to share in the happy occasion, and it reminded Heidi of the times at Fort Bragg when she didn't care about being there for Brett or Olivia's sports. Her actions constantly gave her the impression she wasn't interested in her or her siblings. The only thing she cared about was herself.

Jenna begrudgingly did as she was asked, even though she was slightly embarrassed to make the call. The school explained all seating was on a first come, first served basis, and no accommodation would be made ahead of time for anyone. They suggested the party get to the arena early so they would be able to find a suitable seat and felt confident there were many handicap accessible seats available.

Donna was dissatisfied with the school's response and decided she wouldn't come at all.

If she was protesting the school, they didn't know and didn't care—but Heidi did.

Instead of coming, Donna sent a gift, wrongly assuming her step granddaughter's feelings could be bought. In a rare moment of generosity, she allowed her husband to book a flight for himself so he could attend.

It was ironic when graduation day came, the entire family got there early and was able to sit in a section that didn't require going upstairs at all. They walked straight into the arena at ground level.

It was even more ironic when shortly after Heidi's graduation, Donna posted pictures of her standing at the top of the Ponce de Leon Inlet Lighthouse, the third tallest lighthouse in the United States. She climbed up two hundred and three steps for the photo op.

The pattern of rejection continued when Heidi was a freshman at UNF and she asked if she could visit her grandfather and Donna's new house on a weekend when she wanted to get away from school. Sometimes college life got exhausting and she needed a break. It was too far to go home for just a weekend, but Tom and Donna were only an easy drive away, straight up I-95. Heidi thought it would be nice to spend some time on their dock or by the pool at the vacation home.

Tom agreed to let Heidi come and they were both looking forward to the visit. However, it never happened. Donna canceled on Heidi at the last minute because she needed to go to HomeGoods to pick up some fall decorations she had specially ordered. The store had just phoned her and told her she needed to collect her items as soon as possible. She was afraid they would be re-shelved if she didn't go immediately, and it was imperative Tom drive her since it was quite a distance from their house. Even though she drove all over the state on a regular basis, she demanded Tom play chauffeur on this occasion because he drove faster than she did. She couldn't risk not getting her glass gourds.

Heidi couldn't understand why this necessitated canceling the entire weekend or why she couldn't just go to their house and wait for them. She was in college and not a small child.

Donna promised her they would reschedule, but they never did. Everything was always more important than her.

Heidi brushed off their rejection because she was used to it and decided to visit her other grandma, Paul's mother, instead. Beverly had moved to Florida a few years before Heidi started college and lived only an hour away in the other direction.

Beverly had an open-door policy and made sure Heidi knew she was welcome anytime, day or night. No invitation was necessary. Heidi was given the code to the automatic garage door and knew where the hideaway key was kept. If Paul's mother wasn't there, she instructed her to just let herself in and make herself at home. So, she did.

Any time Heidi suffered girl drama or heartbreak, she went to her grandmother's house. Any time she was overwhelmed with schoolwork and needed a quiet place to study, she went to her grandmother's house. Any time she needed someone to push her to stay focused and write a paper, she went to her grandmother's house. Any time she needed to feel loved because college was sometimes lonely, she went to her grandmother's house. She was always welcome there, and because of this, never asked if she could go to her Pop Pop and Donna's again. They also never invited her.

After Donna canceled her visit, Heidi called her mother and said, "My mission trips weren't important to them, my high school graduation wasn't a priority for Donna, and now fall decorations outrank me. What could possibly happen next?"

Jenna was afraid to even try to answer her daughter's question. It was all so inconceivable. She thanked God Paul's mother was a constant source of love for her daughter and modeled what a grandparent should be like, since her own father and Donna did not.

Tom and Donna only tried two more times to see Heidi over the entire course of her undergraduate college experience, despite being so close in proximity, and never at their own home.

Shortly after canceling her visit to see them, Donna invited Heidi to attend a play with them at the Historic Ritz Theatre in Brunswick. It wasn't going to take place until March of her freshman year, but they needed to know right then if she could go. Tickets were sure to sell out. Heidi told them she had no way of knowing what her schedule would be like five months in the future since she hadn't even registered for second semester classes yet, but they bought the tickets anyway. They knew it was a gamble to buy the tickets when they made the purchase.

The week of the play turned out to be Heidi's midterm exams and she had to prepare. It had been a tough semester, and she couldn't afford to sacrifice any study time. Donna was indignant she canceled at the last minute, making sure to point out how much money she had cost them.

At the time Heidi thought to herself, *exams are way more important than fall decor*, but kept it to herself. She also held back her desire to say, "I hope you get ground floor seats in the auditorium." She didn't want to add any more fuel to Donna's fire, and she knew being petty was unchristian like.

The next time Donna and Tom invited Heidi to do anything was two years later, when she was a junior. They had business to attend to in Jacksonville, so they planned a visit to see her at school and offered to take her out to lunch. When they arrived, Heidi gave them a tour of the campus. They had a lovely lunch and went to Heidi's favorite coffee shop afterward. Heidi thought they had a wonderful time but sensed a little tension at various points throughout the visit. She had no idea why it was there, so she tried to dismiss it. When it was over, they hugged and said their goodbyes. Heidi returned to campus thinking all went well. *Had she actually had a good time with her Pop Pop and Donna?*

However, when Tom reported back to Jenna on how the visit went, he said, "Donna didn't feel there were any lasting bonds created between her and Heidi." He indicated he would be surprised if she ever agreed to make plans with her again. And they never did.

It was maddening to Jenna. She didn't realize Heidi was on an audition trying to earn the role of granddaughter. She mistakenly believed she already had the part in the bag. Twenty years of experience apparently didn't count for anything.

Tom and Donna rarely spoke to Heidi after the lunch date, but if they did, it was only to inquire about her boyfriends or remind her what strong Christians they were. It felt like they were comparing their faith to hers since she was a religious studies major and planned to become a minister.

It never made sense to Heidi why they did this or why they needed to let her know they knew more than she did. She wasn't in a faith competition and had no desire to be. She just wanted to be their granddaughter and for them to be "regular" grandparents. No knitting required.

Heidi also saw every vindictive Facebook post Donna made directed at her family. No matter how many times her step grandmother made passive aggressive posts, she was always felt lambasted. She was never prepared for the hurt that would wash over her.

It was difficult to see other people visiting her grandparents' house, the vacation home on Beachview Drive, or enjoying her Pop Pop's yacht. She had never even set foot on his new boat, and it had been so many years since she was allowed in either of his homes.

It was hurtful to see her grandfather riding horses with Sydney, and Donna spending time with her, because she had not been given the same opportunity. She was annoyed every time she saw pictures of Olivia in her flower girl dress posted repeatedly, knowing Donna hadn't seen her sister in real life in many years and was just using her for likes. And the nonstop barrage of quotes about toxic people pilfered from Pinterest was almost more than she could stand.

The worst post Donna ever made, though, as far as Heidi was concerned, came on the same day she had been accepted to college. It had been a magical day for the Millers because Heidi's dreams were coming true. She had been accepted to the University of North Florida with a very large scholarship offer and she was filled with excitement for her future. Her mother had posted a picture of her holding a banner that said, "Future Osprey!" And of course, they had called her grandfather to tell him the good news.

Heidi didn't expect anything to bother her on that day because she was so happy, however, she failed to anticipate being the victim of a sneak attack on social media from someone who was supposed to love her—or at least like her. It was very upsetting when she saw Donna had shared an article on her Facebook page about "how it was far more important for parents to teach their children to learn to be decent human beings and learn how to be respectful than for them to go to college." The timing of the post felt like a sucker punch.

Heidi knew this was a personal attack. *Was Donna insinuating she wasn't a good person or that she had bad parents—or both?* Either way, it was mean and cast a dark shadow on Heidi's wonderful news.

Moving On

Jenna tried to forget about her dad and wished thoughts of him and Donna would stop filling her head. They had caused so much pain in the family, and she didn't want them to occupy her brain another second. She wanted to enjoy the last moments she had with Brett and Heidi before they left. Being present in the moment with her children was all that mattered right now. She loved Heidi, Brett, Paul, and Olivia more than life itself and vowed nothing would ever come between them.

It was her dad's loss he wasn't a part of their lives. He had missed multiple graduations and countless accomplishments of his grandchildren over the years. He didn't even know them anymore or understand how amazing they were. They were loving, kind, intelligent, respectful, and successful, yet he had no idea.

He stopped sending them anything for their birthdays or Christmas after the letter informing them he was stepping away and never even bothered to text them to see how they were doing. He was clearly happier in his marriage without his daughter or grandchildren in his life.

With each passing week, month, and year he stayed away, the children missed him less and less, and their anger toward Donna increased more and more because they blamed her for everything. Memories of Tom began to fade, and they no longer thought of him as often as they had before.

Jenna was glad her children were moving on from the pain he had inflicted. She just wished she could do the same.

Fighting Cancer

Shortly after Jenna received her diagnosis of breast cancer, she had the nagging feeling she should tell her father. It seemed like too big of a secret to keep from him, after all, he was her dad. Even though he had walked away from their relationship and chose to exclude her from his current life, he was still the man who had wrapped her up in a towel after her bath when she was little and swung her through the air like she was Superwoman. He was still the man who had made her oatmeal with sliced bananas and brown sugar every morning before school. He was still the man who had walked her down the aisle on her wedding day.

She was confident he would want to know she had breast cancer, and despite all the pain he had caused her, she felt he deserved to know. Jenna couldn't imagine how she would feel if something was terribly wrong with one of her own children and she was kept in the dark.

Since the fateful day Jenna received the scornful letter from her father notifying her she was being cut out of his will and his life, they had only exchanged emails once. Jenna had learned from a mutual acquaintance her dad had been very ill, and being immediately concerned about him, she reached out to him via email—her only allowable form of communication. She wanted to be sure he truly was okay. He responded he had made a full recovery but did not elaborate with any details.

Jenna knew he had been extremely sick but was minimizing the severity of his illness in his response. He gave no details and made it sound as if he had only had the common cold.

Their mutual acquaintance had told Jenna her dad had been through a very serious bout of bacterial pneumonia, and he wasn't telling her the truth. He had run a dangerously high-grade fever for days and was so weak at times he could barely lift his head. He had suffered from a painful cough and experienced extreme chest pain that had been unbearable. He had spent a considerable amount of time in the hospital and his recovery was slow. After extensive breathing therapies, heavy doses of antibiotics, and rest, he finally recovered but was still experiencing lingering side effects from the illness.

Jenna was relieved to know he wasn't going to die. She hated to think about something happening to him with so much unresolved conflict in their relationship. She was greatly bothered she was never notified of his illness or told he was in the hospital. She only found out by happenstance. Neither her father nor Donna had the decency to tell her. They were not blocked on her phone and could have easily called her with the news, but instead, they were willing to risk him dying without ever speaking to his daughter again.

It was very upsetting, and it was exactly what she told her father would happen if they ever found themselves in this situation. Several years ago, they had a frank conversation about Jenna's fears that Donna would not notify her if something serious happened to him. He had dismissed her concerns and said she was foolish to feel this way. He assured her his wife was honorable and would do the right thing.

Jenna now knew her thinking was justified and was confident her dad would deny this conversation ever happened if he was asked. *She wondered if she would find out about his death on Facebook.*

She also knew her assumption about not being included in the will, if it was left up to Donna, was also correct. Donna had shown her true character many times, leading them to where they currently stood. Jenna wasn't sure how her father could believe she would do right by his children. It was obvious to everyone who knew the whole truth she would not feel any obligation to make good on Tom's promise to Grace.

Jenna decided she would not let her dad find out she had cancer from a mutual acquaintance. She knew from firsthand experience learning about serious things through the grapevine was hurtful. The right thing to do was to tell him directly and give him all the information she had up to that point.

She laid out her diagnosis in a short email that was straight to the point.

He was shocked by the news and said how thankful he was she contacted him. His email reply also said, "I'm glad I thought ahead of time to keep email available to you for important information such as this."

Jenna was annoyed by his arrogance and thought, *good for him to have such foresight.*

She informed him she would be having a lumpectomy and would undergo radiation treatment but was unsure if chemotherapy would be required at this point.

She reasoned her diagnosis might be just the thing to make him want to reconnect with her and fully expected him to call. *How could a father not call his daughter when he found out she had cancer and would be having serious surgery? Only the most cold-hearted of souls would not reach out. Right?*

She also convinced herself God was going to use her cancer to bring reconciliation in the family. She trusted He would find a way to bring something good out of a bad situation.

As it got closer and closer to her surgery, her father never called. Jenna regularly checked her voicemail and missed call log, but to no avail. Rather than phoning, he emailed her he would be praying for her and said, "I am sorry, but I am unable to help in any other way."

If he had offered to come for a visit, Jenna would have agreed to let him come. But he never did.

Jenna couldn't help but feel he wasn't allowed to visit or reach out to her, and that if he even brought up the idea of traveling to see his daughter, it would have been viewed as a deliberate violation against Donna's rules. He would have suffered backlash from his wife, and he wasn't willing to put himself in that position. His daughter wasn't worth compromising the peace in his house or in his marriage.

Apparently, even cancer wasn't a good enough reason to put the matrimonial boundaries aside.

Jenna's surgery date approached, and then finally arrived, and her dad still didn't call.

He sent her roses as if this was an appropriate substitute for being there for her. However, when Jenna looked at them, they served as a painful reminder that he wasn't.

Donna sent her a note and a gift from the Christian Supply Center, a bookstore operated by the Assembly of God church. Both the note and the gift rubbed Jenna the wrong way.

Donna had the audacity to write, "I know we have had our troubles in the past, but I really am praying for your full recovery."

Her use of the word "really" hit a nerve with Jenna. *Did Donna use it because she wanted her to know she actually meant what she was saying this time? Was she acknowledging her multitude of previous lies?*

Her pitiful attempt to reach out to Jenna made her think Donna felt a gift and a note could absolve her from the role she played in destroying the Jacobs family.

It did not.

Donna had willfully come between Jenna and Tom and ruined their relationship. She had said and done truly unimaginable things. Because of her, Jenna was disowned! Her jealousy and need to control every aspect of Tom's life had caused more hurt, stress, and damage than Jenna ever dreamed possible, and her father let it happen.

Jenna was also agitated Donna had written, "I put you on the prayer list at my church."

She was glad for people to pray for her and was thankful she had made her way onto the prayer lists at many of her friends' home churches because she believed in the power of prayer. Knowing so many people were lifting her up, especially on days when she didn't have the energy to pray herself, gave her great peace.

What bothered her about Donna, though, was she felt she put her on the prayer list so she could receive attention for herself. It bugged her to think people would shower Donna with comfort because of Jenna's illness. They would say things like, "Oh Donna, this must be so difficult on you," and "I can't imagine what you are going through!"

Donna wasn't a part of Jenna's life, and she certainly had no active participation in her cancer journey. She had no idea what Jenna was experiencing. Jenna didn't want people to assume there was a deep love between them when there was not. She felt used.

She pushed her father's lack of support out of her mind, because she was surrounded by friends and family who inundated her with their love, prayers, attention, phone calls, visits, meals, and gifts. It was obvious who was on her side. She was amazed to see she had a humongous support system behind her. She needed to focus on healing, not on hurt feelings.

Jenna was even more surprised when she received a picture of Brett's entire company at The Citadel the morning of her surgery. Her support system went far beyond those she knew well and extended to the friends of her inner circle. In the photo, the cadets were holding handmade posters wishing her luck and telling her they were praying for her. She believed their warm wishes to be sincere, and she was touched by their kindness. She couldn't believe this group of young people had taken time out of their busy schedules to do this for her. It made her tear up with gratitude. They also collected money and sent her a card and a gift basket. Their gestures were incredibly thoughtful and heartfelt. Jenna knew if they supported her, they supported Brett. It was difficult for him to be away from her because of her diagnosis and seeing the love from his company brought her great peace of mind.

Out of courtesy for Tom, believing it was the right thing to do, Jenna and Paul continued to keep him in the loop via email regarding her cancer. Paul even made sure to send him surgery updates. Tom thanked them for the information, but still never called.

Unfortunately, as with many cancer stories, things didn't go as smoothly as they hoped. Even Jenna's doctors were surprised by the curveballs being thrown at them.

Jenna's lumpectomy was unsuccessful. Pathology reports showed her cancer was much larger than the eleven millimeters initially detected by the mammogram, but they weren't sure exactly how large it was yet. It was also confirmed Jenna had a genetic mutation known as CHEK-2 that was probably responsible for her developing cancer in the first place. The last bit of bad news was they had discovered micro metastatic disease in three of her lymph nodes during the lumpectomy. Although they successfully removed the lymph nodes, more extensive surgery was going to be necessary to get the cancer out of Jenna's body.

With her new diagnosis, Jenna was confident her mother must have had the same gene. By discovering the source of her own cancer, she now believed she had uncovered the reason why her mother had also contracted the disease. She was grateful it had been caught much earlier in her and wished it had been the same with her mom. She also prayed she did not pass it on to any of her own children. She couldn't bear this thought.

Jenna and her doctors scheduled her second surgery for the twentieth of December, right before Christmas. Although this might seem like a bad time for major surgery to some people, it made perfect sense to the Millers. Paul had time off from work for the holidays and could devote all his time and attention to his wife. All the Miller children, and even their future son-in-law, would be able to come to their home for the holidays and assist with her recovery. Jenna knew they would all pitch in wherever they were needed and would make sure Christmas went off without a hitch. And finally, it was soon.

Jenna didn't want the cancer growing inside of her for a minute longer than was necessary. She felt like her body had been invaded by a silent intruder and the faster it was apprehended, the better.

Jenna was more scared this time than she was for the lumpectomy because no one knew the extent of the cancer growing inside her right breast. She felt very unsettled since there were so many unknowns. She was also worried because of her genetic predisposition, she might develop a tumor in the left breast, so she opted to be proactive.

Jenna's doctors had similar concerns and suggested a double mastectomy might be the best option for her, and she agreed. They also advised against reconstruction until at least a year after radiation treatment.

After extensive research, Jenna decided against reconstruction entirely. She would be flat for the rest of her life, but she would be cancer free if the plan worked.

Her doctors and her family fully supported her decision. She wasn't defined as a woman or a person by her breasts. She was defined by her heart, her faith, and her character.

Jenna joined several online support groups in preparation for going flat and quickly learned how lucky she was to have Paul as her husband. Many husbands were not nearly as supportive. She was shocked by how many marriages fell apart because of cancer and because husbands are unable to accept their wives' changed bodies or reduced sex drives after cancer.

Paul agreed wholeheartedly with her decision to stay flat and was against reconstruction even more than she was. He wanted to be sure if anything came back, it would be found easily, and not obstructed from view. He repeatedly reminded Jenna how beautiful she was, and it wasn't because of her breasts.

Paul loved her more than she thought possible. She laughed when he teased her about scars being sexy.

Deep down all Paul wanted was for his wife to survive. He was terrified but didn't want Jenna to know. She needed him and he would be strong for her. He wasn't ready to even consider losing her yet. They had way too many plans for their future to allow doubt or fear to enter his mind.

Jenna kept her dad informed of her decisions and next steps via email. They had a somewhat regular back and forth between each other for a while, and Jenna thought they might be on the road to reconciliation, but she couldn't help but be bothered by her father's tone in each message. His emails lacked the compassion and love she was looking for. She pointed out to him it was hurtful he didn't ask how her kids were handling the news and she informed him it felt like he was more concerned about being reassured than he was about her health. He wanted facts but didn't offer any emotional support.

This probably wasn't totally true, and Jenna could admit she was overly sensitive to anything from her dad because of the tremendous hurt he had inflicted, but she couldn't help the way she felt. A phone call would have made her feel he cared much more than emails, and she would have been able to hear concern in his voice. It is very difficult to discern true emotion from words on a screen.

Jenna went in for surgery as planned, a few days before Christmas, and this time it was successful. Her tumor was five point six centimeters, much larger than expected. Jenna's diagnosis had gone from a barely Stage One, best case scenario, to a full Stage Two with a variety of variables to consider. But, regardless of the notes in her medical record, the cancer was finally out, and all margins were clear. Thank God!

Paul kept her father informed via email every step of the way.

Tom still never called.

Jenna's team of oncologists recommended chemotherapy, radiation, and endocrine hormone therapy as preventative measures to keep the cancer from returning. She also had a choice to make after chemo and radiation were complete. Since her cancer was estrogen and progesterone positive, she would either need to receive monthly injections to force her into medical menopause or have her ovaries removed entirely. Jenna agreed to the entire treatment plan and opted for surgical removal of her ovaries. She wanted to do everything in her power to keep from ever going through this again.

Also, God forbid it ever did return, she could look her children in the eyes and tell them she truly did everything possible. She would be able to honestly say she had fought cancer with every weapon available.

A month after the double mastectomy, Jenna had healed enough to go to the next phase of her treatment plan. Even though she still had limited range of motion in her right arm, gnarly incisions that were only just starting to heal, and was unable to sleep on her stomach or move her torso without pain, the doctors approved her for chemotherapy. A port was surgically placed into her chest to make receiving infusions easier. It was uncomfortable, and the tubing that extended up into her neck poked her every time she turned to the left. The place on her chest where the port was placed was constantly sore, but she knew it was necessary for the next step of her treatment, and she tried to keep her complaining to a minimum.

Her infusion schedule was built around Heidi and Caleb's wedding, which was planned for March. She would have two treatments before their wedding and two after. Her infusions were planned with the wedding date in mind and designed so she would hopefully only experience minimal side effects on the actual day.

Jenna was heartbroken when her hair started falling out in clumps only twelve days after the first session—and before the wedding. She decided to shave it entirely since she was shedding at a rapid pace, and her hair follicles were extremely tender. She hadn't expected chemo to even make her hair hurt. She resigned herself to the fact she would have to wear a wig to the wedding, but nothing was going to stop her from being there.

Her daughter's wedding became the most important focus of her life. Not only did it help take her mind off her treatment and keep her busy, but it also had significant emotional importance. Jenna was grateful she would be there and wanted it to be perfect. She spent countless hours making phone calls to vendors, crafting when she felt up to it, and surfing the internet for items that would add to the overall experience.

She feared if the cancer came back, she would miss Brett's and Olivia's weddings, and it broke her heart to think these thoughts. If she was only going to be able to attend one of her children's weddings, it would need to be amazing. She prayed constantly for God to grant her healing and to end the cycle of cancer in her family with her making a full recovery.

Her doctors were very hopeful with the extensive treatment plan, she would beat the cancer and go on to have a full life. There was some concern about her young age, because they needed to keep her healthy for another forty years. Her treatment was far more aggressive than if she had been in her seventies when she was diagnosed, but she was young and otherwise healthy, so she could handle it.

Jenna had full faith in her oncology team and believed God had blessed her with amazing doctors. She forced herself to remain positive and push her fear to the wayside.

Jenna decided to keep her bucket list the same as before she had cancer. She would plan for many years of living and make sure her mindset reflected positivity as much as possible. On her list was: to be a grandma, to see Olivia graduate and become an architect, to see Brett become a commissioned officer, to see Heidi officially ordained, and to grow old with Paul. Everything on this list could only happen if she was given time. She didn't need to skydive or climb Mount Everest. She just needed to be there for her family.

Do You Love Me?

Just a few weeks before Heidi and Caleb's wedding, Paul received an email from Tom. Although the message was intended to be nice, it infuriated both Paul and Jenna, as most things from her father did.

He was attempting to provide support to Paul, as Jenna's caretaker, and empathized with him because he had cared for Grace.

They could appreciate the purpose of the message; however, he came off as all-knowing and like a self-proclaimed expert regarding being a good husband. He didn't see anything offensive in telling Paul "Since Jenna has cancer, it is a good opportunity for you to show her you love her." He explained, "this is the perfect time to prove to her you love her with your actions, not just your words."

Jenna couldn't believe her dad would have the nerve to try to tell Paul how to love her or to infer that showing her love wasn't important prior to her diagnosis. Her dad certainly didn't know how to show Jenna love, and if he did, he hadn't followed his own advice in years.

Jenna and Paul felt the message was another example of his hypocrisy.

Paul responded angrily via email, still his only option for communication. He said, "Cancer doesn't change anything for me. Every day since I said "I do" has been an opportunity to show my wife I love her. I vowed to love her in sickness and in health, and for more than two decades the health part has fully applied. I didn't wait until the sickness part to shower my wife with love, affection, and appreciation." He continued, "I have worked hard for a quarter of a century to make Jenna feel valued and have never given her a reason to even question my love for her. Cancer didn't change my feelings for my wife or my actions. I was there for her before cancer, I will be there for her during cancer, and I will be there after cancer. I will love her all the days of our marriage, just as I promised her and God."

After Jenna read the letter from her father, it stirred up a lot of emotions she had bottled up inside for so long. She still longed for things to be the way they used to be in her family, but she knew the chances of that ever happening was a long shot.

The nostalgia she felt for the family she had before her mother's death made her miss her childhood home, which she hardly thought about anymore. She decided to look up her old address on the internet and see if she could find some pictures. She assumed when she typed in the address, the sales listing from many years ago might show up on Zillow. It would be marked as "off the market." She thought it would comfort her to see photos of her once happy home and transport her back in time when family was simple, love for her from her parents was abundant, her mom was alive and well, and any hard feelings were always forgiven.

Jenna was surprised when her quick Google search returned information about an estate sale that happened just after she cleaned out the home. She did not remember her father telling her about hiring a professional company to help him clear the house. She could understand the practicality of it but didn't know why he would keep it a secret. He had told her he was getting rid of things, but never gave details as to how he would accomplish this. If he had, she wouldn't have been so shocked to find the ad.

Also, if he had been honest with her at that time, she would have driven right back down to Georgia and saved her great aunt's paintings. She couldn't believe what she was seeing in the ad! Some of the family's beloved paintings were photographed and highlighted in the "Items for Sale" section of the advertisement. A painting of a beautiful monarch butterfly that had hung in her parents' home for decades was staring back at her from the computer screen. She was utterly flabbergasted her father would be so cold as to sell his late wife's family heirlooms as easily as he sold an old couch.

Her dad did not store the paintings as promised and had sold them off, most likely for the value of their frames, with no regard to their sentimental value. He had no intention of keeping his promise to her and had lied to her face when he told her he thought she and Katie had taken them all. He knew what their fate had been but was too ashamed or too heartless to tell her the truth.

Jenna was furious. Anger pumped through her veins. *How dare her dad try to tell her husband how to love her. How dare he sell off her great aunt's artwork and lie about it. How dare he let his daughters and grandchildren be kicked out of his life. How dare he not call his daughter with cancer even one time!*

Jenna was beside herself with frustration and grief. She knew she had made the right decision when she opted not to invite him to

Heidi's wedding. He didn't value family at all, and his actions were proof of that.

Jenna sat on her discovery until after the wedding. She couldn't allow it to occupy any more of her thoughts. She had so many last details to tie up for Heidi and Caleb's special day and didn't want to be distracted.

A few days after the wedding, and after her third round of chemo, Jenna sent her dad an email telling him she had learned about the estate sale from years ago. She questioned why he got rid of the artwork he promised to keep? She also told him she didn't even know if he loved her. His advice to Paul made her wonder because she could not tell by his actions that he cared at all, much less felt love for her.

He had treated her like a dog that was dumped on the side of the road and then blamed for its fate because it was too much of a puppy, and thus, too much trouble. A puppy couldn't help being a puppy any more than Jenna could help that she was Grace's daughter, the reason Donna had wanted her kicked to the curb.

She typed furiously, and as she did, every other question she ever had for her father came to mind. She made her own questionnaire in her head about what answers she would need to see in his reply if she was ever going to talk to him again. For her own sanity, it was finally time to either move forward or end it all.

She asked her dad if he still wanted to be buried next to her mother when he died—he had ignored the question multiple times over the years after meeting Donna. She asked him why the only thing he seemed to be interested in about her children was their romantic relationships. Donna seemed to have a strange fascination with other peoples' love lives.

Tom had asked her in his last email if she could send him some pictures of Heidi's wedding. His request rubbed Jenna the wrong way and she snapped back at him angrily. She wondered, *why had he never asked for pictures of anything else before? Why didn't he ask for pictures of Brett's high school graduation or first day of college? Did he care about Heidi's college graduation or Olivia winning the Science Fair? Did he ever just want to see his grandchildren's faces and see how much they had grown?*

Jenna thought it was interesting in his last email he also mentioned he wasn't invited to the wedding, as if Jenna didn't know. *Did he honestly not know Jenna and Heidi were as thick as thieves and Jenna was included in every facet of wedding planning?* She was the one who addressed every envelope by hand.

Jenna no longer cared about holding back and told him she was fully aware he wasn't invited. She reminded him he was the one who notified her via mail long ago he was taking a break and walking away from her family. He was the one who blocked their ability to talk to him. He was the one who allowed his wife to establish "matrimonial boundaries," making a relationship with him impossible.

She concluded her email by telling him she was sad their relationship was in such a terrible state. She read over her message one more time, no longer caring how it would make her father feel.

She hit Send.

The only question he had to answer in his reply was, "Did he love her?" If he answered yes to that, she would continue to share her cancer journey with him and attempt to keep communication open. If he didn't respond with a clear yes, she knew in her heart she would be done once and for all. Her heart had been broken so many times, it was reaching the point where it could no longer be pieced back together. For her own self-preservation, she could no longer spend so much emotional currency on someone who didn't love her back.

Test Failed

A few days after her anger-driven email was sent, she received a reply from her father. He told her, "You only remember what suits you."

Lie.

He said, "I told you about the estate sale."

Lie.

He tried to twist the facts by telling her "you and your friend came to the house and were given every opportunity to take what you wanted." He failed to mention her phone call to him while she was there or the promise he made to her about storing the pictures. He also told her, "I will not discuss my matrimonial boundaries with you," which obviously meant they were still in place.

The worst part of his response was when he implied perhaps her sadness was God's way of trying to humble her for her behavior. Then he took the opportunity to remind her about the commandment to honor your mother and father.

Was he even serious?

How dare he try to shame her and use God as a weapon against her—again. He had been doing this for years, and it made her blood boil every time. He was unable to see his own hypocrisy in the whole situation. The irony of telling someone to humble themselves without a trace of humility was not lost on Jenna.

He blamed her entirely for their division and said, "Donna and I were forced to withdraw from you because of your inability to accept our marriage."

Jenna laughed out loud at his self-righteousness, blaming her for their problems. He still did not answer her question about where he wanted to be buried. But most importantly he did not address her question if he loved her. He had failed her test. She imagined writing a big F in red ink.

Instead of responding with love, humility, sadness, or compassion, he had responded with aggression, accusations, and blame shifting. He had attempted to shame her as a Christian and a daughter.

The whole situation came into perfect clarity for her. He was never going to accept responsibility. He was never going to work on their relationship. He was emotionally abusive. He was harsh. He was a liar. He was a hypocrite. He was toxic.

She could have retaliated with 1 Corinthians 15:33 (NIV) which says, "Do not be misled: Bad company corrupts good character," referring to Donna. Or she could have quoted Proverbs 5:3-4 (NKJV) which says, "For the lips of an immoral woman are as sweet as honey, and her mouth is smoother than oil. But in the end, she is as bitter as poison, as dangerous as a double-edged sword."

Both verses were extremely applicable.

But she did not. She would not use the Bible this way. She would turn to its pages for support, guidance, and comfort, like her grandmother had taught her.

Instead of being angry anymore or consumed by her emotions, at that moment God gave her peace. He gave her permission to let it all go. The peace she had been praying for since her father's wedding day descended upon her like a dove. She sat in silence, listening to her Heavenly Father and feeling His grace and the warmth of His love. True, unconditional, abiding love.

She knew with certainty it was time for her relationship with her dad to end.

She had felt this same feeling several times over the years but had never been able to fully listen. This time she would.

Jenna knew she had the promise that God the Father would never leave her, and this was more than enough for her.

There would be no heated response to his email.

She was done, once and for all.

A Loyal Family Member

Jenna closed her laptop and went out to her back porch. She sat down on her loveseat and admired the bright lemon patterned pillows which always made her happy. No dark thoughts were on her mind. She was simply content.

She mindlessly petted her black Labradoodle puppy, Doah, who lounged on the loveseat next to her. Doah was short for Shenandoah Valley, which was the dog's birthplace, located between the Blue Ridge and Allegheny Mountains in Virginia. She was half Poodle and half Labrador Retriever. She was the kindest and most loving dog Jenna had ever known.

It had always been a dream of Olivia's to have a dog, and she had been pleading for one for years. She had even done research to determine which breed would best suit their family and made a PowerPoint presentation to plead her case. What she didn't know as she made her presentation for the gazillionth time after Jenna's first chemotherapy treatment, was her mother was also wanting a dog for the first time in her adult life.

Since Jenna was home so much now due to her cancer treatments, it was finally the perfect time for the Millers to get a dog. She had more time on her hands than she had ever had before. When they found Doah online, Jenna and Olivia both fell in love, and because Paul loved them so much, he agreed.

Paul also knew his wife wanted an extra source of love for Olivia in the house, and her desire for a dog went far beyond wanting a cute, fluffy creature underfoot. He was keenly aware Jenna felt terrible her youngest daughter had to see her going through treatment and was constantly reminded her mom had cancer. She thought a puppy would be a nice distraction for her and would shower her with love and wet kisses.

Grimly, Jenna also considered the dog would be an extra source of comfort to her daughter if she died, but she tried to shake this morbid thought away as quickly as it came.

More importantly, it felt good for Jenna to make a long-term decision that would affect their family for hopefully at least the next fifteen years. She wanted to allow herself to plan for the future again and was feeling hopeful her treatment was working.

Doah made the house a lot less lonely for Jenna during the days when Paul was at work and Olivia was at school. Best yet, she didn't even shed because she was hypoallergenic. Jenna had lost more hair when it was falling out from chemo than the dog!

Doah nestled in even closer to Jenna, enjoying the feel of the warm sun shining on her back through the screen and the calm attention from her owner. The only feeling either of them were experiencing at that moment was peace.

Peace at Last

Several months after Jenna made the choice to walk away—years after her father made the choice—she received one final email from her dad. He pointed out he had not heard from her for months and wanted an update on her treatment.

She had completed chemotherapy, had her port removed, and had finished thirty grueling rounds of radiation. She had begun taking daily medications, and her surgery to remove her ovaries was scheduled. A lot had happened since their last communication, and he had no idea about any of it. She had been through so much over the last year, and as she sat there now with her chest covered with radiation burns and painful, oozing blisters, she realized her dad's failure to phone had been more painful than any treatment she received.

She made the choice after his last email, in which he blamed her for all the problems in the family, to be done communicating with him. So again, she chose not to respond. She was still done, and she was still at peace with her decision.

Two days after she chose to ignore his email, she learned his cousins, who she was friends with on social media, had visited him and Donna in Georgia. They had praised them for their hospitality on Facebook, and it seemed like her dad's wife had pulled out all the stops to ensure they had a wonderful time.

Jenna realized then that the timing of his email and their visit was most likely not a coincidence. It appeared as if he was only interested in an update on her health because he wanted to look like an involved, loving parent. He wanted to be able to report to them on her condition. He was worried they would see he had no information on Jenna's health and would wonder why.

She could only imagine what story about her he had concocted to make him look good and her look bad, but she honestly didn't care. She knew the truth, and God knew the truth.

Jenna was confident her decision to walk away was best for her and her family. She was moving on from the hurt and the anger. She had forgiven her father and Donna fully so her heart could heal along with her radiation burns and surgical scars.

God is Great

Sixteen months had passed since Heidi and Caleb's picture-perfect wedding. Time had flown by for the newlyweds and the entire Miller family. Paul was preparing to drop his retirement paperwork to the Army after twenty-six years of service, Brett was home for the summer before he started his junior year at The Citadel, and Olivia was going into high school in the fall. Doah had grown from eighteen pounds to sixty-six pounds and was still a bundle of energy. Jenna was cancer free and completely healthy.

God had sustained them every step of the journey, blessed them, and had been ever faithful to them. He had used Jenna's cancer to bring her nuclear family to an unshakeable place of unity, bonded by love. Her children had grown closer to one another by supporting each other through her cancer, and Paul and Jenna's marriage reached a level of trust they didn't know was possible. Jenna's friendships were strengthened and relationships with people she hadn't seen in years renewed. God had been so wonderful to the Millers, and He had made so much good come out of a bad situation.

Bucket List

Jenna sat in the rocking chair in the nursery at Heidi and Caleb's new house. It was the same chair she had taken from her childhood home years ago, and the same one that had been in her grandmother and great-grandmother's house before that.

She tenderly held her beautiful grandson in her arms and kissed him on his head. She was overwhelmed with thankfulness for her life, her family, her health, and for the little bundle of joy nuzzled up against her chest. Holding him was a dream come true.

She could hear the rest of the family laughing in the living room. Everyone she loved was under this roof. Paul, Heidi, Brett, Olivia, Caleb, Katie and her children, Beverly, and of course, Doah, who was nestled on the couch. Jenna was content where she was and happily enjoying the quiet peace of being alone with Henry, the newest and most adorable member of the family.

Although he was only a week old, Jenna's heart was overflowing with love for him. As she stared into his sleepy eyes, she prayed God would protect her grandson, and she vowed to love him unconditionally all the days of her life, however many He gave her.

God had graciously granted her one of her bucket list items. She was now a grandmother. Her whole life had led to this exact moment. This exact perfect moment.

It was now up to her to become a part of her own grandson's heart by loving him fully, regardless of life's circumstances, just as her grandmothers had done with her. She would pray for him, love him, and support him until she took her last breath on Earth. She believed it was possible for the bond between them to last for eternity.

As she rocked Henry, she gently patted him on the back and snuggled him even closer to her. She could feel the presence of her mother in the room and knew she was smiling down at them both.

Jenna's entire life had been defined by the matriarchs of her family, and she was so thankful they had been the kind of women they were. If they hadn't modeled love above all else, she was sure her life would have turned out very differently and she would not be the mother or grandmother she was today. She would not have become a matriarch in her own right. Perhaps she would not even be sitting in this room, holding her grandson.

Jenna knew at that moment her mother's life's work had not been in vain. Even though the family she had been born into had fallen apart in some ways, the family she and Paul had created had been strengthened because of her legacy of love.

Jenna's mother had taught her right from wrong, holy from unholy, and unconditional love from conditional love. Jenna had passed on the lessons she learned from Grace to her children, and they would pass it on to their children.

Jenna could now see the torches of the matriarchs who came before her were still burning bright, and with each generation another torch was lit. She was the newest torch in her lineage. She no longer feared for the future of her family because she now knew the fire would burn as long as love was the source of the flame.

She was doubly grateful Paul also had a line of amazing matriarchs who were unyielding in their faith and their love for family. Her children had been witnesses to the power of women from both sides of the family who used their influence for good. They had taken care of others, served God and their families, worked hard, and loved without abandon. They had encouraged unity and forgiveness and offered grace when it was needed. Just like Grace, and Jenna's grandmothers, the women in Paul's family had also been beautiful inside and out and their torches still burned on.

Jenna was confident if her mom was looking down from Heaven, she would be pleased with what she saw. Since Heaven is a place of joy, she would only see the love between Jenna and her family. She would see the blessing of her great-grandson and the unity between Heidi and Caleb. She would see Jenna healthy. She would be proud. She would be happy. She would be satisfied.

Grace's legacy was just as strong twelve years after her death as it was when she was alive, and there was no indication it would ever diminish.

As Jenna sat in the quiet, it became clear to her a matriarch's influence lasts long after they are placed in the grave. She had been silly to worry about her mother's impact being damaged by her father's choices.

Tom's legacy, unfortunately, would be very different from Grace's. Hatred, pettiness, and self-serving interests will never beat out love, righteousness, and forgiveness.

In the end love wins, and all else is forgotten.

Jenna also realized she and Paul had done all they could to ensure their family unit would remain intact after they are gone. They had followed the lead of the matriarchs who came before them. They had created a strong foundation, built to weather any type of storm. She trusted they had taught their children how to nurture it and how to patch any cracks, long before structural damage could occur.

Her family freely communicated with one another without fear of judgment or grudges and looked for every opportunity to get together they could. Jenna knew her children had had their own private text thread for years, talked on the phone every day, and were each other's Snapchat best friends. They had established a pattern of friendship and love by their own doing, and their bonds were already strong. They would only grow stronger through the next stages of their lives.

Jenna felt nothing but happiness and thankfulness. She thanked God for her grandmothers, her mother, her family, and her grandson for the millionth time that day, knowing she could never thank Him enough; then she sat back in peace and thought intently about her mom and how much she missed her. Instead of being sad, she allowed herself to be comforted by the fact she knew she would see her again one day in Heaven.

Jenna refocused on Henry's sweet face, and as she rocked him in the familiar chair, she felt her own light burning bright. She said, "Henry, I want to tell you the story of the most beautiful woman that ever lived. She had a heart made of gold, a laugh as loud as a hyena, and the softest hands I have ever touched. Her name was Grace, and she was your great grandmother..."

Epilogue

Claire patted her ever-growing belly as she sat in the rocking chair that had been in her family for as long as anyone still living could remember. She had fond memories of sitting in it herself as a child, listening to her Grandma O tell her stories. She could smell her grandmother's perfume when she closed her eyes and could feel her lips kissing the top of her head as they snuggled in the chair. In fact, she still kisses her on the head every time she visits.

Claire sat in silence, dreaming about the daughter she would be holding in her arms in just a few short weeks. She was excited and nervous to become a mother but also confident because she had such strong examples to model after. Her own mother and her Grandma O had been lights in her life, and she was thankful they were both still living and would be there to help her navigate motherhood.

She knew with certainty she would pass on the stories her Grandma O had told her about the amazing matriarchs in her family line. She had heard them so many times she felt like she knew the women personally.

She couldn't wait for her daughter to meet her own dear grandmother, whose real name was Olivia. She was certain she would tell her she had loved her name as a child because her favorite singer, Taylor Swift, had had a cat with the same name. She told everyone that because it made her happy.

As Claire rocked, she decided the first story she would tell her daughter would be the one about where she got her name. She would begin by saying, "Let me tell you a story about the two most beautiful women that ever lived. They both had hearts made of gold, laughs as loud as hyenas, and the softest hands anyone ever touched. You are named after them both, my sweet girl, my Jenna Grace..."

The End.

Acknowledgements

I would like to give my sincere thanks to everyone who helped me make my dream of becoming a published author come true. This book, hopefully the first of many, was a labor of love and your encouragement and support sustained me every step of the way.

To my fabulous family, thank you for allowing me to write day and night, and for understanding I needed five more hours every time I said, "Give me five more minutes."

To my mother-in-law who read my book in its entirety more times than I can count and provided unconditional support.

To my friends who helped me work out the story in my head and listened to me talk about this book incessantly for the last eighteen months.

To Elizabeth Johns, thank you for teaching me the ropes and connecting me with some of the most fabulous people in the business. I will be eternally grateful.

To Stefanie, thank you for designing a cover that represents the story so beautifully.

To Kristyn, Paula, Jessica, and Polly thank you for believing in me and devoting your time to help make publishing my book a reality.

And to every reader out there who is willing to give me a chance, thank you from the bottom of my heart.

Made in the USA
Middletown, DE
15 February 2025